DEEP WATERS

DEEP WATERS

Murder on the Waves

EDITED AND
INTRODUCED
BY MARTIN EDWARDS

Poisoned Pen
PRESS

CONTENTS

Introduction

Welcome to an anthology which plumbs the murky depths of murder and mystery. Readers are invited to dip into a collection of sixteen crime stories which are connected, in one way or another, with water. The contributors range from the legendary Arthur Conan Doyle, through once-famous names such as E. W. Hornung and R. Austin Freeman, and Golden Age doyens Michael Innes and Edmund Crispin, to those relatively unknown figures, James Pattinson (not to be confused with the American bestseller James Patterson) and Kem Bennett.

Deep Waters is the thirteenth themed anthology to appear in the British Library's Crime Classics series; the books aim to illustrate the range of writing in the genre and the varied and often ingenious ways in which different authors tackle a particular subject or type of story. Here we have crime on the high seas, naturally, but there are also mysterious goings-on associated with a river, a canal, even the humble swimming pool.

The first victim to be fished from a watery grave in a detective story was, to the best of my knowledge, Marie Roget in 1842. Her corpse was found in the River Seine in 'The Mystery of Marie Roget', the second of three stories to feature that brilliant sleuth, Chevalier C. Auguste Dupin. Edgar Allan Poe based the story on a real life tragedy concerning the murder of Mary Cecilia Rogers, known as 'the beautiful cigar girl' whose remains were found in the Hudson River. The case remains officially unsolved, but Poe's tale pioneered 'armchair detection' as well as the technique of basing a work of detective fiction on an actual crime.

Since then, crime writers across the world have employed an infinite variety of approaches in producing mysteries with a water-related setting. British authors have been responsible for many notable examples, in novels as well as in short stories. Is it because the British are an island race that they have shown a particular enthusiasm for writing about crime on the ocean wave, as well as closer to home? Whatever the answer, several of the authors featured in this collection had a genuine passion for sailing and the sea. Conan Doyle and C. S. Forester are well-known examples from the past; others include two writers who lived into the twenty-first century, James Pattinson and Andrew Garve.

Mystery writers have long made effective use of a maritime background for a crime scene. Take cruising, for instance. This was once exclusively a pastime of the rich, and stories set on cruises enabled readers to experience vicariously the glamour of shipboard life and exotic foreign destinations while puzzling over a murder mystery. One of the acknowledged masterpieces of Golden Age fiction is Agatha Christie's *Death on the Nile*, in which Hercule Poirot solves the murder of wealthy Linnet Doyle. The novel appeared in 1937; four years earlier, Christie had published a short story with the same title, but featuring a different detective, Parker Pyne.

Christie loved sailing, and in 1922 had embarked on a ten-month voyage around the world as part of a trade mission promoting the British Empire Exhibition; her letters and photographs from this remarkable journey were brought together ninety years later in *The Grand Tour*.

Freeman Wills Crofts, her colleague in the Detection Club, was another Golden Age author whose love of travelling on cruise ships is reflected in his fiction. In *Found Floating* (1937), members of a family which has fallen victim to a mysterious poisoning set off on a cruise to the Greek Islands in search of peace and quiet; unfortunately, one of their number goes missing, and is found in the Straits of Gibraltar. In recent times, novels as diverse as L. C. Tyler's humorous *Herring on the Nile* (2011) and Ruth Ware's bestselling *The Woman in Cabin 10* (2016) have illustrated the continuing possibilities of travel by cruise ship for inventive crime writers.

Inventive use of settings on or by the water is made in innumerable British crime stories. A. P. Herbert's *The House by the River* (1920) is a splendid early example of the psychological crime story strengthened by its setting on the Thames, as is the much more recent *Tideline* (2012) by Penny Hancock. Cyril Hare's *Death is No Sportsman* (1938) is a Golden Age angling mystery set on the river Didder, a fictionalised version of the river Test. In Colin Dexter's *The Wench is Dead* (1989), Inspector Morse, laid up in hospital, investigates an old murder case on the Oxford canal; as with the Marie Roget story, the fiction draws heavily on the facts of a real life crime. C. P. Snow's enjoyable detective novel *Death under Sail* (1932) concerns the intrusion of murder into a boating holiday on the Norfolk Broads. Flooding in Fenland makes for a dramatic climax to one of Dorothy L. Sayers' finest novels, *The Nine Tailors* (1934), and my own love of the Lake District is reflected in books such as *The Frozen Shroud* (2013), set around Ullswater, while the valley of the river Lune provides an evocative setting for several novels by E. C. R. Lorac, starting with *Fell Murder* (1944). Several authors have made use of the drying-up of lakes or reservoirs as a means of revealing evidence of long-ago crimes; especially accomplished examples include Reginald Hill's *On Beulah Height* (1998) and Peter Robinson's *In a Dry Season* (1999). The title of Paula Hawkins's follow-up to *The Girl on the Train* (2015) speaks for itself: *Into the Water* (2017) concerns an unexplained death in the mysterious Drowning Pool.

In putting this book together, I've benefited from the help of a number of friends and fellow detective fiction enthusiasts. Jamie Sturgeon tracked down for me the obscure stories by Kem Bennett, Phyllis Bentley, and Andrew Garve, while Nigel Moss and John Cooper again provided invaluable advice and support. I would also like to express my continuing appreciation for the support of the team in the Publishing Department of the British Library: my thanks go to John Lee, Abbie Day, Maria Vassilopoulos, and Jonny Davidson, as well as to my former editor Rob Davies, who originally commissioned this book.

Deep Waters offers an eclectic mix of stories. There are cases for classic detective characters such as Sherlock Holmes and Dr Thorndyke; a diverse mix of literary styles, from the careless gusto of Gwyn Evans to the meticulously scientific R. Austin Freeman; and a scattering of long-forgotten mysteries, including one which was turned into a film. This collection has been a pleasure to put together, and I hope readers enjoy immersing themselves in it. Go on now: it's time to take the plunge…

Martin Edwards
www.martinedwardsbooks.com

The Adventure of the 'Gloria Scott'

Arthur Conan Doyle

Arthur Conan Doyle (1859–1930) loved the sea. At the age of twenty, after completing the third year of his medical studies, he signed on as ship's surgeon on the Greenland whaler *Hope*. His duties as a doctor were undemanding, and he had the time to try his hand at whaling, becoming so proficient that the captain offered him handsome terms if he would act as doctor and harpoonist on the ship's next voyage. Doyle declined, but after graduating he served as ship's surgeon on board the SS *Mayumba*, travelling to the coast of West Africa. In later life, he remained an enthusiastic sailor, and even played cricket on the deck of the RMS *Dunottar Castle*.

The sea plays a recurrent part in Doyle's fiction. 'The Adventure of the *Gloria Scott*,' a striking example, was first published in *The Strand Magazine* in April 1893. This story recounts Sherlock Holmes's very first case and, together with 'The Musgrave Ritual,' is the major source of information for Holmesians about the consulting detective's early life. Victor

Trevor, a central character in the story, is one of only three people in the canon whom Holmes acknowledged as his friend. They met at college, and Holmes's failure to identify that college has fuelled endless speculation as to where he studied.

'I have some papers here,' said my friend, Sherlock Holmes, as we sat one winter's night on either side of the fire, 'which I really think, Watson, it would be worth your while to glance over. These are the documents in the extraordinary case of the *Gloria Scott*, and this is the message which struck Justice of the Peace Trevor dead with horror when he read it.

He had picked from a drawer a little tarnished cylinder, and, undoing the tape, he handed me a short note scrawled upon a half-sheet of slate-grey paper.

'The supply of game for London is going steadily up,' it ran. 'Head-keeper Hudson, we believe, has been now told to receive all orders for fly-paper, and for preservation of your hen pheasant's life.'

As I glanced up from reading this enigmatical message I saw Holmes chuckling at the expression upon my face.

'You look a little bewildered,' said he.

'I cannot see how such a message as this could inspire horror. It seems to me to be rather grotesque than otherwise.

'Very likely. Yet the fact remains that the reader, who was a fine, robust old man, was knocked clean down by it, as if it had been the butt-end of a pistol.'

'You arouse my curiosity,' said I. 'But why did you say just now that there were very particular reasons why I should study this case?'

'Because it was the first in which I was ever engaged.'

I had often endeavoured to elicit from my companion

what had first turned his mind in the direction of criminal research, but I had never caught him before in a communicative humour. Now he sat forward in his armchair and spread out the documents upon his knees. Then he lit his pipe and sat for some time smoking and turning them over.

'You never heard me talk of Victor Trevor?' he asked. 'He was the only friend I made during the two years that I was at college. I was never a very sociable fellow, Watson, always rather fond of moping in my rooms and working out my own little methods of thought, so that I never mixed much with the men of my year. Bar fencing and boxing I had few athletic tastes, and then my line of study was quite distinct from that of the other fellows, so that we had no points of contact at all. Trevor was the only man I knew, and that only through the accident of his bull-terrier freezing on to my ankle one morning as I went down to chapel.

'It was a prosaic way of forming a friendship, but it was effective. I was laid by the heels for ten days, and Trevor used to come in to inquire after me. At first it was only a minute's chat, but soon his visits lengthened, and before the end of the term we were close friends. He was a hearty, full-blooded fellow, full of spirit and energy, the very opposite to me in most respects; but we found we had some subjects in common, and it was a bond of union when I learned that he was as friendless as I. Finally, he invited me down to his father's place at Donnithorpe, in Norfolk, and I accepted his hospitality for a month of the long vacation.

'Old Trevor was evidently a man of some wealth and consideration, a J.P. and a landed proprietor. Donnithorpe is a little hamlet just to the north of Langmere, in the country of the Broads. The house was an old-fashioned, wide-spread, oak-beamed, brick building, with a fine lime-lined avenue leading up to it. There was excellent wild duck shooting in the fens, remarkably good fishing, a small but select library, taken over, as I understood, from a former occupant, and a tolerable cook, so that it would be a fastidious man who could not put in a pleasant month there.

'Trevor senior was a widower, and my friend was his only son. There had been a daughter, I heard, but she had died of diphtheria while on a visit to Birmingham. The father interested me extremely. He was a man of little culture, but with a considerable amount of rude strength both physically and mentally. He knew hardly any books, but he had travelled far, had seen much of the world, and had remembered all that he had learned. In person he was a thick-set, burly man with a shock of grizzled hair, a brown, weather-beaten face, and blue eyes which were keen to the verge of fierceness. Yet he had a reputation for kindness and charity on the countryside and was noted for the leniency of his sentences from the bench.

'One evening, shortly after my arrival, we were sitting over a glass of port after dinner when young Trevor began to talk about those habits of observation and inference which I had already formed into a system, although I had not yet appreciated the part which they were to play in my life. The old man evidently thought that his son was exaggerating in his description of one or two trivial feats which I had performed.

'"Come now, Mr Holmes," said he, laughing good-humouredly, "I'm an excellent subject, if you can deduce anything from me."

'"I fear there is not very much," I answered. "I might suggest that you have gone about in fear of some personal attack within the last twelve months."

'The laugh faded from his lips, and he stared at me in great surprise.

'"Well, that's true enough," said he. "You know, Victor," turning to his son, "when we broke up that poaching gang, they swore to knife us; and Sir Edward Hoby has actually been attacked. I've always been on my guard since then, though I have no idea how you know it."

'"You have a very handsome stick," I answered. "By the inscription, I observed that you had not had it more than a year. But you have taken some pains to bore the head of it and pour melted lead into the hole, so as to make it a formidable weapon. I argued that you would not take such precautions unless you had some danger to fear."

'"Anything else?" he asked, smiling.

'"You have boxed a good deal in your youth."

'"Right again. How did you know it? Is my nose knocked a little out of the straight?"

'"No," said I. "It is your ears. They have the peculiar flattening and thickening which marks the boxing man."

'"Anything else?"

'"You have done a great deal of digging, by your callosities."

'"Made all my money at the gold-fields."

'"You have been in New Zealand."

'"Right again."

'"You have visited Japan."

'"Quite true."

'"And you have been most intimately associated with someone whose initials were J. A., and whom you afterwards were eager to entirely forget."

'Mr Trevor stood slowly up, fixed his large blue eyes on me with a strange, wild stare, and then pitched forward on his face among the nutshells which strewed the cloth, in a dead faint.

'You can imagine, Watson, how shocked both his son

and I were. His attack did not last long, however, for when we undid his collar and sprinkled the water from one of the finger glasses over his face, he gave a gasp or two and sat up.

'"Ah, boys!" said he, forcing a smile. "I hope I haven't frightened you. Strong as I look, there is a weak place in my heart, and it does not take much to knock me over. I don't know how you manage this, Mr Holmes, but it seems to me that all the detectives of fact and of fancy would be children in your hands. That's your line of life, sir, and you may take the word of a man who has seen something of the world."

'And that recommendation, with the exaggerated estimate of my ability with which he prefaced it, was, if you will believe me, Watson, the very first thing which ever made me feel that a profession might be made out of what had up to that time been the merest hobby. At the moment, however, I was too much concerned at the sudden illness of my host to think of anything else.

'"I hope that I have said nothing to pain you," said I.

'"Well, you certainly touched upon rather a tender point. Might I ask how you know and how much you know?" He spoke now in a half-jesting fashion, but a look of terror still lurked at the back of his eyes.

'"It is simplicity itself," said I. "When you bared your arm to draw that fish into the boat, I saw that 'J. A.' had been tattooed in the bend of the elbow. The letters were still legible, but it was perfectly clear from their blurred appearance, and from the staining of the skin round them, that efforts had been made to obliterate them. It was obvious, then, that those initials had once been very familiar to you, and that you had afterwards wished to forget them."

'"What an eye you have!" he cried, with a sigh of relief. "It is just as you say. But we won't talk of it. Of all ghosts the ghosts of our old loves are the worst. Come into the billiard-room and have a quiet cigar."

'From that day, amid all his cordiality, there was always a touch of suspicion in Mr Trevor's manner towards me. Even his son remarked it. "You've given the governor such a turn," said he, "that he'll never be sure again of what you know and what you don't know." He did not mean to show it, I am sure, but it was so strongly in his mind that it peeped out at every action. At last I became so convinced that I was causing him uneasiness that I drew my visit to a close. On the very day, however, before I left, an incident occurred which proved in the sequel to be of importance.

'We were sitting out upon the lawn on garden chairs, the three of us, basking in the sun and admiring the view across the Broads, when the maid came out to say that there was a man at the door who wanted to see Mr Trevor.

'"What is his name?" asked my host.

'"He would not give any."

'"What does he want, then?"

'"He says that you know him, and that he only wants a moment's conversation."

'"Show him round here." An instant afterwards there appeared a little weazened fellow, with a cringing manner and a shambling style of walking. He wore an open jacket, with a splotch of tar on the sleeve, a red and black check shirt, dungaree trousers, and heavy boots badly worn. His face was thin and brown and crafty, with a perpetual smile upon it, which showed an irregular line of yellow teeth, and his crinkled hands were half closed in a way that is distinctive of sailors. As he came slouching across the lawn I heard Mr Trevor make a sort of hiccoughing noise in his throat, and, jumping out of his chair, he ran into the house. He was back in a moment, and I smelt a strong reek of brandy as he passed me.

'"Well, my man," said he, "what can I do for you?"

'The sailor stood looking at him with puckered eyes, and with the same loose-lipped smile upon his face.

'"You don't know me?" he asked.

'"Why, dear me, it is surely Hudson!" said Mr Trevor, in a tone of surprise.

'"Hudson it is, sir," said the seaman. "Why, it's thirty year and more since I saw you last. Here you are in your house, and me still picking my salt meat out of the harness cask."

'"Tut, you will find that I have not forgotten old times," cried Mr Trevor, and, walking towards the sailor, he said something in a low voice. "Go into the kitchen," he continued out loud, "and you will get food and drink. I have no doubt that I shall find you a situation."

'"Thank you, sir," said the seaman, touching his forelock. "I'm just off a two-yearer in an eight-knot tramp, short handed at that, and I wants a rest. I thought I'd get it either with Mr Beddoes or with you."

'"Ah!" cried Mr Trevor, "you know where Mr Beddoes is?"

'"Bless you, sir, I know where all my old friends are," said the fellow, with a sinister smile, and slouched off after the maid to the kitchen. Mr Trevor mumbled something to us about having been shipmates with the man when he was going back to the diggings, and then, leaving us on the lawn, he went indoors. An hour later, when we entered the house we found him stretched dead drunk upon the dining-room sofa. The whole incident left a most ugly impression upon my mind, and I was not sorry next day to leave Donnithorpe behind me, for I felt that my presence must be a source of embarrassment to my friend.

'All this occurred during the first month of the long

vacation. I went up to my London rooms, where I spent seven weeks working out a few experiments in organic chemistry. One day, however, when the autumn was far advanced and the vacation drawing to a close, I received a telegram from my friend imploring me to return to Donnithorpe, and saying that he was in great need of my advice and assistance. Of course I dropped everything and set out for the north once more.

'He met me with the dog-cart at the station, and I saw at a glance that the last two months had been very trying ones for him. He had grown thin and careworn, and had lost the loud, cheery manner for which he had been remarkable.

'"The governor is dying," were the first words he said.

'"Impossible!" I cried. "What is the matter?"

'"Apoplexy. Nervous shock. He's been on the verge all day. I doubt if we shall find him alive."

'I was, as you may think, Watson, horrified at this unexpected news.

'"What has caused it?" I said.

'"Ah, that is the point. Jump in, and we can talk it over while we drive. You remember that fellow who came upon the evening before you left us?"

'"Perfectly."

'"Do you know who it was that we let into the house that day?"

'"I have no idea."

'"It was the Devil, Holmes!" he cried.

'I stared at him in astonishment.

'"Yes; it was the Devil himself. We have not had a peaceful hour since—not one. The governor has never held up his head from that evening, and now the life has been crushed out of him, and his heart broken, all through this accursed Hudson."

'"What power had he, then?"

'"Ah, that is what I would give so much to know. The kindly, charitable, good old governor! How could he have fallen into the clutches of such a ruffian? But I am so glad that you have come, Holmes. I trust very much to your judgment and discretion, and I know that you will advise me for the best."

'We were dashing along the smooth, white country road, with the long stretch of Broads in front of us glimmering in the red light of the setting sun. From a grove upon our left I could already see the high chimneys and the flagstaff which marked the squire's dwelling.

'"My father made the fellow gardener," said my companion, "and then, as that did not satisfy him, he was promoted to be butler. The house seemed to be at his mercy, and he wandered about and did what he chose in it. The maids complained of his drunken habits and his vile language. The dad raised their wages all round to recompense them for the annoyance. The fellow would take the boat and my father's best gun and treat himself to little shooting parties. And all this with such a sneering, leering, insolent face, that I would have knocked him down twenty times over if he had been a man of my own age. I tell you, Holmes, I have had to keep a tight hold upon myself all this time, and now I am asking myself whether, if I had let myself go a little more, I might not have been a wiser man.

'"Well, matters went from bad to worse with us, and this animal, Hudson, became more and more intrusive, until at last, on his making some insolent reply to my father in my presence one day, I took him by the shoulder and turned him out of the room. He slunk away with a livid face, and two venomous eyes which uttered more threats than his tongue could do. I don't know what passed between the poor dad and him after that, but the dad came to me next day and asked me whether I would mind apologising to Hudson. I refused, as you can imagine, and asked my father how he could allow such a wretch to take such liberties with himself and his household.

'"Ah, my boy," said he, "it is all very well to talk, but you don't know how I am placed. But you shall know, Victor. I'll see that you shall know, come what may! You wouldn't believe harm of your poor old father, would you, lad?" He was very much moved, and shut himself up in the study all day, where I could see through the window that he was writing busily.

'"That evening there came what seemed to be a grand release, for Hudson told us that he was going to leave us. He walked into the dining-room as we sat after dinner and announced his intention in the thick voice of a half-drunken man.

'"I've had enough of Norfolk," said he, "I'll run down to Mr Beddoes, in Hampshire. He'll be as glad to see me as you were, I dare say."

'"You're not going away in an unkind spirit, Hudson, I hope?" said my father, with a tameness which made my blood boil.

'"I've not had my 'pology," said he sulkily, glancing in my direction.

'"Victor, you will acknowledge that you have used this worthy fellow rather roughly?" said the dad, turning to me.

'"On the contrary, I think that we have both shown extraordinary patience towards him," I answered.

'"Oh, you do, do you?" he snarled. "Very good, mate. We'll see about that!" He slouched out of the room, and half an hour afterwards left the house, leaving my father in a state of pitiable nervousness. Night after night I heard him pacing his room, and it was just as he was recovering his confidence that the blow did at last fall.

'"And how?" I asked eagerly.

'"In a most extraordinary fashion. A letter arrived for my father yesterday evening, bearing the Fordingbridge postmark. My father read it, clapped both his hands to his head, and began running round the room in little circles like a man who has been driven out of his senses. When I at last drew him down on to the sofa, his mouth and eyelids were all puckered on one side, and I saw that he had had a stroke. Dr Fordham came over at once, and we put him to bed; but the paralysis has spread, he has shown no sign of returning consciousness, and I think that we shall hardly find him alive."

'"You horrify me, Trevor!" I cried. "What, then, could have been in this letter to cause so dreadful a result?"

'"Nothing. There lies the inexplicable part of it. The message was absurd and trivial. Ah, my God, it is as I feared!"

'As he spoke we came round the curve of the avenue, and saw in the fading light that every blind in the house had been drawn down. As we dashed up to the door, my friend's face convulsed with grief, a gentleman in black emerged from it.

'"When did it happen, doctor?" asked Trevor.

'"Almost immediately after you left."

'"Did he recover consciousness?"

'"For an instant before the end."

'"Any message for me?"

'"Only that the papers were in the back drawer of the Japanese cabinet."

'My friend ascended with the doctor to the chamber of death, while I remained in the study, turning the whole matter over and over in my head, and feeling as sombre as ever I had done in my life. What was the past of this Trevor: pugilist, traveller, and gold-digger; and how had he placed himself in the power of this acid-faced seaman? Why, too, should he faint at an allusion to the half-effaced initials upon his arm, and die of fright when he had a letter from Fordingbridge? Then I remembered that Fordingbridge was in Hampshire, and that this Mr Beddoes, whom the seaman had gone to visit, and presumably to blackmail, had also been mentioned as living in Hampshire. The letter, then, might either come from Hudson, the seaman, saying that he had betrayed the guilty secret which appeared to exist, or it might come from Beddoes, warning an old confederate that such a betrayal was imminent. So far it seemed clear enough. But, then, how could the letter be trivial and grotesque as described by the son? He must have misread it. If so, it must have been one of those ingenious secret codes which mean one thing while they seem to mean another. I must see this letter. If there were a hidden meaning in it, I was confident that I could pluck it forth. For an hour I sat pondering over it in the gloom, until at last a weeping maid brought in a lamp, and close at her heels came my friend Trevor, pale but composed, with these very papers which lie upon my knee held in his grasp. He sat down opposite to me, drew the lamp to the edge of the table, and handed me a short note scribbled, as you see, upon a single sheet of grey paper. "The supply of game for London is going steadily up," it ran. "Head-keeper Hudson, we believe, has been now told to receive all orders for fly-paper and for preservation of your hen pheasant's life."

'I dare say my face looked as bewildered as yours did just now when first I read this message. Then I re-read it very carefully. It was evidently as I had thought, and some second meaning must be buried in this strange combination of words. Or could it be that there was a prearranged significance to such phrases as "fly-paper" and "hen pheasant"? Such a meaning would be arbitrary, and could not be deduced in any way. And yet I was loath to believe that this was the case, and the presence of the word "Hudson" seemed to show that the subject of the message was as I had guessed, and that it was from Beddoes rather than the sailor. I tried it backwards, but the combination, "Life pheasant's hen," was not encouraging. Then I tried alternate words, but neither "The of for" nor "supply game London" promised to throw any light upon it. Then in an instant the key of the riddle was in my hands, and I saw that every third word beginning with the first would give a message which might well drive old Trevor to despair.

'It was short and terse, the warning, as I now read it to my companion:

'"The game is up. Hudson has told all. Fly for your life."

'Victor Trevor sank his face into his shaking hands. "It must be that, I suppose," said he. "This is worse than death, for it means disgrace as well. But what is the meaning of these 'head-keepers' and 'hen pheasants'?"

'"It means nothing to the message, but it might mean a good deal to us if we had no other means of discovering the sender. You see that he has begun by writing, 'The… game… is,' and so on. Afterwards he had, to fulfil the prearranged cipher, to fill in any two words in each space. He would naturally use the first words which came to his mind, and if there were so many which referred to sport among them, you may be tolerably sure that he is either an ardent shot or interested in breeding. Do you know anything of this Beddoes?"

'"Why, now that you mention it," said he, "I remember that my poor father used to have an invitation from him to shoot over his preserves every autumn."

'"Then it is undoubtedly from him that the note comes," said I. "It only remains for us to find out what this secret was which the sailor Hudson seems to have held over the heads of these two wealthy and respected men."

'"Alas, Holmes, I fear that it is one of sin and shame!" cried my friend. "But from you I shall have no secrets. Here is the statement which was drawn up by my father when he knew that the danger from Hudson had become imminent. I found it in the Japanese cabinet, as he told the doctor. Take it and read it to me, for I have neither the strength nor the courage to do it myself."

'These are the very papers, Watson, which he handed to me, and I will read them to you as I read them in the old study that night to him. They are indorsed outside as you see: "Some particulars of the voyage of the barque *Gloria Scott*, from her leaving Falmouth on the 8th October, 1855, to her destruction in N. lat 15 ´ 29° W. long. 25° 14 ´, on November 6th." It is in the form of a letter, and runs in this way:

'My dear, dear son,—Now that approaching disgrace begins to darken the closing years of my life, I can write with all truth and honesty that it is not the terror of the law, it is not the loss of my position in the county, nor is it my fall, in the eyes of all who have known me, which cuts me to the heart; but it is the thought that you should come to blush for me— you who love me, and who have seldom, I hope, had reason to do other than respect me. But if the blow falls which is for ever hanging over me, then I should wish you to read this that you may know straight from me how far I have been to blame. On the other hand, if all should go well (which may kind God Almighty grant!), then if by any chance this paper should be still undestroyed, and should fall into your hands, I conjure you by all you hold sacred, by the memory of your dear mother, and by the love which has been between us, to hurl it into the fire, and never to give one thought to it again.

'If, then, your eye goes on to read this line, I know that I shall already have been exposed and dragged from my home, or, as is more likely—for you know that my heart is weak—by lying with my tongue sealed for ever in death. In either case the time for suppression is past, and every word which I tell you is the naked truth; and this I swear as I hope for mercy.

'My name, dear lad, is not Trevor. I was James Armitage in my younger days, and you can understand now the shock that it was to me a few weeks ago when your college friend addressed me in words which seemed to imply that he had surmised my secret. As Armitage it was that I entered a London banking house, and as Armitage I was convicted of breaking my country's laws, and was sentenced to trans-portation. Do not think very harshly of me, laddie. It was a debt of honour, so-called, which I had to pay, and I used money which was not my own to do it, in the certainty that I could replace it before there could be any possibility of its being missed. But the most dreadful ill-luck pursued me. The money which I had reckoned upon never came to hand; and a premature examination of accounts exposed my deficit. The case might have been dealt leniently with, but the laws were more harshly administered thirty years ago than now, and on my twenty-third birthday I found myself chained as a felon with thirty-seven other convicts in the 'tween decks of the barque *Gloria Scott*, bound for Australia.

'It was the year '55, when the Crimean War was at its height, and the old convict ships had been largely used as transports in the Black Sea. The Government was compelled therefore to use smaller and less suitable vessels for sending out their prisoners. The *Gloria Scott* had been in the Chinese tea trade, but she was an old-fashioned, heavy-bowed, broad-beamed craft, and the new clippers had cut her out. She was a 500-ton boat, and besides her thirty-eight jailbirds, she carried twenty-six of a crew, eighteen soldiers, a captain, three mates, a doctor, a chaplain, and four warders. Nearly a hundred souls were in her, all told, when we set sail from Falmouth.

'The partitions between the cells of the convicts, instead of being of thick oak, as is usual in convict ships, were quite thin and frail. The man next to me upon the aft side was one whom I had particularly noticed when we were led down to the quay. He was a young man with a clear, hairless face, a long thin nose, and rather nut-cracker jaws. He carried his head very jauntily in the air, had a swaggering style of walking, and was above all else remarkable for his extraordinary height. I don't think any of our heads would come up to his shoulder, and I am sure that he could not have measured less than six and a half feet. It was strange among so many sad and weary faces to see one which was full of energy and resolution. The sight of it was to me like a fire in a snowstorm. I was glad then to find that he was my neighbour, and gladder still when, in the dead of the night, I heard a whisper close to my ear, and found that he had managed to cut an opening in the board which separated us.

'"Halloa, chummy!" said he. "What's your name, and what are you here for?"

'I answered him, and asked in turn who I was talking with.

'"I'm Jack Prendergast," said he, "and, by God, you'll learn to bless my name before you've done with me!"

'I remembered hearing of his case, for it was one which had made an immense sensation throughout the country, some time before my own arrest. He was a man of good family and of great ability, but of incurably vicious habits, who had, by an ingenious system of fraud, obtained huge sums of money from the leading London merchants.

'"Ah, ah! You remember my case?" said he, proudly.

'"Very well indeed."

'"Then maybe you remember something queer about it?"

'"What was that, then?"

'"I'd had nearly a quarter of million, hadn't I?"

'"So it was said."

'"But none was recovered, eh?"

'"No."

'"Well, where d'ye suppose the balance is?" he asked.

'"I have no idea," said I.

'"Right between my finger and thumb," he cried. "By God, I've got more pounds to my name than you have hairs on your head. And if you've money, my son, and know how to handle it and spread it, you can do *anything*! Now, you don't think it likely that a man who could do anything is going to wear his breeches out sitting in the stinking hold of a rat-gutted, beetle-ridden, mouldy old coffin of a China coaster? No, sir, such a man will look after himself, and will look after his chums. You may lay to that! You hold on to him, and you may kiss the Book that he'll haul you through."

'That was his style of talk, and at first I thought it meant nothing, but after a while, when he had tested me and sworn me in with all possible solemnity, he let me understand that there really was a plot to gain command of the vessel. A dozen of the prisoners had hatched it before they came aboard: Prendergast was the leader, and his money was the motive power.

'"I'd a partner," said he, "a rare good man, as true as a stock to a barrel. He's got the dibs, he has, and where do you think he is at this moment? Why, he's the chaplain of this ship—the chaplain, no less! He came aboard with a black coat and his papers right, and money enough in his box to buy the thing right up from keel to maintruck. The crew are his body and soul. He could buy 'em at so much a gross with a cash discount, and he did it before ever they signed on. He's got two of the warders and Mercer the second mate, and he'd get the captain himself if he thought him worth it."

'"What are we to do, then?" I asked.

'"What do you think?" said he. "We'll make the coats of some of these soldiers redder than ever the tailor did."

'"But they are armed," said I.

'"And so shall we be, my boy. There's a brace of pistols for every mother's son of us, and if we can't carry this ship, with the crew at our back, it's time we were all sent to a young Miss's boarding school. You speak to your mate on the left tonight, and see if he is to be trusted."

'I did so, and found my other neighbour to be a young fellow in much the same position as myself, whose crime had been forgery. His name was Evans, but he afterwards changed it, like myself, and he is now a rich and prosperous man in the South of England. He was ready enough to join the conspiracy, as the only means of saving ourselves, and before we had crossed the Bay there were only two of the prisoners who were not in the secret. One of these was of weak mind, and we did not dare to trust him, and the other was suffering from jaundice, and could not be of any use to us.

'From the beginning there was really nothing to prevent us taking possession of the ship. The crew were a set of ruffians, specially picked for the job. The sham chaplain came into our cells to exhort us, carrying a black bag, supposed to be full of tracts; and so often did he come that by the third day we had each stowed away at the foot of our bed a file, a brace of pistols, a pound of powder, and twenty slugs. Two of the warders were agents of Prendergast, and the second mate was his right-hand man. The captain, the two mates, two warders, Lieutenant Martin, his eighteen soldiers, and the doctor were all that we had against us. Yet, safe as it was, we determined to neglect no precaution, and to make our attack suddenly at night. It came, however, more quickly than we expected, and in this way:

'One evening, about the third week after our start, the doctor had come down to see one of the prisoners, who was ill, and, putting his hand down on the bottom of his bunk, he felt the outline of the pistols. If he had been silent he might have blown the whole thing; but he was a nervous little chap, so he gave a cry of surprise and turned so pale that the man knew what was up in an instant and seized him. He was gagged before he could give the alarm, and tied down upon the bed. He had unlocked the door that led to the deck, and we were through it in a rush. The two sentries were shot down, and so was a corporal who came running to see what was the matter. There were two more soldiers at the door of the state-room, and their muskets seemed not to be loaded, for they never fired upon us, and they were shot while trying to fix their bayonets. Then we rushed on into the captain's cabin, but as we pushed open the door there was an explosion from within, and there he lay with his head on the chart of the Atlantic, which was pinned upon the table, while the chaplain stood, with a smoking pistol in his hand, at his elbow. The two mates had both been seized by the crew, and the whole business seemed to be settled.

'The state-room was next the cabin, and we flocked in there and flopped down on the settees all speaking together, for we were just mad with the feeling that we were free once more. There were lockers all round, and Wilson, the sham chaplain, knocked one of them in, and pulled out a dozen of brown sherry. We cracked off the necks of the bottles, poured the stuff out into tumblers, and were just tossing them off, when in an instant, without warning, there came the roar of muskets in our ears, and the saloon was so full of smoke that we could not see across the table. When it cleared away again the place was a shambles. Wilson and eight others were wriggling on the top of each other on the floor, and the blood and brown sherry on that table turn me sick now when I think of it. We were so cowed by the sight that I think we should have given the job up if it had not been for Prendergast. He bellowed like a bull and rushed for the door with all that were left alive at his heels. Out we ran, and there on the poop were the lieutenant and ten of his men. The swing skylights above the saloon table had been a bit open, and they had fired on us through the slit. We got on them before they could load, and they stood to it like men, but we had the upper hand of them, and in five minutes it was all over. My God! was there ever a slaughter-house like that ship? Prendergast was like a raging devil, and he picked the soldiers up as if they had been children and threw them overboard, alive or dead. There was one sergeant that was horribly wounded, and yet kept on swimming for a surprising time, until someone in mercy blew out his brains. When the fighting was over there was no one left of our enemies except just the warders, the mates, and the doctor.

'It was over them that the great quarrel arose. There were many of us who were glad enough to win back our freedom, and yet who had no wish to have murder on our souls. It was one thing to knock the soldiers over with their muskets in their hands, and it was another to stand by while men were being killed in cold blood. Eight of us, five convicts and three sailors, said that we would not see it done. But there was no moving Prendergast and those who were with him. Our only chance of safety lay in making a clean job of it, said he, and he would not leave a tongue with power to wag in a witness-box. It nearly came to our sharing the fate of the prisoners, but at last he said that if we wished we might take a boat and go. We jumped at the offer, for we were already sick of these bloodthirsty doings, and we saw that there would be worse before it was done. We were given a suit of sailor's togs each, a barrel of water, two casks, one of junk and one of biscuits, and a compass. Prendergast threw us over a chart, told us that we were shipwrecked mariners whose ship had foundered in lat. 15° N. and long. 25° W., and then cut the painter and let us go.

'And now I come to the most surprising part of my story, my dear son. The seamen had hauled the foreyard aback during the rising, but now as we left them they brought it square again, and, as there was a light wind from the north and east, the barque began to draw slowly away from us. Our boat lay, rising and falling, upon the long, smooth rollers, and Evans and I, who were the most educated of the party, were sitting in the sheets working out our position and planning what coast we should make for. It was a nice question, for the Cape de Verde was about 500 miles to the north of us, and the African coast about 700 miles to the east. On the whole, as the wind was coming round to north, we thought that Sierra Leone might be best, and turned our head in that direction, the barque being at that time nearly hull down on our starboard quarter. Suddenly as we looked at her we saw a dense black cloud of smoke shoot up from her, which hung like a monstrous tree upon the skyline. A few seconds later a roar like thunder burst upon our ears, and as the smoke thinned away there was no sign left of the *Gloria Scott*. In an instant we swept the boat's head round again, and pulled with all our strength for the place where the haze, still trailing over the water, marked the scene of this catastrophe.

'It was a long hour before we reached it, and at first we feared that we had come too late to save anyone. A splintered boat and a number of crates and fragments of spars rising and falling on the waves showed us where the vessel had foundered, but there was no sign of life, and we had turned away in despair when we heard a cry for help, and saw at some distance a piece of wreckage with a man lying stretched across it. When we pulled him aboard the boat he proved to be a young seaman of the name of Hudson, who was so burned and exhausted that he could give us no account of what had happened until the following morning.

'It seemed that after we had left, Prendergast and his gang had proceeded to put to death the five remaining prisoners: the two warders had been shot and thrown overboard, and so also had the third mate. Prendergast then descended into the 'tween decks, and with his own hands cut the throat of the unfortunate surgeon. There only remained the first mate, who was a bold and active man. When he saw the convict approaching him with the bloody knife in his hand, he kicked off his bonds, which he had somehow contrived to loosen, and rushing down the deck he plunged into the afterhold.

'A dozen convicts who descended with their pistols in search of him found him with a match-box in his hand seated beside an open powder barrel, which was one of a hundred carried on board, and swearing that he would blow all hands up if he were in any way molested. An instant later the explosion occurred, though Hudson thought it was caused by the misdirected bullet of one of the convicts rather than the mate's match. Be the cause what it may, it was the end of the *Gloria Scott*, and of the rabble who held command of her.

'Such, in a few words, my dear boy, is the history of this terrible business in which I was involved. Next day we were picked up by the brig *Hotspur*, bound for Australia, whose captain found no difficulty in believing that we were the survivors of a passenger ship which had foundered. The transport ship, *Gloria Scott*, was set down by the Admiralty as being lost at sea, and no word has ever leaked out as to her true fate. After an excellent voyage the *Hotspur* landed us at Sydney, where Evans and I changed our names and made our way to the diggings, where among the crowds who were gathered from all nations, we had no difficulty in losing our former identities.

'The rest I need not relate. We prospered, we travelled, we came back as rich colonials to England, and we bought country estates. For more than twenty years we have led peaceful and useful lives, and we hoped that our past was for ever buried. Imagine, then, my feelings when in the seaman who came to us I recognised instantly the man who had been picked off the wreck! He had tracked us down somehow, and had set himself to live upon our fears. You will understand now how it was that I strove to keep peace with him, and you will in some measure sympathise with me in the fears which fill me, now that he has gone from me to his other victim with threats upon his tongue.'

'Underneath is written, in a hand so shaky as to be hardly legible, "Beddoes writes in cipher to say that H. has told all. Sweet Lord, have mercy on our souls!"

'That was the narrative which I read that night to young Trevor, and I think, Watson, that under the circumstances it was a dramatic one. The good fellow was heartbroken at it, and went out to the Terai tea planting, where I hear that he is doing well. As to the sailor and Beddoes, neither of them was ever heard of again after that day on which the letter of warning was written. They both disappeared utterly and completely. No complaint had been lodged with the police, so that Beddoes had mistaken a threat for a deed. Hudson had been seen lurking about, and it was believed by the police that he had done away with Beddoes, and had fled. For myself, I believe that the truth was exactly the opposite. I think it is most probable that Beddoes, pushed to desperation, and believing himself to have been already betrayed, had revenged himself upon Hudson, and had fled from the country with as much money as he could lay his hands on. Those are the facts of the case, Doctor, and if they are of any use to your collection, I am sure that they are very heartily at your service.'

The Eight-Mile Lock

L. T. Meade and Robert Eustace

Elizabeth Thomasina Meade Smith (1844–1914) was a clergyman's daughter from County Cork who earned fame writing as L. T. Meade. During her lifetime, she was best known for stories written for girls, but she also enjoyed considerable success as an author of detective fiction, often writing in collaboration; with Dr Clifford Halifax, she produced a number of books, and her other principal literary partner was also a medical man, whose main role was to supply plot material. Robert Eustace was the pen name of Eustace Robert Barton (1854–1943), who later co-wrote short stories with Edgar Jepson and a novel with Dorothy L. Sayers.

In 1899, Meade and Eustace published *The Gold Star Line*, and the relative seniority (and, perhaps, contribution) of the authors is reflected in the fact that although both their names are included on the title page of the first edition, only Meade's appears on the front cover and spine. The book collects half a dozen lively mystery stories narrated by George

Conway, the much-travelled purser of the *Morning Star*, a passenger liner of the Gold Star shipping line. This story, however, is set on the river Thames. The detective is John Bell, whose specialism in debunking supposed manifestations of the supernatural earns him the nickname 'the Ghost Exposer'. Bell was introduced in *Cassell's Family Magazine* in June 1897; this story appeared in the September issue, and his exploits were gathered in *A Master of Mysteries* the following year.

It was in the August of 1889, when I was just arranging my annual holiday, that I received the following letter. I tore it open and read:

> '*Theodora* House-boat, Goring.
>
> *Dear Mr Bell,*
>
> Can you come down on Wednesday and stay with us for a week? The weather is glorious and the river looking its best. We are a gay party, and there will be plenty of fun going on.
>
> *Yours very truly,*
> *Helena Ridsdale.*

This was exactly what I wanted. I was fond of the river, and scarcely a summer passed that I did not spend at least a fortnight on the Thames. I could go for a week to the Ridsdales, and then start off on my own quiet holiday afterwards. I had known Lady Ridsdale since she was a girl, and I had no doubt my visit would prove a most enjoyable one. I replied immediately, accepting the invitation, and three days later arrived at Goring.

As the well-cushioned little punt, which had been sent to bring me across the river, drew up alongside the *Theodora*, the Countess came down from the deck to welcome me.

'I am so glad you could come, Mr Bell,' she said. 'I was afraid you might be away on some of your extraordinary campaigns against the supernatural. This is Mr Ralph Vyner; he is also, like yourself, devoted to science. I am sure you will find many interests in common.'

A short, thickset, wiry little man, dressed in white flannels, who had been lolling in a deck chair, now came forward and shook hands with me.

'I know of you by reputation, Mr Bell,' he said, 'and I have often hoped to have the pleasure of meeting you. I am sure we shall all be anxious to hear of some of your experiences. We are such an excessively frivolous party that we can easily afford to be leavened with a little serious element.'

'But I don't mean to be serious in the least,' I answered, laughing; 'I have come here to enjoy myself, and intend to be as frivolous as the rest of you.'

'You will have an opportunity this evening,' said the Countess; 'we are going to have a special band from town, and intend to have a moonlight dance on deck. Ah! here comes Charlie with the others,' she added, shading her eyes and looking down the stream.

In a few moments a perfectly appointed little electric launch shot up, and my host with the rest of the party came on board. We shortly afterwards sat down to lunch, and a gayer and pleasanter set of people I have seldom met. In the afternoon we broke up into detachments, and Vyner and I went for a long pull upstream. I found him a pleasant fellow, ready to talk at any length not only about his own hobbies, but about the world at large. I discovered presently that he was a naval engineer of no small attainments.

When we returned to the house-boat, it was nearly time to prepare for dinner. Most of the ladies had already retired to their cabins. Lady Ridsdale was standing alone on deck. When she saw us both, she called to us to come to her side.

'This quite dazzles me,' she said in a low, somewhat mysterious tone, 'and I must show it to you. I know you at least, Mr Vyner, will appreciate it.'

As she spoke she took a small leather case out of her pocket—it was ornamented with a monogram, and opened with a catch. She pressed the lid, it flew up, and I saw, resting on a velvet bed, a glittering circlet of enormous diamonds. The Countess lifted them out, and slipped them over her slender wrist.

'They are some of the family diamonds,' she said with excitement, 'and of great value. Charlie is having all the jewels reset for me, but the rest are not ready yet. He has just brought this down from town. Is it not superb? Did you ever see such beauties?'

The diamonds flashed on her white wrist; she looked up at me with eyes almost as bright.

'I love beautiful stones,' she said, 'and I feel as if these were alive. Oh, do look at the rays of colour in them, as many as in the rainbow.'

I congratulated Lady Ridsdale on possessing such a splendid ornament, and then glanced at Vyner, expecting him to say something.

The expression on his face startled me, and I was destined to remember it by-and-by. The ruddy look had completely left it; his eyes were half starting from his head. He peered close, and suddenly, without the slightest warning, stretched out his hand, and touched the diamonds as they glittered round Lady Ridsdale's wrist. She started back haughtily, then, recovering herself, took the bracelet off and put it into his hand.

'Charlie tells me,' she said, 'that this bracelet is worth from fifteen to twenty thousand pounds.'

'You must take care of it,' remarked Vyner; 'don't let your maid see it, for instance.'

'Oh, nonsense!' laughed Lady Ridsdale. 'I would trust Louise as I would trust myself.'

Soon afterwards we separated, and I went down to my little cabin to prepare for dinner. When we met in the dining saloon I noticed that Lady Ridsdale was wearing the diamond bracelet. Almost immediately after dinner the band came on board and the dancing began.

We kept up our festivities until two o'clock, and more than once, as she flashed past me, I could not help noticing the glittering circlet round her wrist. I considered myself a fair judge of precious stones, but had never seen any diamonds for size and brilliancy to equal these.

As Vyner and I happened to stand apart from the others he remarked upon them.

'It was imprudent of Ridsdale to bring those diamonds here,' he said. 'Suppose they are stolen?'

'Scarcely likely,' I answered; 'there are no thieves on board.'

He gave an impatient movement.

'As far as we *know* there are not,' he said slowly, 'but one can never tell. The diamonds are of exceptional value, and it is not safe to expose ordinary folk to temptation. That small circlet means a fortune.'

He sighed deeply, and when I spoke to him next did not

answer me. Not long afterwards our gay party dispersed, and we retired to our respective cabins.

I went to mine and was quickly in bed. As a newly-arrived guest I was given a cabin on board, but several other members of the party were sleeping in tents on the shore. Vyner and Lord Ridsdale were amongst the latter number. Whether it was the narrowness of my bunk or the heat of the night, I cannot tell, but sleep I could not. Suddenly through my open window I heard voices from the shore near by. I could identify the speakers by their tones—one was my host, Lord Ridsdale, the other Ralph Vyner. Whatever formed the subject of discourse, it was evidently far from amicable. However much averse I might feel to the situation, I was compelled to be an unwilling eavesdropper, for the voices rose, and I caught the following words from Vyner:

'Can you lend me five thousand pounds till the winter?'

'No, Vyner, I have told you so before, and the reason too. It is your own fault, and you must take the consequences.'

'Do you mean that to be final?' asked Vyner.

'Yes.'

'Very well, then I shall look after myself. Thank God, I have got brains if I have not money, and I shall not let the means interfere with the end.'

'You can go to the devil for all I care,' was the angry answer, 'and, after what I know, I won't raise a finger to help you.'

The speakers had evidently moved further off, for the last words I could not catch. But what little I heard by no means conduced to slumber. So Vyner, for all his jovial and easy manner, was in a fix for money, and Ridsdale knew something about him scarcely to his credit!

I kept thinking over this, and also recalling his words when he spoke of Lady Ridsdale's diamonds as representing a fortune. What did he mean by saying that he would not let the means interfere with the end? That brief sentence sounded very much like the outburst of a desperate man. I could not help heartily wishing that Lady Ridsdale's diamond circlet was back in London, and, just before I dropped to sleep, I made up my mind to speak to Ridsdale on the subject.

Towards morning I did doze off, but I was awakened by hearing my name called, and, starting up, I saw Ridsdale standing by my side. His face looked queer and excited.

'Wake up, Bell,' he cried; 'a terrible thing has happened.'

'What is it?' I asked.

'My wife's bracelet is stolen.'

Like a flash I thought of Vyner, and then as quickly I knew that I must be careful to give no voice to hastily-formed suspicions.

'I won't be a moment dressing, and then I'll join you,' I said.

Ridsdale nodded and left my cabin.

In five minutes I was with him on deck. He then told me briefly what had happened.

'Helena most imprudently left the case on her dressing-table last night,' he said, 'and owing to the heat she kept the window open. Some one must have waded into the water in the dark and stolen it. Perhaps one of the bandsmen may have noticed the flashing of the diamonds on her wrist and returned to secure the bracelet—there's no saying. The only too palpable fact is that it is gone—it was valued at twenty thousand pounds!'

'Have you sent for the police?' I asked.

'Yes, and have also wired to Scotland Yard for one of their best detectives. Vyner took the telegram for me, and was to call at the police station on his way back. He is nearly as much upset as I am. This is a terrible loss. I feel fit to kill myself for my folly in bringing that valuable bracelet on board a house-boat.'

'It was a little imprudent,' I answered, 'but you are sure to get it back.'

'I hope so,' he replied moodily.

Just then the punt with Vyner and a couple of policemen on board was seen rapidly approaching. Ridsdale went to meet them,and was soon in earnest conversation with the superintendent of police. The moment Vyner leapt on board he came to the part of the deck where I was standing.

'Ah, Bell,' he cried, 'what about my prognostications of last night?'

'They have been verified too soon,' I answered. I gave him a quick glance. His eyes looked straight into mine.

'Have you any theory to account for the theft?' I asked.

'Yes, a very simple one. Owing to the heat of the evening the Countess slept with her window open. It was an easy matter to wade through the water, introduce a hand through the open window and purloin the diamonds.'

'Without being seen by any occupants of the tents?' I queried.

'Certainly,' he answered, speaking slowly and with thought.

'Then you believe the thief came from without?'

'I do.'

'What about your warning to Lady Ridsdale yesterday evening not to trust her maid?'

I saw his eyes flash. It was the briefest of summer lightning that played in their depths. I knew that he longed to adopt the suggestion that I had on purpose thrown out but dared not. That one look was enough for me. I had guessed his secret.

Before he could reply to my last remark, Lord Ridsdale came up.

'What is to be done?' he said; 'the police superintendent insists on our all, without respect of persons, being searched.'

'There is nothing in that,' I said; 'it is the usual thing. I will be the first to submit to the examination.'

The police went through their work thoroughly, and, of course, came across neither clue nor diamonds. We presently sat down to breakfast, but I don't think we any of us had much appetite. Lady Ridsdale's eyes were red with crying, and I could see that the loss had shaken both her nerve and fortitude. It was more or less of a relief when the post came in. Amongst the letters I found a telegram for myself. I knew what it meant before I opened it. It was from a man in a distant part of the country whom I had promised to assist in a matter of grave importance. I saw that it was necessary for me to return to town without delay. I was very loth to leave my host and hostess in their present dilemma, but there was no help for it, and soon after breakfast I took my leave. Ridsdale promised to write me if there was any news of the diamonds, and soon the circumstance passed more or less into the background of my brain, owing to the intense interest of the other matter which I had taken up. My work in the north was over, and I had returned to town, when I received a letter from Ridsdale.

'We are in a state of despair,' he wrote; 'we have had two detectives on board, and the police have moved heaven and earth to try and discover the bracelet—all in vain; not the slightest clue has been forthcoming. No one has worked harder for us than Vyner. He has a small place of his own further down the river, and comes up to see us almost daily. He has made all sorts of suggestions for the recovery of the diamonds, but hitherto they have led to nothing. In short, our one hope now turns upon you, Bell; you have done as difficult things as this before. Will you come and see us, and give us the benefit of your advice? If any man can solve this mystery, you are the person.'

I wrote immediately to say that I would return to the *Theodora* on the following evening, and for the remainder of that day tried to the best of my ability to think out this most difficult problem. I felt morally certain that I could put my hand on the thief, but I had no real clue to work upon—nothing beyond a nameless suspicion. Strange as it may seem, I was moved by sentiment. I had spent some pleasant hours in Vyner's society—I had enjoyed his conversation; I had liked the man for himself. He had abilities above the average, of that I was certain—if he were proved guilty, I did not want to be the one to bring his crime home to him. So uncomfortable were my feelings that at last I made up my mind to take a somewhat bold step. This was neither more nor less than to go to see Vyner himself before visiting the house-boat. What I was to do and say when I got to him I was obliged to leave altogether to chance; but I had a feeling almost amounting to a certainty that by means of this visit I should ultimately return the bracelet to my friends the Ridsdales.

The next afternoon I found myself rowing slowly down the river, thinking what the issue of my visit to Vyner would be. It happened to be a perfect evening. The sun had just set. The long reach of river stretched away to the distant bend, where, through the gathering twilight, I could just see the white gates of the Eight-Mile Lock. Raising my voice, I sang out in a long-drawn, sonorous monotone the familiar cry of 'Lock! lock! lock!' and, bending to the sculls, sent my little skiff flying down stream. The sturdy figure of old James Pegg, the lock-keeper, whom I had known for many years, instantly appeared on the bridge. One of the great gates slowly swung open, and, shipping my sculls, I shot in, and called out a cheery good-evening to my old friend.

'Mr Bell!' exclaimed the old fellow, hurrying along the edge of the lock. 'Well, I never! I did not see it was you at first, and yet I ought to have known that long, swinging stroke of yours. You are the last person I expected to see. I was half afraid it might be some one else, although I don't know that I was expecting any one in particular. Excuse me, sir, but was it you called out "Lock" just now?'

'Of course it was,' I answered, laughing. 'I'm in the deuce of a hurry tonight, Jimmy, as I want to get on to Wotton before dark. Look sharp, will you, and let me down.'

'All right, sir—but you did frighten me just now. I wish you hadn't called out like that!'

As I glanced up at him, I was surprised to see that his usually ruddy, round face was as white as a sheet, and he was breathing quickly.

'Why, what on earth is the matter, Jimmy?' I cried; 'how can I have frightened you?'

'Oh, it's nothing, sir; I suppose I'm an old fool,' he faltered, smiling. 'I don't know what's the matter with me, sir—I'm all of a tremble. The fact is, something happened here last night, and I don't seem to have got over it. You know, I am all by myself here now, sir, and a lonely place it is.'

'Something happened?' I said; 'not an accident, I hope?'

'No, sir, no accident that I know of, and yet I have been half expecting one to occur all day, and I have been that weak I could hardly wind up the sluices. I am getting old now, and I'm not the man I was; but I'm right glad to see you, Mr Bell, that I am.'

He kept pausing as he spoke, and now and then glanced up the river, as if expecting to see a boat coming round the bend every moment. I was much puzzled by his extraordinary manner. I knew him to be a steady man, and one whose services were much valued by the Conservancy; but it needed only a glance now to show that there was something very much amiss with him.

The darkness was increasing every moment, and, being anxious to get on as soon as possible, I was just going to tell him again to hurry up with the sluices, when he bent down close to me, and said,—

'Would you mind stepping out for a moment, sir, if you can spare the time? I wish to speak to you, sir. I'd be most grateful if you would wait a minute or two.'

'Certainly, Jimmy,' I answered, hauling myself to the side with the boat-hook, and getting out. 'Is there anything I can do for you? I am afraid you are not well. I never saw you like this before.'

'No, sir; and I never felt like it before, that I can remember. Something happened here last night that has taken all the nerve out of me, and I want to tell you what it was. I know you are so clever, Mr Bell, and I have heard about your doings up at Wallinghurst last autumn, when you cleared up the Manor House ghost, and got old Monkford six months.'

'Well, fire away,' I said, filling my pipe, and wondering what was coming.

'It is this way, sir,' he began. 'Last night after I had had my supper I thought I'd like a stroll and a quiet smoke along the towing path before turning in. I did not expect any more boats, as it was getting on for ten o'clock. I walked about three-quarters of a mile, and was just going to turn round, when I saw a light down on the surface of the water in mid-stream. It was pretty dark, for the moon was not up yet, and there was a thick white mist rising from the water. I thought it must be some one in a canoe at first, so I waited a bit and watched. Then it suddenly disappeared, and the next instant I saw it again about a hundred yards or so higher up the stream, but only for a second, and then it went out. It fairly puzzled me to know what it could be, as I had never seen anything like it before. I felt sure it wasn't any sort of craft, but I had heard of strange lights being seen at times on the water—what they call jack-o'-lanterns, I believe, sir. I reckoned it might be one of them, but I thought I'd get back to the lock, so that, if it was a canoe, I could let it through. However, nothing came of it, and I waited and watched, and worried all the evening about it, but couldn't come to any sort of idea, so I went to bed. Well, about one o'clock this morning I suddenly woke up and thought I could hear some one a long way off calling exactly as you did just now, "Lock! lock! lock!" but it sounded ever so far away.

'"It's some of those theatre people coming back to the *Will-o'-the-Wisp* house-boat," I said to myself, "and I'm not going to turn out for them." The lock was full at the time, so I thought I would just let them work it for themselves. I waited a bit, expecting to hear them every minute come up, singing and swearing as they do, but they never came, and I was just dropping off when I heard the call again. It was not an ordinary sort of voice, but a long, wailing cry, just as if some one was in trouble or drowning. "Hi! hi! Lock! lo-oock!" it went.

'I got up then and went out. The moon was up now and quite bright, and the mist had cleared off, so I went to the bridge on the upper gates and looked upstream. This is where I was standing, sir, just as we are standing now. I could see right up to the bend, and there was not the sign of a boat. I stood straining my eyes, expecting to see a boat come round every moment, when I heard the cry again, and this time it sounded not fifty yards upstream. I could not make it out at all, so I shouted out as loud as I could, "Who are you? What's the matter?" but there was no answer; and then suddenly, the next instant, close below me, from *inside* the lock this time, just here, came a shout, piercing, shrill, and loud, "Open the lock, quick, quick! Open the lock!"

'I tell you, sir, my heart seemed to stand dead still, and I nearly fell back over the bridge. I wheeled round sharp, but there was nothing in the lock, that I'll swear to my dying day—for I could see all over it, and nothing could have got in there without passing me. The moon was quite bright, and I could see all round it. Without knowing what I was doing, I rushed down like mad to the lower gates, and began to wind up one of the sluices, and then I stood there and waited, but nothing came. As the lock emptied I looked down, but there was no sign of anything anywhere, so I let down the sluice without opening the gates, and then filled up the lock again. I stood by the post, hardly daring to move, when, about half-past five, thank God, I heard the whistle of a tug, and, after seeing her through, it was broad daylight.

'That's the whole story, sir, and how I'm going to live through the night again I don't know. It was a spirit if ever there was one in the world. It's a warning to me, sir; and what's going to happen I don't know.'

'Well, Jimmy,' I answered, 'it certainly is a most extraordinary story, and if I didn't know you as well as I do, I should say you had taken something more than a smoke before you turned in last night.'

'I never touch a drop, sir, except when I go into Farley and have a glass of beer, but I have not been there for more than a week now.'

I confess that Jimmy's story had left a most unpleasant

impression on me. I had little doubt that the whole thing was some strange subjective hallucination, but for a weird and ghostly experience it certainly beat most of the tales I had ever heard. I thought for a moment—it was now quite dark, and I felt little inclined to go on to Wotton. My keenest interests were awakened.

'Look here,' I said, 'what do you say if I stay here tonight? Can you give me a shake-down of any sort?'

'That I will, sir, and right gladly, and thank God if you will but stay with me. If I was alone here again, and heard that voice, I believe it would kill me. I'll tie up your boat outside, and bring your things in, and then we'll have supper. I'll feel a new man with you staying here, sir.'

In a few minutes we were both inside old Jimmy's cosy quarters. His whole bearing seemed to have changed suddenly, and he ran about with alacrity, getting supper ready, and seeming quite like himself again. During the whole evening he kept harping at intervals on the subject of the mysterious voice, but we heard no sound whatever, and I felt more and more certain that the whole thing was due to hallucination on the part of the old man. At eleven o'clock a skiff came up through the lock, and almost immediately afterwards I bade Jimmy goodnight and went into the little room he had prepared for me.

I went quickly to bed, and, tired after my long pull, despite the originality of the situation, fell fast asleep. Suddenly I awoke—some one was bending over me and calling me by my name. I leapt up, and, not realising where I was for the moment, but with a sort of dim idea that I was engaged in some exposure, instinctively seized the man roughly by the throat. In a moment I remembered everything, and quickly released my grip of poor old Jimmy, who was gurgling and gasping with horror. I burst out laughing at my mistake, and begged his pardon for treating him so roughly.

'It is all right, sir,' he panted. 'I hope I didn't frighten you, but I have heard it again, not five minutes ago.'

'The deuce you have,' I said, striking a match and looking at my watch.

It was nearly two o'clock, and before the minute was up I heard distinctly a cry, as if from some great distance, of 'Lock, lock, lock!' and then all was silence again.

'Did you hear it, sir?' whispered the old man, clutching me by the arm with a trembling hand.

'Yes, I heard it,' I said. 'Don't you be frightened, Jimmy; just wait till I get my clothes on; I am going to see this thing through.'

'Be careful, sir; for God's sake, be careful,' he whispered.

'All right,' I said, slipping on some things. 'Just get me a good strong boat-hook, and don't make too much noise. If this mystery is flesh and blood I'll get to the bottom of it somehow. You stay here; and if I call, come out.'

I took the thick, short boat-hook which he had brought me and, softly unlatching the door, went out.

The moon was now riding high overhead and casting black fantastic shadows across the little white cottage. All my senses were on the keenest alert, my ears were pricked up for the slightest sound. I crept softly to the bridge on the upper gate which was open. I looked up stream and thought I could see some little ripples on the surface of the water as if a swift boat had just passed down, but there was no sign of any craft whatever to be seen. It was intensely still, and no sound broke the silence save the intermittent croaking of some bull-frogs in the dark shadows of the pollards on the further bank. Behind me could also be heard the gurgling twinkle of the overflow through the chinks of the lower gate.

I stood quite still, gripping the boat-hook in my hand, and looking right and left, straining my eyes for the slightest movement of anything around, when suddenly, close below me from the water, inside the lock, came a loud cry—

'Open the lock, for God's sake, open the lock!'

I started back, feeling my hair rise and stiffen. The sound echoed and reverberated through the silent night, and then died away; but before it had done so I had sprung to the great beam and closed the upper gate. As I did so I caught sight of the old man trembling and shaking at the door of the cottage. I called to him to go and watch the upper gate, and, racing down to the lower ones, wound up one of the sluices with a few pulls, so as to let out the water with as little escape room as possible. I knew by this means if there were any creature of tangible form in the water we must find it when the lock was emptied, as its escape was cut off.

Each of the following minutes seemed stretched into a lifetime as, with eyes rivetted on the dark water in the lock, I watched its gradual descent. I hardly dared to think of what I expected to see rise to the surface any moment. Would the lock never empty? Down, down sank the level, and still I saw nothing. A long, misshapen arm of black cloud was slowly stretching itself across the moon.

Hark! there was something moving about down in the well of darkness below me, and as I stood and watched I saw that the water was uncovering a long, black mass and that something ran slowly out of the water and began to clamber up the slimy, slippery beams. What in the name of heaven could it be? By the uncertain light I could only see its dim outline; it seemed to have an enormous bulbous head and dripping, glistening body. The sound of a rapid patter up the tow-path told me that the old man had seen it and was running for his life.

I rushed down to where the thing was, and as its great head appeared above the edge, with all my force struck it a terrific blow with the boat-hook. The weapon flew into splinters in my hand, and the next moment the creature had leapt up beside me and dashed me to the ground with almost super-human force. I was up and on to it again in a second, and as I caught and closed with it saw that I had at least to deal with a human being, and that what he lacked in stature he more than made up for in strength. The struggle that ensued was desperate and furious. The covering to his head that had splin-tered the boat-hook was, I saw, a sort of helmet, completely protecting the head from any blow, and the body was cased in a slippery, closely fitting garment that kept eluding my grasp. To and fro we swayed and wrestled, and for a moment I thought I had met my match till, suddenly freeing my right arm, I got in a smashing blow in the region of the heart. The creature uttered a cry of pain and fell headlong to the ground.

Old Jimmy Pegg had hurried back as soon as he heard our struggles and knew that he was not dealing with a being of another world. He ran up eagerly to me.

'Here's your ghost, you old coward!' I panted; 'he has got the hardest bone and muscle I ever felt in a ghost yet. I am not used to fighting men in helmets, and he is as slippery as an eel, but I hope to goodness I have not done more than knock the wind out of him. He is a specimen I should rather like to take alive. Catch hold of his feet and we'll get him inside and see who he is.'

Between us we carried the prostrate figure inside the cottage and laid him down like a log on the floor. He never moved nor uttered a sound, and I was afraid at first that I had finished him for good and all. I next knelt down and pro-ceeded to unfasten the helmet, which, from its appearance, was something like the kind used by divers, while the old man brought the lantern close to his face. At the first glance I knew in an instant that I had seen the face before, and the next second recognised, to my utter astonishment and horror, that it belonged to Ralph Vyner.

For the moment I was completely dumbfounded, and gazed at the man without speaking. It was obvious that he had only fainted from the blow, for I could see that he was breathing, and in a few minutes he opened his eyes and fixed them on me with a dull and vacant stare. Then he seemed to recall the situation, though he evidently did not recognise me.

'Let me go,' he cried, making an effort to rise. 'My God! you have killed me.' He pressed his hand to his side and fell back again: his face was contorted as if in great pain.

There was obviously only one thing to be done, and that was to send for medical assistance at once. It was clear that the man was badly injured, but to what extent I could not determine. It was impossible to extract the slightest further communication from him—he lay quite still, groaning from time to time.

I told Jimmy to go off at once to Farley and bring the doctor. I scribbled a few directions on a piece of paper.

The old man hurried out of the cottage, but in less than a minute he was back again in great excitement.

'Look here, sir, what I have just picked up,' he said; 'it's something he has dropped, I reckon.'

As Jimmy spoke he held out a square leather case: there was a monogram on it. I took it in my hand and pressed the lid; it flew open, and inside, resting on its velvet bed, lay the glittering circlet of diamonds. I held Lady Ridsdale's lost bracelet in my hand. All my suspicions were confirmed: Vyner was the thief.

Without saying a word I shut the box and despatched the old man at once for the doctor, bidding him go as fast as he could. Then I sat down by the prostrate man and waited. I knew that Jimmy could not be back for at least two hours. The grey dawn was beginning to steal in through the little latticed window when Vyner moved, opened his eyes and looked at me. He started as his eyes fell on the case.

'You are Mr Bell,' he said slowly. 'Ridsdale told me that you were coming to the *Theodora* on purpose to discover the mystery of the lost diamonds. You didn't know that I should give you an opportunity of discovering the truth even before you arrived at the house-boat. Bend down close to me—you have injured me; I may not recover; hear what I have to say.'

I bent over him, prepared to listen to his words, which came out slowly.

'I am a forger and a desperate man. Three weeks ago I forged one of Ridsdale's cheques and lessened my friend's balance to the tune of five thousand pounds. He and his wife were old friends of mine, but I wanted the money desperately, and was impervious to sentiment or anything else. On that first day when you met me, although I seemed cheery enough, I was fit to kill myself. I had hoped to be able to restore the stolen money long before Ridsdale was likely to miss it. But this hope had failed. I saw no loophole of escape, and the day of reckoning could not be far off. What devil prompted Ridsdale to bring those diamonds on board, Heaven only knows. The moment I saw them they fascinated me and I knew I should have a try for them. All during that evening's festivity I could think of nothing else. I made up my mind to secure them by hook or by crook. Before we retired for the night, however, I thought I would give Ridsdale a chance. I asked him if he would lend me the exact sum I had already stolen from him, five thousand pounds, but he had heard rumours to my discredit and refused point-blank. I hated him for it. I went into my tent under the pretence of lying down, but in reality to concoct and, if possible, carry out my plot. I waited until the quietest hour before dawn, then I slipped out of my tent, waded into the water, approached the open window of the Countess's cabin, thrust in my hand, took out the case, and, going down the river about a quarter of a mile, threw the diamonds into the middle of the stream. I marked well the place where they sank; I then returned to my tent and went to bed.

'You know what occurred the following morning. I neither feared Ridsdale nor his wife, but you, Bell, gave me a considerable amount of uneasiness. I felt certain that in an evil moment on the night before I had given you a clue. To a man of your ability the slightest clue was all-sufficient. I felt that I must take the bull by the horns and find out whether you suspected me or not. I talked to you, and guessed by the tone of your remarks that you had your suspicions. My relief was immense when that telegram arrived which hurried you away from the *Theodora*. On the following day I returned to my own little place on the banks of the river four miles below this lock. I knew it was necessary for me to remain quiet for a time, but all the same my plans were clearly made, and I only waited until the first excitement of the loss had subsided and the police and detectives were off their guard. In the meantime I went to see Ridsdale almost daily, and suggested many expedients for securing the thief and getting hold of the right clue. If he ever suspected me, which I don't for a moment suppose, I certainly put him off the scent. My intention was to take the diamonds out of the country, sell them for all that I could get, then return the five thousand pounds which I had stolen from his bank, and leave England for ever. As a forger I should be followed to the world's end, but as the possessor of stolen diamonds I felt myself practically safe. My scheme was too cleverly worked out to give the ordinary detective a chance of discovering me.

'Two days ago I had a letter from Ridsdale in which he told me that he intended to put the matter into your hands. Now this was by no means to my mind, for you, Bell, happened to be the one man in the world whom I really dreaded. I saw that I must no longer lose time. Under my little boat-house I had a small submarine boat which I had lately finished, more as a hobby than anything else. I had begun it years ago in my odd moments on a model I had seen of a torpedo used in the American War. My boat is now in the lock outside, and you will see for yourself what ingenuity was needed to construct such a thing. On the night before the one which has just passed, I got it ready, and, as soon as it was dark, started off in it to recover the diamonds. I got through the lock easily by going in under the water with a barge, but when I reached the spot where I had sunk the diamonds, found to my dismay that my electric light would not work. There was no help for it—I could not find the bracelet without the aid of the light, and was bound to return home to repair the lamp. This delay was fraught with danger, but there was no help for it. My difficulty now was to get back through the lock; for though I waited for quite three hours no boats came along. I saw the upper gates were open, but how to get through the lower ones I could not conceive. I felt sure that my only chance was to frighten the lock-keeper, and get him to open the sluices, for I knew I could pass through them unobserved if they were open, as I had done once before.

'In my diver's helmet was a thick glass face-piece. This

had an opening, closed by a cap, which could be unscrewed, and through which I could breathe when above water, and also through which my voice would come, causing a peculiar hollowness which I guessed would have a very startling effect, especially as I myself would be quite invisible. I got into the lock, and shouted to Pegg. I succeeded in frightening him; he hurried to do what I ordered. He wound up the lower sluice, I shot through under water, and so got back unseen. All yesterday I hesitated about trying the experiment again, the risk was so great; but I knew that Ridsdale was certain to see his bank-book soon, that my forgery was in imminent danger of being discovered, also that you, Bell, were coming upon the scene.

'Yes, at any risk, I must now go on.

'I repaired my light, and again last night passed through the lock on my way up, by simply waiting for another boat. As a matter of fact, I passed up through this lock under a skiff about eleven o'clock. My light was now all right, I found the diamond case easily, and turned to pass down the stream by the same method as before. If you had not been here I should have succeeded, and should have been safe, but now it is all up.'

He paused, and his breath came quickly.

'I doubt if I shall recover,' he said in a feeble voice.

'I hope you will,' I replied; 'and hark! I think I hear the doctor's steps.'

I was right, for a moment or two later old Jimmy Pegg and Dr Simmons entered the cottage. While the doctor was examining the patient and talking to him, I went out with Jimmy to have a look at the submarine boat. By fixing a rope round it we managed to haul it up, and then proceeded to examine it. It certainly was the most wonderful piece of ingenious engineering I had ever seen. The boat was in the shape of an enormous cigar, and was made of aluminium. It was seven feet long, and had a circular beam of sixteen inches. At the pointed end, close to where the occupant's feet would be, was an air chamber capable of being filled or emptied at will by means of a compressed air cylinder, enabling the man to rise or sink whenever he wished to. Inside, the boat was lined with flat chambers of compressed air for breathing purposes, which were governed by a valve. It was also provided with a small accumulator and electric motor which drove the tiny propeller astern. The helmet which the man wore fitted around the opening at the head end.

After examining the boat it was easy to see how Vyner had escaped through the lock the night before I arrived, as this submarine wonder of ingenuity would be able to shoot through the sluice gate under water, when the sluice was raised to empty the lock.

After exchanging a few remarks with Jimmy, I returned to the cottage to learn the doctor's verdict.

It was grave, but not despairing. The patient could not be moved for a day or two. He was, in Dr Simmons's opinion, suffering more from shock than anything else. If he remained perfectly quiet, he would in all probability recover; if he were disturbed, the consequences might be serious.

An hour afterwards I found myself on my way upstream sculling as fast as I could in the direction of the *Theodora*. I arrived there at an early hour, and put the case which contained the diamonds into Lady Ridsdale's hands.

I shall never forget the astonishment of Ridsdale and his wife when I told my strange tale. The Countess burst into tears, and Ridsdale was terribly agitated.

'I have known Vyner from a boy, and so has my wife,' he

exclaimed. 'Of course, this proves him to be an unmitigated scoundrel, but I cannot be the one to bring him to justice.'

'Oh, no, Charlie, whatever happens we must forgive him,' said Lady Ridsdale, looking up with a white face.

I had nothing to say to this, it was not my affair. Unwittingly I had been the means of restoring to the Ridsdales their lost bracelet; they must act as they thought well with regard to the thief.

As a matter of fact, Vyner did escape the full penalty of his crime. Having got back the diamonds Lord Ridsdale would not prosecute. On the contrary, he helped the broken-down man to leave the country. From the view of pure justice he was, of course, wrong, but I could not help being glad.

As an example of what a desperate man will do, I think it would be difficult to beat Vyner's story. The originality and magnitude of the conception, the daring which enabled the man, single-handed, to do his own dredging in a submarine boat in one of the reaches of the Thames have seldom been equalled.

As I thought over the whole scheme, my only regret was that such ability should not have been devoted to nobler ends.

The Gift of the Emperor

E. W. Hornung

Ernest William Hornung (1866–1921) was Arthur Conan Doyle's brother-in-law and was himself an accomplished storyteller. His Hungarian-born father had worked in a shipping firm in Hamburg before emigrating to England, and 'Willie' Hornung also travelled widely in Europe. At the age of seventeen, he went to Australia, hoping that the climate would improve his fragile health, and spent two years there. After returning to Britain, he worked as a journalist at the time of the Jack the Ripper murders, and started writing fiction.

Hornung created several interesting detective characters, but by far the most popular was A. J. Raffles, the cricketing cracksman. 'The Gift of the Emperor' first appeared in *Cassell's Magazine* in 1898, and formed the concluding episode in *The Amateur Cracksman* (1899). The story was later televised, with a script by the prolific screenwriter Philip Mackie, as an episode in the Yorkshire Television series *Raffles*. First broadcast on 13 May 1977, it starred Anthony Valentine as the gentlemanly burglar and Christopher Strauli as Bunny Manders. Ninety years after the story was written, a BBC radio version featured Jeremy Clyde and Michael Cochrane in the lead roles.

I

When the King of the Cannibal Islands made faces at Queen Victoria, and a European monarch set the cables tingling with his compliments on the exploit, the indignation in England was not less than the surprise, for the thing was not so common as it has since become. But when it transpired that a gift of peculiar significance was to follow the congratulations, to give them weight, the inference prevailed that the white potentate and the black had taken simultaneous leave of their fourteen senses. For the gift was a pearl of price unparalleled, picked aforetime by British cutlasses from a Polynesian setting, and presented by British royalty to the sovereign, who seized this opportunity of restoring it to its original possessor.

The incident would have been a godsend to the Press a few weeks later. Even in June there were leaders, letters, large headlines, leaded type; the *Daily Chronicle* devoted half its literary page to a charming drawing of the island capital which the new *Pall Mall*, in a leading article headed by a pun, advised the Government to blow to flinders. I was myself driving a poor but not dishonest quill at the time, and the topic of the hour goaded me into satiric verse which obtained a better place than anything I had yet turned out. I had let my flat in town, and taken inexpensive quarters at Thames Ditton, on a plea of a disinterested passion for the river.

'First-rate, old boy,' said Raffles (who must needs come and see me there), lying back in the boat while I sculled and steered. 'I suppose they pay you pretty well for these, eh?'

'Not a penny.'

'Nonsense, Bunny! I thought they paid so well? Give them time, and you'll get your cheque.'

'Oh no, I shan't,' said I gloomily. 'I've got to be content with the honour of getting in; the editor wrote to say so, in so many words,' I added. But I gave the gentleman his distinguished name.

'You don't mean to say you've written for payment already?'

No; it was the last thing I had intended to admit. But I had done it. The murder was out; there was no sense in further concealment. I had written for my money because I really needed it; if he must know, I was cursedly hard up. Raffles nodded as though he knew already. I warmed to my woes. It was no easy matter to keep your end up as a raw freelance of letters; for my part, I was afraid I wrote neither well enough nor ill enough for success. I suffered from a persistent ineffectual feeling after style. Verse I could manage; but it did not pay. To personal paragraphs and the baser journalism I could not and I would not stoop.

Raffles nodded again, this time with a smile that stayed in his eyes as he leant back watching me. I knew that he was thinking of other things I had stooped to, and I thought I knew what he was going to say. He had said it before so often; he was sure to say it again. I had my answer ready, but evidently he was tired of asking the same question. His lids fell, he took up the paper he had dropped, and I sculled the length of the old red wall of Hampton Court before he spoke again.

'And they gave you nothing for these! My dear Bunny, they're capital, not only *qua* verses, but for crystallising your subject and putting it in a nutshell. Certainly you've taught me more about it than I knew before. But is it really worth fifty thousand pounds—a single pearl?'

'A hundred, I believe; but that wouldn't scan.'

'A hundred thousand pounds!' said Raffles, with his eyes shut. And again I made certain what was coming, but again I was mistaken. 'If it's worth all that,' he cried at last, 'there would be no getting rid of it at all; it's not like a diamond that you can subdivide. But I beg your pardon, Bunny. I was forgetting!'

And we said no more about the emperor's gift; for pride thrives on an empty pocket, and no privation would have drawn from me the proposal which I had expected Raffles to make. My expectation had been half a hope, though I only knew it now. But neither did we touch again on what Raffles professed to have forgotten—my 'apostasy,' my 'lapse into virtue,' as he had been pleased to call it. We were both a little silent, a little constrained, each preoccupied with his own thoughts. It was months since we had met, and, as I saw him off towards eleven o'clock that Sunday night, I fancied it was for more months that we were saying good-bye.

But as we waited for the train I saw those clear eyes peering at me under the station lamps, and when I met their glance Raffles shook his head.

'You don't look well on it, Bunny,' said he. 'I never did believe in this Thames Valley. You want a change of air.'

I wished I might get it.

'What you really want is a sea voyage.'

'And a winter at St Moritz, or do you recommend Cannes or Cairo? It's all very well, A.J., but you forget what I told you about my funds.'

'I forget nothing. I merely don't want to hurt your feelings. But, look here, a sea voyage you shall have. I want a change myself, and you shall come with me as my guest. We'll spend July in the Mediterranean.'

'But you're playing cricket—'

'Hang the cricket!'

'Well, if I thought you meant it—'

'Of course I mean it. Will you come?'

'Like a shot—if you go.'

And I shook his hand, and waved mine in farewell, with the perfectly good-humoured conviction that I should hear no more of the matter. It was a passing thought, no more, no less. I soon wished it were more; that week found me wishing myself out of England for good and all. I was making nothing. I could but subsist on the difference between the rent I paid for my flat and the rent at which I had sublet it, furnished, for the season. And the season was near its end, and creditors awaited me in town. Was it possible to be entirely honest? I had run no bills when I had money in my pocket, and the more downright dishonesty seemed to me the less ignoble.

But from Raffles, of course, I heard nothing more; a week went by, and half another week; then, late on the second Wednesday night, I found a telegram from him at my lodgings, after seeking him vainly in town, and dining with desperation at the solitary club to which I still belonged.

'Arranged to leave Waterloo by North German Lloyd special,' he wired, '9.25 a.m. Monday next will meet you Southampton aboard *Uhlan* with tickets, am writing.'

And write he did, a light-hearted letter enough, but full of serious solicitude for me and for my health and prospects; a letter almost touching in the light of our past relations, in the twilight of their complete rupture. He said that he had booked two berths to Naples, that we were bound for Capri, which was clearly the Island of the Lotus-eaters, that we would bask there together, 'and for a while forget.' It was a charming letter. I had never seen Italy; the privilege of initiation should be his. No mistake was greater than to deem it an impossible country for the summer. The Bay of Naples was never so divine, and he wrote of 'faery lands forlorn,' as though the poetry sprang unbidden to his pen. To come back to earth and prose, I might think it unpatriotic of him to choose a German boat, but on no other line did you receive such attention and accommodation for your money. There was a hint of better reasons. Raffles wrote, as he had telegraphed, from Bremen; and I gathered that the personal use of some little influence with the authorities there had resulted in a material reduction in our fares.

Imagine my excitement and delight! I managed to pay what I owed at Thames Ditton, to squeeze a small editor for a very small cheque, and my tailors for one more flannel suit. I remember that I broke my last sovereign to get a box of Sullivan's cigarettes for Raffles to smoke on the voyage. But my heart was as light as my purse on the Monday morning, the fairest morning of an unfair summer, when the special whirled me through the sunshine to the sea.

A tender awaited us at Southampton. Raffles was not on board, nor did I really look for him till we reached the liner's side. And then I looked in vain. His face was not among the many that fringed the rail; his hand was not of the few that waved to friends. I climbed aboard in a sudden heaviness. I had no ticket, nor the money to pay for one. I did not even know the number of my room. My heart was in my mouth as I waylaid a steward and asked if a Mr Raffles was on board. Thank Heaven—he was! But where? The man did not know; was plainly on some other errand, and a-hunting I must go. But there was no sign of him on the promenade deck, and none below in the saloon; the smoking-room was empty but for a little German with a red moustache twisted into his eyes;

nor was Raffles in his own cabin, whither I inquired my way in desperation, but where the sight of his own name on the baggage was certainly a further reassurance. Why he himself kept in the background, however, I could not conceive, and only sinister reasons would suggest themselves in explanation.

'So there you are! I've been looking for you all over the ship!'

Despite the graven prohibition, I had tried the bridge as a last resort; and there, indeed, was A. J. Raffles, seated on a skylight, and leaning over one of the officers' long chairs, in which reclined a girl in a white drill coat and skirt—a slip of a girl with a pale skin, dark hair, and rather remarkable eyes. So much I noted as he rose and quickly turned; thereupon I could think of nothing but the swift grimace which preceded a start of well-feigned astonishment.

'Why—Bunny?' cried Raffles. 'Where have you sprung from?'

I stammered something as he pinched my hand.

'And you are coming in this ship? And to Naples too? Well, upon my word!—Miss Werner, may I introduce him?'

And he did so without a blush, describing me as an old schoolfellow whom he had not seen for months, with wilful circumstance and gratuitous detail that filled me at once with confusion, suspicion, and revolt. I felt myself blushing for us both, and I did not care. My address utterly deserted me, and I made no effort to recover it, to carry the thing off. All I would do was to mumble such words as Raffles actually put into my mouth, and that I doubt not with a thoroughly evil grace.

'So you saw my name in the list of passengers, and came in search of me? Good old Bunny! I say, though, I wish you'd share my cabin? I've got a beauty on the promenade deck, but they wouldn't promise to keep me by myself. We ought to see about it before they shove in some alien. In any case we shall have to get out of this.'

For a quartermaster had entered the wheel-house, and even while we had been speaking the pilot had taken possession of the bridge; as we descended, the tender left us with flying handkerchiefs and shrill good-byes; and as we bowed to Miss Werner on the promenade deck, there came a deep, slow throbbing underfoot, and our voyage had begun.

It did not begin pleasantly between Raffles and me. On deck he had overborne my stubborn perplexity by dint of a forced though forceful joviality; in his cabin the gloves were off.

'You idiot,' he snarled, 'you've given me away again!'

'How have I given you away?'

I ignored the separate insult in his last word.

'How? I should have thought any clod could see that I meant us to meet by chance!'

'After taking both tickets yourself?'

'They know nothing about that on board; besides, I hadn't decided when I took the tickets.'

'Then you should have let me know when you did decide. You lay your plans, and never say a word, and expect me to tumble to them by light of nature. How was I to know you had anything on?'

I had turned the tables with some effect. Raffles almost hung his head.

'The fact is, Bunny, I didn't mean you to know. You—you've grown such a pious rabbit in your old age!'

My nickname and his tone went far to mollify me; other things went further, but I had much to forgive him still.

'If you were afraid of writing,' I pursued, 'it was your business to give me the tip the moment I set foot on board. I would have taken it all right. I am not so virtuous as all that.'

Was it my imagination, or did Raffles look slightly ashamed? If so, it was for the first and last time in all the years I knew him; nor can I swear to it even now.

'That,' said he, 'was the very thing I meant to do—to lie in wait in my room and get you as you passed. But—'

'You were better engaged?'

'Say otherwise.'

'The charming Miss Werner?'

'She is quite charming.'

'Most Australian girls are,' said I.

'How did you know she was one?' he cried.

'I heard her speak.'

'Brute!' said Raffles, laughing; 'she has no more twang than you have. Her people are German, she has been to school in Dresden, and is on her way out alone.'

'Money?' I inquired.

'Confound you!' he said, and, though he was laughing, I thought it was a point at which the subject might be changed.

'Well,' I said, 'it wasn't for Miss Werner you wanted us to play strangers, was it? You have some deeper game than that, eh?'

'I suppose I have.'

'Then hadn't you better tell me what it is?'

Raffles treated me to the old cautious scrutiny that I knew so well; the very familiarity of it, after all these months, set me smiling in a way that might have reassured him; for dimly already I divined his enterprise.

'It won't send you off in the pilot's boat, Bunny?'

'Not quite.'

'Then—you remember the pearl you wrote the—'

I did not wait for him to finish his sentence.

'You've got it!' I cried, my face on fire, for I caught sight of it that moment in the state-room mirror.

Raffles seemed taken aback.

'Not yet,' said he; 'but I mean to have it before we get to Naples.'

'Is it on board?'

'Yes.'

'But how—where—who's got it?'

'A little German officer, a whipper-snapper with perpendicular moustaches.'

'I saw him in the smoke-room.'

'That's the chap; he's always there. Herr Captain Wilhelm von Heumann, if you look in the list. Well, he's the special envoy of the emperor, and he's taking the pearl out with him!'

'You found this out in Bremen?'

'No, in Berlin, from a newspaper man I know there. I'm ashamed to tell you, Bunny, that I went there on purpose!'

I burst out laughing.

'You needn't be ashamed. You are doing the very thing I was rather hoping you were going to propose the other day on the river.'

'You were hoping it?' said Raffles, with his eyes wide open. Indeed, it was his turn to show surprise, and mine to be much more ashamed than I felt.

'Yes,' I answered, 'I was quite keen on the idea, but I wasn't going to propose it.'

'Yet you would have listened to me the other day?'

Certainly I would, and I told him so without reserve; not brazenly, you understand; not even now with the gusto of a man who savours such an adventure for its own sake, but doggedly, defiantly, through my teeth, as one who had tried to live honestly and had failed. And, while I was about it, I told him much more. Eloquently enough, I dare say, I gave him chapter and verse of my hopeless struggle, my inevitable defeat; for hopeless and inevitable they were to a man with my record, even though that record was written only in one's own soul. It was the old story of the thief trying to turn honest man; the thing was against nature, and there was an end of it.

Raffles entirely disagreed with me. He shook his head over my conventional view. Human nature was a board of chequers; why not reconcile oneself to alternate black and white? Why desire to be all one thing or all the other, like our forefathers on the stage or in the old-fashioned fiction? For his part, he enjoyed himself on all squares of the board, and liked the light the better for the shade. My conclusion he considered absurd.

'But you err in good company, Bunny, for all the cheap moralists who preach the same twaddle: old Virgil was the first and worst offender of you all. I back myself to climb out of Avernus any day I like, and sooner or later I shall climb out for good. I suppose I can't very well turn myself into a Limited Liability Company. But I could retire and settle down and live blamelessly ever after. I'm not sure that it couldn't be done on this pearl alone!'

'Then you don't still think it too remarkable to sell?'

'We might take a fishery and haul it up with smaller fry. It would come after months of ill-luck—just as we were going to sell the schooner; by Jove, it would be the talk of the Pacific!'

'Well, we've got to get it first. Is this von What's-his-name a formidable cuss?'

'More so than he looks; and he has the cheek of the devil!'

As he spoke a white drill skirt fluttered past the open state-room door, and I caught a glimpse of an upturned moustache beyond.

'But is he the chap we have to deal with? Won't the pearl be in the purser's keeping?'

Raffles stood at the door, frowning out upon the Solent, but for an instant he turned to me with a sniff.

'My good fellow, do you suppose the whole ship's company knows there's a gem like that aboard? You said that it was worth a hundred thousand pounds; in Berlin they say it's priceless. I doubt if the skipper himself knows that von Heumann has it on him.'

'And he has?'

'Must have.'

'Then we have only him to deal with?'

He answered me without a word. Something white was fluttering past once more, and Raffles, stepping forth, made the promenaders three.

II

I do not ask to set foot aboard a finer steamship than the *Uhlan* of the Norddeutscher Lloyd, to meet a kindlier gentleman than her then commander or better fellows than his officers. This much at least let me have the grace to admit. I hated the voyage. It was no fault of anybody connected with the ship; it was no fault of the weather, which was monotonously ideal. Not even in my own heart did the reason reside; conscience and I were divorced at last, and the decree made absolute. With my scruples had fled all fear, and I was ready to revel between bright skies and sparkling sea with the light-hearted detachment of Raffles himself. It was Raffles himself who prevented me, but not Raffles alone. It was Raffles and that Colonial minx on her way home from school.

What he could see in her—but that begs the question. Of course he saw no more than I did, but to annoy me, or perhaps to punish me for my long defection, he must turn his back on me and devote himself to this chit from Southampton to the Mediterranean. They were always together. It was too absurd. After breakfast they would begin, and go on until eleven or twelve at night; there was no intervening hour at which you might not hear her nasal laugh, or his quiet voice talking soft nonsense into her ear. Of course it was nonsense! Is it conceivable that a man like Raffles, with his knowledge of the world, and his experience of women (a side of his character upon which I have purposely never touched, for it deserves another volume)—is it credible, I ask, that such a man could find anything but nonsense to talk by the day together to a giddy young schoolgirl? I would not be unfair for the world. I think I have admitted that the young person had points. Her eyes, I suppose, were really fine, and certainly the shape of the little brown face was charming, so far as mere contour can charm. I admit also more audacity than I cared about, with enviable health, mettle, and vitality. I may not have occasion to report any of this young lady's speeches (they would scarcely bear it), and am therefore the more anxious to describe her without injustice. I confess to some little prejudice against her. I resented her success with Raffles, of whom, in consequence, I saw less and less each day. It is a mean thing to have to confess, but there must have been something not unlike jealousy rankling within me.

Jealousy there was in another quarter—crude, rampant, undignified jealousy. Captain von Heumann would twirl his moustaches into twin spires, shoot his white cuffs over his rings, and stare at me insolently through his rimless eye-glasses; we ought to have consoled each other, but we never exchanged a syllable. The captain had a murderous scar across one of his cheeks, a present from Heidelberg, and I used to think how he must long to have Raffles there to serve the same. It was not as though von Heumann never had his innings. Raffles let him go in several times a day, for the malicious pleasure of bowling him out as he was 'getting set'; those were his words when I taxed him disingenuously with obnoxious conduct towards a German on a German boat.

'You'll make yourself disliked on board!'

'By von Heumann merely.'

'But is that wise when he's the man we've got to diddle?'

'The wisest thing I ever did. To have chummed up with him would have been fatal—the common dodge.'

I was consoled, encouraged, almost content. I had feared Raffles was neglecting things, and I told him so in a burst. Here we were near Gibraltar, and not a word since the Solent. He shook his head with a smile.

'Plenty of time, Bunny, plenty of time. We can do nothing before we get to Genoa, and that won't be till Sunday night. The voyage is still young, and so are we; let's make the most of things while we can.'

It was after dinner on the promenade deck, and as Raffles spoke he glanced sharply fore and aft, leaving me next moment with a step full of purpose. I retired to the smoking-room, to smoke and read in a corner, and to watch von Heumann, who very soon came to drink beer and to sulk in another.

Few travellers tempt the Red Sea at midsummer; the *Uhlan* was very empty indeed. She had, however, but a limited supply of cabins on the promenade deck, and there was just that excuse for my sharing Raffles's room. I could have had one to myself downstairs, but I must be up above. Raffles had insisted that I should insist on the point. So we were together, I think, without suspicion, though also without any object that I could see.

On the Sunday afternoon I was asleep in my berth, the lower one, when the curtains were shaken by Raffles, who was in his shirt-sleeves on the settee.

'Achilles sulking in his bunk!'

'What else is there to do?' I asked him as I stretched and yawned. I noted, however, the good-humour of his tone, and did my best to catch it.

'I have found something else, Bunny.'

'I daresay!'

'You misunderstand me. The whippersnapper's making his century this afternoon. I've had other fish to fry.'

I swung my legs over the side of my berth and sat forward, as he was sitting, all attention. The inner door, a grating, was shut and bolted, and curtained like the open port-hole.

'We shall be at Genoa before sunset,' continued Raffles. 'It's the place where the deed's got to be done.'

'So you still mean to do it!'

'Did I ever say I didn't?'

'You have said so little either way.'

'Advisedly so, my dear Bunny; why spoil a pleasure trip by talking unnecessary shop? But now the time has come. It must be done at Genoa or not at all.'

'On land?'

'No, on board, tomorrow night. Tonight would do, but tomorrow is better, in case of mishap. If we were forced to use violence we could get away by the earliest train, and nothing be known till the ship was sailing and von Heumann found dead or drugged—'

'Not dead!' I exclaimed.

'Of course not,' assented Raffles, 'or there would be no need for us to bolt; but if we should have to bolt, Tuesday morning is our time, when this ship has got to sail, whatever happens. But I don't anticipate any violence. Violence is a confession of terrible incompetence. In all these years how many blows have you known me strike? Not one, I believe; but I have been quite ready to kill my man every time, if the worst came to the worst.'

I asked him how he proposed to enter von Heumann's state-room unobserved, and even through the curtained gloom of ours his face lighted up.

'Climb into my bunk, Bunny, and you shall see.'

I did so, but could see nothing. Raffles reached across me and tapped the ventilator, a sort of trap-door in the wall above his bed, some eighteen inches long and half that height. It opened outwards into the ventilating shaft.

'That,' said he, 'is our door to fortune. Open it if you like; you won't see much, because it doesn't open far; but loosening a couple of screws will set that all right. The shaft, as you may see, is more or less bottomless; you pass under it whenever you go to your bath, and the top is a skylight on the bridge. That's why this thing has to be done while we're at Genoa, because they keep no watch on the bridge in port. The ventilator opposite ours is von Heumann's. It again will only mean a couple of screws, and there's a beam to stand on while you work.'

'But if anybody should look from below?'

'It's extremely unlikely that anybody will be astir below, so unlikely that we can afford to chance it. No, I can't have you there to make sure. The great point is that neither of us should be seen from the time we turn in. A couple of ship's boys do sentry-go on these decks, and they shall be our witnesses; by Jove, it'll be the biggest mystery that ever was made!'

'If von Heumann doesn't resist.'

'Resist! He won't get the chance. He drinks too much

beer to sleep light, and nothing is so easy as to chloroform a heavy sleeper; you've even done it yourself on an occasion of which it's perhaps unfair to remind you. Von Heumann will be past sensation almost as soon as I get my hand through his ventilator. I shall crawl in over his body, Bunny, my boy!'

'And I?'

'You will hand me what I want, and hold the fort in case of accidents, and generally lend me the moral support you've made me require. It's a luxury, Bunny, but I found it devilish difficult to do without it after you turned pi!'

He said that von Heumann was certain to sleep with a bolted door, which he, of course, would leave unbolted, and spoke of other ways of laying a false scent while rifling the cabin. Not that Raffles anticipated a tiresome search. The pearl would be about von Heumann's person; in fact, Raffles knew exactly where and in what he kept it. Naturally I asked how he could have come by such knowledge, and his answer led up to a momentary unpleasantness.

'It's a very old story, Bunny. I really forget in what book it comes; I'm only sure of the Testament. But Samson was the unlucky hero and one Delilah the heroine.'

And he looked so knowing that I could not be in a moment's doubt as to his meaning.

'So the fair Australian has been playing Delilah?' said I.

'In a very harmless, innocent sort of way.'

'She got his mission out of him?'

'Yes, I've forced him to score all the points he could, and that was his great stroke, as I hoped it would be. He has even shown Amy the pearl.'

'Amy, eh! and she promptly told you?'

'Nothing of the kind. What makes you think so? I had the greatest trouble in getting it out of her.'

His tone should have been a sufficient warning to me. I had not the tact to take it as such. At last I knew the meaning of his furious flirtation, and stood wagging my head and shaking my finger, blinded to his frowns by my own enlightenment.

'Wily worm!' said I. 'Now I see through it all; how dense I've been!'

'Sure you're not still?'

'No; now I understand what has beaten me all the week. I simply couldn't fathom what you saw in that little girl. I never dreamt it was part of the game.'

'So you think it was that and nothing more?'

'You deep old dog—of course I do!'

'You didn't know she was the daughter of a wealthy squatter?'

'There are wealthy women by the dozen who would marry you tomorrow.'

'It doesn't occur to you that I might like to draw stumps, start clean, and live happily ever after—in the bush?'

'With that voice? It certainly does not!'

'Bunny!' he cried so fiercely that I braced myself for a blow. But no more followed.

'Do you think you would live happily?' I made bold to ask him.

'God knows!' he answered. And with that he left me, to marvel at his look and tone, and, more than ever, at the insufficiently exciting cause.

III

Of all the mere feats of cracksmanship which I have seen Raffles perform, at once the most delicate and most difficult was that which he accomplished between one and two o'clock on the Tuesday morning, aboard the North German steamer *Uhlan*, lying at anchor in Genoa harbour.

Not a hitch occurred. Everything had been foreseen; everything happened as I had been assured everything must. Nobody was about below, only the ship's boys on deck, and nobody on the bridge. It was twenty-five minutes past one when Raffles, without a stitch of clothing on his body, but with a glass phial, corked with cotton-wool, between his teeth, and a tiny screwdriver behind his ear, squirmed feet first through the ventilator over his berth; and it was nineteen minutes to two when he returned, head first, with the phial still between his teeth, and the cotton-wool rammed home to still the rattling of that which lay like a great grey bean within. He had taken screws out and put them in again; he had unfastened von Heumann's ventilator and had left it fast as he had found it—fast as he instantly proceeded to make his own. As for von Heumann, it had been enough to place the drenched wad first on his moustache, and then to hold it between his gaping lips; thereafter the intruder had climbed both ways across his shins without eliciting a groan.

And here was the prize—this pearl as large as a filbert—with a pale pink tinge like a lady's finger-nail—this spoil of the filibustering age—this gift from a European emperor to a South Sea chief. We gloated over it when all was snug. We toasted it in whisky and soda-water laid in overnight in view of the great moment. But the moment was greater, more triumphant, than our most sanguine dreams. All we had now to do was to secrete the gem (which Raffles had prised from its setting, replacing the latter), so that we could stand the strictest search and yet take it ashore with us at Naples; and this Raffles was doing when I turned in. I myself would have landed incontinently, that night, at Genoa, and bolted with the spoil; he would not hear of it, for a dozen good reasons which will be obvious.

On the whole I do not think that anything was discovered or suspected before we weighed anchor; but I cannot be sure. It is difficult to believe that a man could be chloroformed in his sleep and feel no tell-tale effects, sniff no suspicious odour, in the morning. Nevertheless, von Heumann reappeared as though nothing had happened to him, his German cap over his eyes and his moustaches brushing the peak. And by ten o'clock we were quit of Genoa; the last lean, blue-chinned official had left our decks; the last fruit-seller had been beaten off with bucketsful of water and left cursing us from his boat; the last passenger had come aboard at the last moment—a fussy greybeard who kept the big ship waiting while he haggled with his boatmen over half a lira. But at length we were off, the tug was shed, the lighthouse passed, and Raffles and I leaned together over the rail, watching our shadows on the pale green, liquid, veined marble that again washed the vessel's side.

Von Heumann was having his innings once more; it was part of the design that he should remain in all day, and so postponed the inevitable hour; and, though the lady looked bored, and was for ever glancing in our direction, he seemed only too willing to avail himself of his opportunities. But Raffles was moody and ill at ease. He had not the air of a successful man. I could but opine that the impending parting at Naples sat heavily on his spirit.

He would neither talk to me, nor would he let me go.

'Stop where you are, Bunny. I've things to tell you. Can you swim?'

'A bit.'

'Ten miles?'

'Ten?' I burst out laughing. 'Not one! Why do you ask?'

'We shall be within a ten miles' swim of the shore most of the day.'

'What on earth are you driving at, Raffles?'

'Nothing; only I shall swim for it if the worst comes to the worst. I suppose you can't swim under water at all?'

I did not answer his question. I scarcely heard it: cold beads were bursting through my skin.

'Why should the worst come to the worst?' I whispered. 'We aren't found out, are we?'

'No.'

'Then why speak as though we were?'

'We may be; an old enemy of ours is on board.'

'An old enemy?'

'Mackenzie.'

'Never!'

'The man with the beard who came aboard last.'

'Are you sure?'

'Sure! I was only sorry to see you didn't recognise him too.'

I took my handkerchief to my face; now that I thought of it, there had been something familiar in the old man's gait, as well as something rather youthful for his apparent years; his very beard seemed unconvincing, now that I recalled it in the light of this horrible revelation. I looked up and down the deck, but the old man was nowhere to be seen.

'That's the worst of it,' said Raffles. 'I saw him go into the captain's cabin twenty minutes ago.'

'But what can have brought him?' I cried miserably. 'Can it be a coincidence—is it somebody else he's after?'

Raffles shook his head.

'Hardly this time.'

'Then you think he's after you?'

'I've been afraid of it for some weeks.'

'Yet there you stand!'

'What am I to do? I don't want to swim for it before I

must. I begin to wish I'd taken your advice, Bunny, and left the ship at Genoa. But I've not the smallest doubt that Mac was watching both ship and station till the last moment. That's why he ran it so fine.'

He took a cigarette and handed me the case, but I shook my head impatiently.

'I still don't understand,' said I. 'Why should he be after you? He couldn't come all this way about a jewel which was perfectly safe for all he knew. What's your own theory?'

'Simply that he's been on my track for some time, probably ever since friend Crawshay slipped clean through his fingers last November. There have been other indications. I am really not unprepared for this. But it can only be pure suspicion. I'll defy him to bring anything home, and I'll defy him to find the pearl! Theory, my dear Bunny! I know how he's got here as well as though I'd been inside that Scotchman's skin, and I know what he'll do next. He found out I'd gone abroad, and looked for a motive; he found out about von Heumann and his mission, and here was his motive cut and dried. Great chance—to nab me on a new job altogether. But he won't do it, Bunny; mark my words, he'll search the ship and search us all, when the loss is known; but he'll search in vain. And there's the skipper beckoning the whipper snapper to his cabin: the fat will be in the fire in five minutes!'

Yet there was no conflagration, no fuss, no searching of the passengers, no whisper of what had happened in the air; instead of a stir there was portentous peace; and it was clear to me that Raffles was not a little disturbed at the falsification of all his predictions. There was something sinister in silence under such a loss, and the silence was sustained for hours, during which Mackenzie never reappeared. But he was abroad during the luncheon-hour—he was in our cabin! I had left my book in Raffles's berth, and in taking it after lunch I touched the quilt. It was warm from the recent pressure of flesh and blood, and on an instinct I sprang to the ventilator; as I opened it the ventilator opposite was closed with a snap.

I waylaid Raffles. 'All right. Let him find the pearl.'

'Have you dumped it overboard?'

'That's a question I shan't condescend to answer.'

He turned on his heel, and at subsequent intervals I saw him making the most of his last afternoon with the inevitable Miss Werner. I remember that she looked both cool and smart in quite a simple affair of brown holland, which toned well with her complexion, and was cleverly relieved with touches of scarlet. I quite admired her that afternoon, for her eyes were really very good, and so were her teeth, yet I had never admired her more directly in my own despite. For I passed them again and again in order to get a word with Raffles, to tell him I knew there was danger in the wind; but he would not so much as catch my eye. So at last I gave it up. And I saw him next in the captain's cabin.

They had summoned him first; he had gone in smiling; and smiling I found him when they summoned me. The state-room was spacious, as befitted that of a commander. Mackenzie sat on the settee, his beard in front of him on the polished table; but a revolver lay in front of the captain; and when I had entered, the chief officer, who had summoned me, shut the door and put his back to it. Von Heumann completed the party, his fingers busy with his moustache.

Raffles greeted me.

'This is a great joke!' he cried. 'You remember the pearl you were so keen about, Bunny, the emperor's pearl, the pearl money wouldn't buy? It seems it was entrusted to our little friend here, to take out to Canoodle Dum, and the poor little chap's gone and lost it; *ergo*, as we're Britishers, they think we've got it!'

'But I know ye have,' put in Mackenzie, nodding to his beard.

'You will recognise that loyal and patriotic voice,' said Raffles. 'Mon, 'tis our auld acquaintance Mackenzie, o' Scoteland Yarrd an' Scoteland itsel'!'

'Dat is enought,' cried the captain. 'Have you submid to be searge, or do I vorce you?'

'What you will?' said Raffles, 'but it will do you no harm to give us fair play first. You accuse us of breaking into Captain von Heumann's state-room during the small hours of this morning, and abstracting from it this confounded pearl. Well, I can prove that I was in my own room all night long, and I have no doubt my friend can prove the same.'

'Most certainly I can,' said I indignantly. 'The ship's boys can bear witness to that.'

Mackenzie laughed, and shook his head at his reflection in the polished mahogany.

'That was vera clever,' said he, 'and like enough it would ha' served ye had I not stepped aboard. But I've just had a look at they ventilators, and I think I know how ye worrked it.—Anyway, captain, it makes no matter. I'll just be clappin' the darbies on these young sparks, an' then—'

'By what right?' roared Raffles in a ringing voice, and I never saw his face in such a blaze. 'Search us if you like; search every scrap and stitch we possess; but you dare to lay a finger on us without a warrant!'

'I wouldna' dare,' said Mackenzie gravely, as he fumbled in his breast pocket, and Raffles dived his hand into his own. 'Haud his wrist!' shouted the Scotchman; and the huge Colt that had been with us many a night, but had never been fired in my hearing, clattered on the table and was raked in by the captain.

'All right,' said Raffles savagely to the mate. 'You can let go now. I won't try it again.—Now, Mackenzie, let's see your warrant!'

'Ye'll no mishandle it?'

'What good would that do me? Let me see it,' said Raffles peremptorily, and the detective obeyed. Raffles raised his eyebrows as he perused the document; his mouth hardened, but suddenly relaxed; and it was with a smile and a shrug that he returned the paper.

'Wull that do for ye?' inquired Mackenzie.

'It may. I congratulate you, Mackenzie; it's a strong hand, at any rate.—Two burglaries and the Melrose necklace, Bunny!' And he turned to me with a rueful smile.

'An' all easy to prove,' said the Scotchman, pocketing the warrant.—'I've one o' these for you,' he added, nodding to me, 'only not such a long one.'

'To thingk,' said the captain reproachfully, 'that my shib should be made a den of thiefs! It shall be a very disagreeable madder. I have been obliged to pud you both in irons until we ged to Nables.'

'Surely not!' exclaimed Raffles.—'Mackenzie, intercede with him; don't give your countrymen away before all hands!—Captain, we can't escape; surely you could hush it up for the night? Look here, here's everything I have in my pockets; you empty yours too, Bunny, and they shall strip us stark if they suspect we've weapons up our sleeves. All I ask is that we are allowed to get out of this without gyves upon our wrists.'

'Webbons you may not have,' said the captain; 'but wad about der bearl dat you were sdealing?'

'You shall have it!' cried Raffles. 'You shall have it this minute if you guarantee no public indignity on board!'

'That I'll see to,' said Mackenzie, 'as long as you behave yourselves. There now, where is't?'

'On the table under your nose.'

My eyes fell with the rest, but no pearl was there; only the contents of our pockets—our watches, pocket-books, pencils, penknives, cigarette-cases—lay on the shiny table along with the revolvers already mentioned.

'Ye're humbuggin' us,' said Mackenzie. 'What's the use?'

'I'm doing nothing of the sort,' laughed Raffles. 'I'm testing you. Where's the harm?'

'It's here, joke apart?'

'On that table, by all my gods.'

Mackenzie opened the cigarette cases and shook each particular cigarette. Thereupon Raffles prayed to be allowed to smoke one, and, when his prayer was heard, observed that the pearl had been on the table much longer than the cigarettes. Mackenzie promptly caught up the Colt and opened the chamber in the butt.

'Not there, not there,' said Raffles; 'but you're getting hot. Try the cartridges.'

Mackenzie emptied them into his palm, and shook each one at his ear without result.

'Oh, give them to me!'

And, in an instant, Raffles had found the right one, had bitten out the bullet, and placed the emperor's pearl with a flourish in the centre of the table.

'After that you will perhaps show me such little consideration as is in your power.—Captain, I have been a bit of a villain, as you see, and as such I am ready and willing to lie in irons all night, if you deem it requisite for the safety of the ship. All I ask is that you do me one favour first.'

'That shall debend on wad der vafour has been.'

'Captain, I've done a worse thing aboard your ship than any of you know. I have become engaged to be married, and I want to say good-bye!'

I suppose we were all equally amazed; but the only one to express his amazement was von Heumann, whose deep-chested German oath was almost his first contribution to the proceedings. He was not slow to follow it, however, with a vigorous protest against the proposed farewell; but he was overruled, and the masterful prisoner had his way. He was to have five minutes with the girl, while the captain and Mackenzie stood within range (but not earshot), with their revolvers behind their backs. As we were moving from the cabin in a body, he stopped and gripped my hand.

'So I've let you in at last, Bunny—at last and after all! If you knew how sorry I am... But you won't get much—I don't see why you should get anything at all. Can you forgive me? This may be for years, and it may be for ever, you know! You were a good pal always when it came to the scratch; some day or other you mayn't be so sorry to remember you were a good pal at the last!'

There was a meaning in his eye that I understood; and my teeth were set, and my nerves strung ready as I wrung that strong and cunning hand for the last time in my life.

How that last scene stays with me, and will stay to my death! How I see every detail, every shadow on the sunlit deck! We were among the islands that dot the course from Genoa to Naples; that was Elba falling back on our starboard quarter, that purple patch with the hot sun setting over it.

The captain's cabin opened to starboard, and the starboard promenade deck, sheeted with sunshine and scored with shadow, was deserted but for the group of which I was one, and for the pale, slim, brown figure further aft with Raffles. Engaged? I could not believe it, cannot to this day. Yet there they stood together, and we did not hear a word; there they stood out against the sunset, and the long, dazzling highway of sunlit sea that sparkled from Elba to the *Uhlan's* plates; and their shadows reached almost to our feet.

Suddenly—an instant—and the thing was done—a thing I have never known whether to admire or to detest. He caught her—he kissed her before us all—then flung her from him so that she almost fell. It was that action which foretold the next. The mate sprang after him, and I sprang after the mate.

Raffles was on the rail, but only just.

'Hold him, Bunny!' he cried. 'Hold him tight!'

And as I obeyed that last behest with all my might, without a thought of what I was doing, save that he bade me do it, I saw his hands shoot up and his head bob down, and his lithe, spare body cut the sunset as cleanly and precisely as though he had plunged at his leisure from a diver's board!

Of what followed on deck I can tell you nothing, for I was not there. Nor can my final punishment, my long imprisonment, my everlasting disgrace, concern or profit you, beyond the interest and advantage to be gleaned from the knowledge that I at least had my deserts. But one thing I must set down, believe it who will—one more thing only and I am done.

It was into a second-class cabin, on the starboard side, that I was promptly thrust in irons, and the door locked upon me as though I were another Raffles. Meanwhile a boat was lowered, and the sea scoured to no purpose, as is doubtless on record elsewhere. But either the setting sun, flashing over the waves, must have blinded all eyes, or else mine were victims of a strange illusion.

For the boat was back, the screw throbbing, and the prisoner peering through his porthole across the sunlit waters that he believed had closed for ever over his comrade's head. Suddenly the sun sank behind the Island of Elba, the lane of dancing sunlight was instantaneously quenched and swallowed in the trackless waste, and in the middle distance, already miles astern, either my sight deceived me or a black speck bobbed amid the grey. The bugle had blown for dinner; it may well be that all save myself had ceased to strain an eye. And now I lost what I had found, now it rose, now sank, and now I gave it up utterly. Yet anon it would rise again, a mere mote dancing in the dim grey distance, drifting towards a purple island, beneath a fading western sky, streaked with dead gold and cerise. And night fell before I knew whether it was a human head or not.

Bullion!

William Hope Hodgson

William Hope Hodgson (1877–1918), the son of an Anglican priest, ran away to sea at the age of thirteen. He was duly returned to his family, but obtained his father's permission to fulfil his ambition by becoming a cabin boy. Whilst on board the ship, he experienced bullying, and the need to be able to defend himself prompted a keen interest in physical fitness. In 1898 he received the Royal Humane Society's medal for heroism after rescuing a fellow sailor from shark-infested waters off the coast of New Zealand. Returning to England, he opened a school of physical culture in Blackburn, and wrote a number of articles about physical fitness before turning his attention to fiction. He became an accomplished and influential author of horror, supernatural, and crime stories before being killed by an artillery shell while serving at Ypres in 1918.

Hodgson's understanding of ships and sailing and his keen awareness of the dangers and mysteries of the sea are evident in much of his best work, notably the chilling and brilliant horror story, 'The Voices in the Night'. His novel *The Ghost Pirates* (1909) was admired by H. P. Lovecraft. 'Bullion!' first appeared in *Everybody's Weekly* in 1911. It's a lively example of the 'impossible crime' or 'sealed room' story with a nicely evoked maritime setting.

This is a most peculiar yarn. It was a pitchy night in the South Pacific. I was the second mate of one of the fast clipper-ships running between London and Melbourne at the time of the big gold finds up at Bendigo. There was a fresh breeze blowing, and I was walking hard up and down the weather side of the poop-deck, to keep myself warm, when the captain came out of the companionway and joined me.

'Mr James, do you believe in ghosts?' he asked suddenly, after several minutes of silence.

'Well, sir,' I replied, 'I always keep an open mind; so I can't say I'm a proper disbeliever, though I think most ghost yarns can be explained.'

'Well,' he said in a queer voice, 'someone keeps whispering in my cabin at nights. It's making me feel funny to be there.'

'How do you mean whispering, sir?' I asked.

'Just that,' he said. 'Someone whispering about my cabin. Sometimes it's quite close to my head, other times it's here and there and everywhere—in the air.'

Then, abruptly, he stopped in his walk and faced me, as if determined to say the thing that was on his mind.

'What did Captain Avery die of on the passage out?' he asked quick and blunt.

'None of us knew, sir,' I told him. 'He just seemed to sicken and go off.'

'Well,' he said, 'I'm not going to sleep in his cabin any

longer. I've no special fancy for just sickening and going off. If you like I'll change places with you.'

'Certainly, sir,' I answered, half pleased and half sorry. For whilst I had a feeling that there was nothing really to bother about in the captain's fancies yet—though he had only taken command in Melbourne to bring the ship home—I had found already that he was not one of the soft kind by any means. And, so, as you will understand, I had vague feelings of uneasiness to set against my curiosity to find out what it was that had given Captain Reynolds a fit of the nerves.

'Would you like me to sleep in your place tonight, sir?' I asked.

'Well,' he said with a little laugh 'when you get below you'll find me in your bunk, so it'll be a case of my cabin or the saloon table.' And with that it was settled.

'I shall lock the door,' I added. 'I'm not going to have anyone fooling me. I suppose I may search?'

'Do what you like,' was all he replied.

About an hour later the captain left me, and went below. When the mate came up to relieve me at eight bells I told him I was promoted to the captain's cabin and the reason why. To my surprise, he said that he wouldn't sleep there for all the gold that was in the ship; so that I finished by telling him he was a superstitious old shellback.

When I got down to my new cabin I found that the captain had made the steward shift my gear in already, so that I had nothing to do but turn in, which I did after a good look round and locking the door.

I left the lamp turned about half up, and meant to lie awake a while listening; but I was asleep before I knew, and only waked to hear the 'prentice knocking on my door to tell me it was one bell.

For three nights I slept thus in comfort, and jested once or twice with the captain that I was getting the best of the bargain.

Then, just as you might expect, on the fourth night something happened. I had gone below for the middle watch, and had fallen asleep as usual, almost so soon as my head was on the pillow. I was wakened suddenly by some curious sound apparently quite near me. I lay there without moving and listened, my heart beating a little rapidly; but otherwise I was cool and alert. Then I heard the thing quite plainly with my waking senses—a vague, uncertain whispering, seeming to me as if someone or something bent over me from behind, and whispered some unintelligible thing close to my ear. I rolled over, and stared around the cabin; but the whole place was empty.

Then I sat still, and listened again. For several minutes there was an absolute silence, and then abruptly I heard the vague, uncomfortable whispering again, seeming to come from the middle of the cabin. I sat there, feeling distinctly nervous; then I jumped quietly from my bunk, and slipped silently to the door. I stopped, and listened at the keyhole, but there was no one there. I ran across then to the ventilators, and shut them; also I made sure that the ports were screwed up, so that there was now absolutely no place through which anyone could send his voice, even supposing that anyone was idiot enough to want to play such an unmeaning trick.

For a while after I had taken these precautions I stood silent; and twice I heard the whispering, going vaguely now in this and now in that part of the air of the cabin, as if some unseen spirit wandered about, trying to make itself heard.

As you may suppose, this was getting more than I cared to tackle, for I had searched the cabin every watch, and it seemed to me that there was truly something unnatural in the thing I heard. I began to get my clothes and dress, for, after this, I felt inclined to adopt the captain's suggestion of the saloon table for a bunk. You see, I had got to have my sleep, but I could not fancy lying unconscious in that cabin, with that strange sound wandering about; though awake, I think I can say truthfully I should not really have feared it. But to lie defenceless in sleep with that uncanniness near me was more than I could bear.

And then, you know, a sudden thought came blinding through my brain. The bullion! We were bringing some thirty thousand ounces of gold in sealed bullion chests, and these were in a specially erected wooden compartment, standing all by itself in the centre of the lazarette, just below the captain's cabin. What if some attempt were being made secretly on the treasure, and we all the time idiotically thinking of ghosts, when perhaps the vague sounds we had heard were conducted in some way from below! You can conceive how the thought set me tingling, so that I did not stop to realise how improbable it was, but took my lamp and went immediately to the captain.

He woke in a moment, and when he had heard my suggestion he told me that the thing was practically impossible; yet the very idea made him sufficiently uneasy to determine him on going down with me into the lazarette, to look at the seals on the door of the temporary bullion-room.

He did not stop to dress, but, reaching the lamp from me, led the way. The entrance to the lazarette was through a trapdoor under the saloon table, and this was kept locked. When this was opened the captain went down with the lamp, and I followed noiselessly. At the bottom of the ladder the captain held the lamp high, and looked round. Then he went over to where the square bulk of the bullion-room stood alone in the centre of the place, and together we examined the seals on the door; but of course they were untouched, and I began to realise now that my idea had been nothing more than unreasoned suggestion. And then, you know, as we stood there silent, amid the various creaks and groans of the working bulkheads, we both heard the sound—a whispering somewhere near to us, that came and went oddly, being lost in the noise of the creaking woodwork, and again coming plain, seeming now to be in this place, and now in that.

I had an extraordinary feeling of superstitious fear; but the captain was unaffected. He muttered in a low voice that there was someone inside the bullion-room, and began quickly and coolly to break the sealed tapes. Then telling me to hold the lamp high, he threw the door wide open. But the place was empty, save for the neat range of bullion-boxes, bound sealed, and numbered, that occupied half the floor.

'Nothing here!' said the captain, and took the lamp from my hand. He held it low down over the rows of little chests.

'The thirteenth!' he said, with a little gasp. 'Where's the thirteenth—No. 13?'

He was right. The bullion-chest which should have stood between No. 12 and No. 14 was gone. We set to and counted every chest, verifying the numbers. They were all there, numbered up to 60, except for the gap of the thirteenth. Somehow, in some way, a thousand ounces of gold had been removed from out of the sealed room. In a very agitated but thorough manner the captain and I made a close examination of the room; but it was plain that any entry that had been made could only have been through the sealed doorway. Then he led the way out, and having tried the lock several times, and found it showed no signs of having been tampered with, he locked and sealed up the door again, sealing the tape also right across the keyhole. Then, as a thought came to him, he told me to stay by the door whilst he went up into the saloon.

In a few minutes he returned with the purser, both armed and carrying lamps. They came very quietly, and paused with me outside the door, and examined the old seals and the door itself. Then, at the purser's request, the captain removed the new seals, and unlocked the door.

As he opened it the purser turned suddenly and looked behind him. I heard it also—a vague whispering, seeming to be in the air, then it was drowned and lost in the creaking of the timbers. The captain had heard the sound, and was standing in the doorway holding his lamp high and looking in, pistol ready in his right hand, for to him it had seemed to come from within the bullion-room. Yet the place was as empty as we had left it but a few minutes before—as, indeed, it was bound to be—of any living creature. The captain went to where the bullion-chest was missing, and stooped to point out the gap to the purser.

A queer exclamation came from him, and he remained stooping, whilst the purser and I pressed forward to find what new thing had happened now. When I saw what the captain was staring at, you will understand that I felt simply dazed, for there right before his face, in its proper place, was the thirteenth bullion-chest, as, indeed, it must have been all the while.

'You've been dreaming,' said the purser, with a burst of relieved laughter. 'My goodness, but you did give me a fright!'

The captain and I stared at the rematerialised treasure-chest, and then at one another.

'That chest was not there a few minutes ago!' the captain said at length. Then he brushed the hair off his forehead, and looked again at the chest. 'Are we dreaming?' he said at last, and looked at me. He touched the chest with his foot, and I did the same with my hand; but it was no illusion, and we could only suppose that we had made some extraordinary mistake.

I turned to the purser.

'But the whispering!' I said. '*You* heard the whispering!'

'Yes,' said the captain. 'What was that? I tell you there's something queer knocking about, or else we're all mad.'

The purser stared, puzzled and nodding his head.

'I heard something,' he said. 'The chief thing is, the stuff is there all right. I suppose you'll put a watch over it?'

'By Moses! Yes!' said the captain. 'The mates and I'll sleep with that blessed gold until we hand it ashore in London!'

And so it was arranged. We three officers took it in turn to sleep actually inside the bullion-room itself, being sealed and locked in with the treasure. In addition to this, the captain made the petty officers keep watch and watch with him and the purser, through the whole of each twenty-four hours, trapesing round and round that wretched bullion-room until not a mouse could have gone in or out without being seen. In addition, he had the deck above and below thoroughly examined by the carpenter once in every twenty-four hours, so that never was a treasure so scrupulously guarded.

For our part, we officers began to grow pretty sick of the job, once the touch of excitement connected with the thought of robbery had worn off. And when, as sometimes happened, we were aware of that extraordinary whispering, it was only the captain's determination and authority which made us submit to the constant discomfort and breaking of our sleep; for every hour the watchman on the outside of the bullion-room would knock twice on the boards of the room, and the sleeping officer within would have to rouse, take a look round and knock back twice, to signify that all was well.

Sometimes I could almost think that we got into the way of doing this in our sleep, for I have been roused to my watch on deck, with no memory of having answered the watchman's knock, though a cautious inquiry showed me that I had done so.

Then, one night when I was sleeping in the bullion-room, a rather queer thing happened. Something must have roused me between the times of the watchman's knocks, for I wakened suddenly and half sat up, with a feeling that something was wrong somewhere. As in a dream, I looked round, and all the time fighting against my sleepiness. Everything seemed normal; but when I looked at the tiers of bullion-chests I saw that there was a gap among them. Some of the chests had surely gone.

I stared in a stupid, nerveless way, as a man full of sleep sometimes will do, without rousing himself to realise the actuality of the things he looks at. And even as I stared I dozed over and fell back, but seemed to waken almost immediately and look again at the chests. Yet it was plain that I must have seen dazedly and half-dreaming, for not a bullion-chest was missing, and I sank back again thankfully to my slumber.

Yet when at the end of my 'treasure watch' (as we had grown to call our watch below) I reported my queer half-dream to the captain, he came down himself and made a thorough examination of the bullion-room, also questioning the sail-maker, who had been the watchman outside. But he said there had been nothing unusual, only that once he had thought he heard the curious whispering going about in the air of the lazarette.

And so that queer voyage went on, with over us all the

time a sense of peculiar mystery, vague and indefinable; so that one thought a thousand strange weird thoughts which one lacked the courage to put into words. And the other times there was only a sense of utter weariness of it all, and the one desire to get to port and be shut of it and go back to a normal life in some other vessel. Even the passengers— many of whom were returning diggers—were infected by the strange atmosphere and of uncertainty that prompted our constant guarding of the bullion, for it had got known among them that a special guard was being kept, and that certain inexplicable things had happened. But the captain refused their offers of help, preferring to keep his own men about the gold, as you may suppose.

At last we reached London and docked; and now occurred the strangest thing of all. When the bank officials came aboard to take over the gold, the captain took them down to the bullion-room, where the carpenter was walking round as outside watchman, and the first mate was sealed inside, as usual.

The captain explained that we were taking unusual precautions, and broke the seals. When, however, they unlocked and opened the door, the mate did not answer to the captain's call, but was seen to be lying quiet beside the gold. Examination showed that he was quite dead; but there was nowhere any mark or sign to show that his death was unnatural. As the captain said to me afterwards, 'Another case of "just sickening and going off." I wouldn't sail again in this packet for anything the owners liked to offer me!'

The officials examined the boxes, and, finding all in order had them taken ashore up to the bank, and very thankful I was to see the last of it. Yet this is where I was mistaken, for about an hour later, as I was superintending the slinging out of some heavy cargo, there came a message from the bank to the effect that every one of the bullion-chests was a dummy filled with lead, and that no one be allowed to leave the ship until an inquiry and search had been made.

This was carried out rigorously, so that not a cabin or a scrap of personal luggage was left unexamined, and afterwards the ship herself was searched, but nowhere was there any signs of the gold; yet as there must have been something like a ton of it, it was not a thing that could have been easily hidden.

Permission was now given to all that they might go ashore, and I proceeded once more to supervise the slinging out of heavy stuff that I had been 'bossing' when the order came from the bank. And all the time, as I gave my orders, I felt in a daze. How could nearly seventeen hundredweight of gold have been removed out of that guarded bullion-room? I remembered all the curious things that had been heard and seen and half-felt. Was there something queer about the ship? But my reason objected: there was surely some explanation of the mystery.

Abruptly I came out of my thoughts, for the man on the shore-gear had just let a heavy case down rather roughly, and a dandy-looking person was cursing him for his clumsiness. It was then that a possible explanation of the mystery came to me, and I determined to take the risk of testing it. I jumped ashore and swore at the man who was handling the gear, telling him to slack away more carefully, to which he replied, 'Ay, ay, sir.' Then, under my breath, I said:

'Take no notice of the hard talk, Jimmy. Let the next one come down good and solid. I'll take the responsibility if it smashes.'

Then I stood back and let Jimmy have his chance. The next case went well up to the block before Jimmy took a turn and signalled to the winch to vast heaving.

'Slack away handsome!' yelled Jimmy and he let his own rope smoke round the bollard. The case came down, crashing from a height of thirty feet, and burst on the quay. As the dust cleared I heard the dandy cursing at the top of his voice.

I did not bother about him. What was attracting my attention was the fact that among the heavy timbers of the big case was a number of the missing bullion-chests. I seized my whistle and blew it for one of the 'prentices. When he came I told him to run up the quay for a policeman. Then I turned to the captain and the third mate, who had come running ashore, and explained. They ran to the lorry on which the other cases had been placed, and with the help of some of the men pulled them down again on to the quay. But when they came to search for the swell stranger, who had been looking after the unloading of the stolen gold, he was nowhere to be found; so that, after all, the policeman had nothing to do when he arrived but mount guard over the recovered bullion, of which, I am glad to say, not a case was missing.

Later, a more intelligent examination into things revealed how the robbery had been effected. When we took down the temporary bullion-room we found that a very cleverly concealed sliding panel had been fitted into the end opposite to the door. This gave us the idea to examine a wooden ventilator which came up through the deck near by from the lower hold. And now we held the key to the whole mystery.

Evidently there had been quite a gang of thieves aboard the ship. They had built the cases ashore, and packed them with loaded dummy bullion-chests, sealed and banded exactly like the originals. These had been placed in the hold at Melbourne as freight, under the name of 'specimens.' In the meanwhile some of the band must have got our carpenter, who had built the bullion-room, and promised him a share of the gold if he would build the secret panel into one end. Then, when we got to sea, the thieves got down into the lower hold through one of the forrard hatches, and, having opened one of the cases, began to exchange the dummies for the real chests, by climbing up inside the wooden ventilator shaft, which the carpenter had managed to fit with a couple of boards that slid to one side, just opposite to the secret panel in the wooden bullion-room.

It must have been very slow work, and their whispering to one another had been carried up the ventilator shaft, which passed right through the captain's cabin, under the appearance of a large ornamental strut, or upright, supporting the arm-racks. It was this unexpected carrying of the sound which had brought the captain and me down unexpectedly, and nearly discovered them; so that they had not even had time to replace the thirteenth chest with its prepared dummy.

I don't think there is much more to explain. There is very little doubt in my mind that the captain's extraordinary pre-cautions must have made things difficult for the robbers, and that they could only get to work then when the carpenter happened to be the outside watchman. It is also obvious to me that some drug which threw off narcotic fumes must have been injected into the bullion-room, to ensure the officer not waking at inconvenient moments, so that the time that I did waken, and felt so muddled I must have been in a half-stupefied condition, and did *really* see that some of the chests were gone; but these were replaced so soon as I fell back asleep. The first mate must have died from an over-prolonged inhalation of the drug.

I think that is all that has to do with this incident. Perhaps, though, you may be pleased to hear that I was handsomely rewarded for having solved the mystery. So that, altogether, I was very well satisfied.

The Echo of a Mutiny

R. Austin Freeman

Like Doyle and Eustace, Richard Austin Freeman (1862–
1943) qualified as a doctor before establishing himself as an
author of detective stories. Buying a practice was beyond his
financial means, and he joined the Colonial Service, sailing
to Accra on Africa's Gold Coast in 1887 to take up a post
as Assistant Colonial Surgeon. After contracting blackwa-
ter fever, he returned to Britain and during the long process
of recovery, he started writing as a means of supplementing
his income. His first book, *Travels and Life in Ashanti and
Jaman*, appeared in 1898, and was well reviewed, but sales were
modest. Undaunted, he published articles and stories in magazines, and wrote a series of detective stories about the rogue
Romney Pringle in collaboration with another doctor, Dr
John James Pitcairn, under the pseudonym Clifford Ashdown.

Freeman's breakthrough came with the creation of Dr John
Evelyn Thorndyke, the handsome 'medical jurispractitioner'
based at 5A, King's Bench Walk, Inner Temple. Thorndyke's

meticulous detective work and expertise in forensic science earned a large and appreciative readership, while the stories collected in *The Singing Bone* are generally regarded as the first significant examples of the 'inverted mystery,' in which an account of a seemingly ingenious crime is followed by an explanation of how Thorndyke unravelled the mystery. 'The Echo of a Mutiny' is a classic of this sub-genre. Freeman's careful research was a key factor in the success of the Thorndyke stories. According to his biographer Norman Donaldson, the author used for background 'his memories of his stay in Ramsgate, his journeys down the Thames estuary, and the investigations he had made for his articles in *Cassell's Magazine* on lighthouses.'

CHAPTER ONE

DEATH ON THE GIRDLER

Popular belief ascribes to infants and the lower animals certain occult powers of divining character denied to the reasoning faculties of the human adult, and is apt to accept their judgment as finally over-riding the pronouncements of mere experience.

Whether this belief rests upon any foundation other than the universal love of paradox it is unnecessary to inquire. It is very generally entertained, especially by ladies of a certain social status; and by Mrs Thomas Solly it was loyally maintained as an article of faith.

'Yes,' she moralised, 'it's surprisin' how they know, the little children and the dumb animals. But they do. There's no deceivin' *them*. They can tell the gold from the dross in a moment, they can, and they reads the human heart like a book. Wonderful, I call it. I suppose it's instinct.'

Having delivered herself of this priceless gem of philosophic thought, she thrust her arms elbow deep into the foaming wash-tub and glanced admiringly at her lodger as he sat in the doorway, supporting on one knee an obese infant of eighteen months and on the other a fine tabby cat.

James Brown was an elderly seafaring man, small and slight in build and in manner suave, insinuating, and perhaps a trifle sly. But he had all the sailor's love of children and animals, and the sailor's knack of making himself acceptable to them, for, as he sat with an empty pipe wobbling in the grasp of his toothless gums, the baby beamed with humid smiles, and the cat, rolled into a fluffy ball and purring like a stocking-loom, worked its fingers ecstatically as if it were trying on a new pair of gloves.

'It must be mortal lonely out at the lighthouse,' Mrs Solly resumed. 'Only three men and never a neighbour to speak to; and, Lord! what a muddle they must be in with no woman to look after them and keep 'em tidy. But you won't be overworked, Mr Brown, in these long days; daylight till past nine o'clock. I don't know what you'll do to pass the time.'

'Oh, I shall find plenty to do, I expect,' said Brown, 'what with cleanin' the lamps and glasses and paintin' up the ironwork. And that reminds me,' he added, looking round at the clock, 'that time's getting on. High water at half-past ten, and here it's gone eight o'clock.'

Mrs Solly, acting on the hint, began rapidly to fish out the washed garments and wring them out into the form of short ropes. Then, having dried her hands on her apron, she relieved Brown of the protesting baby.

'Your room will be ready for you, Mr Brown,' said she, 'when your turn comes for a spell ashore; and main glad me and Tom will be to see you back.'

'Thank you, Mrs Solly, ma'am,' answered Brown, tenderly placing the cat on the floor; 'you won't be more glad than what I will.' He shook hands warmly with his landlady, kissed the baby, chucked the cat under the chin, and, picking up his little chest by its becket, swung it on to his shoulder and strode out of the cottage.

His way lay across the marshes, and, like the ships in the offing, he shaped his course by the twin towers of Reculver that stood up grotesquely on the rim of the land; and as he trod the springy turf, Tom Solly's fleecy charges looked up at him with vacant stares and valedictory bleatings. Once, at a dyke-gate, he paused to look back at the fair Kentish landscape: at the grey tower of St Nicholas-at-Wade peeping above the trees and the far-away mill at Sarre, whirling slowly in the summer breeze; and, above all, at the solitary cottage where, for a brief spell in his stormy life, he had known the homely joys of domesticity and peace. Well, that was over for the present, and the lighthouse loomed ahead. With a half-sigh he passed through the gate and walked on towards Reculver.

Outside the whitewashed cottages with their official black chimneys a petty-officer of the coast guard was adjusting the halyards of the flagstaff. He looked up as Brown approached and hailed him cheerily.

'Here you are, then,' said he, 'all figged out in your new togs, too. But we're in a bit of a difficulty, d'ye see. We've got to pull up to Whitstable this morning, so I can't send a man out with you and I can't spare a boat.'

'Have I got to swim out, then?' asked Brown.

The coast guard grinned. 'Not in them new clothes, mate,' he answered. 'No, but there's old Willett's boat; he isn't using her today; he's going over to Minster to see his daughter, and he'll let us have the loan of the boat. But there's no one to go with you, and I'm responsible to Willett.'

'Well, what about it?' asked Brown, with the deep-sea sailor's (usually misplaced) confidence in his power to handle a sailing-boat. 'D'ye think I can't manage a tub of a boat? Me what's used the sea since I was a kid of ten?'

'Yes,' said the coast guard, 'but who's to bring her back?'

'Why, the man that I'm going to relieve,' answered Brown. 'He don't want to swim no more than what I do.'

The coast-guard reflected with his telescope pointed at a passing barge. 'Well, I suppose it'll be all right,' he concluded; 'but it's a pity they couldn't send the tender round. However, if you undertake to send the boat back, we'll get her afloat. It's time you were off.'

He strolled away to the back of the cottages, whence he presently returned with two of his mates, and the four men proceeded along the shore to where Willett's boat lay just above high-water mark.

The *Emily* was a beamy craft of the type locally known as a 'half-share skiff,' solidly built of oak, with varnished planking and fitted with main and mizzen lugs. She was a good handful for four men, and, as she slid over the soft chalk rocks with a hollow rumble, the coast-guards debated the advisability of lifting out the bags of shingle with which she was ballasted. However, she was at length dragged down, ballast and all, to the water's edge, and then, while Brown stepped the main-mast, the petty-officer gave him his directions. 'What you've got to do,' said he, 'is to make use of the flood-tide. Keep her nose nor'-east, and with this trickle of nor'-westerly breeze you ought to make the lighthouse in one board. Anyhow, don't let her get east of the lighthouse, or, when the ebb sets in, you'll be in a fix.'

To these admonitions Brown listened with jaunty indifference as he hoisted the sails and watched the incoming tide creep over the level shore. Then the boat lifted on the gentle swell. Putting out an oar, he gave a vigorous shove off that sent the boat, with a final scrape, clear of the beach, and then, having dropped the rudder on to its pintles, he seated himself and calmly belayed the main-sheet.

'There he goes,' growled the coast-guard; 'makin' fast his sheet. They *will* do it' (he invariably did it himself), 'and that's how accidents happen. I hope old Willett'll see his boat back all right.'

He stood for some time watching the dwindling boat as it sidled across the smooth water; then he turned and followed his mates towards the station.

Out on the south-western edge of the Girdler Sand, just inside the two-fathom line, the spindle-shanked lighthouse stood a-straddle on its long screw-piles like some uncouth red-bodied wading bird. It was now nearly half-flood tide. The highest shoals were long since covered, and the lighthouse rose above the smooth sea as solitary as a slaver becalmed in the 'middle passage.'

On the gallery outside the lantern were two men, the entire staff of the building, of whom one sat huddled in a chair with his left leg propped up with pillows on another, while his companion rested a telescope on the rail and peered at the faint grey line of the distant land and the two tiny points that marked the twin spires of Reculver.

'I don't see any signs of the boat, Harry,' said he.

The other man groaned. 'I shall lose the tide,' he complained, 'and then there's another day gone.'

'They can pull you down to Birchington and put you in the train,' said the first man.

'I don't want no trains,' growled the invalid. 'The boat'll be bad enough. I suppose there's nothing coming our way, Tom?'

Tom turned his face eastward and shaded his eyes. 'There's a brig coming across the tide from the north,' he said. 'Looks like a collier.' He pointed his telescope at the approaching vessel, and added: 'She's got two new cloths in her upper fore top-sail, one on each leech.'

The other man sat up eagerly. 'What's her trysail like, Tom?' he asked.

'Can't see it,' replied Tom. 'Yes, I can, now: it's tanned. Why, that'll be the old *Utopia*, Harry; she's the only brig I know that's got a tanned trysail.'

'Look here, Tom,' exclaimed the other, 'if that's the *Utopia*, she's going to my home and I'm going aboard of her. Captain Mockett'll give me a passage, I know.'

'You oughtn't to go until you're relieved, you know, Barnett,' said Tom doubtfully; 'it's against regulations to leave your station.'

'Regulations be blowed!' exclaimed Barnett. 'My leg's more to me than the regulations. I don't want to be a cripple all my life. Besides, I'm no good here, and this new chap, Brown, will be coming out presently. You run up the signal, Tom, like a good comrade, and hail the brig.'

'Well, it's your look-out,' said Tom, 'and I don't mind saying that if I was in your place I should cut off home and see a doctor, if I got the chance.' He sauntered off to the flag-locker, and, selecting the two code-flags, deliberately toggled them on to the halyards. Then, as the brig swept up within range, he hoisted the little balls of bunting to the flagstaff-head and jerked the halyards, when the two flags blew out making the signal 'Need assistance.'

Promptly a coal-soiled answering pennant soared to the brig's main-truck; less promptly the collier went about, and, turning her nose down stream, slowly drifted stern-forwards towards the lighthouse. Then a boat slid out through her gangway, and a couple of men plied the oars vigorously.

'Lighthouse ahoy!' roared one of them, as the boat came within hail. 'What's amiss?'

'Harry Barnett has broke his leg,' shouted the lighthouse-keeper, 'and he wants to know if Captain Mockett will give him a passage to Whitstable.'

The boat turned back to the brig, and after a brief and bellowed consultation, once more pulled towards the lighthouse.

'Skipper says yus,' roared the sailor, when he was within earshot, 'and he says look alive, 'cause he don't want to miss his tide.'

The injured man heaved a sigh of relief. 'That's good news,' said he, 'though, how the blazes I'm going to get down the ladder is more than I can tell. What do you say, Jeffreys?'

'I say you'd better let me lower you with the tackle,' replied Jeffreys. 'You can sit in the bight of a rope and I'll give you a line to steady yourself with.'

'Ah, that'll do, Tom,' said Barnett; 'but, for the Lord's sake, pay out the fall-rope gently.'

The arrangements were made so quickly that by the time the boat was fast alongside everything was in readiness, and a minute later the injured man, dangling like a gigantic spider from the end of the tackle, slowly descended, cursing volubly to the accompaniment of the creaking of the blocks. His chest and kit-bag followed, and, as soon as these were unhooked from the tackle, the boat pulled off to the brig, which was now slowly creeping stern-foremost past the lighthouse. The sick man was hoisted up the side, his chest handed up after him, and then the brig was put on her course due south across the Kentish Flats.

Jeffreys stood on the gallery watching the receding vessel and listening to the voices of her crew as they grew small and weak in the increasing distance. Now that his gruff companion was gone, a strange loneliness had fallen on the lighthouse. The last of the homeward-bound ships had long since passed up the

Princes Channel and left the calm sea desolate and blank. The distant buoys, showing as tiny black dots on the glassy surface, and the spindly shapes of the beacons which stood up from invisible shoals, but emphasised the solitude of the empty sea, and the tolling of the bell buoy on the Shivering Sand, stealing faintly down the wind, sounded weird and mournful. The day's work was already done. The lenses were polished, the lamps had been trimmed, and the little motor that worked the fog-horn had been cleaned and oiled. There were several odd jobs, it is true, waiting to be done, as there always are in a lighthouse; but, just now, Jeffreys was not in a working humour. A new comrade was coming into his life today, a stranger with whom he was to be shut up alone, night and day, for a month on end, and whose temper and tastes and habits might mean for him pleasant companionship or jangling and discord without end. Who was this man Brown? What had he been? and what was he like? These were the questions that passed, naturally enough, through the lighthouse-keeper's mind and distracted him from his usual thoughts and occupations.

Presently a speck on the landward horizon caught his eye. He snatched up the telescope eagerly to inspect it. Yes, it was a boat; but not the coast guard's cutter, for which he was looking. Evidently a fisherman's boat and with only one man in it. He laid down the telescope with a sigh of disappointment, and, filling his pipe, leaned on the rail with a dreamy eye bent on the faint grey line of the land.

Three long years had he spent in this dreary solitude, so repugnant to his active, restless nature: three blank, interminable years, with nothing to look back on but the endless succession of summer calms, stormy nights and the chilly fogs of winter, when the unseen steamers hooted from the void and the fog-horn bellowed its hoarse warning.

Why had he come to this God-forgotten spot? and why did he stay, when the wide world called to him? And then memory painted him a picture on which his mind's eye had often looked before and which once again arose before him, shutting out the vision of the calm sea and the distant land. It was a brightly-coloured picture. It showed a cloudless sky brooding over the deep blue tropic sea; and in the middle of the picture, see-sawing gently on the quiet swell, a white-painted barque.

Her sails were clewed up untidily, her swinging yards jerked at the slack braces and her untended wheel revolved to and fro to the oscillations of the rudder.

She was not a derelict, for more than a dozen men were on her deck; but the men were all drunk and mostly asleep, and there was never an officer among them.

Then he saw the interior of one of her cabins. The chart-rack, the tell-tale compass and the chronometers marked it as the captain's cabin. In it were four men, and two of them lay dead on the deck. Of the other two, one was a small, cunning-faced man, who was, at the moment, kneeling beside one of the corpses to wipe a knife upon its coat. The fourth man was himself.

Again, he saw the two murderers stealing off in a quarter-boat, as the barque with her drunken crew drifted towards the spouting surf of a river-bar. He saw the ship melt away in the surf like an icicle in the sunshine; and, later, two ship-wrecked mariners, picked up in an open boat and set ashore at an American port.

That was why he was here. Because he was a murderer. The other scoundrel, Amos Todd, had turned Queen's Evidence and denounced him, and he had barely managed to escape. Since then he had hidden himself from the great world, and here he must continue to hide, not from the law—for his person was unknown now that his shipmates were dead—but from the partner of his crime. It was the fear of Todd that had changed him from Jeffrey Rorke to Tom Jeffreys and had sent him to the Girdler, a prisoner for life. Todd might die—might even now be dead—but he would never hear of it: would never hear the news of his release.

He roused himself and once more pointed his telescope at the distant boat. She was considerably nearer now and seemed to be heading out towards the lighthouse. Perhaps the man in her was bringing a message; at any rate, there was no sign of the coast guard's cutter.

He went in, and, betaking himself to the kitchen, busied himself with a few simple preparations for dinner. But there was nothing to cook, for there remained the cold meat from yesterday's cooking, which he would make sufficient, with some biscuit in place of potatoes. He felt restless and unstrung; the solitude irked him, and the everlasting wash of the water among the piles jarred on his nerves.

When he went out again into the gallery the ebb-tide had set in strongly and the boat was little more than a mile distant; and now, through the glass, he could see that the man in her wore the uniform cap of the Trinity House. Then the man must be his future comrade, Brown; but this was very extraordinary. What were they to do with the boat? There was no one to take her back.

The breeze was dying away. As he watched the boat, he saw the man lower the sail and take to his oars; and something of hurry in the way the man pulled over the gathering tide, caused Jeffreys to look round the horizon. And then, for the first time, he noticed a bank of fog creeping up from the east and already so near that the beacon on the East Girdler had faded out of sight. He hastened in to start the little motor that compressed the air for the fog-horn and waited awhile to see that the mechanism was running properly. Then, as the deck vibrated to the roar of the horn, he went out once more into the gallery.

The fog was now all round the lighthouse and the boat was hidden from view. He listened intently. The enclosing wall of vapour seemed to have shut out sound as well as vision. At intervals the horn bellowed its note of warning, and then all was still save the murmur of the water among the piles below, and, infinitely faint and far away, the mournful tolling of the bell on the Shivering Sand.

At length there came to his ear the muffled sound of oars working in the tholes; then, at the very edge of the circle of grey water that was visible, the boat appeared through the fog, pale and spectral, with a shadowy figure pulling furiously. The horn emitted a hoarse growl; the man looked round, perceived the lighthouse and altered his course towards it.

Jeffreys descended the iron stairway, and, walking along the lower gallery, stood at the head of the ladder earnestly watching the approaching stranger. Already he was tired of being alone. The yearning for human companionship had been growing ever since Barnett left. But what sort of comrade was this stranger who was coming into his life? And coming to occupy so dominant a place in it. It was a momentous question.

The boat swept down swiftly athwart the hurrying tide. Nearer it came and yet nearer: and still Jeffreys could catch no glimpse of his new comrade's face. At length it came fairly alongside and bumped against the fender-posts; the stranger whisked in an oar and grabbed a rung of the ladder, and Jeffreys dropped a coil of rope into the boat. And still the man's face was hidden.

Jeffreys leaned out over the ladder and watched him anxiously, as he made fast the rope, unhooked the sail from the traveller and unstepped the mast. When he had set all in order, the stranger picked up a small chest, and, swinging it over his shoulder, stepped on to the ladder. Slowly, by reason of his encumbrance, he mounted, rung by rung, with never an upward glance, and Jeffreys gazed down at the top of his head with growing curiosity. At last he reached the top of the ladder and Jeffreys stooped to lend him a hand. Then, for the first time, he looked up, and Jeffreys started back with a blanched face.

'God Almighty!' he gasped; 'it's Amos Todd!'

As the newcomer stepped on the gallery, the fog-horn emitted a roar like that of some hungry monster. Jeffreys turned abruptly without a word, and walked to the stairs, followed by Todd, and the two men ascended with never a sound but the hollow clank of their footsteps on the iron plates. Silently Jeffreys stalked into the living-room and, as his companion followed, he turned and motioned to the latter to set down his chest.

'You ain't much of a talker, mate,' said Todd, looking round the room in some surprise; 'ain't you going to say "good morning"? We're going to be good comrades, I hope. I'm Jim Brown, the new hand, I am; what might your name be?'

Jeffreys turned on him suddenly and led him to the window. 'Look at me carefully, Amos Todd,' he said sternly, 'and then ask yourself what my name is.'

At the sound of his voice Todd looked up with a start and turned pale as death. 'It can't be,' he whispered, 'it can't be Jeff Rorke!'

The other man laughed harshly, and, leaning forward, said in a low voice: 'Hast thou found me, O mine enemy!'

'Don't say that!' exclaimed Todd. 'Don't call me your enemy, Jeff. Lord knows but I'm glad to see you, though I'd never have known you without your beard and with that grey hair. I've been to blame, Jeff, and I know it; but it ain't no use raking up old grudges. Let bygones be bygones, Jeff, and let us be pals as we used to be.' He wiped his face with his handkerchief and watched his companion apprehensively.

'Sit down,' said Rorke, pointing to a shabby, rep-covered armchair; 'sit down and tell us what you've done with all that money. You've blued it all, I suppose, or you wouldn't be here.'

'Robbed, Jeff,' answered Todd; 'robbed of every penny. Ah! that was an unfortunate affair, that job on board the old *Sea-flower*. But it's over and done with and we'd best forget it. They're all dead but us, Jeff, so we're safe enough so long as we keep our mouths shut; all at the bottom of the sea—and the best place for 'em, too.'

'Yes,' Rorke replied fiercely, 'that's the best place for your shipmates when they know too much; at the bottom of the sea or swinging at the end of a rope.' He paced up and down the little room with rapid strides, and each time that he approached Todd's chair the latter shrank back with an expression of alarm.

'Don't sit there staring at me,' said Rorke. 'Why don't you smoke or do something?'

Todd hastily produced a pipe from his pocket, and having filled it from a moleskin pouch, stuck it in his mouth while he searched for a match. Apparently he carried his matches loose in his pocket, for he presently brought one forth—a red-headed match, which, when he struck it on the wall, lighted with a pale-blue flame. He applied it to his pipe, sucking in his cheeks while he kept his eyes fixed on his companion. Rorke, meanwhile, halted in his walk to cut some shavings from a cake of hard tobacco with a large clasp-knife; and, as he stood, he gazed with frowning abstraction at Todd.

'This pipe's stopped,' said the latter, sucking ineffectually at the mouthpiece. 'Have you got such a thing as a piece of wire, Jeff?'

'No, I haven't,' replied Rorke; 'not up here. I'll get a bit from the store presently. Here, take this pipe till you can clean your own: I've got another in the rack there.' The sailor's natural hospitality overcoming for the moment his animosity, he thrust the pipe that he had just filled towards Todd, who took it with a mumbled 'Thank you' and an anxious eye on the open knife. On the wall beside the chair was a roughly-carved pipe-rack containing several pipes, one of which Rorke lifted out; and, as he leaned over the chair to reach it, Todd's face went several shades paler.

'Well, Jeff,' he said, after a pause, while Rorke cut a fresh 'fill' of tobacco, 'are we going to be pals same as what we used to be?'

Rorke's animosity lighted up afresh. 'Am I going to be pals with the man that tried to swear away my life?' he said sternly; and after a pause he added: 'That wants thinking about, that does; and meantime I must go and look at the engine.'

When Rorke had gone the new hand sat, with the two pipes in his hands, reflecting deeply. Abstractedly he stuck the fresh pipe into his mouth, and, dropping the stopped one into the rack, felt for a match. Still with an air of abstraction he lit the pipe, and, having smoked for a minute or two, rose from the chair and began softly to creep across the room, looking about him and listening intently. At the door he paused to look out into the fog, and then, having again listened attentively, he stepped on tiptoe out on to the gallery and along towards the stairway. Of a sudden the voice of Rorke brought him up with a start.

'Hallo, Todd! where are you off to?'

'I'm just going down to make the boat secure,' was the reply.

'Never you mind about the boat,' said Rorke. 'I'll see to her.'

'Right-o, Jeff,' said Todd, still edging towards the stairway. 'But, I say, mate, where's the other man—the man that I'm to relieve?'

'There ain't any other man,' replied Rorke; 'he went off aboard a collier.'

Todd's face suddenly became grey and haggard. 'Then there's no one here but us two!' he gasped; and then, with an effort to conceal his fear, he asked: 'But who's going to take the boat back?'

'We'll see about that presently,' replied Rorke; 'you get along in and unpack your chest.'

He came out on the gallery as he spoke, with a lowering frown on his face. Todd cast a terrified glance at him, and then turned and ran for his life towards the stairway.

'Come back!' roared Rorke, springing forward along the gallery; but Todd's feet were already clattering down the iron steps. By the time Rorke reached the head of the stairs, the fugitive was near the bottom; but here, in his haste, he stumbled, barely saving himself by the handrail, and when he recovered his balance Rorke was upon him. Todd darted to the head of the ladder, but, as he grasped the stanchion, his pursuer seized him by the collar. In a moment he had turned with his hand under his coat. There was a quick blow, a loud curse from Rorke, an answering yell from Todd, and a knife fell spinning through the air and dropped into the forepeak of the boat below.

'You murderous little devil!' said Rorke in an ominously quiet voice, with his bleeding hand gripping his captive by the throat. 'Handy with your knife as ever, eh? So you were off to give information, were you?'

'No, I wasn't, Jeff,' replied Todd in a choking voice; 'I wasn't, s'elp me God. Let go, Jeff. I didn't mean no harm. I was only—' With a sudden wrench he freed one hand and struck out frantically at his captor's face. But Rorke warded off the blow, and, grasping the other wrist, gave a violent push and let go. Todd staggered backward a few paces along the staging, bringing up at the extreme edge; and here, for a sensible time, he stood with wide-open mouth and starting eyeballs, swaying and clutching wildly at the air. Then, with a shrill scream, he toppled backwards and fell, striking a pile in his descent and rebounding into the water.

In spite of the audible thump of his head on the pile, he was not stunned, for, when he rose to the surface, he struck out vigorously, uttering short, stifled cries for help. Rorke watched him with set teeth and quickened breath, but made no move. Smaller and still smaller grew the head with its little circle of ripples, swept away on the swift ebb-tide, and fainter the bubbling cries that came across the smooth water. At length as the small black spot began to fade in the fog, the drowning man, with a final effort, raised his head clear of the surface and sent a last, despairing shriek towards the lighthouse. The fog-horn sent back an answering bellow; the head sank below the surface and was seen no more; and in the dreadful stillness that settled down upon the sea there sounded faint and far away the muffled tolling of a bell.

Rorke stood for some minutes immovable, wrapped in thought. Presently the distant hoot of a steamer's whistle aroused him. The ebb-tide shipping was beginning to come down and the fog might lift at any moment; and there was the boat still alongside. She must be disposed of at once. No one had seen her arrive and no one must see her made fast to the lighthouse. Once get rid of the boat and all traces of Todd's visit would be destroyed.

He ran down the ladder and stepped into the boat. It was perfectly simple. She was heavily ballasted and would go down like a stone if she filled.

He shifted some of the bags of shingle, and, lifting the bottom boards, pulled out the plug. Instantly a large jet of water spouted up into the bottom. Rorke looked at it critically, and, deciding that it would fill her in a few minutes, replaced the bottom boards; and having secured the mast and sail with a few turns of the sheet round a thwart, to prevent them from floating away, he cast off the mooring-rope and stepped on the ladder.

As the released boat began to move away on the tide, he ran up and mounted to the upper gallery to watch her disappearance. Suddenly he remembered Todd's chest. It was still in the room below. With a hurried glance around into the fog, he ran down to the room, and snatching up the chest, carried it out on the lower gallery. After another nervous glance around to assure himself that no craft was in sight, he heaved the chest over the handrail, and, when it fell with a loud splash into the sea, he waited to watch it float away after its owner and the sunken boat. But it never rose; and presently he returned to the upper gallery.

The fog was thinning perceptibly now, and the boat remained plainly visible as she drifted away. But she sank more slowly than he had expected, and presently, as she drifted farther away, he fetched the telescope and peered at her with growing anxiety. It would be unfortunate if anyone saw her; if she should be picked up here, with her plug out, it would be disastrous.

He was beginning to be really alarmed. Through the glass he could see that the boat was now rolling in a sluggish, water-logged fashion, but she still showed some inches of free-board, and the fog was thinning every moment.

Presently the blast of a steamer's whistle sounded close at hand. He looked round hurriedly and, seeing nothing, again pointed the telescope eagerly at the dwindling boat. Suddenly he gave a gasp of relief. The boat had rolled gunwale under; had staggered back for a moment and then rolled again, slowly, finally, with the water pouring in over the submerged gunwale.

In a few more seconds she had vanished. Rorke lowered the telescope and took a deep breath. Now he was safe. The boat had sunk unseen. But he was better than safe: he was free.

His evil spirit, the standing menace of his life, was gone, and the wide world, the world of life, of action, of pleasure, called to him.

In a few minutes the fog lifted. The sun shone brightly on the red-funnelled cattle-boat whose whistle had startled him just now, the summer blue came back to sky and sea, and the land peeped once more over the edge of the horizon.

He went in, whistling cheerfully, and stopped the motor; returned to coil away the rope that he had thrown to Todd; and, when he had hoisted a signal for assistance, he went in once more to eat his solitary meal in peace and gladness.

CHAPTER TWO

'THE SINGING BONE'

(Related by Christopher Jervis, MD)

To every kind of scientific work a certain amount of manual labour naturally appertains, labour that cannot be performed by the scientist himself, since art is long but life is short. A chemical analysis involves a laborious 'clean up' of apparatus and laboratory, for which the chemist has no time; the preparation of a skeleton—the maceration, bleaching, 'assembling,' and riveting together of bones—must be carried out by someone whose time is not too precious. And so with other scientific activities. Behind the man of science with his outfit of knowledge is the indispensable mechanic with his outfit of manual skill.

Thorndyke's laboratory assistant, Polton, was a fine example of the latter type, deft, resourceful, ingenious, and untiring. He was somewhat of an inventive genius, too; and it was one of his inventions that connected us with the singular case that I am about to record.

Though by trade a watchmaker, Polton was, by choice, an

optician. Optical apparatus was the passion of his life; and when, one day, he produced for our inspection an improved prism for increasing the efficiency of gas-buoys, Thorndyke at once brought the invention to the notice of a friend at the Trinity House.

As a consequence, we three—Thorndyke, Polton and I—found ourselves early on a fine July morning making our way down Middle Temple Lane bound for the Temple Pier. A small oil-launch lay alongside the pontoon, and, as we made our appearance, a red-faced, white-whiskered gentleman stood up in the cockpit.

'Here's a delightful morning, doctor,' he sang out in a fine, brassy, resonant, sea-faring voice; 'sort of day for a trip to the lower river, hey? Hallo, Polton! Coming down to take the bread out of our mouths, are you? Ha, ha!' The cheery laugh rang out over the river and mingled with the throb of the engine as the little launch moved off from the pier.

Captain Grumpass was one of the Elder Brethren of the Trinity House. Formerly a client of Thorndyke's, he had subsided, as Thorndyke's clients were apt to do, into the position of a personal friend, and his hearty regard included our invaluable assistant.

'Nice state of things,' continued the captain, with a chuckle, 'when a body of nautical experts have got to be taught their business by a parcel of lawyers or doctors, what? I suppose trade's slack and "Satan findeth mischief still," hey, Polton?'

'There isn't much doing on the civil side, sir,' replied Polton, with a quaint, crinkly smile, 'but the criminals are still going strong.'

'Ha! mystery department still flourishing, what? And, by Jove! talking of mysteries, doctor, our people have got a queer problem to work out; something quite in your line—quite.

Yes, and, by the Lord Moses, since I've got you here, why shouldn't I suck your brains?'

'Exactly,' said Thorndyke. 'Why shouldn't you?'

'Well, then, I will,' said the captain, 'so here goes. All hands to the pump!' He lit a cigar, and, after a few preliminary puffs, began: 'The mystery, shortly stated, is this: one of our light-housemen has disappeared—vanished off the face of the earth and left no trace. He may have bolted, he may have been drowned accidentally or he may have been murdered. But I'd better give you the particulars in order. At the end of last week a barge brought into Ramsgate a letter from the screw-pile lighthouse on the Girdler. There are only two men there, and it seems that one of them, a man named Barnett, had broken his leg, and he asked that the tender should be sent to bring him ashore. Well, it happened that the local tender, the *Warden*, was up on the slip in Ramsgate Harbour, having a scrape down, and wouldn't be available for a day or two, so, as the case was urgent, the officer at Ramsgate sent a letter to the lighthouse by one of the pleasure steamers saying that the man should be relieved by boat on the following morning, which was Saturday. He also wrote to a new hand who had just been taken on, a man named James Brown, who was lodging near Reculver, waiting his turn, telling him to go out on Saturday morning in the coast guard's boat; and he sent a third letter to the coast guard at Reculver asking him to take Brown out to the lighthouse and bring Barnett ashore. Well, between them, they made a fine muddle of it. The coast-guard couldn't spare either a boat or a man, so they borrowed a fisherman's boat, and in this the man Brown started off alone, like an idiot, on the chance that Barnett would be able to sail the boat back in spite of his broken leg.

'Meanwhile Barnett, who is a Whitstable man, had sig-nalled a collier bound for his native town, and got taken off;

so that the other keeper, Thomas Jeffreys, was left alone until Brown should turn up.

'But Brown never did turn up. The coast guard helped him to put off and saw him well out to sea, and the keeper, Jeffreys, saw a sailing-boat with one man in her, making for the lighthouse. Then a bank of fog came up and hid the boat, and when the fog cleared she was nowhere to be seen. Man and boat had vanished and left no sign.'

'He may have been run down in the fog,' Thorndyke suggested.

'He may,' agreed the captain, 'but no accident has been reported. The coast guards think he may have capsized in a squall—they saw him make the sheet fast. But there weren't any squalls: the weather was quite calm.'

'Was he all right and well when he put off?' inquired Thorndyke.

'Yes,' replied the captain, 'the coast guards' report is highly circumstantial; in fact, it's full of silly details that have no bearing on anything. This is what they say.' He pulled out an official letter and read: '"When last seen, the missing man was seated in the boat's stern to windward of the helm. He had belayed the sheet. He was holding a pipe and tobacco-pouch in his hands and steering with his elbow. He was filling the pipe from the tobacco-pouch." There! "He was holding the pipe in his hand," mark you! not with his toes; and he was filling it from a tobacco-pouch, whereas you'd have expected him to fill it from a coal-scuttle or a feeding-bottle. Bah!' The captain rammed the letter back in his pocket and puffed scornfully at his cigar.

'You are hardly fair to the coast guard,' said Thorndyke, laughing at the captain's vehemence. 'The duty of a witness is to give all the facts, not a judicious selection.'

'But, my dear sir,' said Captain Grumpass, 'what the deuce can it matter what the poor devil filled his pipe from?'

'Who can say?' answered Thorndyke. 'It may turn out to be a highly material fact. One never knows beforehand. The value of a particular fact depends on its relation to the rest of the evidence.'

'I suppose it does,' grunted the captain; and he continued to smoke in reflective silence until we opened Blackwall Point, when he suddenly stood up.

'There's a steam trawler alongside our wharf,' he announced. 'Now what the deuce can she be doing there?' He scanned the little steamer attentively, and continued: 'They seem to be landing something, too. Just pass me those glasses, Polton. Why, hang me! it's a dead body! But why on earth are they landing it on our wharf? They must have known you were coming, doctor.'

As the launch swept alongside the wharf, the captain sprang up lightly and approached the group gathered round the body. 'What's this?' he asked. 'Why have they brought this thing here?'

The master of the trawler, who had superintended the landing, proceeded to explain.

'It's one of your men, sir,' said he. 'We saw the body lying on the edge of the South Shingles Sand, close to the beacon, as we passed at low water, so we put off the boat and fetched it aboard. As there was nothing to identify the man by, I had a look in his pockets and found this letter.' He handed the captain an official envelope addressed to 'Mr J Brown, c/o Mr Solly, Shepherd, Reculver, Kent.'

'Why, this is the man we were speaking about, doctor,' exclaimed Captain Grumpass. 'What a very singular coincidence. But what are we to do with the body?'

'You will have to write to the coroner,' replied Thorndyke. 'By the way, did you turn out all the pockets?' he asked, turning to the skipper of the trawler.

'No, sir,' was the reply. 'I found the letter in the first pocket that I felt in, so I didn't examine any of the others. Is there anything more that you want to know, sir?'

'Nothing but your name and address, for the coroner,' replied Thorndyke, and the skipper, having given this information and expressed the hope that the coroner would not keep him 'hanging about,' returned to his vessel and pursued his way to Billingsgate.

'I wonder if you would mind having a look at the body of this poor devil, while Polton is showing us his contraptions,' said Captain Grumpass.

'I can't do much without a coroner's order,' replied Thorndyke; 'but if it will give you any satisfaction, Jervis and I will make a preliminary inspection with pleasure.'

'I should be glad if you would,' said the captain. 'We should like to know that the poor beggar met his end fairly.'

The body was accordingly moved to a shed, and, as Polton was led away, carrying the black bag that contained his precious model, we entered the shed and commenced our investigation.

The deceased was a small, elderly man, decently dressed in a somewhat nautical fashion. He appeared to have been dead only two or three days, and the body, unlike the majority of seaborne corpses, was uninjured by fish or crabs. There were no fractured bones or other gross injuries, and no wounds, excepting a rugged tear in the scalp at the back of the head.

'The general appearance of the body,' said Thorndyke, when he had noted these particulars, 'suggests death by drowning, though, of course, we can't give a definite opinion until a *post mortem* has been made.'

'You don't attach any significance to that scalp-wound, then?' I asked.

'As a cause of death? No. It was obviously inflicted during life, but it seems to have been an oblique blow that spent its force on the scalp, leaving the skull uninjured. But it is very significant in another way.'

'In what way?' I asked.

Thorndyke took out his pocket-case and extracted a pair of forceps. 'Consider the circumstances,' said he. 'This man put off from the shore to go to the lighthouse, but never arrived there. The question is, where did he arrive?' As he spoke he stooped over the corpse and turned back the hair round the wound with the beak of the forceps. 'Look at those white objects among the hair, Jervis, and inside the wound. They tell us something, I think.'

I examined, through my lens, the chalky fragments to which he pointed. 'These seem to be bits of shells and the tubes of some marine worm,' I said.

'Yes,' he answered; 'the broken shells are evidently those of the acorn barnacle, and the other fragments are mostly pieces of the tubes of the common serpula. The inference that these objects suggest is an important one. It is that this wound was produced by some body encrusted by acorn barnacles and serpulae; that is to say, by a body that is periodically submerged. Now, what can that body be, and how can the deceased have knocked his head against it?'

'It might be the stem of a ship that ran him down,' I suggested.

'I don't think you would find many serpulae on the stem of a ship,' said Thorndyke. 'The combination rather suggests some stationary object between tide-marks, such as a beacon. But one doesn't see how a man could knock his head against a beacon, while, on the other hand, there are no other stationary objects out in the estuary to knock against except buoys, and a buoy presents a flat surface that could hardly have produced this wound. By the way, we may as well see what there is in his pockets, though it is not likely that robbery had anything to do with his death.'

'No,' I agreed, 'and I see his watch is in his pocket; quite a good silver one,' I added, taking it out. 'It has stopped at 12.13.'

'That may be important,' said Thorndyke, making a note of the fact; 'but we had better examine the pockets one at a time, and put the things back when we have looked at them.'

The first pocket that we turned out was the left hip-pocket of the monkey jacket. This was apparently the one that the skipper had rifled, for we found in it two letters, both bearing the crest of the Trinity House. These, of course, we returned without reading, and then passed on to the right pocket. The contents of this were commonplace enough, consisting of a briar pipe, a moleskin pouch, and a number of loose matches.

'Rather a casual proceeding, this,' I remarked, 'to carry matches loose in the pocket, and a pipe with them, too.'

'Yes,' agreed Thorndyke; 'especially with these very inflammable matches. You notice that the sticks had been coated at the upper end with sulphur before the red phosphorous heads were put on. They would light with a touch, and would be very difficult to extinguish; which, no doubt, is the reason that this type of match is so popular among seamen, who have to light their pipes in all sorts of weather.' As he spoke he picked up the pipe and looked at it reflectively, turning it over in his hand and peering into the bowl. Suddenly he glanced from the pipe to the dead man's face and then, with the forceps, turned back the lips to look into the mouth.

'Let us see what tobacco he smokes,' said he.

I opened the sodden pouch and displayed a mass of dark, fine-cut tobacco. 'It looks like shag,' I said.

'Yes, it is shag,' he replied; 'and now we will see what is in the pipe. It has been only half-smoked out.' He dug out the 'dottle' with his pocket-knife on to a sheet of paper, and we both inspected it. Clearly it was not shag, for it consisted of coarsely-cut shreds and was nearly black.

'Shavings from a cake of "hard,"' was my verdict, and Thorndyke agreed as he shot the fragments back into the pipe.

The other pockets yielded nothing of interest, except a pocket-knife, which Thorndyke opened and examined closely. There was not much money, though as much as one would expect, and enough to exclude the idea of robbery.

'Is there a sheath-knife on that strap?' Thorndyke asked, pointing to a narrow leather belt. I turned back the jacket and looked.

'There is a sheath,' I said, 'but no knife. It must have dropped out.'

'That is rather odd,' said Thorndyke. 'A sailor's sheath-knife takes a deal of shaking out as a rule. It is intended to be used in working on the rigging when the man is aloft, so that he can get it out with one hand while he is holding on with the other. It has to be and usually is very secure, for the sheath holds half the handle as well as the blade. What makes one notice the matter in this case is that the man, as you see, carried a pocket-knife; and, as this would serve all the ordinary purposes of a knife, it seems to suggest that the sheath-knife was carried for defensive purposes: as a weapon, in fact. However, we can't get much further in the case without a *post mortem*, and here comes the captain.'

Captain Grumpass entered the shed and looked down commiseratingly at the dead seaman.

'Is there anything, doctor, that throws any light on the man's disappearance?' he asked.

'There are one or two curious features in the case,' Thorndyke replied; 'but, oddly enough, the only really important point arises out of that statement of the coast-guard's, concerning which you were so scornful.'

'You don't say so!' exclaimed the captain.

'Yes,' said Thorndyke; 'the coast-guard states that when last seen deceased was filling his pipe from his tobacco-pouch. Now his pouch contains shag; but the pipe in his pocket contains hard cut.'

'Is there no cake tobacco in any of the pockets?'

'Not a fragment. Of course, it is possible that he might have had a piece and used it up to fill the pipe; but there is no trace of any on the blade of his pocket-knife, and you know how this juicy black cake stains a knife-blade. His sheath-knife is missing, but he would hardly have used that to shred tobacco when he had a pocket-knife.'

'No,' assented the captain; 'but are you sure he hadn't a second pipe?'

'There was only one pipe,' replied Thorndyke, 'and that was not his own.'

'Not his own!' exclaimed the captain, halting by a huge, chequered buoy to stare at my colleague; 'how do you know it was not his own?'

'By the appearance of the vulcanite mouthpiece,' said Thorndyke. 'It showed deep toothmarks; in fact, it was nearly bitten through. Now a man who bites through his pipe usually presents certain definite physical peculiarities, among which is, necessarily, a fairly good set of teeth. But the dead man had not a tooth in his head.'

The captain cogitated a while, and then remarked: 'I don't quite see the bearing of this.'

'Don't you?' said Thorndyke. 'It seems to me highly suggestive. Here is a man who, when last seen, was filling his pipe with a particular kind of tobacco. He is picked up dead, and his pipe contains a totally different kind of tobacco. Where did that tobacco come from? The obvious suggestion is that he had met someone.'

'Yes, it does look like it,' agreed the captain.

'Then,' continued Thorndyke, 'there is the fact that his sheath-knife is missing. That may mean nothing, but we have to bear it in mind. And there is another curious circumstance: there is a wound on the back of the head caused by a heavy bump against some body that was covered with acorn barnacles and marine worms. Now there are no piers or stages out in the open estuary. The question is, what could he have struck?'

'Oh, there is nothing in that,' said the captain. 'When a body has been washing about in a tideway for close on three days—'

'But this is not a question of a body,' Thorndyke interrupted. 'The wound was made during life.'

'The deuce it was!' exclaimed the captain. 'Well, all I can suggest is that he must have fouled one of the beacons in the fog, stove in his boat and bumped his head, though, I must admit, that's rather a lame explanation.' He stood for a minute gazing at his toes with a cogitative frown and then looked up at Thorndyke.

'I have an idea,' he said. 'From what you say, this matter wants looking into pretty carefully. Now, I am going down on the tender today to make inquiries on the spot. What do you say to coming with me as adviser—as a matter of business, of course—you and Dr Jervis? I shall start about eleven; we shall be at the lighthouse by three o'clock, and you can get back to town tonight, if you want to. What do you say?'

'There's nothing to hinder us,' I put in eagerly, for even at Bugsby's Hole the river looked very alluring on this summer morning.

'Very well,' said Thorndyke, 'we will come. Jervis is obviously hankering for a sea-trip, and so am I, for that matter.'

'It's a business engagement, you know,' the captain stipulated.

'Nothing of the kind,' said Thorndyke; 'it's unmitigated pleasure; the pleasure of the voyage and your high well-born society.'

'I didn't mean that,' grumbled the captain, 'but, if you are coming as guests, send your man for your night-gear and let us bring you back tomorrow evening.'

'We won't disturb Polton,' said my colleague; 'we can take the train from Blackwall and fetch our things ourselves. Eleven o'clock, you said?'

'Thereabouts,' said Captain Grumpass; 'but don't put yourselves out.'

The means of communication in London have reached an almost undesirable state of perfection. With the aid of the snorting train and the tinkling, two-wheeled 'gondola,' we crossed and recrossed the town with such celerity that it was barely eleven when we reappeared on Trinity Wharf with a joint Gladstone and Thorndyke's little green case.

The tender had hauled out of Bow Creek, and now lay alongside the wharf with a great striped can buoy dangling from her derrick, and Captain Grumpass stood at the gangway, his jolly, red face beaming with pleasure. The buoy was safely stowed forward, the derrick hauled up to the mast, the loose shrouds rehooked to the screw-lanyards, and the steamer, with four jubilant hoots, swung round and shoved her sharp nose against the incoming tide.

For near upon four hours the ever-widening stream of the 'London River' unfolded its moving panorama. The smoke and smell of Woolwich Reach gave place to lucid air made soft by the summer haze; the grey huddle of factories fell away and green levels of cattle-spotted marsh stretched away to the high land bordering the river valley. Venerable training ships displayed their chequered hulls by the wooded shore and whispered of the days of oak and hemp, when the tall three-decker, comely and majestic, with her soaring heights of canvas, like towers of ivory, had not yet given place to the mud-coloured saucepans that fly the white ensign nowadays and devour the substance of the British taxpayer: when a sailor was a sailor and not a mere seafaring mechanic. Sturdily breasting the flood-tide, the tender threaded her way through the endless procession of shipping barges, billy-boys, schooners, brigs; lumpish Black-seamen, blue-funnelled China tramps, rickety Baltic barques with twirling windmills, gigantic liners, staggering under a mountain of top-hamper. Erith, Purfleet, Greenhithe, Grays greeted us and passed astern. The chimneys of Northfleet, the clustering roofs of Gravesend, the populous anchorage and the lurking batteries, were left behind, and, as we swung out of the Lower Hope, the wide expanse of sea reach spread out before us like a great sheet of blue-shot satin.

About half-past twelve the ebb overtook us and helped us on our way, as we could see by the speed with which the distant land slid past, and the freshening of the air as we passed through it.

But sky and sea were hushed in a summer calm. Balls of

fleecy cloud hung aloft, motionless in the soft blue; the barges drifted on the tide with drooping sails, and a big, striped bell buoy—surmounted by a staff and cage and labelled 'Shivering Sand'—sat dreaming in the sun above its motionless reflection, to rouse for a moment as it met our wash, nod its cage drowsily, utter a solemn ding-dong, and fall asleep again.

It was shortly after passing the buoy that the gaunt shape of a screw-pile lighthouse began to loom up ahead, its dull-red paint turned to vermilion by the early afternoon sun. As we drew nearer, the name *Girdler*, painted in huge, white letters, became visible, and two men could be seen in the gallery around the lantern, inspecting us through a telescope.

'Shall you be long at the lighthouse, sir?' the master of the tender inquired of Captain Grumpass; 'because we're going down to the North-East Pan Sand to fix this new buoy and take up the old one.'

'Then you'd better put us off at the lighthouse and come back for us when you've finished the job,' was the reply. 'I don't know how long we shall be.'

The tender was brought to, a boat lowered, and a couple of hands pulled us across the intervening space of water.

'It will be a dirty climb for you in your shore-going clothes,' the captain remarked—he was as spruce as a new pin himself, 'but the stuff will all wipe off.' We looked up at the skeleton shape. The falling tide had exposed some fifteen feet of the piles, and piles and ladder alike were swathed in sea-grass and encrusted with barnacles and worm-tubes. But we were not such town-sparrows as the captain seemed to think, for we both followed his lead without difficulty up the slippery ladder, Thorndyke clinging tenaciously to his little green case, from which he refused to be separated even for an instant.

'These gentlemen and I,' said the captain, as we stepped

on the stage at the head of the ladder, 'have come to make inquiries about the missing man, James Brown. Which of you is Jeffreys?'

'I am, sir,' replied a tall, powerful, square-jawed, beetle-browed man, whose left hand was tied up in a rough bandage.

'What have you been doing to your hand?' asked the captain.

'I cut it while I was peeling some potatoes,' was the reply. 'It isn't much of a cut, sir.'

'Well, Jeffreys,' said the captain, 'Brown's body has been picked up and I want particulars for the inquest. You'll be summoned as a witness, I suppose, so come in and tell us all you know.'

We entered the living-room and seated ourselves at the table. The captain opened a massive pocket-book, while Thorndyke, in his attentive, inquisitive fashion, looked about the odd, cabin-like room as if making a mental inventory of its contents.

Jeffreys' statement added nothing to what we already knew. He had seen a boat with one man in it making for the light-house. Then the fog had drifted up and he had lost sight of the boat. He started the fog-horn and kept a bright look-out, but the boat never arrived. And that was all he knew. He supposed that the man must have missed the lighthouse and been carried away on the ebb-tide, which was running strongly at the time.

'What time was it when you last saw the boat?' Thorndyke asked.

'About half-past eleven,' replied Jeffreys.

'What was the man like?' asked the captain.

'I don't know, sir: he was rowing, and his back was towards me.'

'Had he any kit-bag or chest with him?' asked Thorndyke.

'He'd got his chest with him,' said Jeffreys.

'What sort of chest was it?' inquired Thorndyke.

'A small chest, painted green, with rope beckets.'

'Was it corded?'

'It had a single cord round, to hold the lid down.'

'Where was it stowed?'

'In the stern-sheets, sir.'

'How far off was the boat when you last saw it?'

'About half-a-mile.'

'Half-a-mile!' exclaimed the captain. 'Why, how the deuce could you see what the chest was like half-a-mile away?'

The man reddened and cast a look of angry suspicion at Thorndyke. 'I was watching the boat through the glass, sir,' he replied sulkily.

'I see,' said Captain Grumpass. 'Well, that will do, Jeffreys. We shall have to arrange for you to attend the inquest. Tell Smith I want to see him.'

The examination concluded, Thorndyke and I moved our chairs to the window, which looked out over the sea to the east. But it was not the sea or the passing ships that engaged my colleague's attention. On the wall, beside the window, hung a rudely-carved pipe-rack containing five pipes. Thorndyke had noted it when we entered the room, and now, as we talked, I observed him regarding it from time to time with speculative interest.

'You men seem to be inveterate smokers,' he remarked to the keeper, Smith, when the captain had concluded the arrangements for the 'shift.'

'Well, we do like our bit of 'baccy, sir, and that's a fact,' answered Smith. 'You see, sir,' he continued, 'it's a lonely life, and tobacco's cheap out here.'

'How is that?' asked Thorndyke.

'Why, we get it given to us. The small craft from foreign shores, especially the Dutchmen, generally heave us a cake or two when they pass close. We're not ashore, you see, so there's no duty to pay.'

'So you don't trouble the tobacconists much? Don't go in for cut tobacco?'

'No, sir; we'd have to buy it, and then the cut stuff wouldn't keep. No, it's hard tack to eat out here and hard tobacco to smoke.'

'I see you've got a pipe-rack, too, quite a stylish affair.'

'Yes,' said Smith, 'I made it in my off-time. Keeps the place tidy and looks more ship-shape than letting the pipes lay about anywhere.'

'Someone seems to have neglected his pipe,' said Thorndyke, pointing to one at the end of the pipe-rack which was coated with green mildew.

'Yes; that's Parsons, my mate. He must have left it when we went off near a month ago. Pipes do go mouldy in the damp air out here.'

'How soon does a pipe go mouldy if it is left untouched?' Thorndyke asked.

'It's according to the weather,' said Smith. 'When it's warm and damp they'll begin to go in about a week. Now here's Barnett's pipe that he's left behind—the man that broke his leg, you know, sir—it's just beginning to spot a little. He couldn't have used it for a day or two before he went.'

'And are all these other pipes yours?'

'No, sir. This here one is mine. The end one is Jeffreys', and I suppose the middle one is his too, but I don't know it.'

'You're a demon for pipes, doctor,' said the captain, strolling up at this moment; 'you seem to make a special study of them.'

'"The proper study of mankind is man," replied Thorndyke, as the keeper retired, 'and "man" includes those objects on which his personality is impressed. Now a pipe is a very personal thing. Look at that row in the rack. Each has its own physiognomy which, in a measure, reflects the peculiarities of the owner. There is Jeffreys' pipe at the end, for instance. The mouth-piece is nearly bitten through, the bowl scraped to a shell and scored inside and the brim battered and chipped. The whole thing speaks of rude strength and rough handling. He chews the stem as he smokes, he scrapes the bowl violently, and he bangs the ashes out with unnecessary force. And the man fits the pipe exactly: powerful, square-jawed and, I should say, violent on occasion.'

'Yes, he looks a tough customer, does Jeffreys,' agreed the captain.

'Then,' continued Thorndyke, 'there is Smith's pipe, next to it; "coked" up until the cavity is nearly filled and burnt all round the edge; a talker's pipe, constantly going out and being relit. But the one that interests me most is the middle one.'

'Didn't Smith say that that was Jeffreys' too?' I said.

'Yes,' replied Thorndyke, 'but he must be mistaken. It is the very opposite of Jeffreys' pipe in every respect. To begin with, although it is an old pipe, there is not a sign of any toothmark on the mouth-piece. It is the only one in the rack that is quite unmarked. Then the brim is quite uninjured: it has been handled gently, and the silver band is jet-black, whereas the band on Jeffreys' pipe is quite bright.'

'I hadn't noticed that it had a band,' said the captain. 'What has made it so black?'

Thorndyke lifted the pipe out of the rack and looked at it closely. 'Silver sulphide,' said he, 'the sulphur no doubt derived from something carried in the pocket.'

'I see,' said Captain Grumpass, smothering a yawn and gazing out of the window at the distant tender. 'Incidentally it's full of tobacco. What moral do you draw from that?'

Thorndyke turned the pipe over and looked closely at the mouth-piece. 'The moral is,' he replied, 'that you should see that your pipe is clear before you fill it.' He pointed to the mouth-piece, the bore of which was completely stopped up with fine fluff.

'An excellent moral too,' said the captain, rising with another yawn. 'If you'll excuse me a minute I'll just go and see what the tender is up to. She seems to be crossing to the East Girdler.' He reached the telescope down from its brackets and went out on to the gallery.

As the captain retreated, Thorndyke opened his pocket-knife, and, sticking the blade into the bowl of the pipe, turned the tobacco out into his hand.

'Shag, by Jove!' I exclaimed.

'Yes,' he answered, poking it back into the bowl. 'Didn't you expect it to be shag?'

'I don't know that I expected anything,' I admitted. 'The silver band was occupying my attention.'

'Yes, that is an interesting point,' said Thorndyke, 'but let us see what the obstruction consists of.' He opened the green case, and, taking out a dissecting needle, neatly extracted a little ball of fluff from the bore of the pipe. Laying this on a glass slide, he teased it out in a drop of glycerine and put on a cover-glass while I set up the microscope.

'Better put the pipe back in the rack,' he said, as he laid the slide on the stage of the instrument. I did so and then turned, with no little excitement, to watch him as he examined the specimen. After a brief inspection he rose and waved his hand towards the microscope.

'Take a look at it, Jervis,' he said, 'and let us have your learned opinion.'

I applied my eye to the instrument, and, moving the slide about, identified the constituents of the little mass of fluff. The ubiquitous cotton fibre was, of course, in evidence, and a few fibres of wool, but the most remarkable objects were two or three hairs—very minute hairs of a definite zigzag shape and having a flat expansion near the free end like the blade of a paddle.

'These are the hairs of some small animal,' I said; 'not a mouse or rat or any rodent, I should say. Some small insectivorous animal, I fancy. Yes! Of course! They are the hairs of a mole.' I stood up, and, as the importance of the discovery flashed on me, I looked at my colleague in silence.

'Yes,' he said, 'they are unmistakable; and they furnish the keystone of the argument.'

'You think that this is really the dead man's pipe, then?' I said.

'According to the law of multiple evidence,' he replied, 'it is practically a certainty. Consider the facts in sequence. Since there is no sign of mildew on it, this pipe can have been here only a short time, and must belong either to Barnett, Smith, Jeffreys, or Brown. It is an old pipe, but it has no tooth-marks on it. Therefore it has been used by a man who has no teeth. But Barnett, Smith, and Jeffreys all have teeth and mark their pipes, whereas Brown had no teeth. The tobacco in it is shag. But these three men do not smoke shag, whereas Brown had shag in his pouch. The silver band is encrusted with sulphide; and Brown carried sulphur-tipped matches loose in his pocket with his pipe. We find hairs of a mole in the bore of the pipe; and Brown carried a moleskin pouch in the pocket in which he appears to have carried his pipe. Finally, Brown's pocket contained a pipe which was obviously not his and which closely resembled that of Jeffreys; it contained tobacco similar to that which Jeffreys smokes and different from that in Brown's pouch. It appears to me quite conclusive, especially when we add to this evidence the other items that are in our possession.'

'What items are they?' I asked.

'First there is the fact that the dead man had knocked his head heavily against some periodically submerged body covered with acorn barnacles and serpulae. Now the piles of this lighthouse answer to the description exactly, and there are no other bodies in the neighbourhood that do: for even the beacons are too large to have produced that kind of wound. Then the dead man's sheath-knife is missing, and Jeffreys has a knife-wound on his hand. You must admit that the circumstantial evidence is overwhelming.'

At this moment the captain bustled into the room with the telescope in his hand. 'The tender is coming up towing a strange boat,' he said. 'I expect it's the missing one, and, if it is, we may learn something. You'd better pack up your traps and get ready to go on board.'

We packed the green case and went out into the gallery, where the two keepers were watching the approaching tender; Smith frankly curious and interested, Jeffreys restless, fidgety and noticeably pale. As the steamer came opposite the lighthouse, three men dropped into the boat and pulled across, and one of them—the mate of the tender—came climbing up the ladder.

'Is that the missing boat?' the captain sang out.

'Yes, sir,' answered the officer, stepping on to the staging and wiping his hands on the reverse aspect of his trousers, 'we saw her lying on the dry patch of the East Girdler. There's been some hanky-panky in this job, sir.'

'Foul play, you think, hey?'

'Not a doubt of it, sir. The plug was out and lying loose in the bottom, and we found a sheath-knife sticking into the kelson forward among the coils of the painter. It was stuck in hard as if it had dropped from a height.'

'That's odd,' said the captain. 'As to the plug, it might have got out by accident.'

'But it hadn't, sir,' said the mate. 'The ballast-bags had been shifted along to get the bottom boards up. Besides, sir, a seaman wouldn't let the boat fill; he'd have put the plug back and baled out.'

'That's true,' replied Captain Grumpass; 'and certainly the presence of the knife looks fishy. But where the deuce could it have dropped from, out in the open sea? Knives don't drop from the clouds—fortunately. What do you say, doctor?'

'I should say that it is Brown's own knife, and that it probably fell from this staging.'

Jeffreys turned swiftly, crimson with wrath. 'What d'ye mean?' he demanded. 'Haven't I said that the boat never came here?'

'You have,' replied Thorndyke; 'but if that is so, how do you explain the fact that your pipe was found in the dead man's pocket and that the dead man's pipe is at this moment in your pipe-rack?'

The crimson flush on Jeffreys' face faded as quickly as it had come. 'I don't know what you're talking about,' he faltered.

'I'll tell you,' said Thorndyke. 'I will relate what happened and you shall check my statements. Brown brought his boat alongside and came up into the living-room, bringing his chest with him. He filled his pipe and tried to light it, but it was stopped and wouldn't draw. Then you lent him a pipe of yours and filled it for him. Soon afterwards you came out on this staging and quarrelled. Brown defended himself with his knife, which dropped from his hand into the boat. You pushed him off the staging and he fell, knocking his head on one of the piles. Then you took the plug out of the boat and sent her adrift to sink, and you flung the chest into the sea. This happened about ten minutes past twelve. Am I right?'

Jeffreys stood staring at Thorndyke, the picture of amazement and consternation; but he uttered no word in reply.

'Am I right?' Thorndyke repeated.

'Strike me blind!' muttered Jeffreys. 'Was you here, then? You talk as if you had been. Anyhow,' he continued, recovering somewhat, 'you seem to know all about it. But you're wrong about one thing. There was no quarrel. This chap, Brown, didn't take to me and he didn't mean to stay out here. He was going to put off and go ashore again and I wouldn't let him. Then he hit out at me with his knife and I knocked it out of his hand and he staggered backwards and went overboard.'

'And did you try to pick him up?' asked the captain.

'How could I,' demanded Jeffreys, 'with the tide racing down and me alone on the station? I'd never have got back.'

'But what about the boat, Jeffreys? Why did you scuttle her?'

'The fact is,' replied Jeffreys, 'I got in a funk, and I thought the simplest plan was to send her to the cellar and know nothing about it. But I never shoved him over. It was an accident, sir; I swear it!'

'Well, that sounds a reasonable explanation,' said the captain. 'What do you say, doctor?'

'Perfectly reasonable,' replied Thorndyke, 'and, as to its truth, that is no affair of ours.'

'No. But I shall have to take you off, Jeffreys, and hand you over to the police. You understand that?'

'Yes, sir, I understand,' answered Jeffreys.

'That was a queer case, that affair on the Girdler,' remarked Captain Grumpass, when he was spending an evening with us some six months later. 'A pretty easy let off for Jeffreys, too—eighteen months, wasn't it?'

'Yes, it was a very queer case indeed,' said Thorndyke. 'There was something behind that "accident," I should say. Those men had probably met before.'

'So I thought,' agreed the captain. 'But the queerest part of it to me was the way you nosed it all out. I've had a deep respect for briar pipes since then. It was a remarkable case,' he continued. 'The way in which you made that pipe tell the story of the murder seems to me like sheer enchantment.'

'Yes,' said I; 'it spoke like the magic pipe—only that wasn't a tobacco-pipe—in the German folk-story of the "Singing Bone." Do you remember it? A peasant found the bone of a murdered man and fashioned it into a pipe. But when he tried to play on it, it burst into a song of its own—

'My brother slew me and buried my bones, Beneath the sand and under the stones.'

'A pretty story,' said Thorndyke, 'and one with an excellent moral. The inanimate things around us have each of them a song to sing to us if we are but ready with attentive ears.'

The Pool of Secrets

Gwyn Evans

Gwyn Evans (1898–1938) was a pulp writer whose memory has been kept alive by fans of old British comics, books, and magazines, notably Steve Holland, author of *Gwyn Evans: The Lunatic, the Lover and the Poet* (2012). On his Bear Alley Books blog, Holland has written: 'Evans created no characters more remarkable than himself. As a journalist and author, he had a talent that could—and occasionally did—earn him riches and recognition. But his Bohemian lifestyle, a daily round of visiting pubs and parties, meant that earnings were soon spent, deadlines were missed and his typewriter often pawned to buy another beer... while some thought him irresponsible, others saw his other side: a carefree spirit, generous and charitable with whatever money he had. "One of the major tragedies of Bohemia," as one friend recorded.'

Evans is best remembered as one of the many authors who wrote stories about Sexton Blake, a detective originally created by Harry Blyth in 1893 as a slightly downmarket rival to Sherlock Holmes. Evans produced a couple of dozen novels and seventy novelettes about the character. He had a facility for writing ripping yarns, but his bibliography is complicated by his habit of rehashing old stories. 'The Pool of Secrets' appeared in *Detective Weekly* on 23 February 1935.

'Ay, there surely be strange goings-on up at the 'All nowadays.'

Old Gorble shook his head dubiously, and gazed ruminatively at his half-empty tankard, and then at the other occupant of the cosy tap-room of the village inn.

'Enough to make poor Sir 'Umphrey turn in his grave,' he added.

The stranger—a tall, distinguished-looking man, clad in comfortable tweeds—smiled pleasantly at the ancient and signalled to the attentive landlord to replenish their tankards.

'So the village doesn't like the change, eh?' he queried.

Old Gorble shook his head emphatically.

'That we don't, sir,' he answered. 'Mind ye, I ain't got nothink to say about the new squire. 'E's open-'anded and pleasant enough, but I don't 'old with these new-fangled ideas of 'is. Bathing beauties, 'ikers and such like,' he added darkly, with a nod of thanks to the landlord, who refilled their china mugs with old ale. ''Ere's your very good health, sir,' said the old man.

His weather-beaten face was seamed and lined, and his gnarled fingers crippled with rheumatism, but his vivid blue eyes twinkled humorously beneath his shaggy white eyebrows.

The stranger stretched out his lean, well-manicured hands towards the comfortable blaze that crackled in the wide old grate.

It was a crisp February afternoon, and the traveller had finished his lunch and had been lured to linger in the cosy bar parlour before setting off again from the quiet Hertfordshire village for London.

'Ay, it'll make a deal of difference to Lyveden village, I reckon,' said Gorble.

He winked shrewdly towards the landlord—a solid, lethargic man, and lowered his voice confidentially.

'Old Smithers 'ere will 'ave it that squire's going to open one of those noodist colonies on the estate, come warmer weather.'

He chuckled as he refilled his clay pipe.

'I wonder what the Silver Bride'd 'ave to say to that?'

'The Silver Bride?' echoed the stranger. 'Who's she?'

Old Gorble leant forward.

'Ain't you 'eard o' the Silver Bride o' Cheriton 'All, sir,' he queried.

The other shook his head. His shrewd, clean-shaven face kindled with interest, and he absently smoothed his iron-grey hair, one lock of which lay in a Napoleonic curl that hid the disfigurement on his wide, smooth forehead.

It was not often that Quentin Drex, that aloof and secretive man, exchanged tap-room gossip with village yokels, but business had taken him into Hertfordshire that morning, and he had been attracted by the old-world charm of the Cheriton Arms.

'She's very famous in these parts, sir,' said Gorble. 'I can't say I've zackly seen 'er meself, but me father 'as—ay, an' me granfer, too! She'm the family ghost o' the Cheritons,' he added. 'I believe the landlord 'ere 'as a cutting in the paper about it.'

He turned to that worthy, who nodded as he produced from his pocket a fat wallet and extracted a newspaper cutting.

Quentin Drex smiled as he took the proffered clipping,

and his deep-set eyes grew abstracted as he scanned the head-lines of the local paper.

'RANCHER BARONET RETURNS—'
'SIR CHARLES CHERITON'S ROMANTIC STORY.—'
'*THE SILVER BRIDE AGAIN.*—'

'The romantic homecoming of the heir to the Cheriton estate recalls once more the legend of the Silver Bride, the apparition which is said to haunt the lake of Cheriton Hall.

'It will be recalled that the new heir is known as the Cowboy Baronet, having lived most of his life on a ranch in Canada, and unaware of his inheritance until the death of his uncle, Sir Hugo Cheriton, two years ago.

'It was thought that the estate would revert to a distant cousin of the late baronet, Mr Stephen Hawksbee, the well-known explorer and antiquary, but a world-wide search by the solicitors resulted in the romantic homecoming of the Cowboy Baronet, and a Cheriton once more is the Lord of the Manor of Lyveden.

'The new baronet is unmarried, tall, a keen athlete, and has already entered into ambitious plans for the development of the estate and the restoration of the old manor house. He is accompanied by his younger brother, Tony Cheriton, who is destined for Oxford next year.

'In an interview Sir Charles states that he intends to remodel the estate on modern lines and to convert the Hall into a luxurious country club with up-to-date sporting amenities, including a swimming pool and a miniature golf course.

'"The upkeep of the estate is far too expensive, even for a confirmed bachelor," said Sir Charles to our representative, and proceeded to outline his plans.

'Recalling the family legend of the Silver Bride, whose tragic ghost is said to haunt the ornamental lake in the beautiful grounds of Cheriton, the Cowboy Baronet said lightly: "I don't believe in ghosts. In any case, a phantom bride would be out of place in a modern swimming pool into which I intend to convert the lake."

'The legend of the Silver Bride is well known and strangely credited in the district, however. Many people claim to have seen the apparition of the unfortunate bride of the third baronet, Sir Nigel Cheriton, when she committed suicide on her wedding eve by drowning herself in the lake.

'Her ghost, arrayed in a silver wedding dress and bridal veil, is said to haunt the grounds when the moon is full, and if seen by a Cheriton to presage disaster and death.'

Quentin Drex folded the clipping and handed it back to the landlord.

'Very interesting,' he commented. 'The new baronet seems to have a mind of his own.'

'He has that, sir. You should see the alterations 'e's 'ad done. Warm water in the swimming-pool, a proper London dance floor, a gymnasium, an' I don't know what else.'

'And noodists!' broke in old Gorble, with a sly wink at the detective. 'We shan't know the village when they starts goin' proper at the 'All. They say as Mr 'Awksbee, Sir Charles' cousin, is fair wild about it, 'im bein' a scholard and sich. Tho' if you ask me, it's only jealousy,' he added.

Quentin Drex rose leisurely to his feet and seized his broad-rimmed hat.

Suddenly the tap-room door burst open and a burly, thick-set figure lurched up to the counter.

'Quick! Give me a brandy, for mercy's sake!' he gasped.

The landlord frowned.

'What's the matter with you, Jem Walker?' he said heavily. 'Bargin' in like this.'

Drex's keen eyes turned towards the newcomer. The man's pale lips twitched and his face was a ghastly grey. His fingers shook as he fumbled in the pockets of his dungarees for the money, and there was fear—deathly fear—in his little close-set eyes.

'What's to do now?' said old Gorble. 'You look as if you've seen a ghost!'

'I 'ave!' replied Walker, with a shudder. 'I've just seen 'er—the Silver Bride!'

'Don't be a fool, man!' snapped the landlord. 'You're drunk, that's what, Jem Walker.'

'S'welp me, I ain't!' he said shakily. 'There she was, in the lake, 'er face all gashly and 'er dress silver. And she killed me dog—sucked 'is blood like the vampire she is!'

'You're crazy!' said the landlord. 'Git out of 'ere, Jem Walker, afore I calls the police!'

'Call 'em!' said the other, with a bitter laugh. 'It's gospel truth, if I drop dead this minute!'

Quentin Drex flung a coin on the counter.

'Give him his brandy!' he said, with quiet authority. 'The man's had a shock, obviously.'

Walker raised his glass to his twitching lips, and the wildness died out of his crafty eyes as he drank.

'Thank 'ee kindly, sir!' he muttered. 'I needed that! My pore l'il dog, Trimmer—dead! Bes' pal I ever 'ad!'

'How did it happen?' queried Drex soothingly.

'Well, sir, I was walkin' past the lake with my dog—a retriever, it were—an' just to amuse 'im like, I flung me stick into the water. He were after it like a flash, and then—the poor beast gave a dreadful howl, and—and I saw 'er with 'er white face and long silver veil streaming behind 'er! She gave a gashly laugh—an' the nex' I see is me dog gorn, and a pool o' red blood in the water!'

Quentin Drex pursed his lips thoughtfully.

'Queer!' he murmured. 'Sounds as if your dog had been attacked by a pike.'

'A pike!' said the other scornfully. 'There ain't no pikes in the lake, sir. There's nowt for 'em to feed on. It's only stagnant water, and shallow at that. Besides, I seed the Silver Bride with me own eyes!' he added obstinately.

Old Gorble shot a significant glance at the landlord.

The dusk had fallen and the short winter day was drawing to its close. The firelight flung fantastic shadows on the ancient rafters of the inn as Quentin Drex turned to the door.

'Interesting, very,' murmured Drex. 'Fill them up again, landlord. I must leave for London before dark!'

He brushed back his long hair from his forehead before donning his hat, revealing for a split second the hideous insignia that marred his brow—the Sign of the Scarlet Skull.

THE STEEL MAN

The grotesque and the bizarre in life never failed to appeal to the complex character of Quentin Drex.

In one way, the skull tattooed on his forehead was symbolic of the strangeness of the man and his love for the fantastic. It was a relic of one of his exploits as a Secret Service man in China, and had been burnt into the skin by a vindictive mandarin, subsequently executed by a rival war lord.

Quentin Ellery Drex's mode of life was as fantastic as his personal character was monastic in tendency. A curious paradox not unfamiliar with men of action. His attitude to humanity in general consisted of the impersonal detachment of a scientist to a problem. A multi-millionaire—owner of London's most luxurious hotel, the Cliffstone—he lived in hermit-like seclusion in a modest suite near the roof of that dominant building above the Thames Embankment.

It was some weeks after Drex's visit to the Cheriton Arms at Lyveden that events occurred which were to recall vividly to his mind the queer story of the Silver Bride and Jem Walker's unfortunate dog.

Things had been quiet of late in the world of crime. Hardly a ripple stirred the unsavoury waters of the underworld, and Drex had devoted himself to a project that satisfied not only his love of the fantastic, but his scientific bent.

He returned one morning to the Hotel Cliffstone after an enlightening call at the Science Museum at Kensington. He avoided the grandiloquent main entrance of the vast hotel and let himself in by his own private lift in a side turning.

He entered the austerely furnished sitting-room, and, taking off his coat, lit one of the Malayan, black rice-paper cigarettes he affected. The door of the adjacent laboratory was ajar, and he pressed an ivory bell-push. There was no sound, but instantly in response to its silent summons a glittering figure glided into the room.

Its height was roughly six feet, and it was clad in a plain serviceable uniform of khaki drill.

Its construction had occupied most of Drex's leisure moments, and combined perfectly his love of the bizarre and the scientific.

The automaton was a triumph of applied mechanism and Drex's scientific genius—a super Robot of shining chromium steel—that responded to every whim of its creator.

In a whimsical moment, Drex had christened his automatic assistant Alpha, for it was the first of its kind. It was uncannily efficient, and save for its blank, expressionless steel face, almost human in its action and response.

Its answer to the silent summons seemed to border on the miraculous, but, in reality, it was Drex's application of wavelength and dynamics that was responsible.

Within the automaton's complex interior, an electric cell, in response to a short wavelength, set its locomotive machinery into action. The delicate mechanism was attuned even to the pitch of the detective's voice, and responded instantly at command.

'Well, Alpha,' said Drex quietly, 'anything to report?'

There came a faint whirring sound as the machinery controlling a wax record was set in action by the timbre of the detective's voice.

'Yes, sir. Phone call from Morgan at ten-twenty-seven a.m. Speaking from Lyveden,' replied the automaton, in a flat metallic voice that was nevertheless perfectly clear and intelligible.

Quentin Drex chuckled.

His bizarre sense of humour had evolved the seeming miracle of making a Robot speak. Actually the phenomenon was simplicity itself.

One of the controls within the Robot's interior was attuned to the exact timbre of a telephone bell—a private 'phone for Drex's exclusive use. In response to the 'phone summons, the Robot automatically lifted the receiver and the wax gramophone disc within its steel skull was set in motion and recorded the voice at the other end of the wire.

It was an ingenious piece of mechanism, but as simple of comprehension as the principles of the dictaphone. Alpha merely repeated mechanically the dictated message.

Drex drew out his notebook and listened intently as the metallic voice continued:

'Morgan speaking, chief. I've kept observation, and there's no doubt there's some funny business happening here. The man Jem Walker seems to have vanished completely since his quarrel with Sir Charles about the dog. The villagers are hinting that there is some sort of foul play going on, and that either Walker, the ghost, or both are at the bottom of it. Two more people claim to have seen the Silver Bride in the past week, and the village is full of rumours.

'The Country Club opens tonight, and there's great excitement locally. I'm standing by until further orders at the Cheriton Arms. Message ends.'

There was a click, and Drex tapped thoughtfully with his pencil on his strong, white teeth.

The Robot stood, motionless as a statue, its steel arms rigid at its sides.

Quentin Drex turned over the pages of his notebook, an abstracted look in his keen eyes.

In his neat, microscopic shorthand he had tabulated the sequel to his visit to Lyveden some weeks before. He refreshed his memory by re-reading a cutting from a local paper reporting a case in which Jem Walker had been charged with assault.

From the evidence, it appeared that the man had repeatedly threatened to molest the cowboy baronet, Sir Charles, unless he was compensated for the loss of his dog. The magistrate pointed out that Walker had already accepted five pounds and that he was trespassing in the first place.

His conduct was aggravated by the assault and he was sentenced to fourteen days.

A curious feature of the evidence, Drex reflected, was that the skeleton of the dog, the bones picked clean, had been found in the lake after it had been drained to make a site for the swimming pool.

And now, after serving his sentence, Jem Walker had disappeared. His wife feared foul play, as he was last seen by a gamekeeper at an early hour in the morning on the Cheriton estate.

Walker had been missing for three weeks now, and Drex had dispatched his outside assistant to investigate the matter. He frowned thoughtfully as he scanned Morgan's report.

What was the mystery of Jem Walker's disappearance? What was the secret of the Silver Bride? That Walker's dog had been killed there was no shadow of doubt, and Drex was sure that the man had not been lying as he spoke of the terror in the lake.

He decided that Cheriton Hall would be worth a visit, especially as it was a full moon that evening, a propitious night for the Silver Bride to walk.

The usually sleepy Herts village was agog with excitement, for tonight the new-fangled wonders of Cheriton Hall were to be opened to the public. The landlord of the Cheriton Arms did a brisk business, and his courtyard was packed with cars belonging to the 'Lunnon' folk.

All sorts of rumours were afoot regarding the novelties and sensations in store for the fortunate guests of the new Country Club.

Quentin Drex reached the inn shortly after eight p.m. and, dodging the garrulous and slightly bibulous Mr Gorble, he held a hurried conference with Morgan.

'Looks like being a success, sir,' the other informed him. 'Sir Charles is certainly a go-getter. They've hired Al Jelks' band for the night, and I'm told there's pretty high stakes in the card-room.'

Quentin Drex pursed his lips thoughtfully.

'Heard nothing further about Walker, I suppose?'

Morgan shook his head.

'No, sir. He seems to have vanished completely, and no one but his poor wife seems to regret it. He was a bit of a bad character, by all accounts.'

'I see. Well, stand by until further orders,' said Drex.

He parked his car at the inn and resolved to walk to the manor house. It was a beautiful moonlit night, but with a chill nip in the air.

Cheriton Hall, a magnificent Tudor mansion, stood in the centre of a rolling deer park, perfect in its seclusion, yet on the main London road.

Drex had easily secured a ticket of admission from Torino, his invaluable *maître d'hôtel*, and though he seldom indulged in Society functions, he was pleasurably anticipating a novel evening in its sylvan setting.

He made a handsome, distinguished figure as he stepped briskly up the long carriage driveway towards the manor. It was a fine old house, well built of creeper-clad brick, and with yellow, friendly lights shining behind the leaded panes of the old mullioned windows.

A butler took his invitation card in the hallway and a moment later he faced his host.

Sir Charles was a lean, tanned young man, with a sharp, hooked nose, high cheekbones, and an air of alert wiry fitness that spoke of the open prairies.

He greeted Drex with breezy cordiality, but it was obvious that he had little idea of his identity.

'Come right in, sir. Let's go to the bar and be friendly,' he said.

Drex glanced appreciatively at the fine oak panelling of the manor as his host led him through the thronged corridor.

It was about nine p.m., and Drex recognised the usual fashionable crowd who frequent first-night functions.

'Looks pretty good, eh?' said Sir Charles complacently. 'A change from a prairie shack.'

Drex smiled.

'I hear you have made many innovations.'

'You bet I have!' said the baronet. 'My uncle only bothered about old parchments and armour—but me, I'm all for the modern stuff. Take a slant at that, sir.'

He waved his hand towards the open door of the conservatory which led to the spacious gardens of the manor. Hundreds of coloured lights glittered like some strange exotic fruits in the trees, and the scene looked ethereally beautiful in the moonlight.

'So that's the famous swimming pool,' said Drex, as he gazed across a velvet lawn to where a silver sheet of water glittered in the moonlight.

The baronet glanced at him sharply.

'Yes, but I'm afraid it's not quite complete yet. In any case, we don't expect bathers tonight. It's too darned chilly.'

He shivered slightly, and excused himself to greet other guests.

Drex strolled through the grounds and studied the decorations. The outlay had evidently been costly, but it seemed worth it. He heard the subdued hum of voices and a gay lilt of laughter from the arbours beneath the trees that surrounded the swimming pool.

The latter was nearly two hundred yards in length and built of green-veined marble. It had two diving-boards, and dominating the deep end was a bronze statue of a Grecian beauty blowing a shell horn.

Drex lit a cigarette and heard a burst of hilarious laughter from a near-by shrubbery. He drew back in the shadows as he saw three young men in evening dress swaying rather uncertainly to the rhythm of the music.

Drex recognised the Hon. Jimmy Welbank, a young racing motorist, and his crony Gillie Fletcher, a wealthy and dissipated young clubman.

He smiled cynically. Judging by their unsteady movements they were evidently enjoying themselves.

'Lesh go and 'ave a swim!' said Fletcher. 'Lesh play mermaids.'

'Not on your life!' echoed his companions. 'Too darn cold. Besides, what about the Silver Bride? The jolly old ghost!'

'Don' marrer! I love ghosts,' hiccoughed Fletcher.

Drex shrugged his shoulders and drew aside as they lurched towards the swimming pool.

Suddenly he heard a loud splash and a gout of silver water jetted skywards.

It was followed instantly by a shrill cackle of drunken laughter, and Drex smiled grimly as the floundering figure of Gillie Fletcher spluttered in the water of the pool.

'Kish the ghost for me!' chuckled Welbank as Fletcher, snorting like a grampus, threshed the water.

He looked a hideous sight in his evening dress and his vacuous, fish-like face spluttered indignantly.

'Drunken young fools!' said Drex impatiently, then suddenly stopped dead.

A shrill scream of terror rang out from the pool, an ear-splitting shriek of mortal agony—a threshing of water, then silence.

Quentin Drex raced towards the pool, his handsome face grim and set.

The two young men, momentarily sobered, were staring in an attitude of frozen terror at the quivering, silver-green water.

'He—he fell in!' gasped one thickly. 'An' the ghos' got him. I—I saw her!'

Drex turned impatiently.

'Nonsense!' he snapped.

'Look there, then!' babbled Welbank.

Drex stared into the pool and saw a shimmering silver radiance that moved like the gauze bridal veil of a woman.

His keen eyes narrowed as he glimpsed a greenish phosphorescent glow from the depth of the pool. For an instant it stayed there and he could have sworn he saw a silvery bridal dress gliding through the water as if a woman were floating there.

Drex peeled off his faultless dress coat.

'Lend a hand with the lifebelt!' he snapped, pointing to a cork buoy on the edge of the pool.

'Look! Blood!' screamed Welbank as Drex poised for a dive on the springboard.

Quentin Drex stared down into the depths of the moonlit pool and, iron-nerved though he was, he gave a shiver of revulsion at the horror that lay in the bottom of the pool.

It was the body of a man in dress clothes, and where the face should have been was the grinning, fleshless bones of a skull.

The Silver Bride had claimed another victim.

SHIMMERING DEATH

Detective-Inspector Blacklock of Scotland Yard frowned gloomily at his colleague, Superintendent Baines of the Hertfordshire Police.

The C.I.D. man's pleasant, oddly boyish face had worn that frown of perplexity for at least a week now since the adjourned inquest on Gillie Fletcher.

'It's moon madness. Stark, raving lunacy, super!' he said. 'This chap Fletcher, for a drunken frolic, dives into a brand-new pool. This fellow Drex turns up to rescue him a few minutes later—and finds Fletcher's skeleton, the bones picked clean and his dress-suit lacerated to ribbons. It's—it's—fantastic—it couldn't have happened!'

The superintendent calmly shrugged his burly shoulders.

'Well, how d'you account for it?' he queried. 'There's no doubt that the skeleton is that of Fletcher. There was enough flesh left for the medical evidence to verify that, to say nothing of the clothes and the contents of the pocket.'

'Yes, and a lot of good the medical evidence is,' growled the C.I.D. man. 'The pool was drained immediately and there was no sign of any of those "sharp instruments" the doctor was so vague about. I tell you this case is getting on my nerves. The man's flesh was lacerated to ribbons and the bathing pool is as smooth as glass. We've searched every inch of it and found nothing.'

The superintendent refilled his pipe.

The two colleagues were sitting in the local police court after the inquest had been adjourned.

A week had elapsed since the Fantastic Horror of Cheriton Hall, as the newspapers described it, and, despite the most rigorous police inquiries, no explanation of the mystery was forthcoming.

The little Hertfordshire village, thanks to the horde of news-hungry pressmen, had provided all England with a nine days' thrill of horror and wonder.

The strange disappearance of Jem Walker was recalled, together with the still unexplained mystery of the Silver Bride.

All sorts of theories were advanced by Press and public alike, ranging from vampires to vultures, to account for

Fletcher's dreadful death. The one person who remained aloof from the case was Quentin Drex. He stated exactly what happened and refused to formulate any theory whatsoever without further evidence.

The coroner had no alternative, therefore, but to adjourn the inquest, and Blacklock, after the most exhaustive investigations in the district, felt up against a blank wall.

'Queer chap, that Drex,' said the super.

The C.I.D. man smiled bitterly.

'Queer? I'd give a lot to know what he suspects. He's got an ice-cold brain, that man. Lives all alone at the Cliffstone Hotel. Must be lousy with money, too. Nobody seems to know much about him. Pleasant enough, but too reticent for my taste.'

The super puffed his briar reflectively.

'Well, it's up to you now, Nick. If we could only find Jem Walker. He might be able to tell us something. His dog was killed in the same way, too, and he swore to old Gorble that the Silver Bride did it.'

'How's Sir Charles taking it all?' queried Nick.

'Pretty bad,' said the super. 'He must have spent a tidy penny on the new alterations to the hall and this scandal's fairly ruined him, they say. Nobody feels like bathing in the pool after what's happened.'

'I don't blame 'em!' said Nick succinctly. 'By the way, what sort of a chap is this cousin of Cheriton's? There's a bit of bad blood between 'em, isn't there?'

The super grunted.

'Well, Captain Hawksbee's naturally a bit sore at the long-lost heir turning up from nowhere when he'd set his heart on living at the manor. You can't blame him, really. He's a quiet, studious fellow, and he's furious about all this country club nonsense.'

'There won't be much future for the club after this, I'm thinking,' commented the Yard man.

The 'phone bell shrilled suddenly and, with a grunt, the superintendent lifted the receiver.

'Hallo! Yes! Speaking!' he barked, then suddenly his manner changed and he became deferential.

'Oh, it's you, Sir Charles!'

He paused and glanced meaningly at Blacklock as he listened.

Suddenly his face became grave, and he gave a soft, astonished whistle.

'What's that, sir? Half an hour ago? But this is dreadful! I'll be along right away, and bring the inspector with me.'

Slowly he replaced the receiver and turned weightily to the Yard man.

'Another of 'em!' he said, in an awe-stricken voice. 'They found the skeleton of Captain Hawksbee at the bottom of the Bride's pool half an hour ago!'

'What?' ejaculated Nick incredulously.

'Gospel truth! That was the squire speaking. He's almost off his rocker—and I don't blame him!'

'Come on!' said Nick Blacklock, grimly. 'Let's go. This devilish business has got to stop, or it'll drive *me* mad!'

In his private suite at the Cliffstone Hotel, Drex sat back in his shining chromium chair, a black Malayan cigarette between his lips.

Opposite sat Morgan, his confidential agent.

On the floor were littered the latest evening papers, where flaring headlines announced:

'NEW HERTFORD HORROR!
CHERITON VAMPIRE AGAIN.'

'This is a ghastly business, chief,' announced Morgan. 'I'm beginning to believe in the supernatural. The whole thing is uncanny. Not a vestige of a clue.'

'On the contrary,' interposed Quentin Drex, 'the problem bristles with clues. The more bizarre and strange a crime appears to be, the easier it is to elucidate. It's your common, featureless murder that is so difficult to solve.'

Morgan sighed.

'Maybe you're right, chief, but this beats me. There's the devil to pay in the village. The folks are scared stiff.'

Drex blew a smoke wreath ceilingwards.

'I presume there's no doubt about the body being Hawksbee's,' he said.

'No doubt at all. Though there wasn't a scrap of flesh on the bones, his sister, poor thing, identified the remains and the clothes as his. There were plenty of papers and personal property on the clothes to make it certain.'

'H'm!' said Drex. 'And Blacklock, I suppose, is still in charge?'

Morgan grinned faintly.

'He is, sir—and you never saw a more worried-looking man.'

'You'd better get back to the Cheriton Arms,' said Drex. 'I'll be along later this evening.'

'You ought to see Sir Charles,' said Morgan. 'He's like a walking ghost!'

'The only ghost I want to see walking is the Silver Bride,' said Drex, with a grim smile. 'By the way, I shall have a companion with me tonight,' he said. 'A new assistant.'

Morgan looked surprised.

'A new assistant, sir?' he queried.

'Yes. Nice fellow. Name of Alpha. You'll like him,' said Drex, with a chuckle.

The wind soughed mournfully in the trees, and a solitary oblong of lemon light shone in the mullioned window of Cheriton Hall.

It was 10 p.m., and the village pub was closed and shut-tered for the night, for since the horror of the Shimmering Death, as some papers called it, not even the bravest would have ventured forth at night.

The latest tragedy of the pool had paralysed the village with terror. True, Captain Hawksbee was not very popular, as he seldom took part in parochial affairs, but he was respected as a scholar and a gentleman.

He lived in a huge, rambling house close to the Cheriton Estate, and had spent a good many years abroad as an explorer.

He was a silent, taciturn man, who lived with his widowed sister, and had been a favourite of old Sir Humphrey, the former baronet.

Inspector Blacklock had returned to Scotland Yard after the formal identification of the body by the sister, then to take conference with his superior at police H.Q. The pool of death had again been drained and subjected to a rigorous search, with no result, and by Blacklock's orders refilled again.

It shimmered now in the watery rays of the moon, a greenish-silver menace in the dark shadows of the ancient elms.

Quentin Drex, at the controls of his ghostly grey gyro-plane, hovered like a hawk over the manor grounds, and his shrewd, intellectual face was grim and unsmiling.

For fully ten minutes he reconnoitred the panorama of the Cheriton Estate, then dropped soundlessly to earth on a grassy plain.

From the pockets of his leather flying-jacket he with-drew a small cylindrical package, and from beneath the seat took out a wire cage in which something stirred and wriggled.

A motionless, grotesque figure sat in the cockpit beside him, and with a sibilant whisper Drex turned to it.

Soundless the robot's steel limbs stirred into activity, and, guided by the detective, emerged from the cockpit.

An owl hooted mournfully from a near-by tree, and the thing in the cage gave a squeak of terror.

Drex smiled grimly.

He thrust the cage into a pocket set in the side of the automaton, and then, soundless as shadows, the two emerged from the clearing to a path that led to the spectral swimming pool.

On the right, near a shrubbery, loomed the ghostly shape of a stone summer-house, or arbour, built as a replica of a Greek temple. Drex softly skirted this, and, guiding the robot with his lean hand, directed it to the marble path that gave access to the pool. Straight ahead the steel figure moved, veering not an inch to right or left.

Quentin Drex stopped suddenly and crouched in the shadow of the bronze figure at the head of the pool.

His agate grey eyes glinted with excitement as he heard a faint stirring from the direction of the Greek temple.

The wind whirred eerily in the trees and the water shimmered with a baleful glitter in the rays of the wan moon. Ahead loomed the bulk of the old manor-house, with one window alight, like a yellow eye bright in the darkness and gloom.

Quentin Drex watched tensely as the steel figure of the automaton lowered itself deliberately into the sinister pool.

Crouched in the shadow, Drex waited.

Not a sound save for the rustling wind in the trees and the

sluggish lap of water. A vein throbbed in his temple as the moments passed. The scar of his maimed forehead glowed dully, as it did in moments of excitement.

From his hiding-place he peered down into the water, then stiffened suddenly. He saw a moving, shimmering phosphorescence in its depths and the vague outline of a cold, deathly face. The silver shimmer was like a bridal veil, and Drex smiled mirthlessly as his hand snaked to his pocket. From it he withdrew the glass cylinder and hurled it against the side of the pool.

Crash!

It scattered into a myriad fragments, and Quentin Drex straightened. Hell itself seemed let loose from the darkness. He heard a demoniacal laugh, and then he was fighting for his life. His fists lashed out, and he felt his knuckles collide with flesh and bone. He chuckled exultantly. This was no phantom. It was something tangible, real.

He felt the bone give beneath the savage ferocity of his blows. His feet moved in the darkness with the poise and surety of a ballet dancer. He was a master-fighter, even in the dark. His keen ears gauged distance merely by the sobbing breathing of his foe.

Something hot slanted along his side, ripping his leather coat, jacket, and shirt to ribbons as a knife blade slashed down. His hands started out, caught the knife-hand as it was raised to strike again. As the weapon fell to the ground, he yanked the man towards him and drove a fist to where he judged his assailant's face was.

He had the satisfaction of feeling his bunched knuckles strike home full and true to his enemy's jaw.

The man wilted in his hands, and at that moment the moon emerged from behind the clouds.

'I thought so!' said Drex, savagely, as he saw that hate-contorted face and recognised it.

The other snarled an oath and again lunged with his knife.

Drex gritted his teeth, exerted all his force, and slammed in his left. It collided with the other's chin with battering-ram force and the man tottered for a split second on the edge of the pool—then toppled with a mighty splash into the dark and ill-omened depths. With his breathing scarcely accelerated, Quentin Drex straightened, then raced for the brass valve which controlled the inflow and outlet of the water.

With a jerk he twisted the lever, but no movement came from the limp figure of his assailant, which had sunk like a stone.

A grim and mirthless smile twisted the features of the Man with the Scarlet Skull.

'Of course,' he murmured. 'The cyanide. It's saved the hangman a job, at least. The end was swifter than he deserved.'

With a gurgle and a roar the water rushed through the waste pipes.

'Come, Alpha!' said Quentin Drex. 'Thank goodness neither prussic acid nor water can harm you!'

Slowly the automaton's steel figure came into motion in response to its master's voice.

The water had no effect on its amazing mechanism, and it was quite impervious even to the shimmering death of the pool.

As it lumbered towards him, Drex stepped forward to the head of the steps.

He placed his hand in the robot's pocket and pulled out the steel cage.

He flashed his torch on to it. Inside was the skeleton of a rat.

From the distance a clock struck eleven.

'Time to get back, Alpha!' said Quentin Drex quietly.

Constable Berry stifled a yawn as he stood on duty beneath the arched portico of that red brick building in Whitehall which houses the C.I.D. of Scotland Yard. He glanced up at the dial of Big Ben, opposite.

It was nearly three a.m., and he sighed regretfully as he resumed his beat of the quadrangle.

'There might have been a chance of a smoke if it wasn't for the conference—confound it!'—he mused with another upward glance at the lighted window, behind which the Big Five were in conclave.

Nocturnal conferences were fairly unusual at Scotland Yard, but the circumstances were exceptional this time.

Berry cursed his superiors heartily as he resumed his measured beat, and he dwelt with gloomy satisfaction on their failure to cope with the notorious 'Hertford Horror.'

'Be another Jack the Ripper case, I expect!' he murmured. 'Old Blacklock won't 'arf go wild if it is. 'Nother unsolved mystery—'

He broke off suddenly as something fell with a metallic rattle almost at his feet.

'Hallo! What's this?' he demanded, staring wrathfully upwards. Far above him hovered a motionless object, like an enormous grey hawk. For a moment it hung there, then with a low hum of its almost soundless engines, vanished.

'Gosh!' said the constable indignantly. 'Might have brained me.'

He stooped down and picked up a small steel container with a label addressed to Detective-Inspector Blacklock and marked 'Urgent.'

'Strewth!' said Constable Berry, and two minutes later burst into the august presence of the Big Five with his story.

Blacklock stared incredulously at his subordinate and at his chiefs.

'Extraordinary!' said the Assistant Commissioner. 'Careful how you handle that, Blacklock! It might be a bomb!'

'It is!' said the Yard man, as he opened the parcel and scanned its contents—two sheets of notepaper in a familiar handwriting.

'Excuse me a moment, sir,' he added, 'but I fancy the Cheriton Case is solved.'

In dead silence he proceeded to read the following missive:

'My Dear Blacklock,—

Having the utmost confidence in your intelligence, I append the following facts for your guidance and necessary action. I am afraid the murderer of poor Gillie Fletcher and the unfortunate Jem Walker will never be arrested, however.

'His body will be found in the swimming pool, together with certain interesting piscatorial fauna, both killed by cyanide of potassium.

'Walker's body will be found in Lyveden Mortuary. The basic facts of the case are comparatively simple, and I am afraid you have allowed village gossip and the spectacular setting of the crime to obscure the issue.

'Briefly, my investigations have shown that Gillie Fletcher was murdered by accident, and that Jem Walker was murdered deliberately.

'The murderer is, of course, Captain Stephen Hawksbee; the motive throughout was his greed and jealousy of his cousin, Sir Charles Cheriton.

'The man was undoubtedly a monomaniac, and

bitterly resented being deprived of what he considered to be his rightful inheritance.

'As an explorer and big game hunter in South America he was also a keen naturalist, and it was undoubtedly on the Amazon that he first met what the papers picturesquely call the Shimmering Death.

'Actually you will find hundreds of specimens of this most ferocious of all fish in the swimming pool, but I have taken the precaution of killing them by cyanide.

'Unfortunately Hawksbee also accidentally fell into the poisoned water.

'Why the man bred these terrible creatures I cannot conjecture. The fish infest certain regions of Brazil and Paraguay, and in appearance are the size of a very small herring.

'It is known as the Pirkana, or Tiger fish, and invariably swims in shoals. It is so ferocious that it can strip the flesh off a horse or an ox in a few minutes, and is the most dreaded of all jungle perils by the natives.

'Perhaps some perverse instinct caused Hawksbee to spawn his devil fish, or perhaps he deliberately cultivated it as a murder weapon. We can never know for certain.

'One thing, however, is sure, he took advantage of the old legend of the Silver Bride, and might have succeeded in his ambition of murdering Sir Charles and his brother and inheriting the manor.

'Incidentally, young Tony Cheriton is safe. I rescued him tonight. He was held prisoner in the Greek Temple where Hawksbee had the hiding-place of his terrible pets in a large tank connected with the feed pipe of the pool.

'The Pirkana are hardly ever satiated, and can sense the presence of flesh at a long distance. Hawksbee used

to tempt the shoal back to their tank by raw meat, and it was discreet inquiries at the local tradesmen that first put me on to the solution of the problem.

'Ostensibly Hawksbee obtained raw meat for his dogs, but I learned later that he had got rid of them months ago.

'Poor Walker's dog was the first victim—and then Walker himself, who must have stumbled across the devilish aquarium by accident.

'He was murdered because he knew too much, and Hawksbee then devised the ingenious idea of arraying Walker's skeleton in his own clothes so that he should be immune from suspicion.

'As for poor Fletcher's tragic end to a drunken frolic, I suspect that the hidden assassin mistook him for Sir Charles. Fletcher and the baronet were both of the same build.

'I fancy I have disposed of all the Pirkana, but I should make sure, my dear fellow, as I had no time to investigate Hawksbee's house.

'His sister is quite innocent of complicity in the crimes. She is, I should say, feeble-minded. Undoubtedly there is insanity in the Hawksbee family, and I do not think he would have ever faced the scaffold.

'One last point; even I was momentarily deceived by the Silver Bride, but on investigation I discovered it was an optical illusion.

'The lights from the decorated Chinese lanterns on the trees reflected on water play strange tricks, especially accompanied by the shimmer of a shoal of Pirkana. It gives the impression of a silver bridal dress.

'A vivid imagination is useful, my dear Blacklock,

but is apt to confuse the issue in the science of pure ratiocination and deduction.

'Yours sincerely,
'Q. E. D.'

'And who the devil is Q. E. D.?' asked the Assistant Commissioner later, knowing nothing of Quentin Ellery Drex.

'Euclid!' said Nick Blacklock, with a rueful grin. 'I always hated him at school. The blighter was always right!'

Four Friends and Death

Christopher St John Sprigg

Long after his tragically early death in the Spanish Civil War, Christopher St John Sprigg (1907–1937) was remembered, primarily as a Marxist poet and commentator. He used the pen-name Christopher Caudwell for his serious writing, while his lively detective fiction appeared under his own name. Whereas several of the writers whose stories appear in this book were highly experienced sailors with a deep knowledge of sea lore, Sprigg's particular expertise lay in the field of aeronautics, and his other publications included *The Airship: Its Design, History, Operation and Future* and *Fly with Me: An Elementary Textbook on the Art of Piloting*.

Recent years have seen a revival of interest in Sprigg's engaging mysteries, fuelled by the republication in 2015 of *Death of an Airman* (1934) as a British Library Crime Classic. His career as a published crime author lasted a mere five years, and he only wrote a handful of short stories, one of which, 'Death at 8.30', is an impossible crime puzzle included in the British Library anthology *Miraculous Mysteries*. This story, which illustrates his all-too-brief enthusiasm for the classic mystery, first appeared in *The 20-Story Magazine* in March 1935.

The small yacht floated motionless, mirrored in the calm waters of Vigo Harbour. Her split headsail, tattered pennant, and stove-in dinghy were mute evidence of the storms that had battered the ketch in the Bay of Biscay, three days out from Falmouth.

In the saloon the four amateur yachtsmen were celebrating their successful completion of the trip by a glass each of excellent cognac, which washed down a meal of tinned salmon, tinned peaches, and coffee extract prepared by Dr Garrett, a well-meaning but indifferent cook.

'Cheerio!' said Dr Garrett, lifting his glass. 'Cheerio!' answered Hopkins, Leathart, and Pickering.

Pickering's greeting seemed particularly hearty, yet immediately after drinking the brandy he gave a moan, flung out his arms, and fell prone.

There was a sudden silence in the cabin. Leathart's rubicund face turned pale; he touched Pickering's livid features with a trembling hand, then helplessly loosened his collar.

Hopkins' eyes gleamed behind their pebble glasses, but he made no move. Garrett, with the expert indifference of the medical man, stepped forward, grasped the fallen man's wrist a moment, and then rolled back his eyelid.

'Dead,' he pronounced solemnly, straightening himself.

'Good heavens!' stammered Leathart incredulously. 'What, why—Has he had a heart attack? Pickering dead! I can't somehow—'

His voice trailed off into silence as he stared at the limp

form of that prosperous banker, their host; a moment ago apparently in the prime of life and now stricken down as if by a physical blow.

Leathart was going to say, 'I can't somehow cotton on to it...' but there was no evading the ghastly reality, the deadness of that inert mass, which had a moment before been living flesh, joking and laughing.

Hopkins still said nothing. His eyes moved from Leathart to Dr Garrett who was busy about the body. Now he was prising open the mouth...

Even at a death, Leathart couldn't help thinking, Hopkins is the same Hopkins; the famous novelist, the remorseless psychological observer, noting, watching, and never showing his hand.

His personality had grated a little on Leathart when they had first met; it was alien to the breezy openness of the Yorkshire Turf commission agent; but they had been brought together by a common love of the sea, and in the ten years that followed Leathart had grown to respect Hopkins' qualities. A good man in an emergency!

Dr Garrett now stood up, and covered the face of the dead man with his handkerchief. He wiped his hands slowly on a table napkin, gazing into space, his saturnine face expressionless, and said;

'No, it's not a heart attack. He's been poisoned.'

'Poisoned, Garrett?' exclaimed Leathart. 'Oh, come! It's impossible!'

'Poisoned!' repeated Hopkins; saying it slowly; almost as if (Leathart thought) he was savouring the phrase on his tongue. But that must be imagination. Just Hopkins' manner. For Pickering had been his friend...

'Hydrocyanic acid,' said Garrett, still gazing away from

them. 'Prussic acid, as the layman calls it. No post-mortem is necessary; it's the most easily detected of poisons.

'I can smell it on his lips and see its traces on his face.' He lifted up the glass of brandy. 'And here is the way it was given him.'

The full horror of this now struck Leathart. He found himself unable to do more than bleat a few inarticulate sounds.

'Well,' said Dr Garrett, with a trace of impatience, 'what are we going to do about it?'

'Yes, what are we going to do about it?' repeated Hopkins, looking at Leathart queerly, almost as if he were amused by this appalling tragedy. But this again could only be Leathart's imagination.

Another long silence followed. The wind had risen and a gentle breeze lapped the ripples softly against the hull; somewhere abeam a siren hooted, as a ship manoeuvred in mid-harbour.

After the buffeting of the Bay, the tension of the incessant pitching and rolling and rattle of the rigging, the scene was a peaceful one; and the faces of the three living men in the cabin might have been those of men calmly resting after a strenuous voyage.

But actually, behind each expressionless face, the thoughts were racing; and it was perhaps natural that Hopkins' mind, used to reflection on complex trains of events, should come to a decision first.

'It would be foolish,' he said quietly, peering for a moment at the dead form, then, his eyes flickering away, at Leathart, 'it would be foolish to deny the obvious implications of this distressing event.

'Poor Pickering has either killed himself or been poisoned. I think we must all agree that it is highly unlikely that he killed himself. No one could be more cheery than Pickering has been during the last two or three days.

'In any event it is inconceivable that a man, however depressed, would kill himself, without a word, in the presence of three guests. Therefore he has been poisoned.'

'Poisoned,' repeated Hopkins, his gaze moving to Garrett, 'by one of us.'

Leathart gave a gasp, or it may have been a sigh; but said nothing. Garrett nodded gravely.

'I am afraid you're right, Hopkins. So here we are, moored in the middle of Vigo Harbour, and one of us a murderer.'

His lean, delicate fingers played thoughtfully with an extinguished cigar stub in front of him. 'It's not as if we were three casual acquaintances. We've known each other now for ten years, and we've been shipmates together twenty or thirty times.

'We all know what that means: it means we know each other's characters as intimately as it is possible for men to know them. The best and the worst of them.'

'By God, you're right!' exclaimed Leathart gruffly. 'And, say what you like, I simply can't believe one of us poisoned Pickering!' In spite of himself, his eyes rested again on the dead man with horror.

'Nonetheless,' Hopkins reminded him coldly, 'one of us did.'

'Yes, one of us did,' went on Garrett. 'We don't know why. Now Pickering was also a friend. We haven't known him as we've known each other, but we've run into him off and on.

'We've chartered his yacht once or twice; and, now, here we are sat; and he's dead, murdered by one of us.

'Sooner or later we've got to turn the thing over to the police. I don't know anything about Spanish police procedure, but even if it's as fair as the English—which I doubt—there's the language, which we don't know; that alone will make things infernally unpleasant.

'We three have pulled through plenty of emergencies alone, and it seems to me that we ought to see if we can't get on top of this one.'

'What exactly are you suggesting?' said Hopkins with a trace of irritation.

'I'm suggesting that we hold a little court of inquiry of our own before we turn the matter over to the police.'

'And give sentence?' asked the novelist sardonically.

'We may or may not do that,' answered Garrett slowly. 'Before we decide we must hear what the law calls the mitigating circumstances. After all, we're friends…'

'I see. In other words, let the murderer spill the beans, and if he's got a good excuse we might help him to escape?'

'And why not?' asked Garrett defensively. 'I may be wrong, but it does seem to me that there are circumstances in which murder might be excusable.'

'You're right,' boomed Leathart, so unexpectedly that the others jumped.

'Blackmail, for instance!'

'Blackmail, Leathart?' queried Hopkins, a surprised note in his voice.

'And what,' he went on suavely, 'makes you think our dear friend Pickering was a blackmailer?'

There was no answer.

'Supposing that after due consideration this court does not find the circumstances justify a recommendation to mercy?'

'Then,' said Garrett soberly, 'I should like to offer to any friend of mine, however guilty, the decent way out.'

'I see. Leave him alone with a revolver, eh?'

'Well, have you any suggestion to make?' countered Garrett. The tension of the atmosphere had frayed his temper a little.

'I have none. I thoroughly agree with you.'

'Yes, and I, too,' said Leathart.

'Carried, then!' exclaimed Hopkins. 'It seems to me that our brains will work a little more clearly without the fourth member of the party.'

Leathart shuddered, and it was Hopkins and Garrett between them who carried the limp form into the forecabin and laid it on one of the bunks.

'The police will complain of our moving the body,' Hopkins reminded his assistant.

'They will have worse than this to complain of before the day's over,' replied Garrett grimly.

Silence fell again. Silence utter and unbroken. Each man was weighing the others up to assess which was the more likely murderer.

Or, rather, two of the three were. The murderer could have no doubt, no scruple, no care but the nerve-stretched eagerness to obliterate all traces of guilt from his face.

The most impartial observer might have hesitated long before he could suggest, from a mere scrutiny or even a deep knowledge of their characters, which man was the most likely.

Could one suspect Leathart, for instance—that genial, kindly Yorkshireman, an impulsive forty-year-old child? Here, one would have said, was a transparent nature. All his failings were on the surface. His easily roused temper so soon over. His schoolboyish greed, which had earned the nickname of the Glutton—greed only in matters of food and drink; in money none was more generous. How could such a man poison, out of long premeditation, in cold blood?

And yet... One didn't succeed in the world of racing

without a fund of native shrewdness. Even the geniality might be all facade. Leathart was, after all, a man of strong emotions. His entanglements with women were notorious. Perhaps...

But then there was Hopkins, with his slow saurian gaze, his complete lack of sentimentality. Wouldn't such a man poison efficiently and ruthlessly?

And yet... Hopkins, by temperament and trade, was a watcher, not a doer. It contented him to stand outside life, peering and prying, and never so much as wetting the soles of his feet in the mud.

It was hard to imagine such a man indulging in the crudity of murder, harder still because he seemed a man capable perhaps of friendship—a thin, attenuated affection—but of nothing so robust as either love or hatred.

What of Garrett—a man to whom the getting of poisons would be easy—efficient, calm, never losing his head? And yet...a doctor, trained to save life, must have a powerful motive to destroy it. What motive could Garrett, in particular, have—he, a successful specialist and famous for his philanthropic activities?

The silence had endured for several minutes now. Outside in the harbour there was the sudden scream of a speed-boat, the wail of its exhaust tearing the silence like a piece of linen.

Leathart jumped. 'For God's sake, let's do something!' he cried. 'What's the good of sitting here like a lot of waxworks not daring to look each other in the eyes?'

His voice was almost hysterical, and Hopkins' eyebrows rose at the tone. 'A sound suggestion,' he said. 'I propose that first of all we find the poison. It must have been in a tube or phial, or something.'

Leathart interrupted him, his voice strained. 'Look here, isn't the first question to find out how the poison got into the brandy? The four drinks came from one bottle and we've all had ours without ill effects.'

'You are doubtless referring,' said Garrett, coldly, 'to the unfortunate fact that it was I who poured out the brandy and passed the glasses round.'

'I just asked,' said Leathart stubbornly, not meeting his eyes, 'how the poison got in the brandy.'

'And I can answer that,' replied Hopkins. Four eyes focused on him instantly. 'You will remember that, after the brandy was poured out, but before we had drunk it, a four-masted Finnish barque came past us to starboard, reaching out of the harbour.

'Naturally, being what we are, we all jumped up and glued our noses to the portholes for several minutes till she'd passed. During that time, any one of us could have poisoned any glass.'

Hopkins' eyes met Leathart's, and a faint, almost imperceptible sigh escaped from between Garrett's lips.

'Right! That clears that up,' said Leathart briskly. 'What were you saying when I interrupted you?'

'Merely that the phial must be somewhere in the cabin.'

'If I had been murdering anyone,' interjected Garrett, 'I should chuck the bottle or what-not overboard.'

'You would have been unable to do so without leaving the saloon,' Hopkins reminded him, 'because the portholes are still screwed up.'

'Well,' retorted Garrett, 'I think it's a silly idea. If the murderer has any cunning he'd plant the phial on an innocent party. So, if we do find it, it will only be misleading. I vote we get on to something more tangible.'

'I think you are wrong to be so emphatic,' commented Hopkins with the utmost gentleness. His pebble glasses were fixed on the doctor's face, and there was a difficult pause.

'Are you suggesting I'm the murderer, then?' shouted Garrett, suddenly flushing and half-rising from his seat.

'Come, come!' said Hopkins, his lips twitching. 'Let us remember we are friends and keep our tempers. What's a murder between friends?'

'Come to that,' answered Garrett more calmly, sinking down into his chair again, 'you seem to be taking it remarkably calmly!'

'I am. To be perfectly frank, I was not at all fond of Pickering. You knew him as a rich and respectable banker. I—with my usual flair for finding out the worst sides of people—happen to know that his bank is a very shady affair, and his past career shadier still. Mr Pickering has put over some pretty raw deals in his time on friends of mine.'

'In that case, why accept his hospitality?'

'Firstly, because I like this yacht—one of the finest hulls that ever came off Champney's drawing-board. And secondly—'

'Secondly?'

'I find Pickering a most interesting character study… Any more questions? No? Then I suggest the court votes on my proposal. That we now search this cabin to find one missing poison phial, tube, or container.'

'Waste of time,' grunted Garrett.

'I think we should do it, old chap,' said Leathart.

Hopkins got up. 'Carried!'

The saloon had many cupboards and lockers, as all well-designed cabins have. Certain of them were for articles used in common-crockery, glasses, cards, books, and so forth.

But at the beginning of the trip two lockers had been offered to each man (and the keys given to him), to stow such private articles as he had—a practice which may sound unfriendly to the uninitiated, but which is carried out by all discreet yachtsmen, for it saves a great deal of argument.

When each man had given up his keys, and the lockers had been searched, an empty phial, smelling strongly of hydrocyanic acid, was found in Dr Garrett's drawer.

More damning still, they found a receipt from a chemist, screwed up in the sheet of brown paper in which the phial had evidently been wrapped: '½ oz. hydrocyanic acid.'

'Good heavens! You, Garrett!' exclaimed Leathart, with surprising scorn. 'No wonder you were so much against the search!'

Garrett had turned pale. 'This is absurd!' he exclaimed. 'I know nothing about this!'

Leathart laughed scornfully. 'Oh, come, I say! Know nothing about it? In your locked drawer? It's as plain as the nose on my face.

'You doped the glass before we sat down to dinner, put away the phial and locked the drawer, and then poured the brandy into glasses, one of which was already charged with poison!'

'It's a lie!' said Garrett furiously.

'Perhaps the Spanish police may have different views!'

'Now, now, Leathart,' said Hopkins, reprovingly. 'Don't start talking about the Spanish police. Let's hear the mitigating circumstances. If there are any.'

'Rot!' said Leathart, angrily. 'There's nothing here but a coldblooded premeditated murder.'

Hopkins peered shrewdly at the flushed face of the Yorkshireman. 'You seem very indignant about it, Leathart! Amazing display of indignation! After all, we don't know yet (a) if Garrett really did poison Pickering, or (b) if he did, why? He may have had some perfectly good reason—eh, Garrett?'

Garrett glared at him furiously. 'All I know is that one of you two is the dirtiest skunk unhanged.'

'I feared,' said Hopkins, with a sigh, 'that we should never be able to discuss this murder without animosity creeping in. However, let us see where we are.

'The poison has been discovered in Garrett's locked drawer. A bad mark against him.

'In defence I should be inclined to urge that no murderer would stow the bottle in his own locker; surely he'd prefer to throw it down anywhere rather than there—particularly as suspicion would be bound to fall on Garrett first through having poured out the brandy.'

'That's all very well for a clever devil like yourself, Hopkins,' broke in Leathart, 'but I'm a plain man, and that argument seems just silly. At that rate the more evidence you discover against him, the less guilty he is.'

'Well, I won't insist on the point. I prefer to leave that kind of argument to my learned and subtle confreres, the writers of detective novels. We will just keep it at the back of our minds. Now, Garrett, have you any contribution to make?'

Garrett stared at them both defiantly.

'No. I prefer to watch you. Being innocent, you see, I happen to know one of you is the murderer, and sooner or later he'll give himself away.'

'A very proper sentiment,' murmured Hopkins. 'Our next task, therefore, is to find some motive. Blackmail has been suggested by Leathart—'

'I didn't actually suggest it,' interrupted Leathart, uneasily.

'I apologise. You are right; you did not suggest it in this case. You merely mentioned it as a justifiable motive for a murder.' Leathart wriggled, but said nothing.

After a keen look at him, Hopkins continued: 'The

murdered man (whom, by the way, I consider perfectly capable of blackmail, with his bland smile and his mean mind)—the murdered man, as the crime stories always call the violently deceased, probably had some documents with which to blackmail—letters and so forth. We had better search his person and his locker.'

'Right,' said Leathart, jumping up, 'I'll look through his clothes.'

'One moment,' remarked Hopkins, suddenly shooting out a long arm and laying it on Leathart's shoulder. 'One moment. We had better go together. And perhaps Garrett had better come too. He might—he just possibly might—try to make a bolt for it.'

They returned with a handful of papers and a wallet. Hopkins read through them. Both watched him with fascinated attention. He made a little noise as if of satisfaction, looked up, and said:

'Well, Leathart, what would you say to this? A letter written to Pickering, in Garrett's own handwriting. And marked "Confidential."'

Garrett started as his eyes fell on the document, and he swore. Without looking up, Hopkins read the letter out:

My dear Pickering,

—I should be infernally grateful if you could give me another thirty days' grace on that promissory note. I've just had a reminder from Leathart about the heavy bill I ran up with him on last month's racing, and I hardly know where to turn for ready cash. I'm safe enough— you know that half a dozen operations will cover the amount—but I happen to be in a temporary corner.

Yours ever, J. GARRETT.

Leathart gave a slow murmur of astonishment. 'So that was it! But why, Garrett, why? Man alive, my reminder to you was a joke! If I'd known you were in any real difficulty, so far from running up any bill I'd have lent you all you wanted!'

Hopkins was watching Leathart's face with an unblinking stare. 'But Garrett didn't know that, eh? And so, when Pickering refused to renew the note, Garrett killed him to gain time.'

Garrett jumped to his feet. Every vestige of self-control had left him. Shaking with anger, he leaned towards Hopkins, his face a few inches from the other man's, and almost spat into his face.

'You rat! You Judas! So this is the little plot you've prepared, sitting there like a spider! God, what a fool I was ever to trust you, you heartless, soulless, gutless devil!

'You killed Pickering. You knew he had that letter on him; he showed it to you, I expect! You hid the poison bottle in my drawer!

'Pickering never refused to renew my promissory note. He told me before we started on this trip not to worry about the note. We were too good friends for him to do anything to embarrass me, he said.

'You told us yourself you hated him. You poisoned him, and wove your slimy little plot, like one of your slimy little stories!'

Hopkins gazed quietly back into the convulsed features of his friend. He seemed to note every line of fury as if he were examining an interesting old picture.

'I understand your fury, Garrett,' he said. 'I was afraid that once we started murdering each other our happy, our almost ideal friendship would be broken up.

'Believe me, however. I bear you no ill-will.' He turned. 'Well, Leathart, what do you say?'

'Guilty as blazes!'

'And do you think the circumstances mitigating? Money affairs are very worrying, you know! Almost the most worrying in the world.'

'Look out!' shouted Leathart; and Hopkins leaped sideways. Wild with fury, Garrett had sprung at him.

Leathart seized Garrett by the elbows. In the huge Yorkshireman's hands he was like a child, and he was flung sullenly back in his chair.

'Very crude!' remarked Hopkins.

'So, Leathart, you consider there are no mitigating circumstances?'

'None!'

'What shall we do, then?'

'Hand him over to the Spanish police.'

Hopkins' eyebrows rose. 'Come, come. An old shipmate of ours! Surely we'll offer him a gentleman's way out?'

'No,' rumbled Leathart, suddenly. 'I wouldn't give him even that, the skunk!'

'I see. Well, well!'

'And what about you, eh, you slimy devil?' said Garrett. 'What's your opinion? You lead others on, but you take darn good care never to give away anything yourself!'

'My opinion? Ah, yes, my opinion.' Hopkins had been smiling, but now the smile vanished; and, behind his thick glasses, he darted at Leathart a glance of piercing malignancy, of utter and biting contempt.

'My opinion, Leathart, is that you're the meanest skunk it has ever been my lot to meet. I thought I was a judge of human character. I turn out to have been a child, a baby.

'You are a murderer, Leathart. Don't look surprised. I repeat, you are a murderer. You murdered Pickering. You had provocation, no doubt. I don't complain of that.

'But not only are you a murderer; you deliberately attempt to fasten on your best friend the guilt of that murder. You had no pity, you pressed for the last ounce of punishment. You won't even permit him to blow his brains out.

'You! Our inoffensive, childish, sporting glutton! Faugh!'

'I kill Pickering?' exclaimed Leathart at last. 'You must be crazy! Why should I want to?'

'I have met you once or twice at Pickering's house,' said Hopkins slowly. 'I'm an observant devil, you know.

'Mrs Pickering is a very beautiful woman, isn't she? And ill-treated by her husband, eh? And ready to tell anyone so? And her husband's jealous of your heart-to-heart talks with her, lunches in town, and so forth? Isn't that so?'

'You're mad!' said Leathart, emphatically. 'It's true that I felt sorry for Mrs Pickering. If you like, I'm in love with her. I don't mind admitting it.

'But, as for murdering him! Confound it, you can't accuse me of murder just because of an admiration for a man's wife!'

'Oh, no,' said Hopkins, 'I happen to have more substantial grounds. I knew you had murdered Pickering the moment he fell dead.'

Leathart laughed aloud, scornfully. 'Oh, and whence this certainty?'

'Well, when we were watching that barque go by, I happened to see the cabin behind me reflected on the porthole glass. I told you I was an observant devil, didn't I?

'And I saw you replacing Pickering's glass, with a guilty air, one eye on our backs to make sure we didn't see you. I wondered what the devil you were playing at… Until Pickering fell down dead.'

'You swine!' exclaimed Garrett, glaring at Leathart. 'You of all people!'

Leathart had flushed; but he seemed strangely uncon-
cerned as he answered, 'Yes, I killed Pickering.'

'You confess?'

'No. Oh, no! For I am not guilty. I killed Pickering. And yet
Garrett is the murderer. And yet Pickering died by accident.'

'Is this madness, Garrett?' asked Hopkins. 'Or is he putting
it on?'

'No, I'm not mad,' replied Leathart. 'I feel peculiarly sane.
I know exactly what happened. I knew from the moment you
found that letter in Pickering's pocket.

'Garrett tried to poison me—me, his best friend—because
of a paltry gambling debt. Do you wonder I wanted to see
him handed over to the police?

'But then Fate, or Chance, stepped in. For, when your
backs were turned, I did a childish thing. Garrett had poured
out for Pickering a much larger portion of brandy than for me.

'Half in genuine greed—you know my weakness for
cognac—and half in joke, I swapped glasses. When we had
drunk I was going to tell you all that I'd swiped the best
share after all. What a joke! What a devil of a joke!'

'Did you give Pickering a larger portion, Garrett?'

'I did,' admitted Garrett. 'As host. But we've only Leathart's
word that he swapped them.'

'No,' said Hopkins. 'I told you I'm an observant devil…
and as we lifted our glasses for the toast, I remember thinking:
trust old Leathart to get the fullest glass!'

'You're both lying!' exclaimed Garrett furiously.

'No,' answered Leathart, firmly and quietly. 'I am not lying.'

A shaft of sunlight lit the troubled faces of the three friends.

Or, rather, former friends. For now they were divided by
abysses of hatred, crime, and a sudden welling up of unbe-
lievable possibilities from their hidden hearts.

And then suddenly Hopkins burst out laughing. A hard, dry, cold laugh so that at first they thought he had gone mad. Both the listeners felt their flesh creep.

'For God's sake, what is it, Hopkins?' cried Leathart.

'What fools we've been! What utter fools!' And now they saw that he was waving the crumpled chemist's bill.

'Look at the date on that! See? July 13!

'All July 13 we three were at Aintree races, 200 miles from this shop. The poor fool! He left this vital clue! Didn't notice it, I expect, when he tore off the brown paper wrapping.'

'But what do you mean?'

'Pickering killed himself!' shouted Hopkins joyously. 'He was hoist with his own petard, with a vengeance! He tried to poison Leathart out of jealousy, and he had everything pre-pared to throw the blame on Garrett, so as to cover his tracks.

'After doping the brandy, he dropped the bottle in the drawer and locked it with a private key—for, as owner, he would have second keys of all lockers. Meanwhile, he had Garrett's letter, which he would produce at the right moment to prove that Garrett owed Leathart money, and so supply a motive.

'He must have been hatching the scheme months before. Perhaps as soon as he got Garrett's letter he saw how it could be used. He must have invited us to go on this trip for that very purpose—you remember we were all a bit surprised by the invitation.

'And he must have been waiting for the first meal that would give him an opportunity for his diabolical scheme; but, thanks to the weather, it wasn't until we beat into Vigo Harbour this afternoon that we sat down together.

'Then he dropped the poison in Leathart's glass; and our dear old Glutton, with his immortal idiocy, swapped the glasses and made the devil drink his own medicine.'

Hopkins' words died away. Leathart gave a strangled groan of relief. Then there was silence for a few moments.

When the wake of another passing ship rocked the yacht, when once again the shaft of sunlight came groping in, it lit the contented faces of three friends and glittered on their upraised glasses, toasting a friendship that had struck dirty weather and come near being cast away, but, at the last moment, had managed to claw off the rocks and make harbour.

The Turn
of the Tide

C. S. Forester

Few authors are as closely associated with sea stories as Cecil Scott Forester (1899–1966), creator of Horatio Hornblower, an officer in the Royal Navy during the Napoleonic era. The success of the Hornblower series has meant that it is sometimes forgotten that Forester, whose real name was Cecil Louis Troughton Smith, also wrote three notable crime novels. *Payment Deferred* (1926) anticipates the ironic tone and plotting of *Malice Aforethought*, a more famous novel by Francis Iles which was published five years later. *Plain Murder* (1930), about advertising men who turn to crime, has a similar flavour. Astonishingly, *The Pursued*, a fascinating novel written in 1935, was lost and forgotten, as Forester concentrated on Hornblower. The manuscript resurfaced in the twenty-first century, and the book was finally published in 2011.

Forester's occasional ventures into the crime short story are well worth reading. A good example is 'The Letters in

Evidence', also known as 'The Editor Regrets', first published in 1937. 'The Turn of the Tide' originally appeared in *The Story-Teller* in April 1936. For all Hornblower's popularity, it is a matter for regret that this talented writer did not contribute more to the crime genre.

'What always beats them in the end,' said Dr Matthews, 'is how to dispose of the body. But, of course, you know that as well as I do.'

'Yes,' said Slade. He had, in fact, been devoting far more thought to what Dr Matthews believed to be this accidental subject of conversation than Dr Matthews could ever guess.

'As a matter of fact,' went on Dr Matthews, warming to the subject to which Slade had so tactfully led him, 'it's a terribly knotty problem. It's so difficult, in fact, that I always wonder why anyone is fool enough to commit murder.'

All very well for you, thought Slade, but he did not allow his thoughts to alter his expression. *You smug, self-satisfied old ass! You don't know the sort of difficulties a man can be up against.*

'I've often thought the same,' he said.

'Yes,' went on Dr Matthews, 'it's the body that does it, every time. To use poison calls for special facilities, which are good enough to hang you as soon as suspicion is roused. And that suspicion—well, of course, part of my job is to detect poisoning. I don't think anyone can get away with it, nowadays, even with the most dunderheaded general practitioner.'

'I quite agree with you,' said Slade. He had no intention of using poison.

'Well,' went on Dr Matthews, developing his logical argument, 'if you rule out poison, you rule out the chance of getting the body disposed of under the impression that the victim died a natural death. The only other way, if a man cares to stand the racket of having the body to give evidence against him, is to fake things to look like suicide. But you know, and I know, that it just can't be done.

'The mere fact of suicide calls for a close examination, and no one has ever been able to fix things so well as to get away with it. You're a lawyer. You've probably read a lot of reports on trials where the murderer has tried it on. And you know what's happened to them.'

'Yes,' said Slade.

He certainly had given a great deal of consideration to the matter. It was only after long thought that he had, finally, put aside the notion of disposing of young Spalding and concealing his guilt by a sham suicide.

'That brings us to where we started, then,' said Dr Matthews. 'The only other thing left is to try and conceal the body. And that's more difficult still.'

'Yes,' said Slade. But he had a perfect plan for disposing of the body.

'A human body,' said Dr Matthews, 'is a most difficult thing to get rid of. That chap Oscar Wilde, in that book of his—*Dorian Gray*, isn't it?—gets rid of one by the use of chemicals. Well, I'm a chemist as well as a doctor, and *I* wouldn't like the job.'

'No?' said Slade, politely.

Dr Matthews was not nearly as clever a man as himself, he thought.

'There's altogether too much of it,' said Dr Matthews. 'It's heavy, and it's bulky, and it's bound to undergo corruption. Think of all those poor devils who've tried it. Bodies in trunks, and bodies in coal-cellars, and bodies in chicken-runs. You can't hide the thing, try as you will.'

Can't I? That's all you know, thought Slade, but aloud he said: 'You're quite right. I've never thought about it before.'

'Of course, you haven't,' agreed Dr Matthews. 'Sensible people don't, unless it's an incident of their profession, as in my case.

'And yet, you know,' he went on, meditatively, 'there's one decided advantage about getting rid of the body altogether. You're much safer, then. It's a point which ought to interest you, as a lawyer, more than me. It's rather an obscure point of law, but I fancy there are very definite rulings on it. You know what I'm referring to?'

'No, I don't,' said Slade, genuinely puzzled.

'You can't have a trial for murder unless you can prove there's a victim,' said Dr Matthews. 'There's got to be a *corpus delicti*, as you lawyers say in your horrible dog-Latin. A corpse, in other words, even if it's only a bit of one, like that which hanged Crippen. No corpse, no trial. I think that's good law, isn't it?'

'By jove, you're right!' said Slade. 'I wonder why that hadn't occurred to me before?'

No sooner were the words out of his mouth than he regretted having said them. He did his best to make his face immobile again; he was afraid lest his expression might have hinted at his pleasure in discovering another very reassuring factor in this problem of killing young Spalding. But Dr Matthews had noticed nothing.

'Well, as I said, people only think about these things if they're incidental to their profession,' he said. 'And, all the same, it's only a theoretical piece of law. The entire destruction of a body is practically impossible. But, I suppose, if a man could achieve it, he would be all right. However strong the suspicion was against him, the police couldn't get him without a corpse. There might be a story in that, Slade, if you or I were writers.'

'Yes,' assented Slade, and laughed harshly.

There never would be any story about the killing of young Spalding, the insolent pup.

'Well,' said Dr Matthews, 'we've had a pretty gruesome conversation, haven't we? And I seem to have done all the talking, somehow. That's the result, I suppose, Slade, of the very excellent dinner you gave me. I'd better push off now. Not that the weather is very inviting.'

Nor was it. As Slade saw Dr Matthews into his car, the rain was driving down in a real winter storm, and there was a bitter wind blowing.

'Shouldn't be surprised if this turned to snow before morning,' were Dr Matthews's last words before he drove off.

Slade was glad it was such a tempestuous night. It meant that, more certainly than ever, there would be no one out in the lanes, no one out on the sands when he disposed of young Spalding's body.

Back in his drawing-room Slade looked at the clock. There was still an hour to spare; he could spend it making sure that his plans were all correct.

He looked up the tide tables. Yes, that was right enough. Spring tides. The lowest of low water on the sands. There was not so much luck about that. Young Spalding came back on the midnight train every Wednesday night, and it was not surprising that, sooner or later, the Wednesday night would coincide with a Spring tide. But it was lucky that this particular Wednesday night should be one of tempest; luckier still that low water should be at one-thirty, the best time for him.

He opened the drawing-room door and listened carefully. He could not hear a sound. Mrs Dumbleton, his housekeeper, must have been in bed some time now. She was as deaf as a post, anyway, and would not hear his departure. Nor his return, when Spalding had been killed and disposed of.

The hands of the clock seemed to be moving very fast. He must make sure everything was correct. The plough chain and the other iron weights were already in the back seat of the car; he had put them there before old Matthews arrived to dine. He slipped on his overcoat.

From his desk, Slade took a curious little bit of apparatus; eighteen inches of strong cord, tied at each end to a six-inch length of wood so as to make a ring. He made a last close examination to see that the knots were quite firm, and then he put it in his pocket; as he did so, he ran through in his mind, the words—he knew them by heart—of the passage in the book about the Thugs of India, describing the method of strangulation employed by them.

He could think quite coldly about all this. Young Spalding was a pestilent busybody. A word from him, now, could bring ruin upon Slade, could send him to prison, could have him struck off the rolls.

Slade thought of other defaulting solicitors he had heard of, even one or two with whom he had come into contact professionally. He remembered his brother-solicitors' remarks about them, pitying or contemptuous. He thought of having to beg his bread in the streets on his release from prison, of cold and misery and starvation. The shudder which shook him was succeeded by a hot wave of resentment. Never, never, would he endure it.

What right had young Spalding, who had barely been qualified two years, to condemn a grey-haired man twenty years his senior to such a fate? If nothing but death would stop him, then he deserved to die. He clenched his hand on the cord in his pocket.

A glance at the clock told him he had better be moving. He turned out the lights and tiptoed out of the house, shutting the door quietly. The bitter wind flung icy rain into his face, but he did not notice it.

He pushed the car out of the garage by hand, and, contrary to his wont, he locked the garage doors, as a precaution against the infinitesimal chance that, on a night like this, someone should notice that his car was out.

He drove cautiously down the road. Of course, there was not a soul about in a quiet place like this. The few street-lamps were already extinguished.

There were lights in the station as he drove over the bridge; they were awaiting there the arrival of the twelve-thirty train. Spalding would be on that. Every Wednesday he went over to his subsidiary office, sixty miles away. Slade turned into the lane a quarter of a mile beyond the station, and then reversed his car so that it pointed towards the road. He put out the sidelights, and settled himself to wait; his hand fumbled with the cord in his pocket.

The train was a little late. Slade had been waiting a quarter of an hour when he saw the lights of the train emerge from the cutting and come to a standstill in the station. So wild was the night that he could hear nothing of it. Then the train moved slowly out again. As soon as it was gone, the lights in the station began to go out, one by one; Hobson, the porter, was making ready to go home, his turn of duty completed.

Next, Slade's straining ears heard footsteps.

Young Spalding was striding down the road. With his head bent before the storm, he did not notice the dark mass of the motor car in the lane, and he walked past it.

Slade counted up to two hundred, slowly, and then he switched on his lights, started the engine, and drove the car out into the road in pursuit. He saw Spalding in the light of the headlamps and drew up alongside.

'Is that Spalding?' he said, striving to make the tone of his voice as natural as possible. 'I'd better give you a lift, old man, hadn't I?'

'Thanks very much,' said Spalding. 'This isn't the sort of night to walk two miles in.'

He climbed in and shut the door. No one had seen. No one would know. Slade let his clutch out, drove slowly down the road.

'Bit of luck, seeing you,' he said. 'I was just on my way home from bridge at Mrs Clay's when I saw the train come in and remembered it was Wednesday and you'd be walking home. So I thought I'd turn a bit out of my way to take you along.'

'Very good of you, I'm sure,' said Spalding.

'As a matter of fact,' said Slade, speaking slowly and driving slowly, 'it wasn't altogether disinterested. I wanted to talk business to you, as it happened.'

'Rather an odd time to talk business,' said Spalding. 'Can't it wait till tomorrow?'

'No, it cannot,' said Slade. 'It's about the Lady Vere trust.'

'Oh, yes. I wrote to remind you last week that you had to make delivery?'

'Yes, you did. And I told you, long before that, that it would be inconvenient, with Hammond abroad.'

'I don't see that,' said Spalding. 'I don't see that Hammond's got anything to do with it. Why can't you just hand over and have done with it? I can't do anything to straighten things up until you do.'

'As I said, it would be inconvenient.'

Slade brought the car to a standstill at the side of the road.

'Look here, Spalding,' he said desperately, 'I've never asked a favour of you before. But now I ask you, as a favour, to forgo delivery for a bit. Just for three months, Spalding.'

But Slade had small hope that his request would be granted. So little hope, in fact, that he brought his left hand out of his pocket holding the piece of wood, with the loop of cord dangling from its ends. He put his arm round the back of Spalding's seat.

'No, I can't, really I can't,' said Spalding. 'I've got my duty to my clients to consider. I'm sorry to insist, but you're quite well aware of what my duty is.'

'Yes,' said Slade, 'but I beg of you to wait. I implore you to wait, Spalding. There! Perhaps you can guess why, now.'

'I see,' said Spalding, after a long pause.

'I only want three months,' pressed Slade. 'Just three months. I can get straight again in three months.'

Spalding had known other men who had had the same belief in their ability to get straight in three months. It was unfortunate for Slade—and for Spalding—that Slade had used those words. Spalding hardened his heart.

'No,' he said. 'I can't promise anything like that. I don't think it's any use continuing this discussion. Perhaps I'd better walk home from here.'

He put his hand to the latch of the door, and as he did so, Slade jerked the loop of cord over his head. A single turn of Slade's wrist—a thin, bony, old man's wrist, but as strong as steel in that wild moment—tightened the cord about Spalding's throat.

Slade swung round in his seat, getting both hands to the piece of wood, twisting madly. His breath hissed between his teeth with the effort, but Spalding never drew breath at all. He lost consciousness long before he was dead. Only Slade's grip of the cord round his throat prevented the dead body from falling forward, doubled up.

Nobody had seen, nobody would know. And what that book had stated about the method of assassination practised by Thugs was perfectly correct.

Slade had gained, now, the time in which he could get his affairs in order. With all the promise of his current speculations, with all his financial ability, he would be able to recoup himself for his past losses. It only remained to dispose of Spalding's body, and he had planned to do that very satisfactorily. Just for a moment Slade felt as if all this were only some heated dream, some nightmare, but then he came back to reality and went on with the plan he had in mind.

He pulled the dead man's knees forward so that the corpse lay back in the seat, against the side of the car. He put the car in gear, let in his clutch, and drove rapidly down the road—much faster than when he had been arguing with Spalding. Low water was in three-quarters of an hour's time, and the sands were ten miles away.

Slade drove fast through the wild night. There was not a soul about in those lonely lanes. He knew the way by heart, for he had driven repeatedly over that route recently in order to memorise it.

The car bumped down the last bit of lane, and Slade drew up on the edge of the sands.

It was pitch dark, and the bitter wind was howling about him, under the black sky. Despite the noise of the wind, he could hear the surf breaking far away, two miles away, across the level sands. He climbed out of the driver's seat and walked round to the other door. When he opened it the dead man fell sideways, into his arms.

With an effort, Slade held him up, while he groped into the back of the car for the plough chain and the iron weights. He crammed the weights into the dead man's pockets, and he wound the chain round the dead man's body, tucking in the ends to make it all secure. With that mass of iron to hold it down, the body would never be found again when dropped into the sea at the lowest ebb of the Spring tide.

Slade tried now to lift the body in his arms, to carry it over the sands. He reeled and strained, but he was not strong enough—Slade was a man of slight figure, and past his prime. The sweat on his forehead was icy in the cold wind.

For a second, doubt overwhelmed him, lest all his plans should fail for want of bodily strength. But he forced himself into thinking clearly—forced his frail body into obeying the vehement commands of his brain.

He turned round, still holding the dead man upright. Stooping, he got the heavy burden on his shoulders. He drew the arms round his neck, and, with a convulsive effort, he got the legs up round his hips. The dead man now rode him pig-a-back. Bending nearly double, he was able to carry the heavy weight in that fashion, the arms tight round his neck, the legs tight round his waist.

He set off, staggering, down the imperceptible slope of the sands towards the sound of the surf. The sands were soft beneath his feet. It was because of this softness that he had not driven the car down to the water's edge. He could afford to take no chances of being embogged.

The icy wind shrieked round him all that long way. The tide was nearly two miles out. That was why Slade had chosen this place. In the depth of winter, no one would go to the water's edge at low tide for months to come.

He staggered on over the sands, clasping the limbs of the body close about him. Desperately, he forced himself forward, not stopping to rest, for he only had time now to reach the water's edge before the flow began. He went on and on, driving his exhausted body with fierce urgings from his frightened brain.

Then, at last, he saw it: a line of white in the darkness which indicated the water's edge. Farther out, the waves were breaking in an inferno of noise. Here, the fragments of the rollers were only just sufficient to move the surface a little.

He was going to make quite sure of things. Steadying himself, he stepped into the water, wading in farther and farther so as to be able to drop the body into comparatively deep water. He held to his resolve, staggering through the icy water, knee deep, thigh deep, until it was nearly at his waist. This was far enough. He stopped, gasping in the darkness.

He leaned over to one side, to roll the body off his back. It did not move. He pulled at its arms. They were obstinate. He could not loosen them. He shook himself, wildly. He tore at the legs round his waist. Still the thing clung to him. Wild with panic and fear, he flung himself about in a mad effort to rid himself of the burden. It clung on as though it were alive. He could not break its grip, no matter how hard he tried.

Then another breaker came in. It splashed about him, wetting him far above his waist. The tide had begun to turn now, and the tide on those sands comes in like a race-horse.

He made another effort to cast off the load, and, when it still held him fast, he lost his nerve and tried to struggle out of the sea. But it was too much for his exhausted body. The weight of the corpse and the iron with which it was loaded overbore him. He fell.

He struggled up again in the foam-streaked, dark sea, staggering a few steps, fell again—and did not rise. The dead man's arms were round his neck, throttling him, strangling him. Rigor mortis had set in and Spalding's muscles had refused to relax.

The Swimming Pool

H. C. Bailey

The literary career of Henry Christopher Bailey (1878–1961) lasted about half a century, but his heyday as an exponent of detective fiction was during the 'golden age of murder' between the two world wars. Bailey began as an author of historical and romantic fiction; his first book, *My Lady of Orange*, appeared in 1901, and later titles included *The Lonely Lady* (1911) and *The Sea Captain* (1913). Reggie Fortune, the character who made Bailey's name, appeared in the half a dozen longish short stories in *Call Mr Fortune* (1920), and during the 1920s Bailey was regarded as one of Britain's leading detective writers.

Bailey was an unorthodox crime writer, whose work shows a passionate loathing of evil, especially when manifested in crimes against young people. There is a seriousness at the heart of his best stories which distinguishes them from many other vintage mysteries. Following the Second World War, readers' tastes changed, and Bailey's idiosyncratic prose style ceased to have widespread appeal. In the twenty-first century, there has been something of a revival of interest in his work; Barry Pike has written a long series of articles for the magazine *CADS* which discuss the Fortune saga, while 2017 saw the publication of Laird R. Blackwell's *H. C. Bailey's Reggie Fortune and the Golden Age of Detective Fiction*. This story first appeared in *Windsor Magazine* in April 1936, and was included in *A Clue for Mr Fortune*, published in the same year.

It was the case of the swimming-pool which made the newspapers put Mr Fortune into headlines. But that is not his only reason for lamentation over the result. He says it was an awful warning.

The late Joseph Colborn made a million or so out of small groceries. His ideas of spending it were old-fashioned. He did not buy a place in society but in the suburbs. Though outer London now stretches far beyond the green ridge of Tootle Heath, on the slopes about that open space some of the houses with which the modest business wealth of last century was content still stand secluded in what are advertised for sale as park-like surroundings half an hour from Piccadilly.

Joe Colborn bought the biggest—Heath Hall, a lump of grey brick with renaissance towers. Whether he made it more hideous by painting it all white has been vainly disputed by the cultured of Tootle. He did nothing else which changed the place, and he died and his nephew Sam Colborn reigned in his stead.

On a sultry afternoon of July, Mr Fortune drove out to Heath Hall with the Chief of the Criminal Investigation Department. Others had come before them. They sat and sweltered in a slow procession of cars along a shadeless road. Reggie opened damp eyelids. 'Where are we?' he groaned.

'Oh, my hat! What a crush! Way to hell, I presume.' Crowds he loves little and a crawling car less.

Lomas smiled. 'That's the spirit, Reginald.'

Their car stopped, and they got out of it into green gloom. The grounds of Heath Hall are encircled by a remnant of the old forest of the London heights, oak and beech. Within that girdle of woodland, the lawns and gardens look as if they were out in the country.

Arch females, giving no change, sold programmes of the delights which, by permission of Samuel Colborn, Esq., Heath Hall offered that afternoon to the philanthropic. The Guild of Grace—President, Her Highness Princess Somebody, who would receive the philanthropists; Chairman, J. Harvey Deal, M.D.—had arranged a tennis fête with the most fashionable foreigners on show. The famous gardens would also be thrown open. Band of the Green Dragoons. Tea. Buffet.

With enquiring eyes Reggie followed Lomas from the shade of the old trees through which a brown brook flowed to the blaze of the gardens. 'Not so bad, what?' Lomas encouraged him.

'Like dining with grandfather,' Reggie answered. 'He had to have everything.'

Heath Hall had a craggy range of rock garden and a Dutch garden and an Italian rose garden and what its maker might have meant for a Japanese garden, and arbours and pergolas and statues spattered among them, and, farther on, borders of lilies and perennials led up to carpet bedding and beds of geraniums and calceolarias.

'"Let me face the whole of it,"' Reggie sighed, '"fare like my peers, the heroes of old." Yes. There's dahlias. I felt he'd grow dahlias. Now we know the worst.'

Resolutely he marched Lomas round the windings of the

path which led to the lawn in the shade of the white house. Her Highness the Princess Whatnot, a Mongolian face above a girlish frock, was receiving the charitable guests with the help of a dapper, officious man. 'Is that Deal or Colborn?' Lomas whispered.

'Oh, my dear chap! Observe that ingratiatin' manner. Dr J. Harvey Deal, the eminent physician.'

As they approached, Dr Deal came out of his bowing and smiling with a jerk of attention, then he glanced behind him, but had a smile ready for them by the time Lomas was taking the Princess's hand.

'One of our busiest men, ma'am,' he explained. 'Mr Lomas is responsible for the public safety.' The Princess said something guttural, and Dr Deal's urbane voice flowed on: 'My dear sir, it's most kind of you to spare an hour for us. Believe me, we do appreciate that. I know what the sacrifice is to a man under such stress of duties. But really it is of the greatest value that someone of your eminence should show his interest in our little work.'

Lomas laughed. 'I hope it may be. I have been interested in your work, Dr Deal.'

'So good of you. I do think the Guild is doing great things.' Dr Deal side-stepped to explain to the Princess that Mr Fortune was one of the most brilliant of the younger men in the profession. 'Will it be surgery or this—er—criminal work, Fortune? A fine future in either, I am sure. So glad to have you here. Do you know Colborn, Mr Lomas?' He looked behind him again. He beckoned to a slouching young man with a sullen, bony face and a shock of red hair. 'Really rather a noble fellow.' He lowered his voice confidentially. 'Takes his great fortune as a duty.'

Reggie slid away, remarking to himself: '"The carpenter

said nothing but: The butter's spread too thick."' He sat down in the shade of a cedar and watched the conversation of Lomas with Deal and Colborn… Colborn was sulky and fidgety… Other people took chairs near Reggie, and he got into talk with them, about the gardens, about Colborn, about his deceased uncle… It appeared that uncle had been popular in Tootle, the most genial, the most hospitable of men, till he had that dreadful illness… Tootle had not made up its mind about the nephew: nobody knew him, he wouldn't go anywhere; never opened the house; didn't seem to have found himself—of course he'd been as poor as a church mouse till his uncle's death. This gossip faded out into looks of silent mysterious meaning…

Colborn had escaped from the triple conversation. Dr Deal was conducting Lomas on a tour. Reggie wandered away, avoided with a shudder the tennis-courts on which the foreign champions were bounding—he objects to modern tennis as a ballet without art—and also Colborn was not stopping there. He made a circuit round the spectators; he vanished.

Taking the same direction, Reggie arrived at the stream which flowed from the wood through the lower level of the laboured gardens in a comparatively natural condition. Willows shaded it; white crowfoot rose from the water above swaying green ribands of vallisneria; the banks were spangled with the gold of St John's wort.

The sound of talk made him stop; a man's voice sulky, a woman's cajoling: 'It's all right, Ann. What's the odds?'—'Oh, silly! Such a funk!'—'Not funking. I've done my stuff.'—'But you haven't. You must show.'—'Dam' all!'—'Me too?'—'You minx'—sounds which were not of talk, movement, a rustle of clothes, a gasp—'Oh, Sam, you bear!'

Reggie stood on a piece of dead wood, made a crack, and,

after a pause of discretion, moved on. He saw Sam Colborn, red of face, departing quickly with a small, dark woman. She had a buxom shape; she had a chin; her walk declared assurance. 'Bear has a leader,' Reggie was thinking, when he saw them come upon another woman.

She did not go well with Ann. Slim and severe in grey silk coat and skirt, which looked like mourning against Ann's abundant apple green, she wore a bob of golden hair, and the tired, pretty face had a complexion so fair that against Ann's bright colour it seemed marble white.

'Hallo! Fancy meeting you,' said Colborn, with no pretence of pleasure.

Ann did much better. 'My dear! How jolly! I haven't seen you for donkey's years. What's the best with you? Come along and have tea and talky.'

'Thanks very much, Miss Deal'—the answering voice had no expression—'I can't stay.'

'Oh, come on, nurse,' Colborn growled.

'No, thank you, Mr Colborn. I only came to look at the place again. Dear place, isn't it? I must go.'

'All right. Sorry. See you again some time.' Colborn marched on.

'But of course we shall.' Ann laughed. 'All the best!' She waved a jaunty farewell and followed him.

The woman in grey stood still for a moment, using her handkerchief, then went on along the stream. Though Ann hung possessive on his arm, Colborn looked back at her. She vanished into the dark of some aged yew-trees.

Reggie strolled that way too. Beyond the yews the stream broadened to make a swimming-pool from which the overflow splashed down a cascade among ferns into the encircling woodland again. The woman stood on the bank looking up at the gardens and the white house, and her pretty face was miserable. As Reggie appeared she turned and hurried into the wood. He saw her go like a grey ghost through the shade to a gate in the palings and let herself out.

'Well, well,' he murmured, and wandered round the pool. It had been elaborately made, with concrete bed and spring-board and diving-stage. It was ill-cared for. On the concrete, greenish slime was thick; through cracks in it weeds grew, and in the glittering yellow water floated scum and leaves and petals. The space within the close boughs of the old yews had been fashioned into two dressing-places, but the seats were dirty and lichened.

'Not swimmers, the Colborns, dead or livin',' Reggie reflected. 'Prehistoric trees.' He was guessing their age over a twisted hollow trunk when he heard brisk footsteps, and turned to see the living Colborn.

'Hallo!' Colborn looked impatient hostility. 'I say, your Mr Lomas is getting peeved with you. He wants to go.'

'Fancy that,' Reggie drawled. 'Wonder why?'

'Bored stiff, by the looks of him. You don't seem to be leading the revels yourself.'

'Not revellin', no. But very interested, thanks.'

'You're easy pleased.'

'Yes. A simple mind. Yes. Lead me to him.'

'He's up there.' Colborn jerked his head towards the house.

'Thanks very much.' Reggie strolled away and left him.

Lomas was found on the outskirts of the tennis crowd with Dr Harvey Deal. 'What, Reginald, you have to go?' He cut through Deal's flow of talk. 'Of course. A most interesting afternoon, Dr Deal. Good-bye. Well, *au revoir.*'

Deal went with them a little way, gushing still. They left him and proceeded to their car in silence.

'Quite interesting, yes,' Reggie murmured, as they drove away. 'Did you send the living Colborn to fetch me? No, I thought you didn't. But he said so.'

'The deuce he did! Why?'

'Because I was where he didn't want me. Which was by a decayed swimmin'-pool.'

'What has that to do with anything?' Lomas frowned.

'Difficult question. The provisional hypothesis is that he wanted somebody else there.' Reggie described the proceedings of Colborn with the two women.

Lomas gave a coarse chuckle. 'Caught by Deal's daughter, is he? Suggestive. And with another girl on his hands. That may be very useful.'

'How happy could he be with either were t'other dear charmer away! Yes. You have a low mind. However. He called the unknown "nurse."'

'What did she look like? Children's nurse?'

'My dear chap!' Reggie moaned. 'I don't know. People don't look like anything. She didn't nurse Colborn's innocent childhood. Or Ann Deal's. Too young. And they both knew her well. I should say she was a hospital nurse. Might have nursed the deceased uncle.'

'Good gad!' said Lomas. 'Devilish suggestive.'

'Yes, it could be. What did you do in the Great War, daddy?'

'You saw the reactions, didn't you? Deal was rattled, badly rattled. And Colborn couldn't be civil. Colborn fled and Deal kept at me with stories of what fine fellows old Colborn and young Colborn were, and how they loved each other and how old Colborn suffered and what a hopeless case it was—and then young Colborn hustled us off the premises. Not bad stuff, Reginald. Better than I expected. But it's generally a sound move to break in on people and shake 'em up over this sort of case. Now we have to consider the next move.'

'Oh, no. No. I want my tea.' Reggie was plaintive. 'I haven't had any tea, Lomas.' He leaned forward and told the chauffeur to stop at his house in Wimpole Street.

Behold him recumbent there, eating a compilation of cream and quince jelly, while Lomas stood before the pots of lilies which filled the fireplace and lectured.

'Now what have we really got? Old Colborn died six months ago, and Deal certified that the cause of death was cancer of the stomach. Colborn left nearly a million: the bulk of it to this nephew Samuel; £5,000 to Deal, and £1,000 to his devoted nurse, Sybil Benan. Will made shortly before death. Two weeks ago the Tootle police received this anonymous letter telling 'em that Mr Joseph Colborn would be alive now if he had been properly treated, and suggesting he was poisoned. Letter in printed letters on common paper, posted in Tootle. Of course we often get that sort of thing when a wealthy man dies. The divisional inspector reported local scandal over old Colborn changing from the local doctor to Harvey Deal. Well, we've had rumours about Deal before. And you confirmed them.'

'No. I wouldn't say that. I told you Deal had a sort of name for passing people out quiet and easy. Nothing more.'

'Quite. Nothing definite. But it was also confirmed by the Tootle doctor. He said he'd advised Colborn that an operation would be necessary and wanted to take him to a surgeon; and Colborn went to Deal on his own, and Deal advised against the operation. All wrong, what?'

'Oh, yes. Yes. Bad choice. Bad opinion. But fashionable. Patients will go after a doctor known to keep 'em off the operatin'-table. Not a criminal offence to do so. However convenient to impatient heirs.'

'Exactly.' Lomas frowned. 'But now we add to all that the alarm of Deal and young Colborn at our interest in 'em—and the connection of Deal's daughter with young Colborn. Very fishy, all this fresh stuff.'

'As you say.' Reggie spoke through a mouthful of éclair. 'And more. Connection with hypothetical nurse.'

'Quite. More than fishy. But I don't see my way. Would you like to exhume old Colborn's body and try your luck?'

'I might, yes,' Reggie said slowly. 'For the good of Dr Deal— his soul, if any. And our Mr Colborn's. But don't expect much. Probably old Colborn had cancer. If so, probably kept under morphia at the last. I should find all that. And you'd be just where you began. Unless I got a lot of morphia. Even then!'

Lomas nodded. 'Very difficult. Looks like a murder by calculated neglect. The worst kind to prove.'

'Bafflin'. Yes. However. There are other possibilities.'

'What are you thinking of?'

'My dear chap! Two obvious possibilities. Find the nurse, Sybil Benan—the thousand-pound nurse. Look after the living Colborn. Put a man or two on his place. I could bear to know who goes there.'

Lomas nodded again. 'I agree. We must put the nurse through it.'

'Yes. That is indicated. But don't forget our Mr Colborn and that gate by the defunct swimming-pool.'

When Reggie talks of the case now he is apt to speculate what would have happened if he had not given this advice. Though it determined the issue, though it was wholly sound, he insists that he gave it expecting quite different conse- quences. Which is one part of the proof of his incapacity to be a good policeman. The other is that he stayed by the swimming-pool.

On the evening of the next day he was warned to attend the exhumation of old Colborn's body, and groaned into the telephone: 'Hasty, aren't you? What about the nurse?'

'The nurse can't be found,' said Lomas. 'Hence the haste.'

'Well, well. You may be right. Have you told Dr Deal of your fell design?'

'I sent Bell round to him. He didn't give anything away. Said he must go on record as protesting we had no justification, and investigation by a competent medical man must confirm his death certificate. He asked who would do the post-mortem, and said he had complete confidence in you and did not desire to be present.'

'Very kind; very gratifyin',' Reggie murmured.

'Sure of himself, isn't he?'

'Yes. He knows the game. What about the nurse?'

'Not at home. Not been at home since yesterday, as far as known. Lived in a one-room flat in Marylebone. Don't seem to have slept there last night. Said nothing about going away.'

'Last night!' Reggie murmured. 'Oh, my Lord.' It was from this moment he became aware that he should not have stayed by the swimming-pool. 'Find her good and quick.'

'We try to please,' said Lomas.

'And the living Colborn?'

'Out in his car. Not informed yet.'

In the dew of next morning Reggie watched the exhumation of Joseph Colborn. The day he spent working upon the corpse. That evening he came into Lomas's room, pale and plaintive. He let himself down into the biggest chair; silently he stretched out a hand to the larger cigar box.

'I thank you.' He blew smoke through his nose. 'Yes. A warm day. "What have I done for thee, England, my England? What is there I would not do, England my own?" I wonder.

However. Speakin' broadly, I've done this job. As stated. As expected. The late Joseph Colborn was full of cancer. Early operation might have postponed death. But he was seventy plus. Not likely he'd have lived long or happy. I shouldn't like to swear it was wrong not to operate.'

'Damme,' Lomas exclaimed, 'that lets Deal out altogether. That leaves us with no case at all. It's natural death.'

'Not a good case. But I should say he didn't die natural. Sharp colour-results to the morphine tests. Must have been quite a lot of morphia in him. Too much morphia, Lomas. Only I can't prove it. After all this time. We didn't get goin' soon enough. We never do.'

'My dear fellow, we can't detect a criminal before we know there's been a crime.'

'That's what I complain of. Essential futility of police work.'

'Not at all.' Lomas was annoyed. 'The effect of your work is to show that no crime has been committed.'

'Oh, no. No. Effect is to leave us where we began. As expected. With suspicion the old man was poisoned.'

'I don't accept that. You show Deal was honest about the cause of death, and probably honest in his treatment. He advised against an operation because it was just a desperate chance for an old man. You admit that you daren't say he was wrong. At the worst, then, he made a sympathetic error of judgment.'

Reggie sat up. 'Sympathetic error? Yes. It could be. By itself. And the morphia. Lomas? Another sympathetic error. Old man in horrid, hopeless pain. An overdose of morphia. Yes. It's done.'

'So I've heard,' said Lomas drily. 'Wouldn't you do it yourself?'

'An overdose? Not me, no. But I'm not sympathetic.'

Lomas looked curiously at his round face, which was drawn into an expression of cold, puzzled anger. 'I shouldn't like to have you out for my blood, Reginald,' he said. 'Well, there it is. You can't get Deal. No case.'

Reggie started. 'What? Wasn't trying for Deal's blood,' he snapped. 'Trying for the truth. That's my job. What about the nurse?'

'Not come home. Not found.'

'Oh, my hat!' Reggie sank back and gazed at him with large reproachful eyes. 'What are you for, Lomas?'

'My dear fellow,' Lomas laughed. 'Sorry I don't give satisfaction. There's nothing very unusual in a young woman going off privately. And we have evidence there's the usual man in the case. The night before last a man was seen coming out of her flat.'

'Night before last. That's just after we called on the livin' Colborn.'

'Quite so. But Colborn hasn't gone. He's at home still. When he isn't buzzing about with Ann Deal. By the way, he blew up over the exhumation. Came down here and cursed at large, Bell says.'

'And the nurse is missing,' Reggie murmured. 'Just after we begin to take an interest in the case. And you say it's over. Well, well. Why are policemen?'

'The case is over,' said Lomas. 'You've finished it. What could we ask the nurse if we found her? What could she say? If she swore Deal poisoned the old man, nobody would believe her against your evidence.'

'No. I'm very useful. I excuse you for doing nothing.' Reggie dragged himself up and looked down at Lomas with weary dislike. 'My only aunt! How I hate you,' he mumbled, and wandered out.

When he discusses his conduct of the case now, he will remark that this was the first point at which he showed some faint intelligence: inadequate, futile, but, so far as it went, sound. He did perceive that something else had happened, would happen, or ought to happen. What it should be, he had not the slightest idea: because, as he always maintains earnestly, he is without imagination.

Late that evening he rang up Lomas. 'Fortune speaking. The mind is almost impotent. But conscience has been invigorated by beef and burgundy. Have you got into the vanished nurse's flat?'

'Good gad! No, of course not. We can't break in. No sort of justification. There never was, and now less than any. What?'

'I said the Lord have mercy on your soul. Which I don't expect. The only evidence she's not there is: she didn't answer when you rang, and a man was seen coming out. Not any evidence.'

'What's in your mind?'

'Nothing. Mind is vacant. Is anybody watchin' the Colborn demesne?'

'Damme, yes, they're still on that,' Lomas chuckled. 'I forgot to cancel the orders.'

'Well, well. Mr Lomas—his defence on the Day of Judgment: "I never did anything without justification. But, please, I did sometimes forget."'

'Oh, go to bed,' said Lomas, and rang off.

Reggie was still in bed next morning, still asleep, when Superintendent Bell rang him up. Reggie squirmed and blinked, and took the receiver and complained.

'Sorry, sir,' said the telephone. 'But this is big stuff, and right up your street. Can you meet me at St Alban's mortuary in half an hour?'

'No. I eat when I get up. I also wash. I will now do so. Go away.'

'I can give you—'

'You cannot,' Reggie snapped, and rang off and rolled out of bed.

Under pressure, however, he will dress and even eat fast. In less than an hour his car slowed to stop at the squalid precincts of the mortuary.

Bell stood in the courtyard, smoking a pipe. 'I'd better give you the outline first, Mr Fortune. There's a dead end to the gates of a little factory just a bit beyond here. This morning, round about six o'clock, some chaps came along to open up the place, and they saw an old brown canvas trunk lying in the roadway where the dead end opens off the main street. Like as if it had fallen off a cab or a car or a van, you see. They told a constable, and it was brought along to the station as lost property. Then the sergeant noticed it was broke a bit, as might be by a fall, and he had a look through the hole and saw a foot inside—a bare foot. So they opened it, and found inside a woman's body without a head. That's what we're up against. I leave it to you.'

'Yes. You do,' said Reggie bitterly. 'Any news of the vanished nurse?'

'There is not.' Bell gave him a stolid stare.

'No. There wouldn't be. Ring up Mr Lomas. Give him my love, and remind him he told me to go to bed last night.' Reggie passed into the mortuary.

The headless body was naked: a young body. Not only at the red neck had there been violence. The right knee was wounded. Elsewhere the flesh was livid white. Reggie inspected it inch by inch, and collected from it yellow flakes, fragments of green leaf... The hands interested him. The palms were dirty with brown slime in the lines, the nails too...

Late in the afternoon he entered Lomas's room and found Bell there also, and subsided into the easiest chair and gazed at them plaintively. 'Well, well. Concentration of the higher intelligence. On the fundamental, painful question. Why are policemen?'

'What are you going to tell me?' said Lomas briskly.

'My dear chap. No answer yet discovered. Your existence seems wholly futile. However. I went to bed. As instructed. I take it you went to bed. Nothing attempted, nothing done, had earned a night's repose. While the corpse was prepared for us. Quite a young corpse, this one. No sympathetic error of judgment. Woman was drowned. Blonde woman, under thirty. Subsequent to death, head detached by an efficient knife. Some cutting operation also performed on right knee.'

'After death?' Lomas asked.

'Oh, yes. Very dead when performed. Small effusion of blood.'

'Why should her knee be cut about?'

'Not havin' known the lady, I can't say. Probably to remove something about the knee which would help us to know her. She may have had a cartilage removed in life. She has now.'

'Quite good, Reginald. That fits very well.'

'What with?' Reggie opened round innocent eyes.

'Why, with the removal of the head. That was cut off to prevent identification.'

'Oh, my Lomas! You do think of things! What a mind! When used. Yes, I should say there was an idea of concealin' identity. Some other little points. Petals of St John's wort adherin' to body. Also scraps of water-weed. And muddy slime about the hands. Suggestin' she was drowned in stream or pond. Curious and interestin' suggestion.'

'It is, begad!' Lomas exclaimed. 'Water-weeds on her body! That suggests she was put into the water naked.'

'Not necessarily, no. Submerged for some time in pond, she would get its odds and ends under her clothes. Common feature of drownin' cases. You miss the point. What is particularly interestin' is the St John's wort. Don't grow much round London except in gardens. The suggestion is therefore that she was drowned in a garden pond: rather dirty pond for a garden; same like our Mr Colborn's swimming-pool.'

'Good gad!' said Lomas.

'Yes. I told you to watch it. And you forgot to stop 'em watchin'. Stroke of genius by Mr Lomas. Any result?'

'There is.' The smile of Lomas was unamiable. 'Not only that back door by the pond, but every gate to Colborn's grounds has been watched. They were still watched last night—while this body was being dumped in the street. You'll be glad to hear, Reginald, that the result is to clear Sam Colborn of suspicion.' Bell coughed. 'What's the matter with you?'

'I wouldn't put it so high myself,' said Bell.

'As regards this woman being drowned in his swimming-pool, he is cleared,' Lomas insisted. 'He ought to be very grateful to you, Reginald.'

'I wonder,' Reggie murmured.

'Since his place has been under observation, no woman except Ann Deal and a servant or two has gone in by any gate. Last night he drove out alone, in evening dress, just after seven; no luggage on his car. Came back about one a.m., quite normal. Apart from his running round with the Deal girl, nothing particular has been noticed at all.'

'Ah, I don't know as I'd say that, sir,' Bell objected again.

'And what would you say?' Reggie turned to him.

'It's like this, sir.' Bell gave Lomas a respectful, apologetic look, and Lomas replied by an ejaculation of contempt. 'Our man on that back gate last night saw a fellow loitering about the heath close by with a bag, pretty much like you do see men loitering with intent; might have been going to crack the house or only just rob the garden—there is a good deal o' that round these big gardens in the suburbs. Mr Lomas thinks it was a job of that sort, nor I shouldn't have any doubt either, in the ordinary way. Well, our man went after the fellow, lost sight of him—no wonder, dodging round on that heath in the dark—went back to the gate, nipped into the grounds, and did a bit o' search; couldn't see anybody, got back to the gate, and had a snap o' the fellow cutting away.'

'Still with bag?' Reggie murmured.

'That's right. And that's all. I'd agree with Mr Lomas, it's the reg'lar stuff, burglar, or sneak thief scared off, only for all this business behind.'

'As you say. Yes. Ordinary in the middle of the extraordinary compels suspicion. For the soul is dead that slumbers. And things are not what they seem. You hadn't noticed that, Lomas. Any description of man and bag?'

'Not much good.' Bell shook his head. 'Slouched hat, long, dark coat, about middle size, quick mover. Squarish, fattish sort o' bag. We ought to have had more, but playing hide-and-seek in the dark you don't often get much of a chance. I don't blame our man, Mr Fortune.'

'Oh, no. No. I think he did very well. So Mr Lomas will now give humble and hearty thanks he forgot to remove the watch on the gate by the pool. Our one bright effort, so far. Genius.' Reggie gazed at Lomas with eyes of dreamy wonder. 'I wish I knew when to forget. Just genius.'

'Always happy to amuse you, Reginald,' said Lomas sharply. 'Even when I don't see the joke.'

'My dear chap!' Reggie was affectionate. 'Spoke very handsome.'

'But I happen to think this gives us nothing relevant. It's a thousand to one the loitering fellow with the bag was a common thief. Suppose he wasn't, the evidence about him is of no use. There's not a hint of an identification. A middle-sized man who moved quick! Of course that would fit Colborn or Deal. And it would fit millions of other men just as well.'

'Oh, yes. That is so. Remains the strikin' fact that a man who might have been Colborn or Deal was pokin' round the Colborn swimmin'-pool, privily and by stealth, with fattish bag, on the night when the body of a young woman, apparently drowned in pool, was dumped on us without a head.'

'You think it was her head in his bag?' Bell grunted and nodded.

'It could be. Yes. One of the possibilities. Rather probable possibility.'

'What are you suggesting?' Lomas demanded, with some vehemence. 'Do you mean the woman was drowned in that swimming-pool last night, and then the head was cut off and removed by this man while the body was carted away in the trunk? Is it likely?'

'No. It is not. And it didn't happen. She was drowned some time ago. Day or two ago. That's one of our few certainties.'

'Very well.' Lomas laughed unpleasantly. 'You're getting more and more muddled, Reginald. You say it's days since she was drowned and she was drowned in that pool. But the place has been watched day and night, ever since we were at the garden-party, and no strange woman has gone in. Yet you ask me to believe that her body was taken away from it unobserved last night, while a man was observed removing her head. The whole thing is preposterous.'

'As you say. Yes. But what you say isn't what I said; it isn't the whole thing, and parts of it aren't anything. I said she was drowned days ago, and there were indications of her being drowned in such water as that of Colborn's decayed swimming-pool. Not proof. Couldn't be proof. Only curious and interestin' indications. Uncomfortable, but irresistible.' He looked at Lomas with large, plaintive eyes. 'I don't like it. But we have to fit 'em in. You said the place had been watched since the garden-party. That isn't true. There was a gap. Watch began next day. Thus leavin' one clear night. At the garden-party people were meetin' round about the pool—Colborn, Ann Deal, unknown young woman called nurse. The same night a man came out of Nurse Benan's flat. But since that day she's sunk without trace—and now we've found a young woman's headless body and we've missed a man with a fattish bag. That's the whole thing, Lomas. Not preposterous. Ghastly. And futile. Why are policemen?'

Lomas sat silent, frowning. Then he exclaimed: 'You are the man in the street, Reginald. Blame the police, whatever happens.'

'Oh, yes. Yes. The natural man. I am. With a reasoned faith in the permanent inefficiency of all officials. Faith justified by works.'

'You talk about reason!' Lomas said, with ferocity. 'Do you suppose you've given me a reasonable theory of the case?'

'No. I haven't. Materials inadequate. That's what I complain of. We're futile.'

'Speak for yourself. You're as futile as a cheap newspaper, cursing at large because we can do nothing without evidence.'

'Oh, my Lomas!' Reggie reproached him. 'A woman's been murdered. Had you noticed that? I'm cursin' because we didn't stop it.'

'How the devil could we?'

'My dear chap! Oh, my dear chap! We didn't try. However. Study to improve. The first-felt want is somebody who knew the departed Nurse Sybil Benan.'

'That's right,' Bell agreed heartily.

'Certainly,' said Lomas. 'But suppose the body can be identified as hers, which isn't too likely, where are we, Reginald? Neither young Colborn nor Deal had any reason for making away with her. She wasn't dangerous to them. Your own evidence is that old Colborn wasn't murdered.'

'Oh, no. I said I couldn't prove he was. But the nurse might have been able to swear to it. And there is another reason possible for the elimination of Nurse Benan, if she was the nurse who met our Mr Colborn and Ann Deal by the pool. That young woman didn't like seeing 'em together. He didn't like her being there. Indications of uneasiness and jealousy strongly marked.'

'You mean the nurse had an affair with Sam Colborn before he took up with Miss Deal,' said Bell eagerly. 'Ah, that's saying something. That puts it on the usual lines of a trunk murder—man getting rid of the woman he didn't want any more. Crime of passion.'

'Yes. I should say there was passion about,' Reggie murmured.

'Quite. We can assume that,' Lomas nodded. 'But how far can you go towards identifying the body in the trunk with the woman you saw by the pool?'

'Same sort of age, same sort of figure, same sort of fair skin. That's all.'

'Doesn't amount to anything,' Lomas said, with contempt.

'No. It doesn't. By itself. But it's quite a lot to work on. Only you won't do any work. I told you to search Nurse Benan's

flat days ago. You wouldn't. You were very correct. Feelin'
correct still, Lomas?'

'I still prefer not to act without justification,' Lomas told
him. 'Of course the case is altered now.'

'Yes. It is. Woman's been murdered. But we've been quite
correct. Grateful and comfortin' reflection. Have you got your
blessed search-warrant?'

'Don't worry.'

'Worry!' Reggie's voice rose, and he stared with round
eyes. 'Oh, my Lord! I want to see the place quick.'

'If you like,' Lomas shrugged. 'Take him along, Bell.'

'What celerity! But I want more. I want young Colborn
asked if he saw Nurse Benan by the swimming-pool at his
party. Question one. And when he saw her last. Question
two. Turnin' to our eminent physician, Dr Harvey Deal. Ask
him what hospital Nurse Benan was trained at. Question one.
If she'd ever had trouble with her right knee. Question two.
And when he saw her last. Question three. Then you can get
on to the hospital for description and identification.'

'Thank you. I had thought of it,' said Lomas acidly.

'Well, well,' Reggie's voice was soft. 'Fancy that! And you
will still forget to remove the men watching Colborn's place,
won't you?'

'What?' Lomas exclaimed.

'My only aunt!' Reggie moaned. 'You would have removed
'em!'

'Of course I shouldn't,' Lomas snapped. 'Not now.'

'Bless you for those kind words,' Reggie smiled sadly.
'Come on, Bell.'

The block of one-room flats to which they came was in a
back street of Marylebone. Bell instructed him that nothing
was known against the place—most respectable—built for

working women—pretty well all of 'em nurses and doctors' secretaries and that sort of thing, with jobs in the medical quarter close by—but you couldn't say it was fishy in itself a man should have been seen coming out of Nurse Benan's flat. No rule against it; not even a custom. Only, nobody would be allowed to stay on who didn't behave decent.

'No. I'm sure she did,' Reggie murmured. 'However. There was a man.'

Bell's assistant, Sergeant Underwood, had no difficulty in opening Nurse Benan's door. They passed from a tiny hall into a bed-sitting-room, the blinds of which were down. When Underwood let the daylight in, they saw a bed draped to look like a divan, a bureau writing-desk, and other cheap, good furniture all in order. Reggie gave a glance round and went on into the bathroom. That also had been left neat and spotless. The towels had been used, but were dry and clean. He opened the white mirrored cupboard, and found in it comb and hairbrush.

Bell joined him. 'Hallo! Left them behind. That don't look like she meant to leave home.'

'No. Unintentional absence is indicated. She didn't take her toothbrush. Or her sponge.' Reggie frowned at the hairbrush and drew out some yellow hairs.

'What about them, sir?' Bell asked. 'Are they the right colour for the woman young Colborn called nurse?'

'Oh, yes. Just about. Also for the woman without a head.' Holding them in the palm of his hand, he continued to frown at them.

'Bobbed yellow hair, eh?' Bell said.

'That is so. Yes. Woman called nurse was bobbed. I wonder.' He put them away in an envelope. 'Hair to match. Collect the brush too. And what has our young friend Underwood found?' He returned to the bed-sitting-room.

'Seems to have left a good lot of clothes, sir,' Underwood told him. 'And a couple of suitcases. No sign of having taken anything.'

'Found a grey silk coat and skirt?'

'No, sir. Nothing like it. Why?'

'That's what the nurse by the swimming-pool was wearing.' Reggie wandered round the room. Bell sat down to the bureau and began to go through drawers and pigeon-holes. 'Hallo! Here's her hospital,' he announced. 'She was trained at St Bede's. Some letters too. Patients and relatives, and one from Dr Harvey Deal, thanking her for work in a very difficult case.'

Reggie glanced round. 'I wonder,' he murmured. 'Date?'

'May twelvemonth, sir.'

'Well, well. Wonder if that patient also died. However.'

'My oath!' Bell muttered, and searched on fiercely. 'Nothing else to signify, sir. Nothing from young Mr Colborn.' Reggie sat down at the bureau, turned over the letters, looked at the blotting-pad beneath. The blotting-paper had been little used and some writing was clear upon it. He started up and took it to the bathroom and held it to the mirror. 'S. Colb… Heath… Toot…' appeared from a corner and in the middle. 'Dear… must speak… meet… fête… if… can't… come… swim… my dear… can't… Syb…'

Reggie looked back into Bell's grim face at his shoulder. 'Nothing from our Mr Colborn. No. Something to him though,' he said.

'Here, we'll have to get this photographed,' Bell growled. 'That might give us the whole letter.'

'Yes. Possible. However. We know what the letter was meant to say. That's enough to put up to our Mr Colborn. Come on.'

They came back to Lomas and showed him the blotting-paper and turned it over to the photographers.

'Good work, Reginald,' Lomas smiled. 'You are getting us somewhere now.'

'Not me. No.' Reggie shook his head. 'Only doin' the obvious and findin' the always probable results. And we're not anywhere. What have you done?'

'I have the answers to your little questions. Young Colborn admits that he did see Nurse Benan down by the pool at his party, and says he's never seen her since. Deal says she was trained at St Bede's and he knows nothing of any knee trouble, and he hasn't seen her for months. The hospital says she was twenty-eight, blonde, blue eyes, about five foot six and nine stone, and she had a cartilage removed from her right knee while on the staff. That tallies with the body in the trunk, what? And I take it the wound on the knee was inflicted to obliterate the scar.'

'Yes. That is the obvious inevitable inference,' Reggie said slowly. 'Body about right. Not a nice case, Lomas.'

'It is not. This won't do for an identification, however sure you feel.'

'I said so,' Reggie complained. 'However, we will now ask Dr Harvey Deal and our Mr Colborn to give us their opinion of the remains. Have 'em brought along to the mortuary.'

'Damme, you don't expect them to identify a headless body? They'd be crazy.'

'Don't expect anything. I haven't expected anything that's yet happened. My error. My gross error. No imagination. I ought to have followed that nurse at the fête. However. I can take pains. I'll try everything. Bring 'em along. It'll shake 'em up. And we might have reactions.'

'I agree.' Lomas nodded. 'Quite justified.' And Reggie made a sorrowful noise at him.

In the mortuary, the headless body lay covered by a sheet, a dim shape under the twilight. Bell brought in Dr Harvey

Deal, who was talking fast: it must be understood that he protested; he could not possibly identify a mutilated body as Nurse Benan even if it was she; he had never been her medical attendant; he—

Reggie came forward from the shadow with a sharp interruption. 'Switch on the lights, Bell,' and as he spoke he drew back the sheet. The body and its wounds gleamed stark.

Deal stood still. 'Really, Fortune,' he gasped.

'Look at her,' said Reggie.

Deal approached the body with mincing steps, and made a perfunctory examination and swallowed and turned away. 'I can only tell you that I am quite unable to give an opinion.'

'You're not doin' yourself justice,' Reggie told him. 'I ask you if you see any reason why that could not be Nurse Benan.'

Deal hesitated. 'It—it is a question to which I should answer No, with every possible reservation. I see nothing definitely incompatible. But you must be aware, Fortune, that is very, very far from evidence of identity.'

'I am. Yes. What about the decapitation?'

'Brutal,' Deal exclaimed.

'Oh, yes. Yes. Would you say it was done with skill?'

'I—I—had not considered,' Deal stammered. 'You know very well it's not a matter on which I should care to claim the authority of an expert.'

'No. But you can give an ordinary medical opinion.'

'If you ask me—but it's quite out of order, Fortune—I should have thought there was very little skill.'

'And the wound on the knee?'

'I can't understand that at all,' Deal said in a hurry.

'Very well. Thank you. Good night.'

'I must be allowed to say, Fortune, that I do consider this most unnecessary and unjustified.'

'You think so?' Reggie murmured. 'Good-bye.' He nodded at Bell and Deal was led out, and a moment later Sam Colborn was brought in.

He came with a swagger but, like Deal, stopped short when he saw the naked, headless body.

He growled something profane, then broke out: 'Expect me to identify that? I told you I couldn't. It's a blasted outrage, whoever she is, bringing a fellow in to stare at her. And Nurse Benan, I never saw her, except like everybody else.'

'Could it be Nurse Benan?' Reggie asked.

'I don't know, damn you. I can't tell what she'd look like, like that. I don't believe she's dead, if you ask me.'

'Why?'

Colborn scowled at him. 'She wasn't the sort to get herself killed.'

'Oh. Compliment?'

'Yes, it is. She knew her way about.'

'You think so? She seems to have lost her way. She's vanished, Mr Colborn. Unless she's on the table there.'

'I don't believe it.'

'Well, well.' Reggie sighed, and went to the door and called Underwood, who brought him a portfolio. 'Thank you.' Reggie turned. 'Mr Colborn, have you had a letter from Nurse Benan lately?'

'No, I have not.' Colborn was truculent.

'Really? You were surprised to see her at your garden-party?'

'I didn't expect to see her, if that's what you mean. No reason why she shouldn't come.'

'You weren't pleased, were you?'

'Oh, I know you were eavesdropping. You think you got on to a bit of scandal, do you? Well, you're wrong.'

'I said nothing about scandal. Do you recognise that writing?' Reggie handed him a photograph of the writing on the blotting-pad. Some more words had come out, and now it read: 'Dear Mr Sam... must speak... meet... fête... if we can't, do come... by the swim... where... you know... my dear... can't, can't... Sybil.'

Colborn flushed as he read, and he crushed the photograph in his hands and looked up at Reggie with a glare in his greenish eyes. 'It's a fake! It's a damned fake!' he roared.

'Oh, no. Written in Nurse Benan's room. Blotted on her blotting-pad. Any explanation?'

'I never had it. I never saw the thing.'

'Had she any claim on you to account'—Reggie paused and directed his eyes to the body—'to account for her writing you that letter?'

Colborn turned his back on the body. 'No, she hadn't. Nothing.'

'Letter's a surprise to you?'

'I say it's a fake! That's all I'm going to say.'

'Do you deny the writing is Nurse Benan's?'

Colborn scowled at him, and decided to say, 'I don't know her writing.'

'Oh. Good night,' said Reggie.

Colborn stood a moment staring at him, then made off without a word. 'Well, well,' Reggie murmured. 'The end of a perfect day.' He drew the sheet over the body, and his round face was pale and miserable. He went out, switching off the lights.

Bell was at the telephone, reporting to Lomas. Underwood whispered: 'Both of 'em being trailed, sir. That's fixed up all right.'

'Yes. Day after the fair. Several days. However. The mind is empty, Underwood. Oh, my Lord—empty!'

Bell turned from the telephone. 'Mr Lomas would like to speak to you, sir.'

'Bless him,' Reggie groaned, and took the receiver. 'Hallo! Yes. Deal did shy at admitting there was any evidence of skill in removal of head and incision on knee. And there isn't. Not exactly. Operations not performed as a medical man should. On the other hand, they're not crude. Either by somebody who only knew a bit, or by somebody who didn't mean to show competent skill.'

'Rather suggests Deal himself, doesn't it?' said Lomas. 'Doctor careful not to leave proof he was a doctor.'

'Yes, one of the possibilities. And heaven only knows what an operation by Harvey Deal would look like afterwards.'

'Don't love him, do you?' Lomas chuckled. 'I don't blame you. On the other hand, that letter was in Nurse Benan's writing. We've got some documents from the hospital, which she did write, and they match. That's not too good for Colborn. So it's about fifty-fifty against each of 'em. And yet it don't make a case, what?'

'Oh, no. No. Not yet. However. I call this a day. No more from Reginald. It's dark—oh, my hat, it's dark.'

'What do you mean?'

'I can't see in the dark,' Reggie was plaintive. 'I want to see the much-advertised swimmin'-pool. And so to bed. Risin' early in the mornin', I proceed to the swimmin'-pool. With an active and intelligent police officer. With our Sergeant Underwood. Will that do?'

'Good luck to you,' said Lomas.

'Luck!' Reggie's voice rose. 'No. The fault, dear Brutus, is not in the stars, but in ourselves that we are underlings. Pleasant dreams.' He hung up and turned to Underwood. 'At my place?' he asked mournfully. 'Bright and early?'

'Six o'clock, sir?' Underwood suggested.

'My dear chap! Oh, my dear chap!' Reggie moaned. 'There isn't such a time. Not to live in. Say seven.'

And when Underwood arrived in the morning, he was already eating strawberries and cream. 'Have some?' he invited. 'No? Coffee? No? Oh, my dear chap. Don't be so superior. Any news?'

'Just a bit, sir. On leaving the mortuary, Deal went home. When Colborn was let go, he went there too, and was in the house a couple of hours. So they thought well to have a confab., you see. Then Colborn went straight back to his own place. Last I've heard is that our chaps there saw nobody about in the night, and Colborn hasn't gone away yet. Deal's still at home too. Looks like they settled to face things out.'

'Looks like anything you please,' said Reggie. 'However.' He finished the strawberries while Underwood fidgeted and disapproved.

It was nevertheless before eight o'clock when Reggie's car set them down on the ridge of Tootle Heath, still in the dewy mist of the prelude to another torrid day. They walked down through clumps of thorn and gorse to the grey palings of Colborn's house and found the back gate. An unshaven loafer sauntered up and grinned at Underwood. 'Not a soul been round here, inspector.'

'Oh. Very well,' Reggie said. 'Show us where the soul went the other night.'

'I couldn't give you the track of him, sir,' the detective protested. 'It was all snooping round these clumps.'

'Yes. But you thought he went inside. And followed. Which way?'

'Oh, I can show you that,' the detective said gloomily, and they passed through the gate into the belt of woodland.

'I couldn't see him here, but I went on thinking I heard foot-steps. But it's like country, for queer sounds o' nights. I came on here, yes; I nearly flopped into that blinking pond, came round it like this, watching the grounds to see if the bloke was making for the house. Not a blink. So I went back to the gate again, and there he was still loitering, and I cut after him and he was off.'

'As you said. Yes,' Reggie murmured. He stood gazing at the pool, and walked round it. The yellowish slimy bottom could be made out clearly enough.

'Nothing in there,' said Underwood.

'There is not. No.' Reggie wandered on into the dressing-places under the old yew-trees, and stood there, looking about him. He made a stride forward, and dropped on his knees where the carpet of brown leaves showed a fragment of something red. Slowly he stood up again, and gazed at the ground all about with a look of fear and surprise, moved to and fro, poring over it. He came back to the twisted hollow trunk of a yew, close by where he had made his find, stared at it, gave a jerk of the head. 'My case, Underwood,' he said sharply, opened it, took out two wooden boxes and a surgical knife. Into one box he scraped the red fragment from the ground. Then he approached the yew-tree, and from the gnarled wood about the gaping hollow removed other fragments, red and pallid, in which yellow hairs were caught. These went into the second box.

He peered down into the hollow trunk. When his face met the light again, it was frowning. He measured across the mouth of the hollow and made a note, and looked up to contemplate Underwood dreamily. 'Well, well,' he sighed. 'This bein' thus, this is all.'

'It's flesh, that stuff, is it?' Underwood asked, in a voice of horror, as they walked away.

'Yes, I think so. However. A little laboratory work is required. Get on the phone to Mr Lomas, and tell him to keep close contact with Colborn and Deal. Then come on to me.'

About half past ten Reggie walked out of his laboratory to the room in which Underwood sat waiting. 'Have you proved it, sir?' Underwood asked eagerly. 'Mr Lomas has just been on the phone again, but you said not to disturb you.'

Reggie took the telephone. 'Is that Lomas? Fortune speaking. Fragments from yew-tree and ground both human tissue: traces of glands in neck.'

'Thanks very much.' A chuckle came from Lomas. 'Nice wedding-present for Mr and Mrs Colborn.'

'What? Who? When? Where?'

'Can it be you didn't foresee this, Reginald? Are you only human after all? You disappoint me sadly. While you've been finding human glands for him, Colborn has been marrying Ann Deal at the Marylebone registry office. Wedding breakfast at Scotland Yard, what?'

Reggie put down the receiver with a clash. 'Come on, Underwood,' he cried, and ran out.

His car brought them to the registry office just before a police car drove up with Superintendent Bell. A loafer approached them. 'Parties gone back to Dr Harvey Deal's house, sir. But Sergeant Smith said Colborn has sent luggage on to Paddington Station.'

'You follow 'em up to Deal's place, Bell,' said Reggie, and told his own chauffeur to drive to the railway station.

On the first departure platform there was a bustle of passengers about a long train to the Devonshire coast. Reggie wandered along with Underwood at his heels till they came to a first-class carriage where a man dressed as a chauffeur stood waiting on guard over luggage which filled the corner seats. Reggie passed on, got into another carriage, and walked back down the corridor, looking in at the luggage as he passed, turned into a neighbouring compartment and sat down. Other people came along the corridor, this way and that.

The chauffeur moved away from the train, lifting his hand. Colborn and Ann appeared, hurrying to him, with a porter who carried more luggage. Colborn spoke to the chauffeur and dismissed him. In the same moment Bell pushed through the crowd and clapped his hand on Colborn's shoulder.

Then Reggie got out of the train and whispered to Underwood, and Underwood slid away and vanished.

Colborn was in a red, stammering fury. Ann clung to his arm. 'No use making a row,' Bell told him. 'Come along, you and your lady.' Detectives closed about them and shouldered a way through the gaping crowd.

Reggie touched Bell's arm. 'And their luggage, please. All the luggage,' he murmured, and watched while it was collected. 'Put it into my car. I'm coming on.'

Three suitcases, a woman's dressing-case, and a square, wide-mouthed bag were in front of him when he drove away. It was the bag which he picked up. He opened it, looked inside, made a small unhappy sound, and still looked long. When he shut the bag again he lay back and closed his eyes, and his round face had a melancholy calm.

Still in a dreamy melancholy he entered Lomas's room carrying that bag. 'Good fellow!' Lomas smiled at him. 'Made a kill at last, what? They tell me Bell's just brought in the happy pair.'

'I suppose so. What about father-in-law—and father?'

'Deal? Oh, we've collected him. I was just going to put 'em through it. But let's get the interpretation of your medical evidence.'

'Yes! That is required,' Reggie's eyelids drooped. 'Not from me, though. Evidence short and sweet. Woman found in trunk was drowned, and on her body vegetable matter like that in the pool. On a yew-tree there, and below, I found, today, human material which came from the interior of a human neck. Old Deal and young Colborn should be asked to explain these things. Also one other thing.' He laid upon Lomas's table the wide-mouthed bag. 'This was found with Colborn's honeymoon luggage. You remember the unknown person who dodged round the pool carried a squarish bag.' Reggie opened it. 'Look.'

Lomas looked, and drew back with a start—gasped. 'Good gad! The head!'

'Yes. I think so. Head of young woman. With yellow hair. Provisionally, fitting body. Face obliterated by vitriol.'

'And that devil Colborn was taking it on his honeymoon!'

'Explanation certainly required,' Reggie murmured.

Colborn was brought into a room where Lomas and Bell sat together with Reggie lounging behind them, the bag on the floor at his feet.

Colborn let out a storm of abusive threats: it was a blank outrage, they had no right, he would give them hell for it, he—

'I am investigating a murder,' Lomas said. 'I have to ask you to explain your actions. Where were you going?'

'I was taking my wife to Dartmouth. I have a yacht there.'

'Really?' Lomas put up his eyeglass. 'Spending your honeymoon at sea?'

'What about it?'

'You didn't tell me you were going to marry Miss Deal. Why not? You didn't tell me you would be at sea tonight. Why not?'

'What the devil is it to do with you?'

'You had been asked to identify a woman's body.'

'And I couldn't. Nothing more to do with me.'

'You said you were unable to recognise that headless woman as Nurse Benan. The woman had been drowned, and on the body were water-weeds like those in your swimming-pool. Beside that swimming-pool we have found fragments of flesh from a human neck. Can you give me any explanation of that?'

The freckles on Colborn's face stood out tawny against pallor. 'What do you say?' he stammered. 'It's mad.'

'No explanation. Very well. The luggage which you and your wife were taking with you to sea has been brought here.' Lomas reached down and put the bag on the table, and opened it. 'Will you give me your reason for taking that?'

Colborn bent forward, saw the dark, misshapen face, cried out an oath, and flung himself back. 'I—I wasn't taking it,' he stammered. 'I never saw it before. That bag's not mine.'

'Not—yours,' Lomas sneered.

'Not ours, damn you!' Colborn roared. 'It's been planted on us.'

'Oh. Who would be likely to plant it on you?' Reggie asked. 'Can you think of anyone? Well, well. Do you recognise the head?'

'Who could recognise it?' Colborn growled.

'Not easy. No. Features chemically obliterated. However. Anyone else connected with you missing besides Nurse Benan? Anyone else about your place with fair hair?'

Colborn glowered at him. 'I say that bag's not ours. I know nothing about it.'

'Better try Deal, Lomas,' Reggie said.

'Quite. Your answers are unsatisfactory, Mr Colborn. You'll be detained.'

'All right. Do your damnedest,' Colborn said loudly. 'What about my wife?'

'She will be detained too,' said Lomas.

As another storm of abuse broke, Reggie went out. A detective was waiting outside the door. 'Anything for me?'

'Yes, sir. Urgent from Sergeant Underwood. He asked for a couple of men to Garnet Mansions, Kennington, and said to let you know.'

Over Reggie's face came a dreamy smile. 'I wonder,' he murmured. 'Lead me to it.'

A detective beside the chauffeur conducted his car to a shabby road in which blocks of flats rose among small old houses. They stopped at the corner of it and walked on to the entry of Garnet Mansions. Underwood came out from behind the stairs. 'He's here in the top flat, sir. Took it furnished from the regular tenant. Name of Edgar Smith. Nothing known about him.'

'Well, well. Let us call on Mr Smith.'

They went up the greasy stone stairs and on the last landing another man joined them, and whispered: 'He's still there all right. He hasn't shown.'

They rang at Mr Smith's door, waited, rang longer, and were not answered. Underwood banged on the panels. The door was opened a little way; a thin, dark face looked round it; an angry voice asked: 'What do you want?'

Underwood and his men pushed in, thrusting before them into the fusty sitting-room of the flat the man who had opened the door, a swarthy man in blue serge. 'I am a police officer,' Underwood said. 'Mr Edgar Smith, I presume?'

'That's my name. What can I do for you?'

'I'm here to ask you where you got the bag you left in a first-class carriage at Paddington this morning?'

The man laughed. 'Oh, that! That's all right, officer. Dr Deal gave it to me to take to Mr Colborn. Sit down. I'll tell you. Have a drink?' He turned to a gimcrack sideboard, and opened one of the cupboards. Reggie moved to the table.

'No drinks, thank you,' said Underwood. 'Come on.'

'Oh, just a spot.' The man laughed, and turned with a bottle and glass in his hands. As he poured the liquor, Reggie plucked off the tablecloth and flung it over his head, and ran at him from behind and pinned his arms.

'Keep clear of the fluid, Underwood,' he cried. Bottle and glass were knocked down and sulphurous fumes rose. Handcuffs snapped on the man's wrists.

Reggie drew back. 'Thanks very much.' He made a little bow to the pinioned man, who grinned and trembled.

Underwood looked down at the smoking, yellowing carpet, and looked at Reggie. 'Oh, yes.' Reggie nodded. 'Vitriol. Meant for you. As used on detached head. Bring her along. She's a felt want.'

'What, sir?' Underwood gasped.

'My dear chap! Oh, my dear chap! Let me introduce you to Nurse Sybil Benan.'

And she began to laugh.

Reggie came into Lomas's room and sank into the biggest chair. 'Where the deuce have you been?' Lomas exclaimed. 'Why did you cut out?'

'Not my job. Your job.' Reggie gazed at him with sad eyes. 'Are we down-hearted? Yes.'

'It is the devil of a case,' Lomas said. 'But I put the wind up Deal, Reginald. And he's told a fool's tale. You remember you asked Colborn if any other woman about the place was missing, and that gravelled him? Not a bad line.'

'My dear chap! You flatter me.'

'I worked that with Deal. And he said old Colborn had a housemaid who'd been discharged for a row with the nurse. I asked what the row was, and he tied himself in knots. I take it that housemaid had her suspicions there was dirty work. She may have tried blackmailing Deal.'

'Yes, it could be,' Reggie murmured. 'I wonder. I always wondered who wrote that anonymous letter which set us going.'

Lomas frowned. 'Damme, do you ask me to believe Deal? What he's after is to make out the housemaid murdered the nurse for revenge, and put it on Colborn and him to make the revenge complete.'

'Ingenious fellow. No. I don't ask you to believe that. Housemaid did not murder nurse. Because Nurse Benan isn't murdered. She's in the cells by now. With black hair and a brown face. But it'll all come out in the wash. Nurse murdered housemaid.'

'Good gad!' Lomas flung himself back in his chair. 'How the devil have you got to that?'

And Reggie told him. 'Bag containin' head was put into the carriage where Colborn's luggage was by a person of middle size in a long coat. Bag and person thus recalled the loiterer with intent round Colborn's place at night. I sent Underwood to see the person home. Person, when embraced by me in the act of throwing vitriol, was found to be female. As expected. Nurse Benan. Kindly convicting herself by possession of head and vitriol. Quite clear now. Nurse Benan, havin' helped old Colborn out of life, which we shall never prove, meant to marry young Colborn and the fortune. She probably tried blackmail for services rendered. He preferred Ann Deal, and he's not a man to be blackmailed. Nurse Benan had lost, and she's not a good loser. Remember the vitriol for Underwood. And she had the housemaid on her shoulders. Probably wanting blackmail also. One brilliant stroke of murdering the house-maid and putting the murder on Colborn and Deal would settle accounts all round. Nurse Benan made it so. She had funds, you remember. A thousand-pound legacy from old Colborn. Even if Deal didn't pay her any hush money. She took the second flat disguised as a man. She'd cut off her hair in the first flat. An error. I found very short yellow hair on her brush. That compelled my attention. However. She also left evidence of a letter making appointment with Sam Colborn by the swimming-pool. Very ingenious. But that also both-ered me. Too convenient. She got the housemaid to call on her in the second flat. Knocked her out and drowned her in the bath. Cut off the head, cut up the knee with the skill of a nurse, and obliterated features by vitriol. Daubed the body with stuff from the pool, collected on the night of the party when we weren't watching. My error. Your error. Dumped body in the trunk from a little old car she has. Then tried to plant head by the swimming-pool. But you had forgotten to remove the watch on the gate. She was nearly caught, head and all, by your active and intelligent police officer, while trying to poke it into the hollow tree. It didn't go easy. Too big. Head had still to be disposed of. Bold and brilliant stroke to plant it on the honeymoon couple. If they were stopped—Colborn was taking the head to throw overboard from his yacht. If they weren't—head would be found in the train they'd travelled by. Clever female. Rather underratin' the male intelligence. As they do. However. Can't blame her. Bad case, Lomas. Very bad case. One of our gross failures. Full of encouragement to the criminal mind.'

'Failure?' Lomas exclaimed. 'Damme, it's great work, Reginald.'

'Oh, my Lomas!' Reggie groaned. 'Frightful. Exemplar of futility. We shall never know the truth of old Colborn's death. We've let a poor wretch of a woman get murdered. And all we do is to hang another. An awful warning. Hopeless trade, our trade. Change the uniform of the police. Should be sackcloth and ashes.'

A Question of Timing

Phyllis Bentley

Like C. S. Forester, Phyllis Eleanor Bentley (1894–1977) became a successful novelist in a field other than detective fiction. The daughter of a mill owner, she grew up in Halifax, and after publishing several books made her breakthrough with *Inheritance* (1932), the first of three novels which formed an exceptionally popular saga about a West Riding mill-owning family called the Oldroyds.

Bentley seems to have had no ambitions to become a detective novelist, although she did write a novel of Gothic suspense, and a juvenile mystery that was nominated by the Mystery Writers of America for an Edgar award. Over a period of more than thirty years, however, she wrote a long series of short detective stories featuring Miss Marian Phipps. Rather like the more famous Miss Marple, she makes effective use of her understanding of human nature to solve crimes. Sixteen of the tales are collected in *Chain of Witnesses: The Cases of Miss Phipps* (2014); the editor, Marvin Lachman, an expert on the short form, describes them as 'some of the best detective stories published in the second half of the 20th century'. This obscure but pleasing tale, which does not feature Miss Phipps, first appeared in the *Poppy Annual* for 1946.

Life's a funny thing. Sometimes there are holes in it big enough to drive a bus through; nothing seems to tie up with anything, if you know what I mean. At other times it works on a mighty close schedule, ties everything up tight without an inch to spare. Yes, indeed; life or fate or whatever it is can time things to a split second. Or if it's chance that manages these things, then it's funnier still.

A month or so ago, one Thursday afternoon, I stopped a murder. But when I think what a chance it was, what a near thing, what trivial things it all depended on—well, I get shudders down my spine.

I'm a writer of sea stories, no great shakes, Robert Beringer by name. I've always done a bit that way—writing I mean—ever since I ran away from the top form at school to sea out of sheer dreaminess, and lately I've taken to it altogether. I have a room in London not too far from the Thames, and when I get stuck in a story, then I go down the hill, wind myself through all that muddle of trams on the Embankment, nip across Westminster Bridge, and limp up and down that stretch of promenade beside the river in front of St Thomas's Hospital. It's quiet there. No traffic; only the river, grey and streaky if it's on the ebb, full and rippling if the tide's going upstream. Across the river there are the Houses of Parliament in a long grey row—the little pointed turrets or minarets or whatever you call them look well against almost any sky. At the end there's Big Ben, which I've always had a fancy for ever since hearing him once on the radio when coming in after a nasty time in convoy across the Atlantic. (It was the next convoy when we were torpedoed, I got my foot crushed, etcetera, and had to leave the sea for good.) Then there are the barges moored together in rows, and little tugs fussing up and down, curtseying their funnels to pass under the bridges, and sometimes police launches, very swift and spick. On the other side of the walk there's the hospital wall and the hospital, which as you know had a bad time during the war, so the river face of it seems quiet. The walk itself is emptyish in the afternoons; on the seats are sometimes a few mothers with babies in prams, some lovers, an invalid or two taking the air in the shelter of the hospital, and walking along will come a father-mother-little-girl selection in good coats who've never been there before and are looking about and liking it, or an occasional man-with-dog. But they're all spaced out, never more than two or three at a time. Not enough to disturb the great mind at work, wrestling with a recalcitrant character or twist of plot.

Well, this Thursday I speak of, I was in the middle of chapter fourteen, blockade-running in the Spanish Civil War, and going on fine. A whole lot of new stuff had come into my mind with a rush while I was shaving that morning, and I couldn't get it down fast enough. At midday I took a sandwich at the desk and went on working.

I had got to the part where the hero, a Merchant Navy man like myself, was about to get engaged to the girl, when the mechanism stuck. I couldn't make those two understand each other to save my life. I struggled a bit; smoked a cigarette, walked up and down, looked out of the window with my hands in my pockets, counted the plant pots on the balcony opposite, and was pleased to see that the dry little sticks in them were beginning to show green. Then I sat down, doodled heavily at the corner of a clean sheet of writing-paper, threw it away, stretched out my hand to the cigarette pack and found it empty.

That settles it, I thought. I put the lid on the typewriter and the paperweight on the typed sheets, turned out the cat and took my hat down from the peg. I debated whether to take my coat, looked at the spring sunshine and decided against it. I'd got down three or four stairs when the telephone bell rang and I had to come back. It proved to be a wrong-number call and didn't detain me long. Just a few seconds.

In the street I found the bright sun was a bit deceptive. There was quite a cold wind blowing, dust rising, smoke careering across the sky. I cursed, for I knew I couldn't risk it without a coat—the Atlantic in mid-winter had seen to that, even though it was all more than three years ago now. 'You should have noticed all those weather signs from the window,' I told myself as I ran back upstairs. 'Call yourself a writer! Call yourself a sailor!' This little vexation made me particularly noticing for the rest of the afternoon, if you know what I mean.

Well, I got my raincoat and ran down again and called in at the tobacconist's round the corner for some fags, had a bit of a clack with him as usual, and set off for my river promenade. The two rows of trams seemed particularly tangling that afternoon; I can't risk much at traffic-crossings, you see, with my tiresome foot. But at last I got across and set off up the Embankment. The tide was flowing and tugs drawing barges were belting up the river with that pleased self-important virtuous look tugs always have. Some seagulls were flying about, screeching, and I stopped to watch. I always wish Walt Disney would do a film about a seagull, and as I stood there I began to imagine how such a film would begin. That delayed me quite a bit, you see.

At last I got to my promenade on the south side of the river. I walked along at a thoughtful sort of pace, stopping at times to look at Big Ben's gilt faces, the westerly one shining in the sun. The place was very empty, it being at a dead time of the afternoon now between three and four when grown-ups are at work, and the day a bit blowy for babies. However, as I went along I saw a youngish fellow, about the mid-thirties I should say, leaning up against one of those tall pillars with dolphins curling round them (very natural too from what I've seen of dolphins) holding glass globes for lights.

'Come now, do your stuff,' I said to myself, being still vexed over my mistake about the weather. 'Be a writer if you can't be a sailor.'

So I observed him, as they say, pretty closely. He was a nice-looking chap, fairish and fair-complexioned, clean-shaven, broad-shouldered, rather above middle height, wearing a blue demob suit. One of his hands, which rested on the parapet, was wound round with a clean bandage, figure-eight style, with some iodine-stained cotton-wool sticking out over the fingers, and a couple of neat turns round the wrist. (I had eighteen months of bandages with my foot, so I know all the bandage lingo.) He had nice firm-set ears, judging from the one I could see. I noticed the ear because that was the view he presented to me; he was flattened sideways between the dolphin pillar and the parapet, rather as though he wanted to hide.

At that I fell to wondering what in fact he was doing, for he couldn't see much from where he stood, and as for sheltering from the wind, that he certainly was not, for the wind was blowing the way I was walking, upstream straight on to him. I got an odd impression he was listening for something, though what he could be listening to or for, in the middle of an empty stretch of embankment, with one man about fifty yards away on a seat and nobody else at all until a seat right at the far end where there seemed to be a woman in a bright blue coat with a child, I really could not see. However it wasn't my affair—as I thought.

'If you'd come round the other side of that dolphin,' I mentally urged him, 'it would be far more effective, believe me, than turning up your collar against the breeze as you are doing now.'

However that was his affair and I walked on, and presently came up level with the man on the seat.

Conscientiously I turned on him my writer's eye. First I thought he was young, then I wasn't sure he was as young as I'd thought. He was dark and small and slight, with pointed features, and had a nice smooth pink cheek, like a girl's, but somehow he looked as though he'd seen a good deal of life. Sophisticated—in fact, almost raffish. He was well turned out; smart cigar-brown suit, shoes and hat to match, striped old-school-looking tie though I daresay it wasn't, fawn shirt very clean, and a fine new off-white raincoat, I noticed this raincoat particularly, because my raincoat had been like that when it was new, before the buttonholes frayed and the straps for the belt came unhitched and the whole thing got dirty. I must say I gave his raincoat an envious, not to say, jaundiced, look, and wondered how it was some people contrived to be clad from head to toe in brand new clothes in spite of coupons, while others like me looked thoroughly shabby. He stared back at me rather insolently, I thought, but perhaps I'd fixed that raincoat rather too long and covetously.

When I'd got a few yards past him I quickened my pace, because now the girl in the blue coat who had been sitting down at the far end got up and began to walk away, holding the child by the hand; and I saw that she was Gerda. I whistled after her, a special whistle which Frank (her husband) and I had always kept for each other; she heard and turned and came towards me, and we met halfway.

Gerda has always been the only girl in the world for me, ever since Frank introduced me to her seven years ago, at the end of our first voyage together. They were already engaged, and anyway Frank was the better man, so there was never any hope for me; but that didn't prevent me feeling the way I did about her, and she knew it, though there was never a word spoken about it between us. Meeting her now always brought it all back—the torpedo I mean, and being in the water with Frank and seeing him get knocked on the head by a bit of wreckage, and towing him towards the corvette which was megaphoning at us impatiently (for the U-boat was still lurking about with plenty of torpedoes left) and helping him up the swaying rope-ladder and being so thankful when we reached the deck. It was all no good though; we buried him two days after, at sea. Gerda wasn't the lively-looking girl now that she was when I first saw her, of course. There were the two children—this one running about with her now was the younger, Frank had never seen him, the other was at school. She had lost her husband, dearly loved (as they say on gravestones) if ever a man was. Her brown eyes had an anxious kind of look and her colour was a little faded and there was even a thread of grey or two in her dark hair. But to me she was Gerda; and to tell you the truth one of the reasons why this riverside walk was a favourite of mine was that I knew she sometimes came there of an afternoon with the little boy. Her uncle and aunt, who had brought her up, had a little house in the Elephant and Castle district, and she was living with them.

Well, so Gerda and I met and had a word or two. The kid, Frankie by name, is my godson and naturally I take a special interest in him. A fine little fellow he is too; very small when born owing to Gerda's upset about Frank, but a fine bouncing three-year-old now. Fair hair like Frank's, brown eyes like Gerda's, rosy cheeks, chubby knees, a very sweet smile somehow when he looks at you, and as much energy as a dynamo. He ran to me now and jumped up and down all round me, and I pretended to lunge out at him with my fist, and he laughed and jumped away and came back asking for more, and Gerda looked at him proudly and smiled, and I smiled too and felt happy. Then Gerda asked after my foot and cough, and to put her off I asked after Dorothy—that's her little girl. This was a mistake, because Gerda started and looked at her watch and said she must go, it was getting time for Dorothy to be coming home and she liked to be there to welcome the kid. She took Frankie's hand and began to walk pretty quickly towards the way she'd come, and I walked along with her. I didn't say much; I was turning over in my mind a question I'd turned over many and many a time before: namely, had I the right to ask Gerda to marry me or hadn't I? A lame foot—though it's true the doctors said it would be right again eventually and certainly it was improving—and this tendency to bronchitis or whatever it was owing to the icy Atlantic water, etcetera, and then no steady job, only this writing business though there again it was sometimes very profitable. I've had an adventurous roving life since I first went to sea and adventure stories seem to come natural to me. Still, it didn't add up to much to offer a woman. I loved the kids as though they were my own, and if Gerda had to marry anyone else I guessed Frank would like it to be me. But I was always diffident where women were concerned. And then, with no steady job and my foot—however, I've said all that before. I wouldn't bother you with it only I just want to explain how it was that when we reached the end of the promenade where it debouches on to the Lambeth Road by the little floating dock, we stood a minute. I had my hand on Frankie's shoulder to delay him and Gerda a moment, trying to decide whether to speak of marriage or not, and Gerda was looking up at me, as I know now hoping I would. I couldn't manage to get out the words, and so I gave a kind of sigh, and said: 'Well, goodbye for the present, Gerda,' or words to that effect, and we parted. I walked back down the prom towards Westminster, and she turned off south towards her aunt's home.

I was a bit upset in my feelings, and didn't notice much of anything at first, hobbling pretty briskly along with my hands in my pockets and my eyes so to speak turned inwards to my mind. I did seem to feel in a half-conscious way that the promenade was very empty. Oh yes, I thought, coming to myself a bit, neither of those men is in sight. Nobody is in sight at all. This is the seat by the bombed bit, where the raincoat man was sitting. Now where's *he* gone, I thought. He's been pretty nippy if he's got right down to the far end by now. Must have gone over the wall into the hospital grounds, I thought—not meaning it, really, just being sarcastic to myself. And where's that chap by the dolphin? Vanished too?

Just then—you'll remember I was now facing the wind—something, a bit of white with a tail, came blowing along the ground towards me, bouncing the way things do before a gusty breeze, sometimes partly trailing, sometimes quite off the ground. It came dancing up to me in company with a lot of dust and an old tram-ticket, skipped across my left shoe, caught a gust and sailed right up into the air over the parapet towards the river, then dropped out of sight.

Ah, I thought. Um. Well. Now what was that, and why does it seem to strike a special note? But good God, I thought, stopping so suddenly I almost fell over my own feet, that was a bandage. That fellow by the dolphin—that was his bandage. But what... But where... But how...

The next few minutes passed like a dream. Without exactly thinking what I was doing, I did a good deal. I sprang to the parapet and looked down, and there sure enough was the dolphin fellow in the water, drowning fast. I could see just his shoulder and sleeve, and then one glimpse of his white face, unconscious, with blood on it, before his body sort of rolled over and submerged, in the sickening way drowning bodies do. For a moment it seemed Frank all over again and I couldn't take it, but habit tells; I found myself sprinting back to the next dolphin post, where there was a lifebuoy in a little wooden cover, and pitching it down into the river and tearing off my coat and following the buoy.

Then it was easy, really. The flowing tide brought him right up into my arms, as you might say, and I got the buoy over him and partly tied him to it by the belt of my raincoat—though how I'd thought quickly enough to plan all that out and bring the belt down with me I just don't know. The tide took us up-river and I helped it as much as I could, and soon enough we were washed up at the little landing-stage, and there we were hauled out by the crew of a police launch, who by one of life's ironies had seen me dive into the river and thought I was an intending suicide and swished across to stop me disposing illegally of myself. They were pretty well puzzled by the set-up when they saw their suicide swimming a strong backstroke towards them, dragging a buoy and a chap with a wound in the back of his head. But as soon as we were near enough to see faces, one of them exclaimed:

'My God! It's Denholme!'

They popped us both into their launch and there were explanations all round.

It seemed this Denholme, the dolphin-bandage man, was a detective-inspector on the track of a black-market racket. One of the crowd had slammed a railway door on him the day before when he was getting rather too hot after them, which explained the bandage. He had tracked down the raincoat man to the embankment—it turned out afterwards that the heads of the racket used to meet there to make plans and hand over the cash. The raincoat man, seeing his danger and his chance, had tried to tip Denholme over the parapet and had succeeded in getting him off his feet; there was a bit of a struggle, the bandage got torn off, the raincoat man knocked out Denholme and gave him a final push. Risky proceeding in broad daylight? It certainly was, and yet nobody saw it. Nobody would have known a thing about it if I hadn't chanced to be walking by during those vital few seconds when the bandage blew along. I described the raincoat man pretty accurately, and the police did some rapid telephoning about him.

He'd got away (through the hospital grounds, it was thought) for that time; but give the police one end of a tangled thread and they'll unwind the whole skein in the end. Denholme recovered, the racket was smashed; I'm getting a life-saving medal, a reward, a clinking good plot for a story and the solution to my problem in chapter fourteen— which proved to be a matter of timing, which I'd got wrong before. I'm getting Gerda too. She read about the affair in the paper and came rushing round to see if being in the Thames had done me any harm. Well, it had thrown me back a bit and I was in bed, and when Gerda saw my room and the way I lived, she told me straight out I was killing myself, I needed home care, and she was going to give it me.

'You mean you'll marry me?' I said stupidly.

'What do you think I mean, Bob?' said Gerda, looking me straight in the eye with a smile.

So there it is. The wedding day is next Monday. But, heavens, when I think what a near thing it all was! The story getting stuck, the cigarettes running out, the telephone call, my coat, me being vexed about the weather and so noticing everything about the two men very particularly; the trams, the seagull, Denholme's bandage and me knowing bandages because of my foot; my talking to Gerda and playing with Frankie, the wind blowing just that way—it was a chance in a million to have synchronised all those properly and brought the thing off. Very messily planned, too, by life or fate or whatever you like to call it. Why bother with so much detail? Every story-teller knows that a big broad way of planning events is simpler, more economical, and far more effective aesthetically speaking, in the long run. Why bring in seagulls and bandages? Poor management on fate's part, I call it. Or if it was chance, then it's stranger still.

Anyway, there it is. A mighty close schedule. Timing to the dot. When I think what a near thing it was, as I say, I get shudders down my spine.

The Thimble River Mystery

Josephine Bell

Josephine Bell was the pseudonym under which Doris Bell Collier (1897–1987) established a reputation as a highly capable author of detective fiction. Like Arthur Conan Doyle, among others, she had previously worked as a physician; her principal series character, David Wintringham, was also a doctor. Over a span of twenty-one years, Wintringham appeared in a dozen books, including *Murder in Hospital* (1937) and *Death at the Medical Board* (1944).

Bell's career in the genre lasted forty-five years, during which time she produced forty-three novels, in addition to numerous short stories. She was elected to membership of the Detection Club in 1954; the previous year she had become a founding member of the Crime Writers' Association. In 1959, she had the distinction of becoming the first woman to chair the CWA, her predecessors having been John Creasey, Bruce Graeme, and Julian Symons. This story originally appeared in the *Evening Standard*, it was included in *The Evening Standard*

Detective Book (1950), and six years after that it resurfaced in a landmark anthology, *Butcher's Dozen*, which Bell co-edited with Symons and Michael Gilbert. This was the first anthology to appear under the auspices of the CWA, which continues to publish collections of members' work to this day.

The Thimble River, running out into Southampton Water, is, like most of the small rivers and creeks of that inlet, as of the Solent, much frequented by yachtsmen. Though it winds for more than five miles inshore and is fed at its upper end by a small stream, which earns it the superior title, it is tidal throughout its length, with a considerable rise and fall, that leaves on the ebb a wide stretch of mud at each bank, where much unlovely junk reveals itself, and the seagulls spatter up to their ankles, looking for titbits in the black ooze. At either side of the deep channel there is a continuous line of fixed moorings, bobbing unused and lonely during the short bitter days and black nights of winter, when all but the biggest yachts are laid up on shore, but in the summer serving to keep their charges in a lovely unbroken line of many-coloured hulls, and tall masts, and graceful cobwebs of rigging. On the shores are the various yards, boat-builders' sheds for construction and maintenance and repairs, and slips for launching or hauling out, and jetties and landing-stages running down to the water. Round these the yachts' pram dinghies cluster all through the season, in a constant traffic to and from the boats moored out in the river.

Most of the boats, whose owners are at work elsewhere during the week, go out only at the week-ends, and for an annual cruise, coast-wise or across the Channel. But some, whose owners have no other home or occupation, or who prefer and can afford to spend the summer afloat, make their yachts their home, coming ashore regularly for their milk and newspapers and stores, perhaps going off for a day's sail, or even moving to another port for a week or two, but on the whole staying where they are, comfortably isolated, wholly master of their world.

Of these Mr Harcourt was the best known and the most notable throughout the length of the Thimble River. He had lived in his yacht, *Helena II*, winter and summer since the end of the Second World War, when the boat-houses, cautiously, because of the necessary restrictions on wood and paint and labour, had begun to put the pleasure boats back on the water. It was said that his son had been killed in the war, and his wife had died at the end of it. His boat, not new, had been laid up for years. She leaked like a sieve when they first put her in the water to test her. But re-caulked and re-fitted, scraped down and painted, she might have been her old self when she was finally out on her moorings, though her lines looked a bit old-fashioned now beside the newer designs all round her.

Tom Winter, who ran the boat-yard and owned the moorings in front of it, was proud of his work of restoration, and pleased to see *Helena II* so smart and like her old self. He often said it gave him a queer feeling not to see the three Harcourts on deck together as in the old days, casting off for a trip to France, or tying up after a week-end down at Yarmouth, Isle of Wight, or busy just fixing the gear, or polishing the bright work.

For Mr Harcourt was very particular about the way his boat was kept. *Helena II* might be old, built in the early twenties, before the Bermuda rig became almost universal. But she still looked smarter than many of the other yachts at Winter's yard, whose owners came down in a hurry on Friday night and sailed hard till Sunday evening, and scrambled ashore in the dusk, to get back to their homes in time to start work again on

Monday. Mr Harcourt had always insisted on absolute order above and below. Order and polish and spotless decks and shining paintwork. Now that he was alone the work took up most of his time. When his friends arrived to crew for him, at those times when he wanted to sail, they were filled with admiration and astonishment. To Mr Harcourt their remarks seemed unnecessary and rather foolish.

One evening, when the old man, rag and can in one hand, for he had just finished oiling a sheet winch, leaned against the combing of his cockpit, idly trying the winch with the other hand, he heard the sound of oars, and looked up to see John Chudley, in his dinghy, pulling past him. Chudley owned the next boat downstream from *Helena II*, and, as he lived in the neighbourhood, was able to get the little jobs on board done in the evening, after he got back from his office in Southampton.

Mr Harcourt did not always feel sociable, but today he decided that he would like to have a chat with young John. He had thought of a way his neighbour might solve one of his problems without too much expense, and by doing his own work. So he put away his oil-can and rag and, going forward along his decks, gave the young man a hail.

John Chudley had nearly reached his own boat by then, and did not feel like going back.

'Care to come aboard for a drink?' Mr Harcourt shouted.

Chudley stopped rowing, smiling and wondering whether to accept.

'I've got an idea for fixing your spinnaker halliard,' went on the old man. 'But don't come if you're pressed for time.'

That decided John. Invitations from Harcourt were rare. The old boy led a lonely existence; perhaps he felt it more often than any of them imagined.

'Thanks awfully,' he said. 'I'll just dump this stuff, and come over.'

A few minutes later he arrived alongside *Helena II*, breathing hard from his stiff, though short, pull against the tide. He found two fenders in place to prevent his pram dinghy scraping the spotless white paint of the yacht's topside, and smiled to himself as Harcourt took the dinghy's painter and made it fast so that the dinghy was carried out behind by the swift current.

'Will you come below, or have it up here?' asked Harcourt.

Chudley had been indoors at his work all day, so they sat in the cockpit and sipped their drinks, while the evening sunshine lay horizontal across the river, turning the white hulls to gold, and the gathering force of the ebb gurgled and slapped its way past, swinging *Helena II* from side to side on her mooring chain. The air was still: not a breath of wind stirred on the glassy water near the shore. Mr Harcourt's burgee hung limp against the mast.

The old man delivered his advice about the halliard, but after that they said very little. Conversation is for the cabin. Sitting in the cockpit with the river and the shipping all about them there was no need of it.

John Chudley finished his drink and as soon as he thought it civil to do so, excused himself on the grounds that he had a lot to do on board his boat and very little time to do it in.

'There'll be trouble at home if I'm not back in good time for supper,' he said. 'And anyway I've only got another hour of the tide.'

Mr Harcourt did not delay him, but drew his dinghy alongside for him, and held it while John climbed in and took up an oar.

'Give me a shove, and the tide'll do the rest,' John said, fitting the oar into the slot in the stern of his dinghy.

Mr Harcourt laughed, and walked up to the bows of *Helena II* to watch his guest moving swiftly across the short gap between their two boats. When Chudley was aboard his own craft he waved to him, called 'good evening,' and picking up the glasses out of the cockpit, went below.

Just after seven John Chudley got back into his pram and rowed away to the landing-stage. He was rather glad that Mr Harcourt was below, because he was in a hurry. He had wasted precious time on that drink on *Helena II*. He hoped the old man was not going to make a habit of hospitality.

He need not have worried, because by the next morning Mr Harcourt was dead.

Bob Goacher was an apprentice in Winter's shipyard. He was a keen, quick-witted lad, with a natural aptitude for working in wood. He already had an eye for it, both inherited and learned from his father, who was a joiner and carpenter. Bob had always intended to follow his father's trade, but living near the river had brought him into contact with boats from the start. He had gone bathing early, had learned to swim, and later to swim out and round the yachts. He had always admired their lines and their smooth shining enamel paint. Later he had acquired an old derelict dinghy for a few shillings, and mended her himself with his father's help, and fitted her with a sail made from a discarded piece of canvas, and took her out proudly, learning to use the wind to drive her along, instead of pulling his arms off with the two sweeps. After Tom Winter took him on, his ambition grew. One day he would have a boat of his own, a real boat. He was never tired of telling his friends and the men at the yard how he would build her, and where he would take her, and how much he despised and envied men like Mr Harcourt who could afford to keep a beautiful boat like *Helena II*, but hardly ever moved off the mooring.

On the morning after John Chudley had drunk with Mr Harcourt, Bob Goacher arrived at Winter's as usual at half-past seven, and as usual, when he had hung up his coat and put on his working dungarees, he opened the big doors at the river end of the shed and looked out across the water. He saw at once a thing that startled him, and waited with impatience for his employer to arrive.

Tom Winter came into the shed at eight to see that the tools were ready for the start of the day's work.

'Mr Winter,' said Bob, coming forward. 'When I got here I saw Mr Harcourt's burgee was still up.'

'Still—?' Winter looked at his watch, saw that it was barely eight, then walked down to the end of the shed and looked out. Across the water, at the masthead of *Helena II*, the small flag with its gay colours flapped in the morning breeze.

'That's funny,' he said.

'He's so particular,' put in Bob.

'You're right there. Looks as if it may have been up all night.'

'He can't have gone away, forgetting to take it down. He must be there. His dinghy is alongside.'

Tom Winter's face hardened.

'Hope the old boy's not been taken ill or anything. I think I'll go off and see.'

With one of the older men from the yard he went off in one of the yard's old grey dinghies.

And they found Mr Harcourt, fully dressed, lying on his cabin floor, with his head beaten in.

They went ashore, hardly speaking a word, and Winter left the other man on the landing-stage to watch anyone coming or going, while he himself went to his office to telephone to the police. In a short time Detective-Inspector Wright, with a police surgeon and two other assistants, arrived. Winter took them out to *Helena II*.

'Before you go aboard,' the latter said, 'I'd like to point out to you that mark on her topside. There, with the smear of green paint along it. Mr Harcourt was very particular about his paint. There'd have been hell to pay if anyone bumped his boat. He'd be equal to going for anyone who did it.'

'You mean there could have been an unpremeditated fight?'

'Yes.'

'I'll bear that in mind,' Inspector Wright said, and climbed on board the yacht.

Later, when the party landed again at the stage, the man who had been left on guard stepped forward and whispered to Tom Winter.

'If you've anything to say, say it to me,' said Inspector Wright, severely.

The man reddened, but he spoke up at once.

'It's just that I saw you looking at that scrape on the top-side,' he said. 'I noticed it myself, same as Mr Winter. And I've been having a look round these prams.' He pointed to the little ships' dinghies, clustered about the stage. 'There's one of them got a white mark on her. It shows because she's painted green.'

'Green!' exclaimed the Inspector, going over to look.

'That's Mr Chudley's,' said Winter, slowly.

'Oh, dear,' said Jill Wintringham at breakfast in her pretty dining-room in Hampstead. 'John Chudley seems to be involved in that affair at Thimble, after all.'

Her husband handed her a letter he had just read, and took the newspaper she gave in exchange.

David read the paragraph she had seen. It was an account

of the inquest on an elderly eccentric named Harcourt, who for the last nine years had been living on board a yacht in the River Thimble, ten miles from Southampton.

His body had been found two days before in the cabin of his boat. A sum of money had disappeared.

The account went on to say that death was caused by a fracture of the skull inflicted by an undiscovered weapon. Verdict—murder by some person or persons unknown.

'Thank God the coroner's jury has been reasonably cautious,' said David, when he had finished the paragraph.

Jill nodded.

'Poor John,' she said. 'What a thing to be mixed up in. Shall you go down?'

'Oh, yes. The sooner this is cleared up the better.'

'You don't think the local police will be competent?'

'I resent the sting concealed in that remark. I have a perfectly open mind about the local police, but John wants me to go down, and he's in a spot, and—'

'Of course you must go, darling,' said Jill, soothingly. 'I'm not trying to stop you. And I think it's a very good thing we've been crewing for the Foresters so often the last two years, and know a little bit about boats now.'

John Chudley met David at Southampton with a car, and drove him to his house above the Thimble.

'How did you get mixed up in this at all?' David asked him.

Chudley answered, 'My boat happens to be moored next to his. I went aboard him that evening for a drink, round about six, but I didn't stay long. Actually I was going off to my own boat when he called me on board. As I had things to do I got off to my own boat after a brief chat, and stayed there till just after seven. I couldn't stay longer than that on account of the tide.'

'Why?'

'The landing-stage at Winter's is on the mud at low water: you can't approach it from the river without wading ankle-deep in mud.'

'That must be very inconvenient sometimes.'

'It is. Perhaps one day Winter will add a piece to his stage.'

'So anyone coming down after you left would not have been able to take a boat away from there?'

'No. Not until there was more water as the tide came in.'

'A couple of hours later?'

'At least that.'

'About this burgee. Mr Harcourt was one of these types who observe the strict drill, I suppose? Flags down at sundown, whatever time that is, and up at 08 hours precisely?'

'Yes.'

'So that the burgee being left up suggests he was killed before sundown. About nine that evening.'

'Then it must have been after seven-fifteen. I was near enough in my boat to have heard anyone going aboard his.'

'And you would have seen a visiting dinghy alongside him as you left to go ashore.'

'Of course.'

'And according to you no one could have gone off after you before the tide made the landing-stage unusable, at least for a few hours. But you got in, didn't you? Couldn't someone have gone down directly after you left and still got off?'

'I doubt it. I had to punt myself over the mud the last few feet, and it dries out very quickly after it reaches that point. The sheds were all locked up, so there wasn't anywhere for anyone to hide. I met no one in the lane coming down from the main road.'

'So you were the last person to see him except the murderer. I suppose that has made the complications for you.'

John Chudley nodded.

'There is a scrape on the old boy's topside with green paint in it. My dinghy is the only green-painted one at the yard. And that's another thing. Harcourt wasn't expecting his visitor, or he would have been up on deck hanging out fenders to prevent just such a scrape.'

Next morning David made his way to the boat-yard early, and after explaining to Winter who he was, persuaded him to take him off to the yacht.

Helena II, he found, was an old-fashioned, gaff-rigged cutter. He noticed that all her many halliards and other ropes were tied out to the shrouds to prevent them banging against the mast: a sensible precaution to take for one who lived on board, and wished to avoid the annoyance of tapping and rustling noises transmitted down the mast into the cabin.

David's eyes followed the thin hoist of the burgee from a cleat to which it was fastened at the foot of the mast up to the little flag, still flapping above the masthead. Evidently no one had thought of taking it down since Harcourt's death.

Turning away, David went carefully over the decks, find nothing of interest until he came to the shrouds on the starboard side. There he checked, stopped, and gathered from the wire, near its foot, a few thin strands, the frayings of a fine rope.

After this he got back into the dinghy, where Winter had been sitting all this time watching him.

David looked him in the eyes.

'Do you think Mr Chudley did it?' he asked.

There was no answer.

'You don't want to suspect him, but you can't be sure he didn't. Any motive, that you know of?'

Tom Winter made up his mind to talk. His words came with a rush.

'I'd have said it was impossible, only Mr Chudley is so dead set on sailing. He needed a lot of repairs this year, and I put them in hand for him. But I'm a small concern and I have to be paid for my material as I go along. Mr Chudley couldn't manage the figure I gave him, so the work had to be suspended *pro tem*.'

'I'm here as Mr Chudley's friend,' said David. 'As I told you. I've not even made contact with the police yet. You may not want to tell me anything if you have your doubts of Chudley, but it would help a lot if you would say what you know about this money that is supposed to have been the incentive.'

'I don't see any harm in that,' answered Winter. 'Mr Harcourt was very regular in his habits. He didn't come ashore more often than he could help, and he only went into Southampton once a month for stores and that. I think he always got his money on these trips, because he'd come into my office and pay his bill for the moorings, and any odd jobs we'd done for him. Regular as clockwork. And he always had a tidy bit of money with him those days.'

'The day of his death was one of those days?'

'Yes. And I noticed he had a lot of money in his wallet, more even than he usually did. There were a lot of five-pound notes, besides the usual thick wad of pound notes. I wasn't really surprised because he was planning to go off down west to the Helford River for a month, starting at the next week-end, when he had a crew joining.'

'I see. Have you any idea which bank he used?'

'Oh, yes. It was on his cheques. We'll get back on shore, and I'll give you the address.'

With this written down on a slip of paper David was leaving the office when he paused and looked back.

'I suppose no one else saw that money?' he asked.

Winter's face showed his annoyance. David repeated his question, adding, 'The police will be sure to ask. It might help to get things clear first.'

Tom Winter nodded.

'They did ask,' he said. 'I told them what I'm telling you. Young Bob Goacher, one of my apprentices, came in just as Mr Harcourt peeled off one of the single notes to give me. He must have seen, too. Couldn't have helped it.'

'Do you mind if I have a word with him?'

'I'll take you down to the shed. Whether he'll speak up or not is his affair.'

Goacher was in the boat-builder's shed, at work on a new fourteen-foot sailing dinghy. David went up to him and began, first of all, to admire his work.

'She'll be a nice job,' agreed the young man, shortly. He seemed disinclined to talk. But as David continued his praise he dropped his reserve and became enthusiastic in his turn.

Very soon he was describing the sort of boat he meant to have for himself, and this seemed likely to continue indefinitely when he suddenly broke off with a muttered 'Castles in the air.'

'Oh, I shouldn't say that,' said David easily. 'You might win your football pools, or get left a legacy.'

Bob swung round on him.

'What do you know?' he asked quickly.

'What about?'

'People are saying I did the poor old beggar in to get his money. I did a lot of odd jobs for him one way and another. He used to say as a bit of a joke, "I'll remember you in my will, Bob." I never took it seriously. Now they're saying I did.'

'Do they say when you are supposed to have done it? Mr Chudley tells me the yard people went home at six and there was no one here when he tied up at seven-fifteen.'

'That's right. But I came back. Mr Harcourt wanted his accumulator. It was being charged and it wasn't ready earlier. I fetched it here from the shop, and took it out to him at half-past seven. Just handed it to him and left.'

'How did you get out over the mud, and back?'

The lad grinned.

'It wasn't quite dried out. But I had to get ashore climbing from one to another of the rest of the dinghies. I doubt anyone could have done it after me.'

'Until well after sundown?'

'That's right.'

David next visited the bank where Mr Harcourt had kept his account. After a few words of explanation to the manager he was allowed to see Denton, the cashier who had served Mr Harcourt on the day he was killed.

'Denton is not allowed to tell you anything about Mr Harcourt's account,' said the manager, as he moved towards the door of his room in order to leave the two men together. 'In fact he will have very little to tell you, I'm afraid. The police told us to say as little as possible to the Press.'

'I'm not the Press,' said David, 'as I told you before. I'm a friend of John Chudley's.'

'We'd like to oblige Mr Chudley,' said the manager, in a guarded manner, 'since he's a customer of ours, too.'

When he had gone David turned to the cashier.

'How many of you are there working here?'

'Just the manager and one other clerk and myself. You see, we're only a small branch for the convenience of people further out. The main branch is in the City centre.'

'I see. Now tell me about Mr Harcourt's visit.'

Denton drew a deep breath.

'The old gentleman came in according to his usual habit at one o'clock precisely. I was on duty. I generally take the one to two break while the manager is out to his lunch. I go off twelve to one. The other chap and the young lady also go from one to two. We do practically no business during that hour.'

'Are you quite alone in the bank at that time?'

'The porter is back. He's handy if wanted.'

'So Mr Harcourt cashed his cheque at that time. Was he the only customer in the bank?'

'Except for Mr Chudley. He was there, too, and spoke to Mr Harcourt. He was in very good form; we had our usual little chat about sailing.'

'Ah!' said David. 'You are one of the breed, are you?'

'I'm very keen. I have a twelve-foot dinghy of my own.'

'Where do you keep her?'

'At Thimble. That's about two miles down-stream from where Mr Harcourt's yacht is.'

'I'd like to see your boat,' said David.

They agreed to meet at Thimble village pub near the riverside at six that evening.

Denton's boat was on a mooring amongst a fleet of other small craft. David was surprised to see that her mainsail was bent on and neatly rolled under a sail-cover.

Denton borrowed a pram and rowed David off.

'I haven't got one of my own,' he explained.

'But you prefer a mooring?' asked David politely.

Most small craft, like this twelve-footer, were pulled up on the hard after use, and the sails and halliards taken away and stowed in the boat-house. It was better for the sails, and prevented weed growing on the boat's bottom.

'Yes,' Denton answered the question. 'I think so. I can go out without wasting time. Less risk to the paint, too. Besides, I'm hoping to have an all aluminium boat before long, larger than this, of course. I secured a mooring when one was available. They are not so easy to come by.'

The two men climbed into the sailing dinghy. She was a smart little craft, painted bright red, with chromium fittings and an aluminium mast.

'I'd like to take you for a sail, and show you what she can do,' Denton said. 'But the tide's still running down for three hours or more, and there doesn't seem to be much wind, and what there is will probably drop in the next hour or so. With no wind and no motor we couldn't make up against the tide.'

'Pity,' said David. 'Another time, perhaps.'

He touched the neatly stowed halliards, all grouped round the aluminium mast.

'I've enjoyed seeing her,' he said politely.

Denton put him on shore, whence he made his way back to Chudley's house. After dinner he got his friend to take him to the police station.

'You're in the clear, old boy—I think,' he explained, as they drove along. 'But the moment has come to declare myself to the official mind, and persuade them how right I am.'

'But it's less than twenty-four hours since you arrived,' said John, doubtfully.

'You've no idea how co-operative everyone has been,' David answered.

At the police station David saw Inspector Wright and explained his position in the case, and also who he was, and why Chudley had asked for his help.

'We know all that,' said Inspector Wright. 'You've been noticed here and there today, and we took the trouble to check up with Winter for the name, which rang a bell, so we were able to get the rest. You have a reputation for poking your nose into this sort of thing, Dr Wintringham.'

David laughed. The Inspector's voice was genial; opposition might not be severe.

'Was that why the bank manager was so cagey?'

It was the Inspector's turn to laugh.

'I'll let you into the detail of the money. Harcourt cashed a cheque for sixty pounds that morning. He spent ten pounds on stores and small bills, Winter's among them. The other fifty has gone.'

'Apart from the bank the only people who knew he had all that money were the people he paid in cash, including Winter, and the ones who saw it, Chudley at the bank, and Goacher at the yard.'

'That's right.'

'About Harcourt. He was fully dressed, wasn't he? That and the evidence of the burgee puts the time early in the evening.'

'His clothes wouldn't. The only irregular thing in his habits was his bed-time. Oh, and his meals. People have seen the light on in his cabin well into the small hours. Not that anyone seems to have noticed it that night. He was getting a bit eccentric the last few years. Not surprising, with his history.'

'So he could have been attacked during the night, when the tide was up again. Provided someone remembered to hoist his burgee again, too. The weapon went overboard, presumably.'

'Not in the vicinity. At least, we've not found it. But it might be anywhere in the river.'

'And the motive was unquestionably money?' said David.

'We haven't come across any other,' said Inspector Wright.

'My friend John, and the boy, Bob Goacher, both have that motive. Winter complained of being short on capital, too. All of those could do with more money. But so, perhaps, could Denton, the bank cashier.'

'Could he?'

'I'm not sure. It's very possible. I can't prove it, but you could.'

'I don't know,' said Wright, eyeing David closely. 'He lives very quietly, he's a bachelor, he pays all his bills, his only hobby is sailing.'

'He wants a two-and-a-half-ton all aluminium yacht,' said David.

The other smiled.

'They all want more than they can afford in the way of boats. It isn't often serious.'

'In the case of these four it was serious enough to drive one of them to murder,' said David.

There was silence for a time, then the Inspector said, 'You've worked out the points about the ebb, I see.'

'I have. But according to my theory they don't matter.'

'No. But have you anything to support it?'

'The evidence is rather slender,' said David. 'Literally slender.'

He produced a few frayed wisps of rope from his wallet.

'These came off Mr Harcourt's boat. Identify them, and I think they will lead you to agree with me.'

He described his visit to the yacht that morning.

'I see what you mean,' said Inspector Wright. 'But I'm dashed if I can see how we can make anything out of it.'

'I'll tell you,' said David.

The next morning Chudley, Goacher, Winter, and Denton were taken out separately to *Helena II*, in turn, and then, after being brought back to land, to the police station.

David followed them there, and on arriving found Chudley, Goacher, and Winter sitting together in the charge-room.

'Where is Denton?' he asked.

'In the superintendent's office. He said would you please go in, sir. This way, sir.'

Denton, white-faced and cringing, swung round as he entered. David looked at him.

'You didn't take enough trouble, Denton,' he said. 'It was quite a neat idea to put up the burgee again after you killed Harcourt. It muddled the time. It made it seem impossible for anyone from your part of the river to come up by water and do it before sundown. There was no wind that evening, we know. You were lucky with the medical evidence, too. It is not always easy to put the time of death within a few hours, and Harcourt must have had his last meal particularly late that evening, which was a bit of luck for you at the post-mortem. You were helped by the fact that Mr Chudley and Goacher both visited the yacht between six and eight, when you were known to have been playing around in your own dinghy down at Thimble. Also your boat is red, and by using Mr Chudley's green dinghy to bump the yacht's side you again suggested local effort. Going off, from Winter's yard, as you did, some time early that night, you had enough water to use the landing-stage and keep the mud off your clothes. You saw his cabin light on, and knew he was up, so you had your weapon handy and your plan of action prepared. You scrambled on board *Helena* quickly, not caring if you bumped her or not, or was that devilishly deliberate? You must have flung a loop of the dinghy painter round the nearest stanchion to make fast, jumped up over the rail, and struck down Mr Harcourt as he began to come up on deck to see what was happening. You took the money and put out the cabin lights. You flung the weapon in the river—or did you row farther off, afterwards, to sink it where it couldn't be picked up? But you ought to have known Mr Harcourt better. You ought to have got to know his yacht better before you tampered with her. Because several people knew him and his ways and his boat very well indeed.'

'You're mad,' Denton spluttered. 'I don't know what you mean.'

'Read him what the other three said,' David suggested.

The Superintendent took up three pieces of paper which Inspector Wright pushed along the desk to him.

'Chudley, Winter, and Goacher all state the same things,' the Superintendent began. 'They were asked separately this morning, as you were, to put down anything unusual you saw on the yacht *Helena*. You put down one word: Nothing. They all pointed out that the burgee hoist is at present fastened to a cleat at the foot of the mast, whereas Mr Harcourt invariably fastened it to the shrouds on the starboard side. He had a thing about halliards flapping. He tied all his strings out away from the mast.'

'That was what I noticed,' said David. 'And moreover, I found some frayed bits of rope on the shrouds. They tally with the hoist, don't they, Superintendent?'

'That's so.'

'Just because you make fast your own burgee halliard to a cleat on your mast is no reason you should do so on another boat. Every man has his own way of fixing things. You ought to have remembered that and gone to look first. After all, you knew it would be dark when you planned to go off to kill an unsuspecting, defenceless old man, in order to steal his money. The money you had counted out to him yourself that very morning.'

'I didn't,' said Denton, breathlessly. 'That's no proof. I didn't notice that burgee halliard, I didn't notice anything wrong, but why should I? I've never been on that boat in my life.'

'Someone put the burgee up again. The man with a motive for murder. You, Denton.'

'Why me? I only saw him once a month. What did I know of his affairs? What should I do it for, anyway? I had no motive.'

'I'm afraid you had,' said David.

He looked at the Superintendent, who nodded to him to go on.

'Your own story of your times of work at the bank showed me that for an hour every day you had the bank to yourself. You *could* have indulged in a spot of embezzling if you had wanted to.'

'And you did,' said Inspector Wright, leaning forward. 'Your manager had already found the leak, and he was expecting you to do something about it, though he naturally never thought of murder. He came to us a couple of days after the murder, because he found that some of the trouble had been put right. That gave us ideas, but there didn't seem to be anything to go on until Dr Wintringham came along with his theory about the burgee.'

'I didn't pin it on Denton until he showed me his own boat,' said David, determined to be honest. 'Seeing his own halliards stowed round the mast, and knowing from the wisps of rope that Harcourt had been in the habit of tying out his burgee halliard like his other ropes, it was obvious.'

'You devil!' the cashier gasped. 'You treacherous devil!'

'That's enough of that,' said the Superintendent.

Denton was charged with the murder and removed. The Superintendent said, 'You'd never think a sailing man would do such a thing.'

'He sailed for show,' said David. 'Haven't you seen his boat? Vulgar little piece, she is. Not the design, of course. The way he had her. Good varnished wood wasn't flashy enough for him; he had to have red paint. And he kept her in the river, away from the other dinghies; fully rigged, too, as if she was a cruising yacht, not a twelve-foot sailing dinghy at all. Also he told me he wanted a bigger craft, all alloy. Metal boats are pretty expensive.'

The Superintendent said, 'I congratulate you, Dr Wintringham. They all have pretty good alibis for that night, and now we know which we have to break. Save us a lot of time. Your observation lets the other three out, too, at the same time it puts Denton in.'

David smiled, then turning to Inspector Wright, said, 'Does that lad, Bob Goacher, really get a legacy from the old man?'

'I believe he does,' answered the Inspector.

'I'm glad of that,' said David. 'He'll build his dream boat with it.'

'And most likely take her out to sea and drown himself.'

They all laughed.

Man Overboard

Edmund Crispin

Robert Bruce Montgomery (1921–78), like J. I. M. Stewart, used his real name for his 'serious' work and a pseudonym for his detective fiction and for his work as an influential anthologist of science fiction. Montgomery was a successful composer, who wrote concert music and film soundtracks; the latter include the music for six *Carry On* films, the thriller *Eyewitness*, and *The Brides of Fu Manchu*. Today he is remembered principally for his detective stories written under the name Edmund Crispin. David Whittle's biography, *Bruce Montgomery/Edmund Crispin: A Life in Music and Books*, was published in 2007.

The Case of the Gilded Fly (1944) introduced the Oxford don and amateur sleuth Gervase Fen, who appeared in all nine of Crispin's novels and the overwhelming majority of his short detective stories. A sparkling blend of wit and ingenuity became Crispin's hallmark. His third novel, *The Moving Toyshop* (1946), benefits from an especially intriguing puzzle and the entertainment value of Crispin's mysteries was consistently high. Poor health and alcoholism meant that after 1951 he published only one further novel, and he died at the age of fifty-six, but his books have enjoyed continuing popularity over the years. 'Man Overboard' was first published in the *Evening Standard* in 1954 and subsequently included in the posthumous collection *Fen Country* (1979).

'Blackmailers?' Detective Inspector Humbleby finished his coffee and began groping in his pocket for a cheroot.

'Well, yes, one does of course come across them from time to time. And although you may be surprised to hear this, in my experience they're generally rather nicer than any other kind of crook.

'Writers of fiction get very heated and indignant about blackmail. Yet, by and large, it's always seemed to me personally to be one of the least odious and most socially useful of crimes. To be a blackmailer's victim you do almost invariably have to be *guilty* of something or other. I mean that, unlike coshing and larceny and embezzlement and so forth, blackmail has a—a punitive function—

'Naturally, I'm not claiming that it ought to be encouraged.' Having at last disinterred his cheroot, Humbleby proceeded to light it. 'At the Yard, we have plenty of occasions for thinking that we're being deprived of evidence against a suspect in order that someone else may use it for private profit.

'On the other hand, a blackmailer can *acquire* such evidence more easily than we can—not having Judges' Rules to hamper him—and like Socrates in the syllogism, he's mortal. The death of a known blackmailer is a great event for us, I can tell you. It's astonishing the number of "Unsolved" files that can be tidied up by a quick run through the deceased's papers.

Sometimes even murders—Saul Colonna, for instance; we'd never have hanged him if a blackmailer hadn't ferreted out an incriminating letter and then got himself run over by a bus.'

'Two Armagnacs, please,' Gervase Fen said to the club waiter. 'Colonna? The name's vaguely familiar, but I can't remember any details.'

'It was interesting,' said Humbleby, 'because the incriminating letter didn't on the surface *look* incriminating at all… There were these two brothers, you see, Americans, Saul and Harry Colonna. They came over here—their first visit to England—early in April of 1951, Saul to work in the office of the London correspondent of a Chicago paper, Harry to write a novel.

'New country—fresh beginning. But they'd hardly had a chance to unpack before Harry succumbed at long last to the cumulative effects of his daily bottle of Bourbon. With the result that *his* first few weeks among the Limeys were spent at a sanatorium in South Wales—Carmarthenshire, to be exact: no alcohol, no tobacco, lots of milk to drink, regular brisk walks in the surrounding countryside—you know the sort of thing.

'Harry didn't like that very much. His brisk walks tended to be in the direction of pubs. But at the same time he did acquire an awe, amounting almost to positive fear, of the formidable old doctor who ran the place. So that when at last he decided that he couldn't stand the régime any longer, he felt constrained to arrange for a rather more than ordinarily unobtrusive departure, such as wouldn't involve him in having to face a lot of reproaches for his failure to stay the course. Quite simply, abandoning his belongings, he went out for one of his walks and failed to return.

'That was on the afternoon of 7 May. About mid-day next

day, *both* brothers arrived by car at Brixham in Devon, where they took rooms at the Bolton Hotel; for after only a month's journalism Saul had been sacked, and so had been free to respond to Harry's SOS from the sanatorium, and to assist in his flight. Once in Brixham, they proceeded to enjoy themselves. Among other things, they bought, actually *bought*, a small Bermudan sloop. And did quite a lot of sailing in it...

'Then, on the evening of the 12th, having ignored numerous warnings from the weather-wise, they got themselves swept out into mid-Channel by a gale. And in the turmoil of wind and darkness Harry was knocked overboard by the boom and drowned.

'That, at least, was Saul's account of the matter, when the Dartmouth lifeboat picked him up; and it was a credible story enough. Even the subsequent discovery that Harry's life had been well insured, and that Saul was the beneficiary, failed to shake it. If a crime *had* been committed, it was undetectable, the police found—with the inevitable result that in due course the insurance companies had to pay up. As to the body, what was left of that came up in a trawl about the beginning of September, near Start Point. By then there wasn't much chance of diagnosing the cause of death. But the teeth identified it as Harry Colonna beyond any reasonable doubt...

'So that without Laking, that would have been the end of that.

'Barney Laking was clever. He was a professional, of course. Though he'd been inside several times, he always went straight back to blackmail as soon as he'd done his term... So you can imagine that when a number 88 ran over him, in Whitehall, we lost no time at all getting to his house. And that was where, among a lot of other very interesting stuff, we found the letter— *the* letter.

'To start with, we couldn't make anything of it at all. Even after we'd linked the "Harry" of the signature with Harry Colonna, it was still a long while before we could make out what Barney had wanted with the thing. However, we did see the light eventually… Wait and I'll do you a copy.'

And Humbleby produced a notebook and began to write. 'I looked at that letter so hard and so often,' he murmured, 'that it's engraved on my heart…'

'Envelope with it?' Fen asked.

'No, no envelope. Incidentally, for the record, our hand-writing people were unanimous that Harry Colonna *had* written it—that it wasn't a forgery, I mean—and also that nothing in it had subsequently been added or erased or altered… There.'

And Humbleby tore the sheet out and handed it to Fen, who read:

You-Know-Where, 6.5.51
Dear Saul,

I'm just about fed with this dump: time I moved. When you get this, drop everything and bring the car to a little place five or six miles from here called Llanegwad (County Carmarthen). There's a beer-house called the Rose, where I risked a small drink this morning: from 6 on I'll be in it: Private Bar (so-called). Seriously, if I don't move around a bit I'll go nuts. This is urgent.

Harry.

'M'm,' said Fen. 'Yes. I notice one thing.'

'Actually, there are two things to notice.'

'Are there? All right. But finish the story first.'

'The rest's short if not sweet,' said Humbleby. 'We had Saul along and confronted him with the letter, and of course he said exactly what you'd expect—that this was the SOS Harry had sent him from the sanatorium, properly dated and with the distance from Llanegwad correct and so on and so forth. So then we arrested him.'

'For murder?'

'Not to start with, no. Just for conspiracy to defraud the insurance companies.'

'I see... Part of it is simple, of course,' said Fen, who was still examining Humbleby's scrawl. 'When an American uses "6.5.51", in writing to another American, he means not the 6th of May but the 5th of June... On the other hand, Saul and Harry, having settled in England, may have decided that it would save confusion if they used the English system of dating all the time.'

'Which is just what Saul—when we pointed the problem out to him—told us they had decided to do.' Humbleby shook his head sadly. 'Not that it helped the poor chap.'

Fen considered the letter again. And then suddenly he chuckled.

'Don't tell me,' he said, 'that 6 May 1951, was a *Sunday*?'

'Bull's eye. It was. Sunday in Wales. No pubs open for Harry to have even the smallest of small drinks at. Therefore, Harry was using the American system of dating, and his letter was written on 5 June, four weeks after he was supposed to have been swept overboard into the Channel. Insurance fraud.'

'And Harry getting restive in his hideout near the sanatorium, and Saul suddenly thinking how nice it would be not to have to share the insurance money...'

'So back to Brixham, unobtrusively, by night, and out to sea again in the sloop. And that time,' Humbleby concluded, 'Harry really did go overboard.'

'And you have found enough evidence for a murder charge?'

'As soon as we stopped worrying about 12 May, and started concentrating on the period after 5 June, we most certainly did. Mind you, it *could* have been difficult. But luckily Saul had had the cabin of the sloop revarnished at the end of May, and we found human blood on top of the new varnish— not much, after all that time, but enough to establish that it belonged to Harry's rather unusual group and sub-groups. Taken with the other things, that convinced the jury all right. And they hanged him…

'But you see now why I'm sometimes inclined to say a kind word for people like Barney Laking. Because really, you know, the credit in the Colonna case was all his.

'Even if I'd possessed that letter at the outset, I could quite easily have missed its significance. I only worked hard on it because it had come from Barney's collection, and I knew he didn't accumulate other people's correspondence just for fun.

'But *he* had no such inducement, bless him. With him it was just a consummate natural talent for smelling out even the most—the most deodorised of rats. What a detective the man would have made… Do you know, they gave me a full month's leave at the end of that case, as a reward for handling it so brilliantly? And it was all thanks to Barney…'

And Humbleby reached for his glass. 'No, Gervase, I don't care what novelists say. I like blackmailers. Salt of the earth. Here's to them.'

The Queer Fish

Kem Bennett

Kem Bennett (1919–1986) is possibly the least celebrated of all the authors whose work appears in this volume, although in his day he achieved a measure of success. I confess that I'd never heard of him until Jamie Sturgeon drew my attention to this story, which first appeared in *Argosy* in 1955, and pointed out that it uses a trick subsequently employed, in a slightly different way, in a novel by Andrew Garve. Bennett's full name was Kemys Deverell Bennett, and he came from St Ives. He wrote a handful of novels, not all of them criminous, and his interest in maritime matters is reflected in several of his publications, including a book called *Look at Rescue at Sea*.

'The Queer Fish' was filmed in 1956 as *Doublecross*; Bennett worked on the screenplay, and a strong cast included Donald Houston, Fay Compton, Anton Diffring, William Hartnell and (long before that more famous film about sailing misadventure, *Jaws*) the young Robert Shaw. A handful of his other scripts were televised during the 1950s, and he also wrote the screenplay for the film *Timebomb*, a.k.a. *Terror on a Train*, which starred Glenn Ford, and concerns a plan to blow up a train loaded with sea mines.

At five-thirty the buzzer went and Albert Pascoe stopped shovelling china clay in the hold of the Danish freighter *Langeland*. At five-thirty-five, in company with fifty other dockers, and with a quarter-litre of smuggled aquavit in a tomato-ketchup bottle in his pocket, Albert walked past the policeman on duty at the dock gates. Then, and then only, did he permit himself to let go a breath of gusty relief which shifted a cloud of white dust from the hairs of his stubby moustache.

The ferry was waiting. Albert went aboard, a short, stiff man in middle age, filled with good nature, argument, and Cornish independence. When they were halfway across the estuary, Harry Sims, the ferryman, came up. 'Evening, Albert.'

'Evening, Harry.'

'They'm running, boy.'

Albert blinked at the ferryman. 'They be?' He went to the side and stared down into the clear water, thinking of great silver fish. A moment later he thought of his fine net, hanging in the woodshed behind his cottage, and of his boat, moored half a mile upstream. Then, sourly, he remembered Herbert Whiteway, the water-bailiff, and spat his disgust overboard.

The law said that the salmon had to be left in peace to finish their journey to the spawning-grounds at the head of the Fowey River. The law enforced its opinion with the threat of a fifty-pound fine. Albert winced; then spat again, in disgust and for the more practical reason that he needed to rid his throat of a layer of china clay.

The ferry came to a stop at the slip below Pendennick,

whose single street plunged like a madman's ski-jump. Albert paid his fare—a penny—and started to clump slowly up the hill to the top, where lay his cottage and where the rolling Cornish farmland started, with its fat cattle, gull-dotted ploughland, and sleek hawks sitting on the telegraph posts. Presently he pushed open the door of his whitewashed cottage. Children fluttered into movement like a flock of starlings and he patted heads absentmindedly. At the stove, Alice turned from frying chipped potatoes. She looked down at him. 'You're back then.'

'Arrh,' Albert said, smiling sheepishly. For fifteen years his beloved wife had been making him feel sheepish. He no longer minded, for it had become a habit, like having children, drinking beer, smuggling aquavit, poaching salmon, and keeping his nose clean. 'What's for tea?' he asked.

'Nice bit of pollack and chips.'

He nodded, without vast enthusiasm. 'Salmon are running.'

Alice turned. Six feet two. Built like an oak tree. 'Let 'em run,' she said. 'You leave your net be, d'you hear?'

'Yes, my dear,' Albert said, then added with grievance in his voice, 'Who said aught about the net? Never crossed my mind.'

Alice grunted. 'Go and get washed. Tea's nearly ready.'

Shortly after seven that evening, Albert shut the door of his cottage behind him and started downhill towards The Lugger. As he walked he leaned slightly backwards to compensate for the gradient and brought his best drinking-boots down hard, so that the nails would bite. He had the ketchup bottle in his pocket and at the back of his mouth there lingered the regurgitant sweetness of well-fried potatoes. He was content.

There were six other customers in the public bar of The Lugger—three regulars, two strangers, and Herbert Whiteway, the water-bailiff. Albert ignored Whiteway; he was not yet in the mood to start pulling his leg, which was all the man was good for. Instead, from his favourite seat on a high-backed oak settle by the fire, he surveyed the strangers. There had been a fat new car outside, he remembered. They must belong to it.

They had white faces and soft hands and their clothes were uncomfortably new. They were restless and when they spoke they did so in undertones. They were drinking brandy, which was unheard of in The Lugger, and they didn't even look as if they were enjoying it. City fellows. No concern of his—not until April, anyway. In April Albert would cease to be a docker and become a boatman instead. Then strangers would have some interest for him, if they wished to go out fishing or take a trip to Polperro or Mevagissey; now they had none.

He dismissed the two men from his thoughts as if they had already returned to London, or Mars, or wherever it was that they followed their mysterious livelihood.

Presently he took the ketchup bottle out of his pocket and stared at it. Unscrewed the top. Sniffed. He put the neck to his lips and tilted his head back. A fire started behind his uvula. Albert happily let it burn for a few seconds, then reached for the pint of bitter beer on the table in front of him. He quenched the fire. Vapours wreathed round the back of his palate. Arrh!

From across the room, Herbert Whiteway was watching, envy in his small eyes. Albert beamed at him. 'Physic,' he said. 'Doctor give it me for me guts. Proper tasty, 'tis.'

The bar shook with laughter. Only Herbert Whiteway did not laugh. Even the strangers smiled palely. Albert took out his pipe. He took a rope of twist from a tin in his pocket and cut slivers from it which he started to roll between the palms of his small, hard hands. Then he said conversationally, 'Harry Sims told me they was running, Herbert.'

Whiteway said, 'So they may be.'

''Tis early for they.' No reply. Albert took a pull at his beer and lit his pipe. 'If you ask me,' he said blandly, 'they'm not Cornish fish at all, boy.'

The bar was suddenly silent. It was the old joke; the good joke; the joke that never failed.

Whiteway fell for it, as usual. 'Gerraway!' he said. 'Talk sense, man.'

'They'm Canadian steelheads.' Albert's voice was pontifical, the voice of a man pronouncing dogma. 'They'm Canadians driven over by the porps, and as such they can be fished.'

Whiteway said nastily, 'If I catch you fishing them before February month I'll have you up before the Bench, all the same. Fifty pound or three months it'll cost you—unless you can get the fish to show a Canadian passport, ha ha!'

Nobody laughed. Albert stared at the bailiff, saying nothing. He let the poor joke fall, flatten, fail, and by its very failure recoil upon its originator. Then, at last, he said smugly, 'You didn't ought to make threats like that, boy. You'm a public servant. 'Tis up to you to keep a civil tongue in your head, now.'

There was a pause, loaded with hatred. Whiteway drained the half-pint of rough cider called 'scrumpy' that was all his parsimony would permit him to drink, and rose to his feet, a long-faced, stooping, miserable man.

'You're a poaching, sneering, smuggling good-for-nothing, Pascoe,' he said thickly. 'One day it'll be my turn to laugh, and I don't mind how soon it comes, so I'm warning you!'

The door slammed shut behind him. Albert stared at it sorrowfully. Always the same trouble; the man'd never stay to have his leg pulled proper.

'Arrh!' he said, 'the—!' and the word he used was libellous.

He tilted his ketchup bottle, wiped his lips on the back of his hand and glanced round the bar. 'Who's for a game of darts?'

At ten o'clock, time was called. The strangers had gone long ago. Only the regulars remained. They drained their glasses slowly, taking their time because beer tasted all the better after hours. Eventually they drifted towards the door.

Somebody said, 'Going upalong, Albert?'

Albert stood in the open door. The night was clear and soft and the stars were out. He was not drunk—half the contents of the ketchup bottle remained, scrupulously saved for another occasion—but he was warm with drink. He shook his head.

'Not yet awhile, Charlie,' he said. 'I got to fetch something from the boat. G'night, all.'

She was called the *Alice*, and she lay at her winter moorings half a mile up-river from Pendennick. She was the pride of Albert's life, a twenty-three-foot fishing-boat converted to a day cruiser with a small, stuffy cabin forward, a glassed-in shelter for the steersman, and a well aft from which the seats were removable when the space was needed for fishing. She had an old-fashioned main engine and a smaller, more modern wing engine. With both going the *Alice* could plough herself through the water at eight knots, but at that speed she was inclined to be smelly and she shook and chattered like a cement-mixer.

The tide was falling. Albert left the road and trudged across shingle to sit on a rock at the water's edge. He had lied when he said he needed to fetch something from the boat; in fact he had just wanted to look at her, to plan the things he would do to her when the time for refitting came, and to dream about Easter. At Easter the tourists started coming, which, for Albert, meant money in the pocket and, better still, liberation from the detestable necessity of working as a docker.

His pipe had gone out. Dreamily, Albert reached in his

pocket for matches. Then, without warning, a voice in the darkness behind him said, 'Don't move, please.'

Albert did move. He jumped uncontrollably.

A man appeared at his side. Albert looked up, his eyes wide with astonishment. It was one of the strangers who had been in The Lugger. The stranger had a pistol in his right hand.

Slowly, Albert put his unlit pipe in his mouth.

'Is that your boat?' the stranger asked. 'If so, my friend and I would like to hire her.'

'I'll not talk to 'ee till that pistol's put away,' Albert said grimly.

'Yes, you will.' The stranger's voice, in which there was a trace of foreign intonation, was harsh and cold. 'Be sensible. We can take the boat if we want to. We're giving you the chance to make a little money, my friend, and to keep your boat into the bargain. Is she seaworthy?'

'She be,' Albert said, with sullen pride in his voice.

'Would she take us to France?'

The pipe came out of Albert's mouth. 'To France! You'm reckoning to go to France—now, in my *Alice*?'

'Yes.'

'Arrh! talk sense, mister.'

'Will she get us there?'

Albert shrugged. He looked lovingly at the *Alice*, and pride stirred his tongue again. 'She would,' he said, 'but she aren't going to.'

'Why not?'

'Because, for one thing, 'tis agin the law.'

The man beside him smiled with one side of his mouth. 'We were in the inn tonight,' he said. 'From what we heard it did not seem that you were a man to take the law too seriously.'

Albert said nothing.

'If you'll take us to France we'll give you fifty pounds,' the stranger continued. 'If not, I shall have to shoot you before we leave because we cannot afford to let you raise the alarm.'

There was a long silence. Albert looked at the *Alice* and at the pistol in the man's hand. He scratched his nose with the stem of his pipe. An inward voice was telling him that this cool-tongued, white-faced stranger did not make empty threats. He would shoot, if necessary. And then Alice and the kids would be alone and he, Albert Pascoe, would be floating, face downwards, in cold, green water with the salmon flashing by on their way to spawn.

Sweat stood on his forehead. He made a sudden, violent gesture with his hand. 'You'm barmy! France! in the middle of the night with no charts!' He pointed his pipe at the *Alice*. 'She'm a day cruiser, mister. She don't belong to do this kind of thing.' A new thought struck him and he added flatly, 'Anyway, there's no more than a gallon of petrol in her tanks, so that's that.'

The stranger said quietly, 'We have petrol—fifty gallons in cans in the back of the car. The need for it had occurred to us.'

The silence returned. Albert shifted on his rock, restless, glancing at the pistol—and at the *Alice*, as if she might be able to tell him what he should do.

The stranger said impatiently, 'Well?'

Albert shrugged. 'Seems I shall have to take 'ee, mister,' he said sullenly. 'But 'tis agin the law and good sense, and you'll maybe not see tomorrow if the weather blows up.'

The stranger smiled. 'We shall be happy to take the risk,' he said. 'Now give my companion some help with the petrol.'

Fifteen minutes later the *Alice* had full tanks and a reserve of six four-gallon jerry-cans aboard.

While Albert made preparations to start the cold engines,

the stranger with the gun stood over him. The other man drove the car away and came back on foot.

Albert said, 'She'm ready to go now if you'm still set on it.'

'We are,' the stranger said. 'Do you know the French coast?'

'I been there.'

'Do you know of a place where you could put us ashore secretly?'

'I reckon I might find a place on the Brittany coast,' Albert said unwillingly. ''Tis a risky business, though.'

'How long will it take?'

''Bout fifteen hours, if the weather holds.'

There was a silence. Then the man with the gun snarled, 'Fifteen hours! You're lying! It should not take so long as that.'

Albert looked at him. 'I'm not lying,' he said quietly. 'If you reckon you'm able to get her there quickerer, you'm welcome to try.'

The back of the stranger's hand came slashing out of the darkness. It caught Albert on the cheek, knocking his head back and making his ears ring painfully. He made a noise in his throat and moved forwards, his hands reaching out. The black eye of the pistol stared at him. He dropped his hands.

'That was for insolence and to show you that we can be harsh if necessary,' the stranger said. 'Now let us go, and if I think you are trying any tricks I shall shoot you. Understand?'

Albert said nothing. He stooped to swing the handle of the main engine. It fired. He set the throttle and turned to the wheel. The second stranger cast off.

As the *Alice* pulled away from her mooring and turned down the estuary towards the sea, Albert was staring fixedly into the darkness ahead, the set of his lips making his moustache jut angrily forwards.

Two men saw the *Alice* creep out of Fowey harbour. One

was the coastguard on duty on the hill above the harbour mouth, who noted down that she had left but took no other action. The second was Herbert Whiteway. Having a one-track mind, Whiteway instantly jumped to the conclusion that Albert was out after salmon.

With excitement gleaming in his pale eyes the water-bailiff wrapped himself in many coats, got out his dinghy, and rowed quietly across the estuary to take up a position of concealment under the lee of the jetties opposite Pendennick. There he stayed, nursing the conviction that Albert was merely waiting for the tide to be right before he started netting.

In the early hours of the morning the south-westerly wind which prevails in Cornish waters sprang up and quickly freshened until it was blowing half a gale. When Herbert Whiteway got home he was a sadder and wetter, if not wiser, man.

However, at breakfast time there was something to cheer him up. He opened his morning paper to see headlines blacker than usual across the front page—CABINET MINISTER'S SUI-CIDE. BLACKMAIL SUSPECTED. And beneath the headlines two photographs, under which the text read:

THE TWO MEN ABOVE ARE WANTED FOR QUESTIONING AND MAY BE CARRYING VITAL STATE SECRETS. THEY WERE PREVENTED FROM LEAVING THE COUNTRY AT SOUTHAMPTON YESTERDAY, BUT BROKE CUSTODY, AND ESCAPED IN A STOLEN CAR.

A few minutes later, in the Fowey police-station, Whiteway leaned eagerly over the counter. 'Them two men,' he panted. 'I seen them in The Lugger last night.'

The policeman behind the counter was infuriatingly calm. He nodded.

'Yes, mate. So did the landlord. You'm a bit late.'

Whiteway scowled. 'Albert Pascoe took the *Alice* out last night,' he said with angry malice. 'She's not back yet. I reckon he took them two fellows with him.'

At half past two in the afternoon Albert cut the *Alice*'s wing engine and throttled down the main. It was blowing hard. The sky was leaden with racing cloud through which there were no gaps for the sun to shine.

A hundred yards away, waves with wind-broken crests crashed into foam against black needles of rock with cliffs behind them. But between the rocks there was a channel and beyond the channel fairly calm water and a cove with a gently sloping beach.

Albert went to the cabin door. 'We'm there,' he said. 'If you'm willing to risk it, I'll try to put you ashore.'

The two strangers were half sitting, half lying in a huddle of sick agony amid the litter of the cabin. The leader, the one with the pistol, looked up, swallowed bile frantically and lurched to his feet. When he was outside, Albert pointed. The stranger stared at the tumult of the waves and shut his eyes. 'France?' he whispered.

'That's right,' Albert said.

'Can you get the boat in… in there?'

'I reckon.'

The stranger nodded, gripping the side of the wheelhouse so hard that his knuckles were as white as chalk. Albert swung the *Alice*'s bows towards the little beach. White water broke over her. She staggered and yawed and swooped like a storm-tossed seagull, but she missed the rocks. Gently, gently, Albert nosed her into the beach. The strangers were ready.

Albert put his hand out. 'Fifty pound,' he said.

A sodden envelope came out of a coat-pocket and was pressed into his hand. In their waterlogged city clothes the two men clambered over the bows and lurched up the beach.

Albert shouted, 'Gimme a shove off!' but they ignored him. He spat. Then smiled a grimly happy smile. At least he was shut of them. That was good.

The *Alice*'s engines throbbed. Water boiled at her stern. Albert hopped over the side, heaved, hopped back in again, soaked to the skin. The *Alice* slid slowly backwards, her keel grating on the sand. Helm hard over. She came round. A tooth of rock reached out for her but she seemed somehow to dodge. She was in open water.

Albert rubbed the salt out of his eyes. He spared a glance over his shoulder and saw the two strangers searching for a way up the cliffs. He grinned again.

Then he opened the envelope he had been given. It was full of wet newspaper.

The police found the strangers' car hidden among bushes close to the place where the *Alice* had been moored. That was at nine o'clock in the morning. By ten o'clock messages had gone to London, and from London to Paris and Paris to Brittany. Watchers on the bleak Brittany coastline saw nothing of the *Alice*, nor of the wanted men.

The R.A.F. were asked to fly sorties in an attempt to locate the boat. They did, but the weather defeated them and they saw nothing.

Alice Pascoe spent the day in the coastguard's hut above Fowey harbour, having left her children in the care of a neighbour.

By half past six in the evening Albert was very tired. He had tied a loop of cord round his wrist and fastened the other end to one of the spokes of the *Alice*'s wheel, so that the tugging of the wheel would awaken him if he chanced to sleep.

The wind had lessened. The waves no longer showed white caps. The *Alice* rode the swell with a neat, swooping motion that would have unravelled the stomach of a landsman but which Albert found soothing. In spite of his tiredness he was glad—glad to be going home, glad to be alive, even glad, in a way that he did not fully understand, that the strangers had robbed him of his promised fifty pounds.

He up-ended his ketchup bottle for the last time at six-thirty-five, stared regretfully at its utter emptiness and pitched it over the side.

Dusk was coming down as he sighted the landmark of the Gribbin, a peak of black and yellow cliff two or three miles west of Fowey. He left the wheel for a moment then, and went to stoop in the cabin entrance in order to light his pipe. It was when he straightened, puffing hard, that he saw the first porpoises.

Three of their black backs wheeled a few yards away, the triangular dorsal fins cutting up, over, and down again into the water in a movement of slow poetry.

And ahead of the gliding porpoises a great salmon leaped. More porpoises wheeled. Another salmon broke the surface; then a third and a fourth—and the fourth was so close to the *Alice* that it almost jumped inboard.

Like a man in a dream, Albert flipped the throttles down and went to the cabin. After rummaging for a few seconds, he found the thing he was looking for, a rusty old gaff on the end of a six-foot pole. He went to the side of the boat and leaned over, staring fixedly down into the water. Porpoises and salmon showed nearby but he did not raise his head.

Then there came a gleam of silver and a splash right

under the lee of the almost stationary boat. Albert struck, his hands as skilled with the gaff as the hands of a pianist on the keyboard. He felt the gaff bite, and he gave a great heave, staggering backwards into the well of the boat.

He stared down with happy incredulity at the full-grown, twenty-pound cock salmon that he had snatched from the beaks of the porpoises.

Then alarm struck at him. Herbert Whiteway. Fifty pound or three months. He glanced about him. The sea was deserted. Arrh, who could have seen?

On his knees he touched the salmon. 'You'm a beauty, my dear. You'm a real beauty!'

They were waiting for him at the Town Quay—Alice, Herbert Whiteway, ten reporters, most of the inhabitants of Fowey, four dogs, and an Inspector of Police. Albert brought the *Alice* in smartly, hugging the splendid guilty knowledge of the salmon to himself. He cut the engines, flicked a rope's end round a bollard and made her fast. He stumped soggily up the steps and kissed Alice. Cameras clicked.

'I'm afraid I shall have to ask you to come with me, Mr Pascoe.'

Albert looked up into the face of the Police Inspector. He nodded. 'Now?'

'Yes.'

In the police car the Inspector said, 'You took two men in your boat last night…'

'I had to,' Albert said gruffly. 'They forced me with a pistol, like.'

'Did you land them?' The policeman's voice was urgent. 'Arrh.'

'Do you know exactly where?'

'Surely,' Albert said. 'I put they ashore in a cove, not far from St Levan.'

The Inspector peered down at a map on his knees, his forefinger following a coastline. Albert watched him. He coughed 'Excuse me.'

'Yes?'

'You got the wrong chart, sir. St Levan, I said. 'Tis not far from Land's End.'

The Police Inspector's head came up and the map of Brittany slid off his lap on to the floor of the car. His eyes were wide with astonishment. 'In Cornwall!'

Albert grinned. ''Twas when I last saw it,' he said, then added, 'I reckoned they two had no business to be asking to go to France in the middle of the night. I reckoned they was bad ones, so I went out to sea for an hour or two and then, when the weather worsened, I come round in a big circle.

'There was no sun to say I was changing course, and anyway they was proper seasick by then. Didn't ask no questions. I told they it was France and they went ashore. Glad to be on dry land, I reckon.'

He chuckled. 'If you'm after those two, sir, they'll be there still unless they swum for it. To my knowledge there's no way up the cliffs from that cove at all.'

As an honoured guest, Albert was driven back to the Town Quay after his visit to the police-station. With the Inspector's friendly hand on his shoulder he walked proudly through the still-waiting crowd.

But when he caught sight of Herbert Whiteway, he stopped in his tracks. The water-bailiff was standing in the *Alice*, his face gleeful with triumph and malice. Albert's salmon lay on a piece of sacking at his feet.

Albert swallowed. Dismay hit him, self-disgust, anger,

and a sense of bitter unfairness. Alice was there, her face glum with disaster. He looked at her for a moment and then lowered his eyes.

Before he could say anything, the Police Inspector's surprisingly soft voice sounded, 'Something wrong, Mr Whiteway?'

'Nothing wrong, sir,' Whiteway said creamily. 'I was watching Pascoe come in through my glasses and I saw him gaff a fish. I found this salmon hidden under tarpaulins in the cabin of his boat.'

There was a silence. Albert looked up. He took a deep breath and was about to launch himself into a futile defence on the grounds that the salmon was a Canadian fish when the Inspector said softly, 'Salmon? That doesn't look like a salmon to me, Mr Whiteway. I'd say it was a fine big bass.'

The water-bailiff stared. He lowered his eyes, glanced for a moment at the salmon at his feet, and looked up again. 'A bass!' he said squeakily. 'You mean…'

'I mean that as far as the police are concerned that is a *bass*, Mr Whiteway. I'm sorry to disappoint you. Good afternoon.'

Albert swallowed again. He looked at the Inspector, at Herbert Whiteway, whose mouth was hanging open, and at the salmon. For once he could think of nothing to say.

Alice stepped into the breach. 'I'll thank you to put that fish back where you found it, Mr Whiteway, and step out of our boat,' she said in a loud voice.

Then, as a roar of delighted laughter rose from the crowded quay, she went down the steps like a duchess, with Albert behind her, smiling.

The Man Who Was Drowned

James Pattinson

James Pattinson (1915–2009) was a Norfolk man whose most popular books were tales of adventure on the high seas. Educated at Thetford Grammar School, he nourished early ambitions to become a writer, but on his own account (quoted in his obituary in the *Daily Telegraph*) his younger days were devoted mainly to 'failing in the Civil Service examinations and poultry farming'. In 1939, he volunteered for the Royal Artillery, and in 1941 he was transferred to the maritime arm to serve as a gunner on Defensively Equipped Merchant Ships (DEMS). On D-Day, he was aboard a 600-ton coaster carrying ammunition to Normandy, and he also served on convoys in the Mediterranean and the Atlantic.

After the war he returned to poultry farming in Norfolk, but found that his war-time experiences supplied valuable raw material for fiction. His first novel, *Soldier, Sail North*, was set on the Arctic convoys to Russia and published in 1954. Once he had broken through, there was no stopping him, and the success of *Last in Convoy* (1958) enabled him to become a full-time writer. Poultry farming's loss proved to be fiction's gain, and he continued to publish novels until late in his long life. 'The Man Who Was Drowned' first appeared in the *John Creasey Mystery Magazine* in January 1958.

The man went overboard from the M.V. *Southern Star* at about 10.30 p.m. A woman was the only person to see him go, and she ran to the bridge and gave the alarm.

The officer of the watch acted promptly. The 15,000 ton liner turned in such a narrow arc and heeled over so acutely that some of the more nervous passengers thought she was about to capsize. Then she straightened, the propellers ceased to revolve, and the vessel came to rest on a sea so calm that scarcely a ripple disturbed its surface.

Searchlight beams cut silver paths across the water and two boats, slipping down from out-swung davits, thrust into the night, seeking one small body in an infinity of ocean.

But the Atlantic has an insatiable appetite for bodies: it had swallowed this man as easily as a whale will swallow the tiniest speck of plankton. After a long and fruitless search the boats returned. Dripping salt water, they were hauled up again, the davits swung inboard, and the *Southern Star* sailed on her way with one passenger the fewer.

At the time of the incident Barton Rice had been drinking the captain's whisky and smoking one of the captain's excellent cigars. Rice and Captain Perry were old friends, though two more dissimilar men, physically, it would have been hard to imagine: Rice, dried-up, stringy, unemotional: the captain, stout, red-faced, jovial.

Captain Perry poured whisky from a square-sided bottle and added soda-water with skilled hands.

'So it was business rather than pleasure that took you to Rio. Pity; it's a fine place for a holiday.'

Rice accepted the drink, wrapping his long, thin fingers round the glass, and answered in his gentle voice:

'Oh, I had time to look around; though certainly it was business that took me there. There was a man Scotland Yard were interested in. They thought I might get something out of him.'

'And did you?'

Rice smiled, but did not answer the question. His pale blue eyes were childishly ingenuous. Captain Perry drew on his cigar and smoke curled away towards the white-painted ceiling of the comfortable stateroom.

'I have never understood,' he said, 'exactly what your position in the forces of law and order is.'

Barton Rice's smile was positively angelic. 'I am not sure that I quite understand it myself. Shall we just say that I am useful?'

When the *Southern Star* suddenly heeled over as she put about, Captain Perry swore vividly and briefly.

'What the devil does Turner think he's playing at?'

Whisky had spilled over on to the captain's neatly creased trousers. He dabbed at them with a handkerchief and lifted a telephone that was in reach of his hand.

'Hello; hello there! What's the trouble? Is that so? Oh, confound it!'

He put the telephone back on its hook. 'Some damn fool's slipped overboard. This'll put us behind schedule. Damn all idiots!'

The woman who had seen the passenger fall overboard appeared to be about twenty-five to thirty years of age. She was dark, attractive, and had a good figure. She spoke English with only the faintest of accents, so that it was difficult to tell whether she was an Englishwoman who had lived a great deal overseas or a foreigner who had spent much of her life in England.

She refused the glass of brandy which Captain Perry offered her, but accepted one of his cigarettes, leaning forward in her chair as he questioned her about what she had seen.

'You say you were standing on the promenade deck, Miss Leblanc?'

'That is so. I was leaning back on the rail and looking back towards the end of the ship, watching the moon shining on the water. It was very beautiful. Then I saw the man. I noticed him especially because there was nobody else in sight. There were some other people strolling along the promenade deck but they were behind me. Where he stood this man was alone, and I am sure that I was the only one who could have seen him.'

'Where exactly was he standing?'

Rice lay back in his chair, watching Miss Leblanc with half-closed eyes. There was an urgent vibration running through the cabin as the *Southern Star* made up for lost time, thrusting forward into the night and opening a gap between herself and the man who had gone to his lonely grave in a wide ocean. It was as though the vessel were shuddering at the memory of the tragedy.

'The man was standing,' said Miss Leblanc, 'just where a kind of iron spout goes through the rails.'

'The garbage chute,' said Captain Perry. 'I know where you mean. Did his actions strike you as being in any way peculiar?'

'Not at first. He just seemed to be gazing out across the water. Then he swayed, threw out his arms, and fell down the chute headfirst. That was when I ran up to the bridge and gave the alarm.'

'You acted most sensibly. That was the quickest way to get something done. My only regret is that we were unable to save this unfortunate man. Whether he fell overboard by accident or threw himself over on purpose I don't suppose we shall ever know.'

Miss Leblanc got to her feet and the two men rose also.

'I am very tired,' she said. 'I think I will go to bed.' Captain Perry walked to the door and opened it; but before Miss Leblanc could leave the cabin Rice said in his gentle voice:

'May I ask one question? Were you standing on the port or the starboard side of the promenade deck?'

The woman hesitated. 'Really, I am so vague about nautical terms. Looking back in the direction from which the ship was coming, I was on the right hand side.'

'That would be the port side,' said Rice. 'Thank you.'

Barton Rice was dozing in a deck-chair in the morning sunshine when Captain Perry came to a halt in front of him.

'We have discovered who it was who left us so abruptly last night,' he said.

Rice's childlike eyes opened. 'Ah! Anyone of interest?'

'A fellow named Schmidt—Walter Schmidt. Came aboard in Buenos Aires.'

'Schmidt, eh? A German?'

'He was travelling on a Mexican passport. May have been German originally. I don't know anything about that.'

Rice digested this information. Then he got up from his chair and stretched himself.

'If you have a moment to spare,' he said, 'I should like to show you something. It won't take more than a minute.'

Under their feet the ship seemed perfectly steady; it was like walking along a pier at the seaside. The tropics had been left behind but the weather was still pleasantly warm. The two men came to the after rail of the promenade deck and halted. They were on the port side.

'This should be about where Miss Leblanc was standing,' said Rice.

Perry agreed. 'From what she said, it must be.'

'Exactly. Now look down towards the poop.' Rice pointed with his finger. 'Does anything strike you as peculiar?'

Captain Perry looked aft at the stern and away towards the creaming wake of her passage. He shook his head.

'Nothing.'

Rice beat a little tattoo on the teak rail, holy-stoned and bleached almost white by sun and water.

'I am surprised you notice nothing strange. You remember Miss Leblanc's story? She said the man—Schmidt—fell down the garbage chute. Now, as you will observe, the chute is not visible from here; there is deck housing in the way. From the starboard side it can be seen, but not from here.'

Perry exclaimed: 'Damned if you aren't right! I ought to have noticed that.' Then he gave a laugh. 'She was confused about port and starboard and obviously made a mistake.'

Rice nodded. 'Oh, certainly she may have done so. But I have a nasty suspicious mind—it's one of the occupational diseases of my profession—and I think she may have been lying.'

Captain Perry stared—surprised and slightly shocked.

'But why should she have lied? Where was the point in telling a story like that if it wasn't true?'

'We will skip that for a moment,' answered Rice, 'and examine her conduct a little further. After she had seen the man fall overboard, doesn't her subsequent action strike you as rather peculiar?'

'In what way?'

'Well now; in such a case what would be the normal reaction, the instinctive conduct of the ordinary person? Wouldn't it be to yell "Man overboard! Man overboard!" and go on yelling until somebody heard? Miss Leblanc herself admits there were other people on the promenade deck whose attention she might easily have attracted. But no; she acted quite differently; without apparently uttering a single cry, she ran some considerable way along the deck, up a number of stairs and on to the bridge to inform the officer of the watch.'

'It was the most sensible thing to do.'

'Sensible no doubt, but not normal. In moments of emergency few people do the sensible thing.'

'Perhaps Miss Leblanc is not an ordinary person.'

Barton Rice smiled. 'There,' he said, 'I think you may well be right.'

Suddenly he changed the subject. 'Wireless telegraphy is a wonderful thing,' he remarked. 'A most useful invention. Don't you agree?

'I have been in touch with Buenos Aires and London since our conversation this morning,' said Barton Rice.

He and Perry were watching, with an interest that was more apparent than real, a game of shuffle-board which some noisy young men and women were playing.

'I have gained quite a lot of interesting information about this fellow Schmidt—Walter Ludwig Schmidt, to give him his full, and apparently genuine, name. It seems he was a pretty well known Communist—a kind of international organiser of unrest. The Argentine police were glad to see the back of him, he'd been in gaol there—and I don't think he'd have been received with joy by the authorities in England. The fact is he was deported some years back as an undesirable alien; he had Anglicised his name to plain Walter Smith then, but it was the same man. Twice he tried to get back into England and was stopped at the ports. It seems he was going to have a third attempt. He must have been very keen on getting into the country.'

'Well, he's lost the chance now,' said Perry. 'Seems to me he was no great loss. But there's one thing—this rules out the suicide theory.'

'Why do you say that?'

'This man had a purpose. It's the people whose lives are empty who do away with themselves. Must have been an accident.'

'Is there not a third alternative?' Rice asked quietly. 'Could it not have been murder?'

Perry looked startled. In the warm afternoon sunshine, watching the gay shuffle-board players and hearing their excited laughter, the idea seemed preposterous.

'Oh, come now,' he said. 'Murder? Where's the reason— the motive?'

Rice stroked his chin thoughtfully. 'A man like Schmidt must have had a lot of enemies; activities such as his breed enemies as bad meat breeds flies. He may have been due for liquidation—communists are notoriously prone to that sort of thing.'

'But,' Perry objected, 'Miss Leblanc saw him fall. She would have known if he had been pushed.'

Rice's thin face creased into its ingenuous smile. 'Ah,' he said, 'but you see there is still an idea in my unpleasant mind that Miss Leblanc was not telling the whole truth.'

'You surely don't think she murdered Schmidt? And if she had a hand in it, why should she give the alarm?'

'Those are questions that have yet to be answered. Meanwhile, it might be instructive to notice with whom she is on friendly terms.'

'As to that,' Perry answered, 'she seems to be friendly with no one. I have never come across anyone so obviously aloof from social contacts—especially a woman as attractive as she is.'

'Which again, my dear Perry, marks her out from the ordinary. I think I shall have to have a talk with her.'

Barton Rice discovered Miss Leblanc in a deck-chair. Casually he dropped into one beside her.

'You don't mind?'

She looked at him coolly. Her face and arms were very brown from the hot sun that they were now leaving behind. So were her legs—very shapely legs, the detective noticed.

'Not at all, Mr Rice.'

Rice took out a cigarette case and offered it to his companion. She took a cigarette with her left hand. The hand, like the rest of her visible body, was burnt to a dark brown, but on one finger was a circle of paler skin, like a ring. Rice noticed the circle, as he noticed all things, but he did not remark upon it.

'Captain Perry and I have been admiring your presence of mind, Miss Leblanc,' he said, holding a match to her cigarette.

Miss Leblanc allowed smoke to float away from her red lips. 'For what reason, may I ask?'

'When this man fell down the chute last night you did not uselessly cry "Man overboard!" You went at once to the one part of the ship where something could be done. Not many would have acted so resourcefully.'

'I am not in the habit of losing my head, Mr Rice.'

Rice wondered whether he detected a hint of mockery in the tone. 'However,' he said, 'there is one point which puzzles us. You said you were standing on the port side of the promenade deck, yet the garbage chute is not visible from there. From the starboard side, yes; from the port, no. How then could you have seen the man?'

He was watching Miss Leblanc closely, but she gave no sign of being disconcerted by this attack.

'It was the left hand side, looking towards the rear of the ship.'

'You said the right hand side last night,' Rice pointed out gently.

'Then I must have made a slip of the tongue.' She smiled, and again Rice suspected mockery. 'We all make slips of the tongue, don't we?'

Rice nodded. 'That is true.'

When he left Miss Leblanc it was with a higher opinion of her self-possession but not of her concern for the truth. He remembered the circle on her finger, however. She should have covered that up, he thought.

That evening Barton Rice went on a journey to a part of the ship unfrequented as a rule by passengers—the forecastle, in which the crew's quarters were situated.

Rice had struck up a friendship with one of the sailors, a man named Tomlinson, soon after the ship left Buenos Aires. He had encountered him on the boat-deck where Tomlinson was at work and the discovery of a mutual interest in detective novels had led to Rice lending the sailor a number of paperbacks.

It was with another of these in his hand that he was now going in search of Tomlinson, but as he was about to enter the forecastle his way was barred by a man wearing a blue jersey and a peaked cap. He was well over six feet tall and heavily built, very dark about the chin and with black eyebrows that sprouted stiffly like flue-brushes.

'No passengers allowed in this part of the ship,' he said gruffly.

Rice answered affably. 'I wanted to speak to one of the ABs—a friend of mine.'

The man did not move to let him pass. 'You can't,' he said. 'Not down here. It's against regulations for passengers to come in the crew's quarters. If everybody was to crowd down here we wouldn't be able to move.'

The man's tone was, to say the least, uncivil. Rice resented it, but did not allow his voice to reflect his feelings.

'Surely regulations are not altogether rigid. They can be waived.'

'Not on my responsibility, they can't. No passengers in the fo'c'sle.'

Rice shrugged. 'Oh, very well then. I suppose I shall have to see him another time.'

But the interview with Tomlinson was not to be thus postponed, for the man himself at that moment appeared in the forecastle doorway. Seeing Rice, he stepped out on to the deck.

'Good evening, sir. Taking a bit of fresh air?'

Tomlinson was a cheerful young man with red hair, his face and hands a mass of freckles like splashings of paint. When he smiled his blue eyes seemed to light up.

'I was bringing this book for you,' Rice said, 'but it appears I am not allowed in the fo'c'sle.'

Tomlinson took the book, glanced at the black-haired man, who scowled back, and began to walk with Rice along the foredeck.

'Who's the unpleasant customer?' Rice asked.

'Oh, that's Pickering,' said Tomlinson. 'Bosun. Proper old nasty and no mistake.'

They came to a halt and leaned on the bulwark, watching the water as it flowed hissing past the ship's side.

Suddenly Tomlinson said: 'Queer business last night, sir. That man, Schmidt. Not the sort of feller I'd have expected to fall overside.'

Rice turned and faced Tomlinson, his interest awakened. 'You knew him then?'

'By sight, sir, very well.'

'What was he like?'

'A big florid sort of man with very fair hair, like straw, cropped close. Proper Jerry type, if you know what I mean. Wore glasses—rimless ones with big round lenses.'

'How did you come to know him?'

'How? Why, he was friends with Pickering. Schmidt used to come down to the bosun's cabin. Used to drink and play cards together, I reckon.'

'In spite of regulations?'

Tomlinson grinned. 'Mebbe it's different rules for bosuns. Him and Pickering were bosom pals. P'raps that's why the bosun is so sour he's gone.'

'Perhaps so,' Rice said. 'I wish I'd seen this Schmidt. If you could find out anything about him from Pickering—in a discreet way, you understand—I should be glad to hear it.'

Barton Rice was enjoying a cigarette in the first class smoke room after lunch the following day when one of the stewards brought him a letter.

'For you, sir.'

Rice took the letter, slit open the envelope and glanced rapidly over the few lines of untidy handwriting.

'Thank you,' he said to the steward. 'That will be all.'

The letter read:

> Come to my cabin at 8.30 this evening. Third door on the left, crews alleyway. I've something important to tell you, something queer. My cabin mate will be on duty, so we won't be disturbed. Look out for the bosun.　A.T.

At 8.30 p.m. Barton Rice was walking quietly across the dimly lighted foredeck, making his way to Tomlinson's cabin and keeping a wary eye open for Pickering. It was not a pleasant evening; scuds of chilly rain were hitting the ship and Rice could hear the slap of waves against the bows as the big liner sliced her way through the Atlantic.

He bent his head to the weather and was glad to come under the shelter of the forecastle. Peering inside, he saw that the alleyway was deserted, and without hesitation he stepped inside.

Third door on the left—that was what Tomlinson had said in his note. Rice did not pause to knock; he turned the handle and walked in, closing the door silently behind him.

It was a small cabin, the steel bulkheads painted white and a naked electric bulb burning overhead. Along one side were two bunks, one above the other.

There was a man lying on the lower bunk with his back to the room. He did not stir as Rice came in.

Rice said: 'Good evening, Bert. Wake up.'

But still the seaman made no movement, and suddenly Rice noticed the man's neck and knew the reason why. With a swift movement he put out his hand and pulled the man over on to his back. It was Tomlinson all right, his sightless, bulging eyes staring from the purple face at the bunk above.

Rice looked down at the bruised neck and distorted features and muttered softly, very softly: 'Strangled.'

Suddenly he put his hands into the folds of the disturbed bed-cover and picked up a fragment of glass, rounded on one edge, jaggedly broken on the other. Holding the glass carefully by the edges, he opened his cigarette case and slipped it inside.

Then he switched the light off, opened the cabin door,

glanced quickly up and down the alleyway to make sure that no one was in sight, and closed the door behind him.

———

Some fifteen minutes elapsed before Barton Rice was again opening the door of Tomlinson's cabin. Now he had Captain Perry with him.

Rice stepped inside the cabin, felt for the light switch and snapped it on. Then he stared in amazement at the lower bunk. Perry also stared at it.

'Damn it all! Is this your idea of a joke?'

Rice did not answer. He moved over to the bunk and fingered the smooth surface of the neatly tucked-in bed-cover. In the cabin there was no longer any sign of violence. He glanced at his wrist-watch.

'They lost no time,' he said.

Perry was shifting his feet impatiently. 'What's the idea of bringing me here on a fool's errand? You said Tomlinson had been strangled. Well, I don't see him. Where is he?'

'At a rough guess,' Rice answered in his gentle voice, 'I should say he is at least a mile astern in a place where dead men certainly tell no tales.'

The Liverpool dock in which the *Southern Star* lay was almost deserted. It was a misty November evening, and in the pearly light of electric lamps the ships, the cranes and the transit sheds looked dark and gloomy.

A man, making his careful way down the gangway, seemed to feel the cold after so recent an experience of tropical warmth. He was dressed in a thick overcoat, the collar of which was turned up to his ears, and he wore a brown felt hat pulled low over his forehead.

As he reached the ground, two policemen, a sergeant and a constable, stepped out of the shadow of a transit shed and accosted him.

'Shore pass, please.'

The man felt in his pocket and held out a slip of paper. The sergeant took it and began reading out in a slow toneless voice: 'Charles Pickering. Boatswain.'

He looked up. 'Would you take your hat off?'

The man shifted his feet nervously, but made no attempt to remove the hat.

Then Barton Rice stepped from behind a packing case. 'Come, Mr Schmidt,' he said. 'For a man who has been five days drowned you are surprisingly reluctant to face the light. Come, let us see beneath the hat.'

And as he spoke, Rice neatly flicked the hat from the man's head and sent it rolling on the ground.

'Fair hair, cropped short,' observed Rice in his gentle voice. 'Eyes obviously short-sighted and in need of glasses.'

The man's breath was coming hard and short; it was like an animal panting. His head was thrust forward as though he were peering into a hazy background, trying to distinguish blurred objects. Suddenly, with a quick, darting movement, he pulled an automatic pistol from his pocket and fired. Rice, in what was almost a reflex action, flung himself to one side and the bullet went whining and ricochetting among the cranes and buildings.

Schmidt fired once more, then turned and ran along the dockside, Rice and the two policemen hard after him, dodging bollards and mooring ropes, crates and packing-cases. For a heavy man Schmidt had a surprising turn of speed, and for a few moments he gained on his pursuers; but the thick overcoat hampered him, and soon the gap narrowed. Feeling the chase close at his heels, he turned and fired three times. The constable stumbled and fell clutching at his chest, and the sergeant tripped over his outstretched legs, falling headlong.

Rice went grimly after Schmidt who turned again to fire on the run. The shot whined harmlessly away, but Schmidt's foot caught in a ring-bolt and his own momentum flung him over the side of the dock. He fell with a scream.

Rice ran to the edge and shone a torch into the dark chasm formed by the concrete side of the dock and the steel hull of a ship made fast there. At the bottom of the chasm was a narrow channel of oily, scum-covered water with empty bottles, pieces of orange peel, and all manner of filth.

Schmidt was wedged head downwards just above the water as securely as if he had been riveted.

His screams came up, echoing hollowly in that narrow space; they rose to a crescendo of terror and agony; then ceased for ever.

'I still don't quite understand it,' said Captain Perry, holding his glass of whisky up to the light.

Rice settled himself more comfortably in his armchair. 'It is simple enough,' he said. 'Schmidt met Pickering in Buenos Aires and between them they arranged this little pantomime. No doubt the bosun was paid pretty heavily for his trouble. Schmidt was very keen to get to England, as you know; but he also knew that the police would be looking out for him when the ship docked, especially as he was travelling under his correct name. That was all part of the plan. The idea was this:

'Schmidt was supposedly to disappear overboard, but in reality he would be hiding in Pickering's cabin until the ship docked. Then he would go ashore on Pickering's pass, which he could easily send back through the post, and nobody would be any the wiser. The police would not be looking for a man who had been lost at sea.

'It was a good plan, and it might have worked if poor Tomlinson hadn't chanced to see him after he was supposed to be dead. That, of course, was what Tomlinson wanted to tell me about, and that was what cost him his life. Men like Schmidt stop at nothing.

'But in the struggle with Tomlinson, Schmidt's glasses were broken and he did not find all the pieces. It was one of them I found when I visited Tomlinson's cabin; and that must have been just at the moment when Schmidt had gone to fetch Pickering to help him dispose of the body.'

'But Miss Leblanc,' Perry said. 'How was she concerned in it?'

Rice smiled. 'Miss Leblanc was an integral part of the plan. Miss Leblanc is in reality Mrs Walter Schmidt, now widowed. She had removed her wedding ring but unfortunately the sun had not had time to cover up the evidence of where it had been.'

Rice sipped his drink. 'So much for a pleasant holiday cruise,' he said.

Seasprite

Andrew Garve

Andrew Garve was the principal pen-name of Leicester-born Paul Winterton (1908–2001), whose father Ernest Winterton was a journalist and, from 1929 to 1931, a Labour Member of Parliament. Paul studied economics at the LSE before himself moving into journalism. His first novel, *Death Beneath Jerusalem* (1938) appeared under the name Roger Bax; he published several Bax novels and also as Paul Somers, but his most successful crime fiction was written as by Garve.

Garve's love of small boat sailing is evident in many of his stories. A notable example is *The Megstone Plot* (1956), which was filmed with James Mason, George Sanders, and Vera Miles as *A Touch of Larceny*. Life on a boat is integral to the storyline of the rather less celebrated *Murderer's Fen* (1966), a.k.a. *Hide and Go Seek*, a fast-paced variant of the 'inverted mystery' invented by Richard Austin Freeman. This story first appeared in the *Evening Standard* in March 1963, as part of a series of ten tales by authors whose novels were published by Collins Crime Club. Puzzled bibliographers should note that we have changed the title to 'Seasprite', on the basis that the original was too much of a spoiler. For those who are curious and wish to do a little detective work of their own, the clue is that Garve's one-word title summarised Jones's motivation.

Guy Lunt tied up his smart motor cruiser *Seasprite* at the quay of the West Country harbour and went ashore to get stores.

He was a handsome man of 30, with a well-heeled, carefree look. His appearance was misleading. In fact he was worried—about money.

His problem was how to make ends meet till his former companions, Gurney and Franks, came out of gaol.

In particular, how to raise enough cash to pay the instalments on the cruiser. He knew he'd no chance of pulling off a lucrative job single-handed—smuggling was a tough racket and you needed a reliable crew.

He missed Gurney and Franks badly—and it would be four months before they came out. Damn bad luck all round.

His thoughts went back to the disastrous March trip. There'd been four of them then—himself and Gurney and Franks, and a new man named Jim Haines, a dour middle-aged fisherman from up the coast. They'd taken Haines because he had a boat and *Seasprite* was in dock with gearbox trouble. Gurney had met him in a pub and talked him into it.

Everything had gone fine until they'd been a mile from home. Then, out of a thick night, had come a challenge from a revenue launch. Their chances had seemed slight. In a patch of fog, they'd decided to split up; Gurney and Franks had taken to the dinghy—and by sheer mischance had blundered straight into the launch and been caught.

Haines had stuck to his boat and Lunt had stayed with him. For a while they'd played hide-and-seek in the fog.

Then as the launch had approached again, there'd come the tragedy. A lurch, a slippery deck—and Haines had gone overboard.

Later, Lunt had learned that he'd managed to reach the shore but had died in hospital next day. Which was just as well, Lunt thought, because otherwise he might have talked and given me away. A new, untried man.

Gurney and Franks, of course, had kept mum. They were trustworthy. So Lunt had come out of it all right. He'd succeeded in beaching Haines's boat and getting away unseen. So he was still free, with nothing against him, and *Seasprite* ready for a trip. But meanwhile there was the problem of the payments.

That evening, as Lunt was sipping whisky in his cockpit, a man appeared out of the darkness of the quay and stood looking down.

'Nice boat,' he commented.

Lunt exchanged some words with him, at first without much interest. Then, gradually, his interest grew.

The man was young and tough-looking and, it turned out, a seafarer. He had a powerful launch of his own which he used for lobster potting and, in the summer, for taking visitors out. Neither venture, Lunt gathered, was paying too well. In fact, the young man, whose name was Jones, seemed to have a financial problem, too.

Lunt wondered how he'd fancy a run to Cherbourg. He invited him aboard for a drink and cautiously sounded him out.

Jones, it soon appeared, had no moral objections to smuggling, but he thought it too risky for what you got out of it. 'If we want quick dough there's a better way,' he said.

'What's that?'

'Salvage. Last summer I towed in a yacht that was in distress. Got three hundred quid.'

'I dare say—but you don't find a yacht in trouble just when you want to.'

Jones grinned. 'This boat insured?'

'You bet.'

'How much for?'

'Three thousand.'

'There you are, then. You take a trip up the coast when there's an onshore wind blowing. I happen to be around tending my pots. You fix your engine so that it conks. You're on a lee shore in a rough sea and if you strike there's not a hope for you. I throw you a line and tow you in. I claim one third of the value as salvage. A thousand quid. And we split it. Can't go wrong'

'There'd be an inquiry,' Lunt said.

'So what? No one's seen us together. No one will if we're careful. Why should they suspect anything?'

'They'd check up on the engine failure. And water in the petrol. That could happen on any boat.'

Lunt grunted. 'We'd have to make it all look genuine. Someone might have glasses on us. A coastguard.'

'We'd choose a place away from coastguards. Off Black Rock, say six miles up the coast. Any rate, we would make it look genuine. I tell you mate, we can't go wrong.'

Lunt poured more whisky. 'Let's look at the chart,' he said.

They had to wait 72 hours for the right weather. Then a southerly wind, force five, was forecast for the following day. They completed their plans in the darkness of the quay.

Lunt left at three o'clock next afternoon. The sea was uncomfortable, but safe enough away from the shore. Lunt cruised along slowly, looking out for the launch. Naturally, he wouldn't tamper with his engine until Jones showed up.

By four he was approaching the rendezvous. Presently he spotted the launch, coming from the opposite direction. Everything was going according to plan. He steered *Seasprite* inshore till she was only three cables from the rocks. Soon he decided the launch was near enough for him to cut the engine safely.

He took the cap off the petrol tank and poured in a little water. Then he went below and dismantled the carburettor. That would show he'd been doing his best. Back on deck, he waved his shirt as a distress signal.

The launch turned towards him. Lunt watched the rocks. They were very close and the wind was dead on shore. But the timing was perfect. The launch closed in and stopped. Jones waved encouragingly from his foredeck, and threw a rope.

Lunt caught the coil—then stared at it in dismay. It was old and worn. 'That's no use!' he shouted.

'It's all I've got,' Jones called back. 'Make it fast.'

Lunt tied it. Jones pulled away. There was a twang, and the rope parted.

Lunt gazed in panic at the closing shore. No time now to reassemble the carburettor.

'You'll have to take me off, Jones,' he yelled.

The launch came alongside—but not close enough for Lunt to jump. Jones's face was as hard as the rocks.

'My name isn't Jones,' he said. 'It's Haines—remember him? I was with him in hospital when he died. He told me what happened. How you jerked him off the deck and didn't even slow down. He told me your name and the name of your boat. So I found you. You meant to kill him, didn't you?… Well, now I'm going to kill you. So long—see you in hell.'

The launch sheered away. Lunt called in a cracked voice: 'For God sake, Jones—you've got it all wrong. I can tell you what happened…'

But before he could think of a story, the cruiser struck.

Death by Water

Michael Innes

Edinburgh-born John Innes Mackintosh Stewart (1906–94) enjoyed a distinguished academic career, culminating in a professorship in English at Oxford University. Writing as J. I. M. Stewart, he published non-fiction books such as *Character and Motive in Shakespeare* (1949) and novels including the quintet *A Staircase in Surrey*. As if this was not enough, he enjoyed a highly successful career as a writer of detective novels and short stories under the pen-name Michael Innes.

Innes's debut, *Death at the President's Lodging* (1936), was bought by the leading publisher Victor Gollancz, and the front cover of the dust jacket of the first edition announced: 'This is the best "first" Detective Story that has ever come our way'. This bold claim was justified by the cleverness and wit of the story, and the novel established both Innes and his detective, Inspector (later Sir John) Appleby. The Appleby series continued for half a century, a remarkable achievement. 'Death by Water' was included in his collection *The Appleby File*

(1975); confusingly, the novel *Appleby at Allington* (1968) has also been given the alternative title *Death by Water*.

Sir John Appleby had been worried about Charles Vandervell for some time. But this was probably true of a good many of the philosopher's friends. Vandervell's speculations, one of these had wittily remarked, could be conceived as going well or ill according to the sense one was prepared to accord that term. His last book, entitled (mysteriously to the uninstructed) *Social Life as a Sign System*, had been respectfully received by those who went in for that kind of thing; but it was clear that something had gone badly wrong with his investments. He was what is called a private scholar, for long unattached to any university or other salary-yielding institution, and had for years lived very comfortably indeed on inherited wealth of an unspecified but doubtless wholly respectable sort.

He was not a landed man. His country house, pleasantly situated a few miles from the Cornish coast, owned extensive gardens but was unsupported by any surrounding agricultural activities. The dividends came in, and that was that. Nobody could have thought of it as a particularly vulnerable condition. Some adverse change in the state of the national economy might be expected from time to time to produce a correspondingly adverse effect upon an income such as his. But it would surely require recessions, depressions, and slumps of a major order to result in anything like catastrophe.

Vandervell himself was vague about the whole thing. This might have been put down to simple incompetence, since it would certainly have been difficult to imagine a man with less of a head for practical affairs. But there were those who maintained that some feeling of guilt was operative as well.

Vandervell was uneasy about living a life of leisure on the labours of others, and was unwilling to face up to considering his mundane affairs at all. He occasionally spoke in an old-fashioned way about his 'man of business'. Nobody had ever met this personage, or could so much as name him; but it was obvious that he must occupy a key position in the conduct of his client's monetary affairs. Vandervell himself acknowledged this. 'Bound to say,' he had once declared to Appleby, 'that my financial wizard earns his fees. No hope of keeping my chin above water at all, if I didn't have him on the job. And even as it is, I can't be said to be doing too well.'

For some months this last persuasion had been gaining on Vandervell rapidly and throwing him into ever deepening gloom. One reading of this was clearly that the gloom was pathological and irrational—a depressive state generated entirely within the unfortunate man's own head—and that a mere fantasy of being hard up, quite unrelated to the objective facts of the case, was one distressing symptom of his condition. One does hear every now and then, after all, of quite wealthy people who have stopped the milk and the newspaper out of a firm conviction they can no longer pay for them. There was a point at which Appleby took this view of Vandervell's state of mind. Vandervell was a fairly prolific writer, and his essays and papers began to suggest that the adverse state of his bank balance (whether real or imagined) was bringing him to a vision of the universe at large as weighted against him and all mankind in an equally disagreeable way. Hitherto his philosophical work had been of a severely intellectual and dispassionate order. Now he produced in rapid succession a paper on Schopenhauer, a paper on von Hartmann, and a long essay called *Existentialism and the Metaphysic of Despair*. All this didn't precisely suggest cheerfulness breaking in.

This was the state of the case when Appleby encountered Vandervell's nephew, Fabian Vandervell, in a picture gallery off Bond Street and took him to his club for lunch.

'How is your uncle getting along?' Appleby asked. 'He doesn't seem to come much to town nowadays, and it's a long time since I've been down your way.'

Fabian, who was a painter, also lived in Cornwall—more or less in a colony of artists in a small fishing village called Targan Bay. As his uncle was a bachelor, and he himself his only near relation, it was generally assumed that he would prove to be his uncle's heir. The prospect was probably important to him, since nobody had ever heard of Fabian's selling a picture. So Fabian too might well be concerned at the manner in which the family fortunes were said to be in a decline.

'He muddles along,' Fabian said. 'And his interests continue to change for the worse, if you ask me. Did you ever hear of a book called *Biathanatos*?'

'It rings a faint bell.'

'It's by John Donne, and is all about what Donne liked to call "the scandalous disease of headlong dying". It caused a bit of a scandal, I imagine. Donne was Dean of St Paul's, you remember, as well as a poet; so he had no business to be fudging up an apology for suicide. Uncle Charles is talking about editing *Biathanatos*, complete with his own learned commentary on the theme. Morbid notion.' Fabian paused. 'Uncommonly nice claret you have here.'

'I'm delighted you approve of it.' Appleby noticed that the modest decanter of the wine with which Fabian had been provided was already empty. 'Do you mean that you are alarmed about your uncle?'

'Well, he does talk about suicide in a general way, as well. But perhaps there's no great cause for alarm.'

'We'll hope not.' Appleby decided not to pursue this topic, which it didn't strike him as his business to discuss. 'I have it in mind to call in on your uncle, incidentally, in a few weeks' time, when I go down to visit my sister at Bude. And now I want you to explain to me those pictures we both found ourselves looking at this morning. Puzzling things to one of my generation.'

Fabian Vandervell proved perfectly willing to accept this invitation. He held forth contentedly for the rest of the meal.

Appleby fulfilled his intention a month later, and his first impression was that Charles Vandervell had become rather a lonely man. Pentallon Hall was a substantial dwelling, yet apart from its owner only an elderly manservant called Litter was much in evidence. But at least one gardener must be lurking around, since the extensive grounds which shielded the place from the general surrounding bleakness of the Cornish scene were all in apple-pie order. Vandervell led Appleby over all this with the air of a country gentleman who has nothing in his head except the small concerns which the managing of such a property must generate. But the role wasn't quite native to the man; and in an indefinable way none of the interests or projects which he paraded appeared quite to be coming off. Vandervell had a theory about bees, but the Pentallon bees were refusing to back it up. In a series of somewhat suburban-looking ponds he bred tropical fish, but even the mild Cornish climate didn't suit these creatures at all. Nor at the moment did it suit the roses Vandervell was proposing to exhibit at some local flower show later in the season; they were plainly (like so much human hope and aspiration, their owner commented morosely) nipped in the bud. All in all, Charles Vandervell was revealing himself more than ever as a man not booked for much success except, conceivably, within certain rather specialised kingdoms of the mind.

Or so Appleby thought until Mrs Mountmorris arrived. Mrs Mountmorris was apparently a near neighbour and almost certainly a widow; and Mrs Mountmorris came to tea. Litter took her arrival distinguishably in ill part; he was a privileged retainer of long standing, and seemingly licensed to express himself in such matters through the instrumentality of heavy sighs and sour looks. Vandervell, on the other hand, brightened up so markedly when the lady was announced that Appleby at once concluded Litter to have rational ground for viewing her as a threat to the established order of things at Pentallon. Moreover Vandervell took considerable pleasure in presenting Appleby to the new arrival, and Mrs Mountmorris obligingly played up by treating her host's friend as a celebrity. It was, of course, a quiet part of the world. But Appleby, being well aware of Vandervell as owning a distinction of quite another flight to any attainable by a policeman, found in this piece of nonsense something a little touching as well as absurd.

Not that, beneath an instant social competence, Mrs Mountmorris was in the least pleased at finding another visitor around. She marked herself at once as a woman of strong character, and perhaps as one who was making it her business to take her philosophic neighbour in hand. If that was it—if she had decided to organise Charles Vandervell—then organised Charles Vandervell would be. On the man's chances of escape, Appleby told himself, he wouldn't wager so much as a bottle of that respectable claret to which he had entertained Vandervell's nephew Fabian at his club. And Fabian, if he knew about the lady, would certainly take as dark a view of her as Litter did.

'Charles's roses,' Mrs Mountmorris said, 'refuse to bloom. His bees produce honey no different from yours, Sir John, or mine.' Mrs Mountmorris paused to dispense tea—a duty which, to Litter's visible displeasure, she had made no bones about taking to herself. 'As for his ships, they just won't come home. *Mais nous changerons tout cela.*'

This, whatever one thought of the French, was nothing if not forthright, and Appleby glanced at the lady with some respect.

'But a philosopher's argosies,' he said a shade pedantically, 'must voyage in distant waters, don't you think? They may return all the more richly freighted in the end.'

'Of *that* I have no doubt.' Mrs Mountmorris spoke briskly and dismissively, although the dismissiveness may have been directed primarily at Appleby's flight of fancy. 'But practical issues have to be considered as well. And Charles, I think, has come to agree with me. Charles?'

'Yes, of course.' Thus abruptly challenged, Vandervell would have had to be described as mumbling his reply. At the same time, however, he was gazing at his female friend in an admiration there was no mistaking.

'Has that man turned up yet?' Mrs Mountmorris handed Vandervell his tea-cup, and at the same time indicated that he might consume a cucumber sandwich. 'The show-down is overdue.'

'Yes, of course.' Vandervell reiterated with a nervous nod what appeared to be his *leit-motif* in Mrs Mountmorris's presence. 'And I've sent for him. An absolute summons, I assure you. And you and I must have a talk about it, *tête-à-tête*, soon.'

'Indeed we must.' Mrs Mountmorris was too well-bred not to accept this as closing the mysterious topic she had introduced. 'And as for *these*'—and she gestured at an unpromising rose-bed in the near vicinity of which the tea-table was disposed—'derris dust is the answer, and nothing else.'

After this, Appleby didn't linger at Pentallon for very long. His own call had been casual and unheralded. It would be tactful to let that *tête-à-tête* take place sooner rather than later. Driving on to his sister's house at Bude, he reflected that Mrs Mountmorris must be categorised as a good thing. Signs were not wanting that she was putting stuffing into Charles Vandervell, of late so inclined to unwholesome meditation on headlong dying. It was almost as if a worm were going to turn. Yet one ought not, perhaps, to jump to conclusions. On an off-day, and to a diffident and resigned man, the lady might well assume the character of a last straw herself. Litter, certainly, was already seeing her in that light. His gloom as he politely performed the onerous duty of opening the door of Appleby's car suggested his being in no doubt, at least, that the roses would be deluged in derris dust before the day was out.

Appleby hadn't, however, left Pentallon without a promise to call in on his return journey, which took place a week later. This time, he rang up to announce his arrival. He didn't again want to find himself that sort of awkward extra whom the Italians style a *terzo incomodo*.

Litter answered the telephone, and in a manner which instantly communicated considerable agitation. Mr Vandervell, he said abruptly, was not in residence. Then, as if recalling his training, he desired Appleby to repeat his name, that he might apprise his employer of the inquiry on his return.

'Sir John Appleby.'

'Oh, yes, sir—yes, indeed.' It was as if a penny had dropped in the butler's sombre mind. 'Pray let me detain you for a moment, Sir John. We are in some distress at Pentallon— really very perturbed, sir. The fact is that Mr Vandervell has disappeared. Without a trace, Sir John, as the newspapers sometimes express it. Except that I have received a letter from him—a letter susceptible of the most shocking interpretation.' Litter paused on this—as if it were a phrase in which, even amid the perturbation to which he had referred, he took a certain just satisfaction. 'To tell you the truth, sir, I have felt it my duty to inform the police. I wonder whether you could possibly break your journey here, as you had proposed? I know your reputation, Sir John, begging your pardon.'

'My dear Litter, my reputation scarcely entitles me to impose myself on the Cornish constabulary. Are they with you now?'

'Not just at the moment, sir. They come and go, you might say. And very civil they are. But it's not at all the kind of thing we are accustomed to.'

'I suppose not. Is there anybody else at Pentallon?'

'Mr Fabian has arrived from Targan Bay. And Mr Truebody, sir, who is understood to look after Mr Vandervell's affairs.'

'It's Mr Truebody whom Mr Vandervell refers to as his man of business?'

'Just so, sir. I wonder whether you would care to speak to Mr Fabian? He is in the library now, sorting through his uncle's papers.'

'The devil he is.' Appleby's professional instinct was alerted by this scrap of information. 'It mightn't be a bad idea. Be so good as to tell him I'm on the telephone.'

Within a minute of this, Fabian Vandervell's urgent voice was on the line.

'Appleby—is it really you? For God's sake come over to this accursed place quick. You must have gathered even from that moronic Litter that something pretty grim has happened to my uncle. Unless he's merely up to some ghastly foolery, the brute fact is that *Biathanatos* has nobbled him. You're a family friend—'

'I'm on the way,' Appleby said, and put down the receiver.

But Appleby's first call was at a police station, since there was a certain measure of protocol to observe. An hour later, and accompanied by a Detective Inspector called Gamley, he was in Charles Vandervell's library, and reading Charles Vandervell's letter.

> *My dear Litter,*
>
> *There are parties one does not quit without making a round of the room, and just such a party I am now preparing to take my leave of. In this instance it must be a round of letters that is in question, and of these the first must assuredly be addressed to you, who have been so faithful a servant and friend. I need not particularise the manner of what I propose to do. This will reveal itself at a convenient time and prove, I hope, not to have been too untidy. And now, all my thanks! I am only sorry that the small token of my esteem which is to come to you must, in point of its amount, reflect the sadly embarrassed state of my affairs.*
>
> *Yours sincerely,*
> *Charles Vandervell*

'Most affecting,' Mr Truebody said. 'Litter, I am sure you were very much moved.' Truebody was a large and power-ful looking man, disadvantageously possessed of the sort of wildly staring eyes popularly associated with atrocious crim-inals. Perhaps it was to compensate for this that he exhibited a notably mild manner.

'It was upsetting, of course.' Litter said this in a wooden

way. Since he had so evident a difficulty in liking anybody, it wasn't surprising that he didn't greatly care for the man of business. 'But we must all remember,' he added with mournful piety, 'that while there is life there is hope. A very sound proverb that is—if an opinion may be permitted me.'

'Exactly!' Fabian Vandervell, who had been standing in a window and staring out over the gardens, turned round and broke in unexpectedly. 'At first, I was quite bowled over by this thing. But I've been thinking. And it seems to me—'

'One thing at a time, Fabian.' Appleby handed the letter back to Gamley, who was in charge of it. 'Was this simply left on Mr Vandervell's desk, or something of that kind?'

'It came by post.'

'Then where's the envelope?'

'Mr Litter'—Gamley favoured the butler with rather a grim look—'has unfortunately failed to preserve it.'

'A matter of habit, sir.' Litter was suddenly extremely nervous. 'When I open a postal communication I commonly drop the outer cover straight into the waste-paper basket in my pantry. It was what I did on this occasion, and unfortunately the basket was emptied into an incinerator almost at once.'

'Did you notice the postmark?'

'I'm afraid not, sir.'

'The envelope, like the letter itself, was undoubtedly in Mr Vandervell's handwriting?'

'No, sir. The address was typewritten.'

'That's another point—and an uncommonly odd one.' Fabian had advanced to the centre of the room. 'It makes me feel the whole thing is merely funny-business, after all. And there's the further fact that the letter isn't dated. I'm inclined to think my uncle may simply have grabbed it from the pile, gone off Lord knows where, and then typed out an envelope and posted the thing in pursuance of some mere whim or fantasy.'

'Isn't that pretty well to declare him insane?' Appleby looked hard at Fabian. 'And just what do you mean by talking about a pile?'

'I believe he was always writing these things. Elegant valedictions. Making sure that nothing so became him in his life as—'

'We've had Donne; we needn't have Shakespeare too.' Appleby was impatient. 'I must say I don't find the notion of your uncle occasionally concocting such things in the least implausible, psychologically regarded. But is there any hard evidence?'

'I've been hunting around, as a matter of fact. In his papers, I mean. I can't say I've found anything. Uncle Charles may have destroyed any efforts of the kind when he cleared out, taking this prize specimen to Litter with him.'

'Isn't all this rather on the elaborate side?' Truebody asked, with much gentleness of manner. 'I am really afraid that we are failing to face the sad simplicity of the thing. Everybody acquainted with him knows that Vandervell has been turning increasingly melancholic. We just have to admit that this had reached a point at which he decided to make away with himself. So he wrote this perfectly genuine letter to Litter, and perhaps others we haven't yet heard of—'

'Why did he take it away and post it?' Inspector Gamley demanded.

'That's obvious enough, I should have thought. He wanted to avoid an immediate hue and cry, such as might have been started at once, had he simply left the letter to Litter behind him.'

'It's certainly a possibility,' Appleby said. 'Would you consider, Mr Truebody, that such a delaying tactic on Vandervell's part may afford some clue to the precise way in which he intended to commit suicide? He tells Litter it isn't going to be too untidy.'

'I fear I am without an answer, Sir John. The common thing, where a country gentleman is in question, is to take out a shot-gun and fake a more or less plausible accident at a stile. But Vandervell clearly didn't propose any faking. The letter-writing shows that his suicide was to be declared and open. I feel that this goes with his deepening morbidity.'

'But that's not, if you ask me, how Mr Vandervell was feeling at all.' Litter had spoken suddenly and with surprising energy. 'For he'd taken the turn, as they say. Or that's my opinion.'

'And just what might you mean by that, Mr Litter?' Gamley had produced a notebook, as if he felt in the presence of too much unrecorded chat.

'I mean that what Mr Truebody says isn't what you might call up to date. More than once, just lately, I've told myself Mr Vandervell was cheering up a trifle—and high time, too. More confident, in a manner of speaking. Told me off once or twice about this or that. I can't say I was pleased at the time. But it's what makes me a little hopeful now.'

'This more aggressive stance on your employer's part,' Appleby asked, 'disposes you against the view that he must indeed have committed suicide?'

'Yes, Sir John. Just that.'

There was a short silence, which was broken by a constable's entering the library. He walked up to Gamley, and then hesitated—as if doubtful whether what he had to say ought to be communicated to the company at large. Then he took the plunge.

'Definite news at last, sir. And just what we've been afraid of. They've discovered Mr Vandervell's body—washed up on a beach near Targan Bay.'

'Drowned, you mean?'

'Yes, sir. Beyond doubt, the report says. And they're looking for his clothes now.'

'His clothes?'

'Just that, sir. The body was stark naked.'

Although the North Cornish coast was only a few miles away, Charles Vandervell owned no regular habit of bathing there—this even although he was known to be an accomplished swimmer. Even if the letter to Litter had never been written, it would have had to be judged extremely improbable that his death could be accounted for as an accident following upon a sudden whim to go bathing. For one thing, Targan Bay and its environs, although little built over, were not so unfrequented that a man of conventional instincts (and Vandervell was that) would have been likely to dispense with some decent scrap of swimming apparel. On the other hand—or this, at least, was the opinion expressed by his nephew—a resolution to drown himself might well have been accompanied by just that. To strip naked and swim straight out to sea could well have come to him as the tidy thing.

Yet there were other possibilities, and Appleby saw one of them at once. The sea—and particularly a Cornish sea—can perform astonishing tricks with a drowned man. It can transform into a nude corpse a sailor who has gone overboard in oilskins, sea-boots, and a great deal else. It can thus cast up a body itself unblemished. Or it can go on to whip and lacerate such a body to a grim effect of sadistic frenzy. Or it can set its own living creatures, tiny perhaps but multitudinous, nibbling and worrying till the bones appear. What particular fate awaits a body is all a matter of rocks and shoals—shoals in either sense—and of currents and tides.

Appleby had a feeling that the sea might yield up some further secret about Charles Vandervell yet. Meantime, it was to be hoped there was more to be learnt on land. The circumstances of the missing man's disappearance plainly needed investigation.

Appleby's first visit to Pentallon had been on a Monday, and it was a Monday again now. According to Litter, the remainder of that first Monday had been uneventful, except in two minor regards. The formidable Mrs Mountmorris had stayed on almost till dinner-time, which wasn't Litter's notion of an afternoon call. There had been a business discussion of some sort, and it had been conducted with sufficient circumspection to prevent Litter, who had been curious, from hearing so many as half a dozen illuminating words. But Litter rather supposed (since one must speak frankly in face of a crisis like the present) that the lady had more than a thought of abandoning her widowed state, and that she was in process of thoroughly sorting out Vandervell's affairs before committing herself. When she had at length gone away Vandervell had made a number of telephone calls. At dinner he had been quite cheerful—or perhaps it would be better to say that he had appeared to be in a state of rather grim satisfaction. Litter confessed to having been a little uncertain of his employer's wave-length.

On the Tuesday morning Mr Truebody had turned up at Pentallon, but hadn't stayed long. Litter had received the impression—just in passing the library door, as he had several times been obliged to do—that Mr Truebody was receiving instructions or requests which were being pretty forcefully expressed. No doubt Mr Truebody himself would speak as to that. There had been no question, Litter opined, of the two gentlemen having words. Or it might be better to say there had been no question of their having a row—not as there had been with Mr Fabian when he turned up on the same afternoon. And about *that*—Litter supposed—Mr Fabian would speak.

This sensational disclosure on Litter's part could have been aimed only at Appleby, since Inspector Gamley turned out to have been treated to it already. And Fabian seemed to have made no secret of what he now termed lightly a bit of a tiff. He had formed the same conjecture about Mrs Mountmorris's intentions as Litter had done, and he was ready to acknowledge that the matter wasn't his business. But between him and his uncle there was some obscure matter of a small family trust. In the changed situation now showing every sign of blowing up he had come to Pentallon resolved to get this clarified. His uncle had been, in his view, quite unjustifiably short with him, saying that he had much more important things on his mind. So a bit of a rumpus there had undoubtedly been. But as he had neither carried Uncle Charles out to sea and drowned him, nor so effectively bullied him as to make him go and drown himself, he really failed to see that Litter's coming up with the matter had much point.

Listening to all this, Appleby was not wholly indisposed to agree. He had a long experience of major catastrophes bringing unedifying episodes of a minor order to light. So he went on to inquire about the Wednesday, which looked as if it might have been the point of crisis.

And Wednesday displayed what Inspector Gamley called a pattern. It was the day of the week upon which Pentallon's two maidservants, who were sisters, enjoyed their free half-day together. Immediately after lunch, Vandervell had started fussing about the non-delivery of a consignment of wine from his merchant in Bristol. He had shown no particular interest about this negligence before, but now he had ordered Litter to get into a car and fetch the stuff from Bristol forthwith. And as soon as Litter had departed in some indignation on this errand (Bristol being, as he pointed out, a hundred miles away, if it was a step) Vandervell had accorded both his gardener and his gardener's boy the same treatment—the quest, this time, being directed to Exeter and a variety of horticultural needs (derris dust among them, no doubt). Apart from its proprietor, Pentallon was thus dispopulated until the late evening. When Litter himself returned it was in a very bad temper, so that he retired to his own quarters for the night without any attempt to report himself to his employer. And as his first daily duty in the way of personal attendance was to serve lunch, and as the maids (as he explained) were both uncommonly stupid girls, it was not until after midday on Thursday that there was a general recognition of something being amiss. And at this point Litter had taken it into his head that he must behave with discretion, and not precipitately spread abroad the fact of what might be no more than eccentric (and perhaps obscurely improper) behaviour on the part of the master of Pentallon.

The consequence of all this was that it took Charles Vandervell's letter, delivered on the Friday, to stir Litter into alerting the police. And by then Vandervell had been dead for some time. Even upon superficial examination, it appeared, the police surgeons were convinced of that.

Establishing this rough chronology satisfied Appleby for the moment, and he reminded himself that he was at Pentallon not as a remorseless investigator but merely as a friend of the dead man and his nephew. That Charles Vandervell *was* now definitely known to be dead no doubt meant for Inspector Gamley a switching to some new routine which he had better be left for a time to pursue undisturbed. So Appleby excused himself, left the house, and wandered thoughtfully through the gardens. The roses were still not doing too well, but what was on view had its interest, all the same. From a raised terrace walk remote from the house, moreover, there was a glimpse of the sea. Appleby had surveyed this for some moments when he became aware that he was no longer alone. Truebody, that somewhat mysterious man of business, had come up behind him.

'Are you quite satisfied with this picture, Sir John?' Truebody asked.

'This picture?' For a second Appleby supposed that here was an odd manner of referring to the view. Then he understood. 'I'd have to be clearer as to just what the picture is supposed to be before I could answer that one.'

'Why should Vandervell clear the decks—take care to get rid of Litter and the rest of them—if he was simply proposing to walk over *there*'—Truebody gestured towards the horizon—'for the purpose of drowning himself? The unnecessariness of the measure worries me. He could simply have said he was going for a normal sort of walk—or even that he was going out to dinner. He could have said half a dozen things. Don't you agree?'

'Yes, I think I do—in a way. But one has to allow for the fact that the mind of a man contemplating suicide is quite likely to work a shade oddly. Vandervell may simply have felt the need of a period of solitude, here at Pentallon, in which to arrive at a final decision about himself. Anyway, he *has* been drowned.'

'Indeed, yes. And his posting that letter immediately before-hand does seem to rule out accident. Unless, of course, he was putting on a turn.'

'A turn, Mr Truebody?'

'One of those just-short-of-suicide efforts which psychologists nowadays interpret as a cry for help.'

'That's often a valid enough explanation of unsuccessful suicide, no doubt. But what would the cry for help be designed to save him from? Would it be the embrace of that predatory Mrs Mountmorris?'

'It hadn't occurred to me that way.' Truebody looked startled. 'But something else has. Say that Vandervell was expecting a visitor here at Pentallon, and that for some reason he didn't want the circumstance to be known. That would account for his clearing everybody out. Then the visit took place, and was somehow disastrous. Or perhaps it just *didn't* take place, and there was for some reason disaster in the mere fact of that. And it was only *then* that he decided to write that letter to Litter as a preliminary to walking down to the sea and drowning himself.' Truebody glanced sharply at Appleby. 'What do you think of that?'

'I think I'd call it the change-of-plan theory of Charles Vandervell's death. I don't know that I'd go all the way with it. But I have a sense of its being in the target area, of there having been some element of improvisation somehow in the affair... Ah! Here is our friend the constable again.'

'Inspector Gamley's compliments, sir.' The constable appeared to feel that Appleby rated for considerable formality of address. 'A further message has just come through. They've found the dead man's clothes.'

'Abandoned somewhere on the shore?'

'Not exactly, sir. Washed up like the body itself, it seems—but in a small cove more than a mile farther west. That's our currents, sir. The Inspector has gone over to Targan Bay at once. He wonders if you'd care to follow him.'

'Thank you. I'll drive over now.'

Vandervell's body had been removed for immediate post-mortem examination, so it was only his clothes that were on view. And of these most were missing. It was merely a jacket and trousers, entangled in each other and grotesquely entwined in seaweed, that had come ashore. Everything else was probably lost for good.

'Would he have gone out in a boat?' Appleby asked.

'I'd hardly think so.' Gamley shook his head. 'One way up or the other, such a craft would have been found by now. I'd say he left his clothes close to the water, and they were taken out by the tide. Now they're back again. Not much doubt they've been in the sea for about as long as Vandervell himself was.'

'Anything in the pockets—wallet, watch, that kind of thing?'

'Both these, and nothing else.' Gamley smiled grimly. 'Except for what you might call one or two visitors. All laid out next door. Would you care to see?'

'Decidedly so, Inspector. But what do you mean by visitors?'

'Oh, just these.' Gamley had ushered Appleby into the next room in the Targan Bay police station, and was pointing at a table. 'Inquisitive creatures, one gets in these waters. The crab was up a trouser-leg, and the little fish snug in the breast-pocket of the jacket.'

'I see.' Appleby peered at these odd exhibits. 'I see,' he repeated, but on a different note. 'Will that post-mortem have begun?'

'Almost sure to have.'

'Then get on to them at once. Tell them—very, very

tactfully—to be particularly careful about the bottom of the lungs. Then I'll put through a call to London myself, Inspector. We must have a top ichthyologist down by the night train.'

'A *what*, sir?'

'Authority on fish, Inspector. And there's another thing. You can't risk an arrest quite yet. But you can make damned sure somebody doesn't get away.'

———

Appleby offered explanations on the following afternoon.

'It has been my experience that the cleverest criminals are often prone to doing some one, isolated stupid thing—particularly when under pressure, and driven to improvise. In this case it lay in the decision to post that letter to Litter, instead of just leaving it around. The idea was to achieve a delaying tactic, and there was a sense in which a typewritten address would be safer than one which forged Vandervell's hand. But it introduced at once what was at least a small implausibility. Vandervell while obsessed with suicide may well have prepared a dozen such letters, and without getting round to either addressing or dating them. But if he later decided that one of them was really to be delivered—and delivered through the post—the natural thing would simply be to pick up an envelope and address it by hand.'

'Was that the chap's only bad slip-up?'

'Not exactly. The crime must be called one of calculation and premeditation, I suppose, since the idea was to get the perpetrator out of a tough spot. But its actual commission was rash and unthinking, so that it left him in a tougher spot still. Consider, for a start, the several steps that led to it. Charles

Vandervell's supposed financial reverses and stringencies were entirely a consequence of sustained and ingenious speculations on Truebody's part. They didn't, as a matter of fact, *need* to be all that ingenious, since our eminent philosopher's practical sense of such matters was about zero. But then Mrs Mountmorris enters the story. She is a very different proposition. Truebody is suddenly in extreme danger, and knows it. His client's attitude stiffens; in fact you may say the worm turns. Truebody is summoned to Pentallon, and appears on Tuesday morning. He is given only until the next day to show, if he can, that everything has been fair and above board, after all. But Charles Vandervell has a certain instinct for privacy. If there is to be a row, he doesn't want it bruited abroad. When Truebody comes back on Wednesday afternoon there is nobody else around. And I suppose that puts ideas in his head.'

'So he waits his chance?' Fabian Vandervell asked.

'Not exactly that. Imagine the two of them, walking around the gardens. Your uncle is a new man; he has this dishonest rascal cornered, and is showing grim satisfaction in the fact. He says roundly that he'll have Truebody prosecuted and gaoled. And, at that, Truebody simply hits out at him. He's a powerful fellow; and, for the moment at least, your uncle is knocked unconscious. It has all happened beside one of those small ponds with the tropical fish. So it is *now* that Truebody sees—or thinks he sees—his chance. He will stage some sort of accident, he tells himself. In a moment he has shoved your uncle into the pool. And there he holds him down until he drowns. So far, so good—or bad. But the accident looks a damned unlikely one, all the same. And then he remembers something.'

'*Biathanatos*, and all that.'

'Precisely so—and something more. Truebody has had

plenty of opportunity, during business visits to Pentallon, to poke about among your uncle's papers. He remembers that batch of elegant farewells by a Charles Vandervell about to depart this life by his own hand—'

'But nobody would drown himself in a shallow fish-pond. It simply couldn't be done.'

'Exactly so, Fabian. And as soon as Truebody had slipped into the empty house and secured that batch of letters, he heaved your uncle's body into his car, and drove hard for the sea. And there, let us just say, he further did his stuff.'

'And later posted that letter to Litter. After which he had nothing to do but lie low—and get busy, no doubt, covering up on the financial side.'

'He didn't quite lie low. Rashly again, he took the initiative in holding rather an odd conversation with me. He thought it clever himself to advance one or two considerations which were bound to be in my head anyway.'

'And now he's under lock and key.' Fabian Vandervell frowned. 'Good Lord! I'm forgetting I still haven't the faintest notion how you tumbled to it all.'

'That was the shubunkin.'

'What the devil is that?'

'Small tropical fish—decidedly not found in the sea off Cornwall. A shubunkin deftly made its way into your uncle's breast-pocket while Truebody was holding him prone in that pool.'

'Well I'm damned! But it doesn't sound much on which to secure a conviction for murder.'

'It's not quite all, Fabian. In your uncle's lungs there was still quite a bit of the water he drowned in. Full of minute freshwater-pond life.'